BLOOD AND THORNE

Eva Thorne Book Three

Lorel Clayton

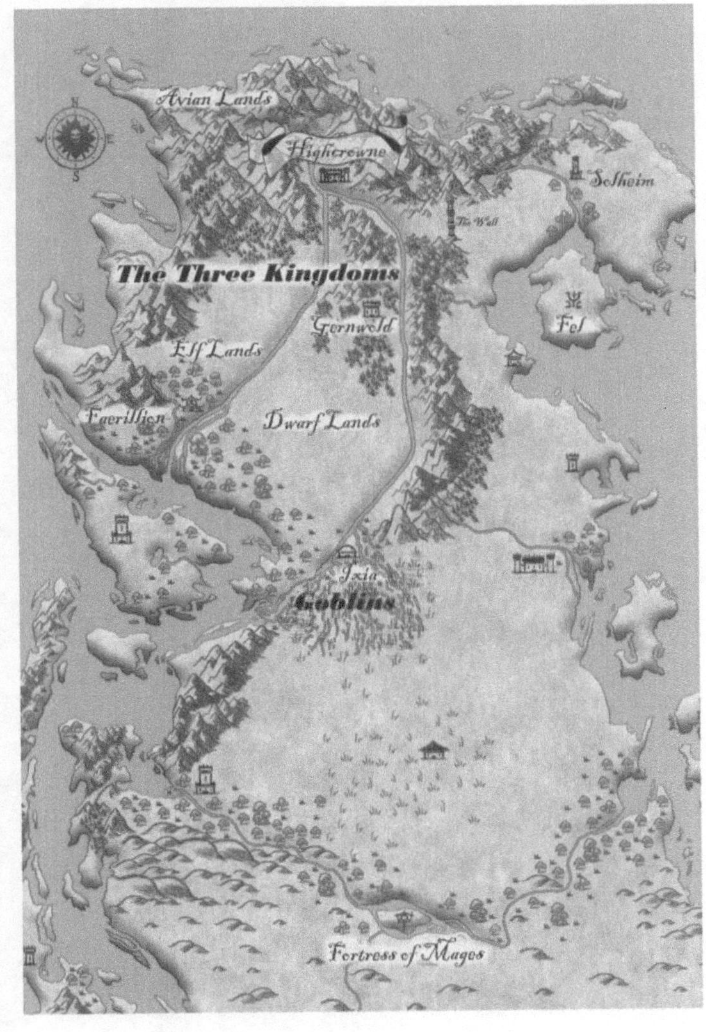

N
W
E
S
Avian Lands
Highcrowne
Solheim
The Wall
The Three Kingdoms
Gornwold
Fel
Elf Lands
Faerillion
Dwarf Lands
Ixia
Goblins
Fortress of Mages

DEDICATION

*To family and friends old and new, who make
us laugh, and to <u>you</u>, our readers for joining Eva
on her adventures. Thank you.*

1 Where Were We?

I was flying. Not good when you're afraid of heights—and dragons. Unlike my phobia of heights, this fear was all new. I'd never been in the clutches of a giant lizard with wings before. I had arm-wrestled a dead wyvern, funny story, and not the best time for it. The point is, I knew a wyvern when I saw one, and this was not it, even if all I could see was a pale belly above and a deadly drop below. Dragons were rare, but lucky me, I'd found one.

Cold wind blew the tatters of my dress. If the dragon wasn't so warm, its insides rumbling with fire, I probably would have frozen to death. I was caught in its talons, arms pinned to my sides, the agony from a broken collarbone making me pass out every once in a while. At least it hadn't swallowed me whole, so maybe it was a friendly dragon? Or maybe it had hungry babies elsewhere.

Last I remembered, I was surrounded by an army of corpses, betrayed by my best friend, and, oh yes, a hairsbreadth away from having my soul given to the god of death in the final act of a macabre wedding ceremony begun before I was born. All in all, this was an improvement.

Every time I opened my eyes—which I didn't do often, because I got woozy—it seemed there was a different landscape below. The plains of Solheim, the eternal winter of Gernwold, and then green hills cut by the Serpent's Ribbon. We followed the river, its surface turning from molten gold in the sunset to liquid silver in moonlight. We flew until dawn and the river vanished into the sea.

Elf lands. A place unwelcoming to humans and Solhans, like me. Dragons too, but that didn't seem to perturb the creature. It carried us to a small island and settled on the sandstone spire of a castle, massive hind talons digging into the stone. A wagon-sized mouth opened, and fangs, each as long as a spear and five times as thick, delicately hooked the iron bars of the window below me and pulled, swinging it open. It placed my sister inside and then me, before closing the barred window again, like placing doves in a cage.

One eye peered at me, a cream-colored moon crowding the view. The black pupil reminded me of the Void between worlds, a place I'd gazed into not long ago.

The dragon looked but did not speak. Maybe I'd imagined its words when it first grabbed me? Then the creature was gone, its golden form vanishing into the yellow glare of the fully risen sun, leaving me to explore the cage in silence.

Ilsa lay where the dragon had left her, trapped in the same unnatural slumber she'd been in ever since Thane took her hostage. She was my twin—same black hair, pale skin and even paler eyes—but she was the cruel one, the murderer, the femme fatale. More than that, she was my warning to myself, a reminder of what not to be, and the one I was always saving when I shouldn't. I hadn't managed to save either of us this time.

"The Dead God. Thane," I whispered into the silence. I was in shock from that experience more than from the dragon. Thane had captured me, but escaping him was no escape. His soul was entangled with mine. A portion of a god in human form, pulling me toward the cold grave of eternity.

It seemed like a nightmare the dragon had stolen me from, and as confused as I was by this imprisonment, I did not want to go back. I would never sleep soundly again, knowing the nightmare was my life.

The room I stood in was ancient, probably not cleaned since the sandstone blocks used to build it were hewn from the cliffs. A single door and a single window were its only features.

I went to the door and pushed. It didn't open of course. There was no handle either. What sort of sick bastard makes a living from crafting doors without handles? I broke a few fingernails trying to pry it open. Nothing. The hinges were on the outside, so the room was built to be a prison. I'd been in one before, and I wasn't impressed. This one had daylight and room to move around, no torture implements either. I scoffed.

"Hardly a prison at all. Probably the tower room where they keep naughty nobles," I said aloud, hearing my voice echo off the empty walls. "Like Princesses. *Bleh.*" I was no princess, waiting for a hero to save me. That never happens. In my experience, the hero often turns out to be the bad guy. You need to get on with things and save yourself.

I tried the window. When it swung open, my heart sped up. I hung my head out, the wind swirling my hair and rushing past my ears. I looked down and down to jagged rocks where waves crashed in white plumes of spray. Not that way.

No other windows above or below. One window in a sheer sandstone spire perched above a rocky death. Even if I managed to climb down without killing myself, I didn't know how to swim.

Okay, I was wrong. It was a very effective prison.

"Great going, Eva," I told myself. I had a tendency to end up in bad situations, but was there anything I could have done this time?

Maybe not have stood so close to the doorway into the Void? Maybe not have been duped for years by my best friend, who turned out to not only be a werewolf but one working for the enemy of humanity? That might have been a good start.

I remembered Thane's look of fear when the dragon came for me.

Why had the dragon come? Had I been the yummiest looking morsel among that vast army of dead and werewolves? Highly unlikely.

I sat down on the floor next to my twin and said, "Ilsa, what are we doing here?"

She didn't answer, of course, still trapped in sleep, and Thane wasn't around to wake her. Thane who was separate from the Dead God but a part of him. The piece that was mine. My betrothed, although we were already husband and wife in his mind, an arrangement made before I was born.

No thanks. I wasn't ready to be married, and certainly not to someone who was trying to destroy the world. He was a god, or something like it, though. That was flattering. And a bit ... mesmerizing.

It was easier to stop thinking about Him when we were across the Kingdoms from one another. A bit easier. Even this far away, Solheim called to me.

My people's ancient home was swallowed whole when the Dead God was summoned into the world by the Nine, the council of necromancers that included my uncle and the mother I'd never known. They had ruled Old Solheim, long fallen to introspection and decay, seeking only power over death. Death was not to be contained, however. Uncle Ulric once said he had come to his senses in time to avert even greater destruction. Almost all the lands beyond the Three Kingdoms of Avian, Elf and Dwarf had been conquered. This was the last sanctuary. It was hard to imagine how much worse it could have been.

Wind whispered through the window, salty and chill, making me clutch my shoulders. My dress had survived a dirigible crash, a train crash and a dragon-napping, but it was wearing a bit thin now. My collarbone ached too.

Enough whining. I searched again for means of escape. The room was bare except for Ilsa, and the landscape outside offered only rusted sandstone cliffs too far away to reach.... And then I looked at my twin again.

The power I'd gained after stealing a piece of Ilsa's soul came to me from time to time as a green light that itched its way out of my skin. The glow was subdued, but it was there, a tiny orb in the palm of my hand, summoned at the mere thought of it. I'd learned to control souls, gained so much control, I wondered if I could compel the dragon when it returned. Force it to set me free? I hadn't dared anything like that before.

I needed to *experiment* first, a useful concept I'd picked up from the goblin professor and his protégé. And I had just the test subject. First experiment was to see if I could wake her up.

"Don't try to kill me this time."

To be safe, I removed her charms and spell tokens. I felt the dark ones, burning my fingers, leaving an acrid oily odor in my nose. That was my sense of them, anyway, before I tossed them aside. I couldn't get at the charms stitched into her dress—she had them even there—and the one in her hair comb felt harmless enough, something to keep her tresses from slipping.

I'd never been able to assess her magic so well before, and I knew I'd changed. Whether it was by practicing or from being so close to Death, a step away through the Void. Something had shifted inside me.

I hovered my hand over her heart and searched for the small remains of her soul, the one bit I hadn't stolen from her. It was like a vicious animal curled up in its burrow to sleep away the winter. I gave it a poke.

Ilsa's eyes opened wide, and she sat up. Her breathing came fast and frantic, as though she'd escaped a terrible dream. Who knew a monster like her could have nightmares?

She seemed almost glad to see me, before her breathing settled and a steely glare took over her face. That was my glare. I didn't like her borrowing it.

"Eva."

She took in the room, her gaze barely straying from me, but I knew she'd quickly seen and judged it all: The barred window, the handle-less door.

"Why am I here?" She demanded answers, as though I'd orchestrated the whole thing.

"How should I know?" I shot back. "What's the last thing you remember?"

"Besides failing to steal back from you what is mine? Let's see. An unfaithful Elf King leaving me behind, crowds of vermin trying to take the escape balloon I set my sights on, and to top it all off—a werewolf grabbing me and taking me to your boyfriend, Conrad. His face was the last thing I saw. That and—"

"—Let me guess. Cinnamon smoke? Eyes like burning suns in the black of the Void? A chill like the grave calling?" I said, thinking of how the Dead God appeared to me.

"No cinnamon, all burning and blackness. It was Our Lord."

"Your Lord maybe, not mine. And Conrad is not my boyfriend. Thane..." Why did I keep wanting to say his name? "...Thane took over Conrad's body. Thane was the Dead God. In the flesh."

"When he touched me there was nothing but darkness."

"Not as appealing as you thought," I said, smirking.

"No. More appealing. The power, like an endless black sea of force—"

"—Before you burst into song, there's plenty of endless sea outside keeping us from escaping. You don't know how to swim do you?" Not that I thought she could be relied on to get us out of here. Then again, Ilsa wanted her soul back, so she might return for me, if only to kill me herself.

She almost dived out the window as she scouted for hand holds, and I instinctively grabbed her legs. She'd always been stupidly unafraid of heights.

"There's no way out. I looked already." I told her. "Our only chance is to face the dragon when it returns."

"The dragon." Ilsa ducked back inside and looked at me like I was the biggest idiot in existence. "You could have mentioned a dragon before."

"I was getting to it. I want to try something first." She was standing close enough, and I wouldn't get a better opportunity.

I touched the center of her chest with my palm and found that bit of soul inside. I wrapped a mental fist around it and commanded it as I would a leashed dog. Dogs never listened to me, but it was an analogy.

"Step away from the window," I commanded.

She obeyed.

It was working.

"Now, stand on one foot." I couldn't think of anything else to command her to do, except possibly change her personality and become a nice, non-murderous person for once.

"Why on earth do you want me to stand on one foot?" She pushed my hand away. "And stop touching me."

It hadn't worked at all. My grip on her soul felt like I was holding smoke rather than a leash, so I released it.

My magical sense was intact, but the ability to control souls as I'd done with the werewolves was lacking. Maybe I could only control wolves? Maybe my twin was immune? Or maybe Solheim was too far away? I didn't know why I thought that last, but it felt right. Like some part of me was stretched thin and out of reach.

No compelling a dragon then.

"Can any of your charms destroy the door?" I asked her.

She glanced at the pile I'd made in the corner of the room and carefully sidled over to retrieve them.

"No," she said, flipping through them and shooting me frustrated looks, as she mentally judged each one to be ineffective against me as well.

"Then we're stuck. Unless you have any ideas?" Trapped in a prison with my twin was my worst nightmare. Perhaps the dragon planned to eat us later. There might be some peace.

"I'll try climbing out the window if need be, but apologies, Sugar, if I don't rely on your assessment."

She spent the next hour testing every inch of the door, the sandstone blocks in the wall, the floor, the ceiling … convincing me to boost her up on my back for that part. I was not happy, as my broken collarbone felt it, and I nearly passed out again. Then she messed with the hinged iron grate over the window, trying to dislodge it. Maybe she planned to bludgeon me with it, as she certainly didn't need to remove it to climb out. I didn't care anymore.

I lay on the cold stone floor staring up at what felt like the lid of my coffin. My mausoleum at least. I could picture my skeleton lying here a century from now, the rags of this ridiculous red dress clinging to the bones and dust. My skeletal fingers would be wrapped around Ilsa's throat and hers around mine.

The sound of her voice grated on my nerves as she searched the room, dropping annoying remarks here and there like she was decorating the place with them.

"Unfortunate that Uncle was not on the dirigible," she said. "He would have dealt with the werewolves, and we wouldn't be in this predicament." Meaning I hadn't dealt with them to her standards. "Then again I might not have come so close to Our Lord. I know you are hiding His purposes from me. Why do you fear the dark so?"

"I'm not afraid of the dark. I'm more afraid you'll never shut up. I don't like your words using my voice."

"My voice."

"I'm the firstborn, so I claim it. And I haven't forgotten what you tried to do with that charm. You had every intention of killing me, or close to it. I don't feel like sharing my feelings with you," I said.

"Feelings? Really, Eva. There are far greater things to talk about. Tell me more about this dragon. Tell me what happened while I slept. I have a sense of great things, of the Lord's voice in my mouth instead of 'yours' ... tell me before my curiosity becomes unbearable and I must throttle it out of you."

One step closer to my skeletal vision.

"You know, every twin I've met, and there were quite a few among the dwarves in Gernwold when I went to school there—"

"—Not another tedious school story," she interrupted.

"Since when have I told you any of my stories? Shut up. I was saying, all the twins I've met are best friends, the girls especially. Even when they were fighting, you'd see those shared glances, the knowing between them. They faced the world together. How come I never wanted to tell them I was a twin? How come I don't see a kindred spirit when I look at you but a dark reflection?"

"Why do you hate me? You tell me, Sugar." She crossed her arms and waited. Listening intently for once.

"Why do you hate me?" I shot back. "How can you try to kill your own sister? How can you threaten Little Viktor in one breath and Nanny, who helped raise us, in another? How can you be so without love, or guilt, or regret for the lives I know you've taken?"

"I'm a good Solhan girl. You should try it sometime."

I was tired of that excuse. Solhans had no more need to be evil than a grall did. It was a choice.

I stared at the ceiling, enjoying silence for a change. I might not have gained any understanding, but at least I'd made her thoughtful. And quiet.

When she did speak, there was a sad note I hadn't heard before. "We were friends once. Don't you remember? You liked our games, and we laughed together. It *was* us against the world. You were the one who changed."

"What?" I sat up. I didn't remember any of that.

The door creaked, and I jumped to my feet. I backed up beside Ilsa. What was coming for us now?

There was no hand on the door. It seemed to be opening of its own accord, and when it was wide enough for me to see the dim corridor outside, I started forward, ready to grab any escape that presented itself.

A girl with honey-colored hair and cream-colored eyes blocked my path, and the door shut behind her. Olyve had on the same lace summer dress she'd been wearing when last I saw her. She also wore that same shadow of dread.

I ignored the doom feeling and hurried past her to pry the door open again. It was stuck fast.

"There's no way out unless they let you out," she said.

"They?" I asked.

"Who are you?" Ilsa's tone was imperious. She was looking down her nose at the girl, but her arms were covered in gooseflesh, so I knew her snobbishness was meant to hide the fear the girl inspired.

Olyve didn't answer either of us and, instead, paced the edge of the room, peeking out the window in the end, as it was the only thing interesting in the bare chamber. Although it wouldn't be bare for much longer if 'they' didn't supply a chamber pot soon. I was already to the point of squeezing my legs together.

"Dreary little space," Olyve commented.

I knew there was more to Olyve than the pre-pubescent elf girl she appeared to be. She was probably the mastermind behind our abduction.

"Then why don't you let us out?" I said. "I'm in dire need of the facilities, and my empty stomach has given up grumbling. It's now resigned itself to gurgling sadly from time to time."

"It's not up to me whether they let you out. You must convince them. Although, I'm sure a chamber pot and a bit of sustenance will arrive shortly."

As soon as she finished speaking, the door opened again. I shot toward it and hit an invisible wall. I bounced back onto my behind, my nose drowning and sore. I felt it to make sure it wasn't broken and watched, incredulous, as a brass chamber pot walked into the room, followed by a pitcher of water, two wooden glasses, and a large platter of fruit, cheese, and meat.

By 'walked' I didn't mean they had little legs, more they seemed to rock back and forth as they moved across the floor, a funny little gait that was almost human. The chamber pot settled in the opposite side of the room from the refreshments, and the door thudded shut again.

"What is this? A fairy story?" Ilsa snorted, disbelieving.

I'd also thought of the enchanted objects in children's stories that could move about, like brooms sweeping on their own and lanterns dancing about with the fireflies, but this was all too real. I touched a glass, and it was just a glass. Or wood, really. Even the pitcher was wood. Nothing that could be broken to create a sharp weapon. I felt no magic in them, sensed no runes.

"You did this," I accused Olyve. "They moved at your bidding."

"No, afraid not. You really do not understand how little sway I have in this situation."

"I felt your power when first you came to see Nanny, and I sense it now. You are not what you seem."

"Of course not. None of us are. And I did not come to see Nanny but you, if you recall. You should have come with me then. Your choice, and the choices that followed, have made them suspect you more. I'm afraid both your lives are in danger now."

"What have you gotten us into, Eva?" Ilsa snarled. "I don't see why I need to be dragged into your imbecilic predicaments. Let me go, child. Keep my sister if you must, but I do have other business to attend to back in Highcrowne. Uncle relies on me."

I snorted at that. Ilsa hoped to take over the family empire of crime and conspiracy, but she was certainly dispensable. Our uncle relied on no one but himself.

"You will not leave this island until certain understandings are acquired," Olyve said. "And you are both necessary for that. If they do not like what they learn, of course, neither of you will survive. I told you this was a matter of life and death, my dear."

She had, back in Highcrowne. I hadn't assumed she meant my life.

"Then tell me what you want. Let's get this over with. Stop being so tediously enigmatic," I demanded. I was pretty used to enigmatic, but it had gone too far now.

"The hearing is tonight. Some prefer midday light, some the moons to be at their zenith, but those that really matter require darkness, and so they have set the time. Until then, eat, drink and be … joyful. For you have at least these hours to live. I will see you again when it is time." She walked sedately to the door, and it opened for her.

I grabbed her wrist before she could get away. "At least tell me who 'they' are," I demanded.

It felt like I had taken the tail of a snake that was about to turn around and bite me, and as much as I wanted to let go, I was too terrified to move. Something monstrous lurked behind her gaze.

She pried my hand loose and kept walking. Before the door shut, she turned and put a finger to her lips. "*Shhh.* We're unmentionable."

2 SISTERS

Unmentionables. I'd heard stories of them all my life, Solhan stories meant to frighten dark-hearted children. Anything that could scare Solhans had to be truly terrifying. I believed in them, left my offerings whenever I could, and was always cautious not to break their rules. But they couldn't be real. Not really real. Could they?

"This is ridiculous," Ilsa said. "Fairy magic and Unmentionables? I recognize that expression. You believe her. Don't be fooled, Sugar. She's trying to rattle you, to make you give up whatever information it is she wants from you. What information is it, anyway? What do 'they' want?"

"I have no idea. I don't know anything." I couldn't imagine what information I had. What kind of things did Unmentionables want? I wracked my memory of the stories Nanny and Morgan told us growing up.

'They' liked offerings of milk and cream. 'They' hated iron, or was it silver? Whatever it was that worked against fairies, I remember those two things were shared among them even if I couldn't recall exactly. Unmentionables travelled across the night and with the rays of sunlight. They could traverse a kingdom in a day—I remembered the dragon doing just that—and they were invisible. Neither the dragon nor Olyve were, but whatever had brought the food was.

I stopped panicking for a moment and took advantage of the chamber pot, making Ilsa look away.

"Please. You have absolutely nothing I haven't seen before," she said, even as she turned her back. She pretended indifference, but I'd seen the fear in her eyes. She'd heard the same stories as me.

'They' could be anywhere at any time, listening, watching, judging. The Unmentionables destroyed empires. Darrub vanished beneath the sands because of them. Anyone who showed disrespect was at risk, no matter how grand or how unimportant, and their acts were unpredictable. A serving maid who left out sour milk might find all her linen shredded, while a Solhan necromancer, whose power was unmatched, might be torn apart silently in the night, with even the necromancer's concubines asleep in his bed unaware of the slaughter. 'They' were the bogeymen of bogeymen.

And no one had ever seen one.

"They will kill us," I told Ilsa. "Olyve revealed she's an Unmentionable, and no one knows what one looks like, which means they kill everyone who's seen them. If we don't learn how to swim in the next few hours, we're doomed."

"You're the one who is doomed. I know how. And who is Olyve?" she asked.

"When did you learn? Highcrowne water is either frozen solid or freezing all year round. Never mind. Question answered: it's about the same temperature as your blood. And Olyve claimed to be a granddaughter of an old friend of Nanny's. Someone who knew our mother. I didn't believe her, which is why I didn't take her case and follow her to Faellion. That must be where we are now."

"Then the water here will be most pleasant." Ilsa tore off the bottom of her white dress and twisted it into a short rope. "Give me your dress as well."

"No. All our clothing combined won't be long enough to reach the ground, or should I say sharp and extremely deadly rocks below. We don't want to go that way."

"How come you were never so nihilistic when I was trying to kill you? It would have been so much simpler, and better for me, if you had given up then."

"I am not giving up." Okay, I'd said the words and now I needed to believe them. I was frightened. Terrified. Unmentionables were real.

Nanny had told particularly vivid stories, but I'm sure she'd made up most of it. If no one had seen the last elf prince vivisected, then no one knew exactly how it happened. Or even if it was Unmentionables. Maybe they liked the mystery and fear and took credit for every dark deed in history?

I made a Solhan sign of protection for even thinking such disrespect. I hoped they wouldn't hold it against me when they brought me in for judgement. Of course, I had no idea what I'd done wrong, but did it matter? Unpredictable I'd said.

I gave Ilsa my underdress and tore off the hem of the outer dress as well. "Ok. Make a rope, but I say let's go up instead."

While she worked—I heard her murmuring enchantments for strength and tracing runes into the fabric with dabs of kohl from her eye makeup—I poured water into the glasses. After gulping a few down and wishing they were whisky, and when the pitcher was empty, I tied Ilsa's rope around the handle. I swung it in a test circle, remembering how Duane had swung his bolas.

Duane. Reginald, Doctor Ghunnan, and Baroness Syla ... They felt like a century away as well as a continent. I hoped they had made it out of the ruins and avoided capture by Gypsum's forces. I hoped I could make it out of here and compare notes with them again. I'd love nothing more than to share funny stories with Bell, laughing about our survival over a spiked cup of kaffe.

I needed to survive first. I stuck my head out the window, felt woozy. Don't look down, I kept telling myself. I looked up, instead, at the decorative battlements above us. A bit higher than I remembered from earlier. I hoped we had enough rope.

"Let me," Ilsa insisted. Trying to steal the makeshift grapnel from me.

"Have you ever scaled a castle before?"

"No. And neither have you."

"Actually, our boarding school in Gernwold was built like a castle..." I trailed off when Ilsa groaned. I did not tell school stories all the time. Really.

I held onto the grapnel and stuck my head out again. I needed to climb out further. "Hold my legs," I said. Ilsa raised an eyebrow, and I never would have let her hold my life in her hands if I didn't know she needed my help to survive. She also needed the right charms to steal my soul before she could kill me, so I was fairly safe. I hoped.

She sighed loudly and held my legs.

"Tighter," I said. Not until I was happy with her grip did I sit on the window ledge and start swinging the rope. I was pretty good if I say so myself, but the pitcher was not the same as a hook; it kept rolling loose.

"Perhaps I should try," Ilsa cooed.

"I already have your soul. Do you really want me holding you?"

"Please. You couldn't harm a fly, and you are too weak to hold my murder in your heart. You've said it plenty of times—you don't want to kill me."

That's where she was wrong. I didn't want to act on my impulses.

"Give me a minute," I said.

The next few attempts I tried to swing around the crenellation instead, thinking once more of Duane and his bola hooking around his opponents' legs. I'd seen him use the weapon in real street fights, but I'd also seen him practicing when we were kids, when he hadn't been so great at it. He always whispered to the leather, telling it where he wanted it to go. I found myself doing the same thing to the rope, and then it worked.

"You are insane," Ilsa said.

"I thought you planned to brave the rocks below? That's insane."

"I was only goading you into action, Sugar. You are too easy to manipulate."

I hated that she was right. But I'd done it. Before I could outthink myself, I started to climb up, but I needed both arms, and my collarbone, while tolerating my earlier maneuvers, refused this.

"Ow, ow, ow," I said like a child, feeling sore and tender from having even tried a two-handed grip.

I climbed back inside before I passed out.

"Is your bone still broken?" Ilsa asked, annoyed.

"It hasn't changed from an hour ago when I told you I couldn't be used as a human step ladder to test the ceiling."

"You're Solhan."

"I don't see how that makes me a better step ladder than a human."

"I've seen your power." There was envy in her voice as she looked at my hands. They weren't glowing now, but she had seen it plenty of times before.

"It's not what you think. I can't heal. Not even the Dead God can heal," I said, remembering how Thane was unable to.

She looked even more envious at mention of Him. It must be killing her that I wouldn't tell her more about the encounter.

"Uncle Ulric can heal," she pointed out. "He goes on and on about you, you know? If he could see his little darling now, he'd be so disappointed."

"I'm an embarrassment to him and the Thorne name, he told me. He's told me that plenty of times. I am not his darling, nor do I want to be."

"Whatever you say, Sugar. So, you really can't heal yourself?"

"If I knew how, I would have done it already."

She rolled her eyes. "You *are* an embarrassment. Here, allow me."

She did a quick inventory of the rune-etched beads on one bracelet and undid the hasp to pull it free. She held it up and came toward me.

I backed away, but I was already wedged against the window.

"How quaint. If I had my Little Death charm still you should be wary, but you threw it away. Remember?"

I didn't sense any menacing dark magic from the bead she held, so I said, "Fine."

She placed the blue glass against my collarbone, digging in a bit so that I gritted my teeth and glared at her. She smiled in such a way I doubted so much roughness was an actual requirement of the spell; another one of her petty vengeances. She spoke a few words in Solhan, something about Mater, which was the ancient god of order, opposing Chaos, and with another sharp pain and a sound like a tree cracking, it was done. The break was fixed, and I could move my arm in a big circle. It felt great.

"Thank you," I said.

"Save me from your insincerity, sister dear. This is only a cease-fire. I do not expect to begin exchanging pleasantries."

I saved my breath for climbing and managed it more nimbly this time around. What a difference not having to endure excruciating pain made. I reached the top and swung my legs over, giving the stone battlements a kiss when I was safe. I had not looked down once, but I needed to now, as Ilsa was calling for me.

"Help, pull me up," she ordered. She had added a loop to the makeshift rope and stood on it like a swing. My attention was caught by the white waves moving far below, roiling and shifting, and I thought I'd be sick.

"Climb," I said.

"I'm not as accustomed to hard labor as you are, sister."

"Then get accustomed, quick."

"Help me, please." She put on the sweet tone she used to collect the swarms of friends and lovers she had in Highcrowne, and I realized how she was so effective. She sounded genuinely helpless and innocent. It was frightening how good people were at lying. Most everyone I knew was a liar.

I gave in and hauled her up. I stood a moment, enjoying the open sky above us. Of course, there might be no way off the island, but at least we had the illusion of freedom.

"Let's find a stair or trapdoor," I said. Confident in my knowledge of castles. There was always a stair or a ladder or a trapdoor.

Of course, there wasn't one this time.

"Now what?" Ilsa snapped. The sweetness didn't last long.

The castle was built of several towers clustered together, some thin, like ours, others broader and flat, like the next tower over, which was about a story below. I was certain I spotted a trapdoor on its roof. If it wasn't a shadow. Still, down was down, and that's where we wanted to go.

"We jump, of course," I said.

"Excuse me?" Ilsa gave me the same look I must have given Duane when he suggested we jump from a moving train. It was a tall one story.

"You do know how to tuck and roll?" I asked.

"I had sword lessons as any proper Solhan lady should, but there is a difference between evading an attack and this. I am not a cat."

"Well, I've learned a few things from a cat burglar, which is close enough." I went back and fetched the loop of rope that we'd made. I retied it around a crenellation on the side we wanted to go down so that as much rope as possible hung freely. It cut the distance in half. I grabbed hold of the cloth and walked my feet down the wall. When I reached the end of the rope, I dropped, tucking and rolling as soon as I landed.

"Too easy," I called up to Ilsa. She had her runes, but I had a few skills of my own.

She mirrored what I had done and smiled sweetly at me. Okay, she was a fast learner.

The trapdoor really was there and unlocked. There was even a ladder. I climbed down, vindicated about my castle knowledge, and went looking for the stairs. There were no torches in the sconces, but the hallway ran along the perimeter of the tower, and small windows let in light every dozen feet or so.

There was no one to be seen or heard. The castle was not a ruin; it had been kept up until recently I could tell. The unlighted candles and lamps were free of dust, as were the floors. I opened doors as I explored and spotted living chambers with furniture and bedclothes still intact. They'd all vanished. I felt a chill, wondering if the Unmentionables had done something to these people. Had they too been judged?

The corridor ended in stone stairs that went down. I decided not to explore the other levels, as I didn't want to risk being caught. I moved as swiftly and silently as I could from one level to the next, Ilsa right behind me and sagely keeping her usual criticisms to herself when I took us down a dead end from time to time. The whole island—which might be nothing but seagulls with the people vanished—had likely heard us squabbling in the high tower, but we didn't want Olyve to guess where we were now.

When we finally exited the castle, I sighed, glad to see the end of stone walls. Stone cliffs greeted me instead. They were sandstone, patched with pale green lichen that made me think of corroded copper slapped onto rusting iron. Cliffs stretched above us, forming parts of the castle wall, and more cliffs plummeted below our feet down to the waves below. I stepped closer to the ledge, but not too close, and looked down to the ocean we'd have to cross.

Turquoise water swirled with blue depths and white crests. The wind blew my hair back, carrying droplets and a salt tang that felt familiar, summoning a faint memory, a fragment of an old dream I couldn't hold onto. I watched a bit of driftwood turn around and around before being crashed against the rocks and lost beneath the waves.

"So, you think you can swim that to the mainland?" I asked Ilsa, incredulous.

"Let's look for a boat," she said, answering my question.

I highly doubted our captors would leave one lying around for us, but then again they didn't seem to be good at imprisoning people, other than locking us in a tower. There was no sign of guards or anyone to stop us as we scrambled along the cliffs. The island, like the castle, seemed deserted.

We came to a beach, trackless golden sand nestled between fingers of rock, and made our way down to it. The waves looked less menacing there at least. We were within jumping distance of the sand when my pulse quickened. There was an overturned rowboat resting against the rocks. Its hull was visible and looked intact. Now if it had oars...?

Ilsa put out an arm to block me. She put a finger to her lips and then pointed down.

Below us were legs. They crossed and uncrossed from time to time, so I assumed they were attached to someone. A well-tanned female someone. I carefully leaned over a bit more and spotted a white bathing suit embroidered with black thread in complex floral patterns. The woman lay on a matching, embroidered white blanket.

I heard a strange click sound and then the woman began to stand up. Ilsa and I backed away, but climbing up the stones backwards was not easy to accomplish at speed. A moment later, the woman's torso was in view, and I doubted if it was a woman. All I could see was a black shroud, one huge black eye covered in glass, and gossamer wings, like a dragonfly's, sprouting from its back.

There was the click sounds again, and I saw the creature had human hands. It had just pressed a silver button on a long black cord. A moment later the black shroud shifted, and a less frightening woman's face was revealed. She frowned at us.

"No, no, no. You've spoiled my shot. Move aside. Stop climbing, now. Come down to the sand here and stand behind me. Come on. Move it." She had a schoolteacher tone I couldn't resist, so I obeyed, dragging Ilsa with me.

When I reached the sand, I realized the woman, although perfectly proportional, was half my height, and those really were wings sticking out of her back. The bathing suit left all but a few places bare, and I could see the chitin joint between tanned flesh and translucent wing. She was a fairy.

Not a pixie or a nymph or a dozen other faerie-like creatures, but a genuine fairy of the sort elves had warred with since time immemorial. They were legend, even more than dragons, hunted to extinction. There was the odd sighting, which no one believed, as it was usually deluded seekers who had devoted their lives to finding a fairy or similar rare creature. I'm not sure for what purpose; hopefully not to mount on their wall, but there were strange hunters as well. Or so I'd heard. I really didn't get out of Highcrowne much, and most of my knowledge about the world came from travelers telling stories at Karolyne's café.

The fairy ducked under the black shroud again, and the click soon followed. She emerged with a sigh, an irritation relieved.

"That's better," she said. "No annoying people ogling you, ruining your daguerreotypes, just an image of perfect stone. Wait a minute, was that there before?" She flicked a purple beetle off a rock and ducked under the shroud again to the accompaniment of another click sound.

She placed a wooden cover over the glass lens and then folded up her apparatus. It had three wooden, collapsible legs, and ended up being the size of a small suitcase when she finished. The fairy turned and started when she saw us.

"Oh. You're still here? Run along now." She waved her hand, trying to shoo us as she'd done the beetle.

"Is that your boat?" Ilsa asked.

"Oh, my, no. Someone left it lying there. You're welcome to it. Just, please, step way back."

We obeyed.

"Further back, please. Let me get around you, and then you can have the boat. A bit further." She was shouting now, as we'd backed all the way to the surf and my boots were sticking in the wet sand.

She nodded with satisfaction and then vanished in a flicker of wings. Her apparatus and blanket vanished with her.

"That was a fairy," I said. "We should have spoken to her, asked her more about her kind, if she's been here all this time, if there are others...."

"All we need is the boat," Ilsa said. "We're not on a natural science expedition."

"Aren't you the least bit curious about anything?"

"No." She grunted, trying to turn the rowboat over. A sliver of wood tore off, and she stuck a bleeding finger in her mouth. She glared at me. "A little help?"

It was a lot heavier than it looked, but we managed to turn it over. There were oars. We were saved.

"Excuse me."

I jumped, for the voice was in my ear. The fairy was back and standing right behind us.

"You're those two who are supposed to be in the tower, aren't you?" she said. Her brow was furrowed, and there was a predatory blackness to her eyes. Her face was beautiful when not covered in the shroud, dusted with a powder than made rainbow sparkles in the sunlight. I swear her eyes were violet or maybe azure before, but now they were certainly black.

Extinct species or not, my hand suddenly itched for my Ashur, and it was only then I realized I didn't have my sword anymore. I remembered having it when the dragon took me, but somewhere along the way it had vanished.

"Why don't you step back now," I said. "Way back."

"There must be some arrangement we can make, Sugar," Ilsa said sweetly. "You don't want us around spoiling things. You said so yourself. No one needs to know we were ever here."

"They won't." The fairy pointed at the boat and it vanished. Only the oars left behind.

Ilsa took a step toward the fairy and then my sister vanished too.

"I'd really like to know more about you—" I began before she cut me off.

"—I don't like people, animals, or conversation. That's all you need to know," the fairy said.

Then she aimed her finger at my forehead and the world vanished.

3   A Matter of Life and Death

"What is this place?" Ilsa wondered.

We hadn't vanished into nothing. We were in a strange, foggy land, Ilsa sitting on the boat that had disappeared from the beach. Forest surrounded us, green leaves and white trees dappled with alternating patterns of light and shadow, but everything was slightly smudged, like we were in an artistically-styled painting. I reached out to touch the nearest tree, to steady myself, but there was nothing there, or it was farther away than it looked. It felt like we were the only real things and everything around a mirage.

"The fairy lands," I said, recalling stories of people being stolen away or wandering here.

It was a place where a century in the real world could pass in what felt like a year and a day, and if you ate the food or drank the water you were trapped forever.

People thought it was myth, that the fairies were an ancient species like the elves, but since I'd encountered Doctor Ghunnan and his explanations of worlds accessible through the Void, eerily similar worlds, it made sense the fairy lands were real and one of these alternative places. It's probably where all the fairies were hiding. But how had the fairy woman sent us here? There were supposed to be doorways to the Void in only certain places, formed naturally. Doctor Ghunnan had said it would take knowledge and power beyond his comprehension to cross to other worlds without them. Perhaps that was what the fairy had? Knowledge and power beyond any of our comprehension.

She must be an Unmentionable, here to judge us.

I touched the air, feeling for an imperfection or tear, a hint of the doorway we'd just come through. The blurred image of forest around us blurred even more, rippling as I moved my hands across it, like skimming my fingers through the surface of a pond or along the soft membrane within an eggshell. We were trapped in a bubble, the fairy lands visible through it but still out of reach, and I felt no imperfection in the surface yet.

"What are you doing?" Ilsa asked, arms folded as she watched me caressing the air.

"You could help me look for a way out."

"Why do I feel we've gone from bad to worse? We should have killed her and taken the boat when we had the chance."

"You can't kill a fairy! Well, maybe you can physically, but I mean you *can't*. Haven't you ever dreamed of meeting one? A real fairy?" I knew my eyes sparkled a bit. Despite the fairy having imprisoned us, possibly for all eternity, I couldn't hide my awe.

"No. When did you become such a pathetic pile of girlishness? Since we've had these wonderful hours together to talk and see each other more than we have in years, I'm losing what little respect I had for you, Sugar."

"Then the feeling is mutual. Actually, wait, I didn't have any respect for you to start with, and you've only met my expectations at every turn, so I really haven't been surprised. Other than perhaps realizing you're even more boring and predictably evil than I thought," I said.

"You toss the term evil about, sister, without having seen true evil I think. Otherwise you would know I am simply practical and ambitious."

"I've faced the Dead God."

"Our Lord is not evil, merely a force of nature. I have slunk through Highcrowne's darkest places, through sewers and refugee towns in search of power and secrets...."

"Secrets like that little death charm of yours I brushed so easily aside?" I cut in, sounding unimpressed.

"I found that charm in my wanderings, yes, but true power is not surrendered by others for any amount of money or promised souls. You must rip it from them. I have grown my collection, but there are the feeblest of creatures lurking in the shanty towns and dark places of Highcrowne I would not dare touch. True evil twists their souls. A taste for pain beyond my games, a hunger for chaos without purpose. They are so far gone in dark dreams they sleep in their own offal and grime without care or notice."

"Sounds like they are a matter of evil by degree, not kind. You need to watch the path you walk, Ilsa, or you could end up like them."

"And you need to stop tripping over your own feet and go somewhere. Oh yes, I needn't bother with any helpful advice, for once our détente is over, I will relieve you of your power and concerns."

"Back to threatening me again so soon? Predictable. Like I said." I pounded harder on the invisible wall that held us, hoping it would shatter.

Even wandering hungry and thirsty through the fairy lands in search of a doorway through the Void sounded like a better plan than one more second trapped in a heart-to-heart chat with my twin. I could not believe we were ever once alike. I'm sure she'd said that to mess with my head.

Then I saw something move outside in the hazy trees. It was a black shape, fast and predatory. The hairs on my arms stood up.

"Now, that feels like evil," Ilsa whispered.

There was a pop sound, and I was terrified I had found a way out only to be eaten by something deadly lurking in the fairy lands. It hadn't been us popping out, however; the fairy had popped her way in. Despite her diminutive form, the bubble felt crowded now.

"Oh, here's where I left you," the fairy said. "We'd best get moving as it's almost time for your hearing. Well, past time. They had to reschedule."

I was relieved to be getting away from the predatory shadow, but I had the feeling I shouldn't be.

"Olyve said that the judgement would be at midnight. What's your name?" I added, not wanting to keep thinking of her as 'fairy'. I'm sure her name was beautiful, like Morninglight or Crystalbell.

"Whilst this little pocket of mine is not my homeland proper, time still slows here," the fairy said. "I love to visit for a nap, keeps me younger than Olyve, but I do sometimes sleep too well and miss whole years at a time. The others are quite vexed with me for misplacing you here. Let's hurry along now. Time is flying by out on the island, and we've lost several midnights already."

"Several—?" I began, but she snapped her fingers and the blurred forest around us vanished.

We were once more on the beach, but it was dark. Stars filled the moonless sky, the white breakers on the water the only thing visible in the vast dark ocean. The sand at our feet was gray, the boat nearby a darker gray against it.

The whites of Ilsa's eyes flashed for a moment, and I knew she was looking at the boat. I saw her outline crouch down and grab a broken white shell from the sand.

Please don't hurt the fairy, I almost said aloud. Then again, if we could escape without facing the judgement of the Unmentionables...?

"Oh, silly me," the fairy said, pointing her finger at the boat. It vanished. So did the shell in Ilsa's hands. My sister patted her neckline and frantically felt along her wrists and the seams of her dress.

"My charms." I heard a note of panic beneath the anger in her voice.

"No weapons allowed when I take you before the gathering," the fairy said. "Not that you had anything dangerous to worry about, but rules are rules. If we don't follow our own, who will? Harbinger gets a bit touchy about these things. Come along now." She headed up the beach toward a high cliff face about a mile away. It was black against the starry sky.

I hesitated.

"Fool. Let's run," Ilsa said, grabbing my arm.

Had I been thinking the same thing?

"There is no running from the Unmentionables," I said, finally. "Our only hope is to follow the rules. Show respect. Beg for our lives."

"I'm not good at begging," Ilsa pointed out.

"Neither am I, but I get the sense from the way Olyve and the fairy talk there are worse things. I think I'll soon get a chance to meet better examples of the true evil you've been telling me about. Let's not piss them off."

I hurried after the fairy, who moved fast despite her small legs. Her wings seemed to be doing most of the work of speeding her ahead of us.

Ilsa's feet scraped across the shifting sand behind me. She was following. Not that I cared what she chose to do. We'd escaped the tower, and I was happy for us to go our separate ways. She could heed my advice or not. I didn't care.

"Wait up," I called to the fairy.

She paused, tapping her foot.

"What's your name again?" I asked, panting a bit. It was hard work trudging across what had become small sand dunes.

"I didn't tell you. I would never reveal my true name. I'm not stupid."

"Oh, yes, sorry." True names gave people power over you. Solhans believed that too, which is why we never revealed our full names to anyone. Only our mothers knew our middle names and passed that secret down when we were of age. My mother had never told me mine.

"You can call me..." she looked around for inspiration, "...Sandy."

"Are you sure? That's not like Moonsong or anything."

"Why would I want to call myself Moonsong? The moons don't sing. I can't sing. It's a stupid name. This is why I don't like conversation. People are always saying ridiculous...."

"Never mind," I said and kept walking.

As we neared the cliffs, I saw a blacker section, the maw of a huge cave. Neither Ilsa nor I with our Solhan night vision had any problem finding our way, but 'Sandy' cursed and summoned a glow of fairy light around herself. She looked like a walking lighthouse. I squinted against her brightness as we stumbled over stones and boulders that had broken from the cave mouth. Deeper inside, the cave narrowed into a large, artificial tunnel before opening again into a proper limestone cavern with dangling stalagmites like huge teeth. I'd been in a few too many caves of late and my hairs stood on end, as they seemed to be a lodestone for dark rituals and things I generally hoped to avoid. I was terrible at avoiding.

The cave was empty as far as I could tell. No altars, no arcane symbols etched in stone, nothing.

"No-Thing is more accurate," a voice in the dark said. "I am here and welcome seeing you again, Miss Thorne."

There was nothing to form No-Thing's voice, and the last time I'd seen that soulless creature of the Void he'd been animating a pile of ropes and canvas at the docks. Now there was no form to focus on and no way to locate the source of the disembodied voice.

"Apologies I did not bring trappings to wear," No-Thing said, answering my unspoken thoughts, as he had an unnerving tendency to do.

"What is that?" Ilsa asked. Whenever she was frightened, a derisive tone entered her voice, and I detected it now, as though my conversing with an invisible creature was distasteful to all civilized beings.

"No-Thing, meet my sister. It is good to have a familiar ... something familiar here. Are you...?"

"An Unmentionable? If you must classify my interest in certain affairs of this world, then yes," No-Thing said.

"I thought Unmentionables were all one race, like fairies?" Ilsa still assumed that air of annoyance at things not being as she thought they should.

"Fairies are not one race either," Sandy chimed in, "but it doesn't keep my particular kind from being blamed for everything. The Unmentionables, though, yes that's a good label to use when assigning blame to dark deeds. We do what we must."

"What we must," No-Thing chorused, as though it was their little club's slogan.

If No-Thing was here, plus I assumed Olyve would come, she who seemed as friendly as a creepy little elf girl can be, and the disinterested Sandy, if this was the gathering of Unmentionables meant to judge us, I was optimistic. *They weren't all that bad.*

I knew as soon as I thought it I shouldn't have. For it was then the rest of them arrived.

It began with a blackness, like pure night that swept across the cave, smothering Sandy's glow and blocking even my keen sight. We were swallowed in darkness, and it had substance to it, unlike No-Thing. It was suffocating, making my heart clench and struggle to beat even as I struggled to breathe.

"Some of us need oxygen," Sandy admonished, but there was even a note of worry in her voice.

The darkness withdrew to the far corner of the cavern and out of it stepped an assembly of horrors. First there was a ghostly woman with three heads, then came a large rabbit whose white fur was matted and caked with blood, as were its steel claws and ivory fangs. A mummified creature, skin shrunk against its bones, scrambled across to a stalagmite and climbed it backwards, its impossibly long limbs moving like a spider's but bent at odd angles. There was a giant spider as well, huge and transparent. It darted about the cave more quickly, passing before Ilsa and me, its mandibles feeling the air, reaching for us.

I shivered and took a step back, but the spider was too fast to avoid, and dry, transparent appendages tickled over my face, my skull, my neck, my back ... I felt violated in an instant, a dozen black eyes looking at me from its face. A scream was tearing its way out of my throat, but then the creature darted back to the others.

Their number now included a normal looking man, plainly handsome and plainly dressed, with hollow features and hollow eyes. Beside him was an Avian— my heart leapt at something familiar again—but next was a demonic woman with blue skin and bat wings, all her joints sprouting sharp, bony protrusions and with a sweep of horns that hung from her skull to her waist instead of hair. Her gaze was even more violating that the spider's limbs.

The tangible darkness solidified then into one last figure who loomed behind them all. A heavily muscled man, skin white as snow, a massive crown of antlers on his head and two small, perfect fangs showing beneath sensuous red lips. His gaze was compelling, like gravity pulling you in.

I'd heard legends of vampires, those who drank blood to feed their immortality, and somehow, I knew here was one right before me. Maybe it was the way he eyed my throat or his very presence that screamed 'predator'. All the new arrivals looked eager to eat me, but only the horned man put such sensuality behind it.

"Harbinger," Sandy whispered, like she felt it too, a quickening of the pulse, an attraction to doom.

I was attracted to Death Himself, so I knew the feeling, and the vampire, although compelling at first, I could resist. Ilsa seemed less immune. She took an involuntary step toward him.

Olyve appeared out of the dark, and the elf girl gently put a hand on my sister's chest. Ilsa stopped and blinked, emerging from her daze.

"Looks like most who want to be here are here. Sorry I'm late," Olyve said cheerfully, before taking her place beside the others.

Now that Olyve had arrived, I remembered she did not have the most reassuring presence, more an aura of looming darkness as powerful as the vampire's but with a flavor all its own. Not even the Avian's expression was reassuring. None of them looked happy.

"You are not the tardiest, Olyvandra," a slow voice said behind me.

I heard the clop of horse's hooves and looked back to see a spindly creature plod toward us. It was almost as tall and bony as the mummy creature, but its arms, sprouting thick-fingered hands, were twice as long as its rear legs, which had horse's hooves. Its face was like that of a horse as well, with huge, liquid brown eyes. When it joined the others, it sat down on its haunches, and its bony knees stuck out oddly. It was the only Unmentionable who smiled at me.

Sandy looked distracted when she went over to join the assembly. I realized there was no one guarding the exit now, and I could run for it, but I suspected the spider at least would catch me before I made it a few steps. What had I walked into? Why had I thought the judgment of the Unmentionables would be fair?

"I'd just like to state for the record that I have always respected you," I said, sounding like the worst kiss up. "I leave cream or milk out regularly, never take your name in vain and … what were some of the other things we're supposed to do?"

"Cream is for fairies," Olyve said, glancing at Sandy.

"What? Oh, yes. I put that stipulation in, I recall. So, there's cream lying about you say? Where?"

"Highcrowne."

"Good to know," Sandy said.

"There are no rituals, no observances for us." The three-headed ghost woman spoke from only one of her mouths, the sound harsh, making me feel like my ear drums were shredded. Each set of eyes on her heads were white and sightless. They were all looking at me though. I sensed it. Another mouth produced a small, sing-song chirp like a bird's, saying "There is only myth. Here is truth: We judge each circumstance as we see fit, and there is no placation."

All a myth? I was deeply disappointed.

"What are we accused of? What gives any of you the right to sit in judgement?" Ilsa said. She was trying not to look at the horned vampire and managed a convincing glare for the others. "I am a Solhan, a Thorne, and only Our Lord can presume to judge us."

"Her," I added quickly. "That's Ilsa who's talking. Me, Eva, I'm not questioning your authority. No Sirs, Madams, Miss ... I say that he, or she, or it, really, who has the power has the right in this day and age. Right?" I was blithering and knew it. And such an unbelievable kiss up. That's what fear did to you. Maybe they'd be lenient if they thought I was simple.

"*You* are Eva?" Olyve asked, looking back and forth between us. "Good of you to point that out. I've always had difficulty telling you two apart, despite being your godmother. I wished I could have spent more time watching over you both, learning your idiosyncrasies, but duty called, and you seemed safe enough in Highcrowne."

Olyve gave the Avian a disapproving look.

"None in Highcrowne are safe anymore," the Avian said. "Our power wanes and the Dead God's waxes. We could not protect them even if they had stayed out of harm's way."

"Instead they blundered right into the arms of their 'Lord' and almost destroyed the world!" the blue-skinned she-devil with the long horns said. She was not happy with us. "I say they are too great a risk and should be destroyed now. Who agrees?"

They were voting already? I hadn't even had a chance to defend myself. Or hear the charges!

"The Dead God is not my lord," I said hastily. "Don't listen to Ilsa. I don't want to destroy the world. I'd save it if I could."

"She can," No-Thing said. I recognized his disembodied voice even if I couldn't see him. "She is the key and can send the Dead God back to where He came from."

"Eva is a blessing, not a danger, and we must give her the opportunity to do what we have been unable," the low-voiced horse man said. It seemed others wanted to interrupt, he spoke so slowly, but there must be some rule among them to hear each other out.

"And me?" Ilsa asked. "I'm not special?"

"Not if Eva has your soul," No-Thing said.

"We do not know enough about the keys to be certain," Olyve interjected as soon as she could. "I say we cannot pass judgement until we have more information, and now that I've brought them here, we can learn what we must about them and about the relic. I say we do not judge until we know, for we could be throwing away our salvation."

What was this about a relic too? I'd heard about keys before from No-Thing, but this was new. I kept my mouth shut. Olyve was clearly trying to protect me, and I didn't want to foul her up.

A pull, like the tide, drew the gazes of all in the room to the muscled vampire who was silent, listening.

Finally, he said, "Eva and Ilsa were on the plains of Solheim when you found them, Olyvandra. The Dead

God's armies had them within their lifeless hands. All they had to do was rip their limbs away and their souls would have gone to Him. He would have all He needs, the keys, as you say, to step fully into this world and end it. Either you were extremely fortunate with the timing of your arrival, or the god did not want them dead. Why?"

He looked at me expectantly, and I felt compelled to answer.

"It was Thane," I said. "He wanted ... he wanted to keep me alive."

"Who is Thane?" the blue demon asked angrily. Maybe that was her accent, and she couldn't do polite.

"A part of the Dead God in human form," I said. "He'd taken over a friend of mine and been with me since we flew out of Highcrowne. Thane had plenty of opportunities to kill me or let me die."

"The Dead God?" Olyve asked, incredulous. "Walking around in Highcrowne? That is a breach of the Compact."

There were a few shocked expressions, but then No-Thing's voice said, "The Compact is not broken by a fragment of the god inhabiting a limited mortal form, for it is exactly what He does when He animates the human dead. It is only broken if He sends His armies or exerts His direct power against the Three King-doms. A primal god such as He would know exactly how to bend the Compact without breaking it."

There were a few moments of thoughtful silence I didn't feel brave enough to fill.

The Avian was the first to speak. "Tell me more of this Thane. He inhabited the body of a living person you knew?"

"Yes, Conrad's body. He said he'd been in other bodies as well, a necromancer named Erick for one." I didn't want to elaborate on the fact Erick had been my lover. Or had it been Thane in his body? I was all confused.

"Why would Thane let you live if he is, as you say, The Dead God?" Olyve asked.

"I'd like to know too," Ilsa said. "She hasn't told me anything."

All eyes of creatures terrible and strange were on me now. I gulped.

"Thane said I was his, and he was the portion of the god that was mine. That ... that I'd been promised to Him. I'm His wife, but not by my reckoning. There's no ring on this finger."

The horse neighed, and I was certain it was a laugh. "Who ever heard of the God of Death in love? You were fooled."

"It's true," I insisted. "The Dead God spoke to him, of him, as a piece of himself. And I sensed Thane's soul. The body he inhabited was Conrad's, but his soul was ... He was not lying."

"You heard the Dead God speak?" the vampire asked.

"Plenty."

"And you did not die?" the gaunt man asked, sounding a bit awed.

"No. Why?" I began, but then I thought about what had happened, and I felt shaky. I had been so close to being His. I knew now why they thought I was a danger.

"Her ability to wield soul magic, her connection to the relic, answers we must gain about the keys and this Thane ... these things are reason enough to defer our judgement. Agreed?" Olyve said.

There was a moment of silence.

"Agreed," Harbinger said. Many of the others immediately joined in then, their voices for once melding together in a chorus that held power, the reverberations sinking into my bones.

A few abstained, and a few were reluctant with their assent, such as the blue demon, who said, "But if what we learn confirms the danger they represent, we will kill them? You assent to that?"

"Yes," Harbinger said. "If the risk is too great, then we must destroy both their souls so utterly they cannot reach The Dead God's side."

4 Impossibles

Destroy our souls utterly? Harbinger's promise to the others meant more than death. This was oblivion. For both of us.

"I'm sorry, Ilsa," I whispered. There was no reaction, so I wasn't sure if she heard.

The threat of eternal nothingness paralyzed me. I suddenly thought of all those I knew who did not believe in the gods like I did, and I understood what they faced every day. To keep walking, to keep living and doing in the face of inevitable, not threatened, but inevitable extinction was courage beyond imagining.

There was silence as the gathering let the weight of their pronouncement sink in. All those terrifying eyes upon us. And then they began to disperse, in blanketing darkness, as most had come, a blur of spider speed, or the rush of air past Avian wings. Only Olyve, Sandy and the horse creature remained behind, but he was trying to make his exit too, albeit slowly.

"Wait," I said, finally getting my mind functioning again. "I need to know. What must I do to satisfy you? How do I stay alive?"

"The only way," the horse man said as he clopped by, "is to demonstrate beyond doubt that you are capable of sending the Dead God back across the Void. We know not how to defeat Him, so you must learn."

"Why am I even a part of this?" Ilsa hissed. "She has my soul, as you all know. Make her give it back and then send me on my way." Her tone was imperious, but it couldn't hide the plea behind it.

"We do not have her power to steal souls, so we cannot take it from her and return it to you," the disembodied voice of No-Thing said. "And even if we managed it somehow, then you would be equal in threat to her. I have heard whisperings of the keys, not key, needed to release the Dead God fully into this world or shut him out."

"As they are only whisperings," Olyve added, "the others will rule that, even with your soul diminished, it will be safest to kill you both. Lack of knowledge is their true fear. We Unmentionables know more than most any living or un-living creature in this world, but we are not omniscient, and when we encounter something beyond our experience, we are ... frightened.

It is not a fit state for those who must decide the fate of the world."

"It sounds like something you do all the time," I said.

"Never to this degree. Kingdoms, bloodlines, and genocide of whole races ... we have ruled on all such fates, but the Dead God threatens even us," Olyve said.

"What else do you think would make me come to a meeting?" Sandy added. She seemed to be in her own world, ignoring us, but apparently, she'd been listening.

"So, you need knowledge?" I said, biting my lip. "That's what detecting is for. Tell me what you know and don't lie or leave anything out. Clients always lie, but in this situation, I'm the client and the investigator too." Actually, I felt like the femme fatale again. I needed to stop reading mysteries as they were warping any normal sense of the world.

"Don't you want something to eat first?" Olyve asked.

My stomach rumbled, but I said, "No. Tell me what you know of the keys, and what was this mention of a relic?"

Ilsa sighed and sat down on a rock next to Sandy, head on her chin.

"Even if you're not hungry," Olyve said, her child's voice turning to a low growl, "I am. No-Thing and

Fairy can answer your questions. I'll meet you at the castle after I feed."

Her form shifted before my eyes, enveloped in a heat haze that seemed out of place in the damp cave, her hands and feet first turning scaled and clawed and huge, and then the rest of her following, the head last. It was a small, blonde elf girl's head on a golden body before it became the familiar wagon-sized head of the dragon who had carried us here, huge cream-colored eyes glowing with hunger. Her jaws snapped, but then I realized she was speaking when I heard her growled voice again.

"You should eat as well. What kind of godmother would I be if I didn't look after you?" Then she was off, flying back through the wide mouth of the cavern we'd walked through, her wings pushing so much air behind her we toppled over.

I had a dragon godmother?

"Olyve suffers from low blood sugar," Sandy explained. "Makes her mighty grumpy when she doesn't have a steady supply of fish or sheep. She's already eaten half the herd the villagers left behind."

"And the villagers?" I asked. The castle was abandoned recently. Or harvested.

"Gone away, most before we arrived," Sandy said. "There was already too much evil, and then Harbinger and the rest came, which sent the stragglers running. We'd best get walking. Olyve said to feed you, so let's return to the tower. I saw a larder somewhere around there, as you can't eat what I eat."

"What do you mean by 'too much evil'?" I asked.

"From the relic," she said, as though I should know all about it. She fluttered ahead, and Ilsa and I hurried to keep up.

My sister was strangely quiet. I was usually her favorite person to ridicule, so her silence was eerie.

When the tunnel opened out into starry night and glowing white sand, the first moon on the rise, I could see Ilsa clearly. The same wide-eyes and rigid lips had greeted me in the mirror plenty of times.

"I'm scared too," I told her.

"Don't speak to me." Her words were lost in the sound of wind and surf. There were things I wanted to say, more to reassure myself, but I left her in peace.

A mini cyclone stirred the sand between us, growing taller than me, and I paused, watching it sprout arms and legs, each a separate funnel of spinning sand. A mouth and dark eyes formed in the hollow areas where its head might be. No-Thing.

"What evil?" I asked him, as Sandy hadn't answered before.

"Predatory creatures and spirits, revenants ... Harbinger. Many of my fellows felt the call and were drawn to the waters off the coast here. They summoned the rest of us when they recognized the effects of the relic. We have seen it before in Solheim."

"In Solheim?"

"Yes, the artifact has been in their possession since ages ago, making them a great and terrible empire. The object draws power to it and then poisons the minds of all those around. Your kind turned to dark thoughts and deeds, finally summoning the God of Death in your madness."

"How? What else do you know about the relic?" I asked. It sounded to me like a too convenient explanation for why my people had a bad reputation. I didn't believe it for a second. Then again ... what Ilsa had said about us once being friends still disturbed me. Was I the anomaly?

"It is called The First Soul," Sandy said. Once again, she'd been listening in when I thought she was oblivious.

"Is it?" I asked.

"What?"

"The first soul."

Sandy shrugged. "It's purported to be a gem, so it's probably more like 'the star of Darrub' or some such."

"It is no mere gem," No-Thing insisted. "It is a relic of the oldest gods, the Primals, and it could well be the result of their first efforts at crafting a soul. That would explain why it is flawed."

"The Primals? Do you mean Lightbringer?" I said. I hadn't dared interrupt the hearing, but I'd been wondering about the term since then.

Sandy snorted but didn't say anything. My questions were funny for some reason.

"There have been three generations of gods," No-Thing said, "beginning with Chaos and Mater. The Primals, including the Dead God, are their children. Lightbringer and the rest people now worship in their temples are the youngest. Or almost the youngest. A fourth generation is on the rise."

This was all new to me, and I wanted to ask more, but Sandy interrupted, impatient. "No-Thing keeps skirting around the real reason you've been brought here, aside from the obvious inevitability of execution."

"Inevitability?" I said, stopping. "They were undecided."

"Don't be naïve." Sandy snorted again. I must be a real hoot. "Harbinger kills a living being every night, and most of the others have grown calloused over the ages as well. Do you think they would hesitate to destroy your soul if there was even the slightest risk you could open the doorway to the Dead God and annihilate this world of theirs? We soft-hearted ones, No-Thing and I, have been burdened with keeping tabs on you. The others would casually see you dead. The only reason they don't risk it is that gem. They want it, and they think you can find it."

"Why me? Because I'm a detective?"

This time Sandy laughed outright, bent over, holding her sides. Ilsa stopped walking, cocking her head back to listen.

When Sandy finally stopped and wiped away tears of mirth, she said, "Detective." And started laughing again.

Okay, I was a crap detective, but I wanted to be better. How could you learn without doing? It wasn't like there was an apprentice program or anything.

"I do not like to interfere," No-Thing said over her giggles, "but there is knowledge the others would impart to you if they were inclined," he must have meant not laughing uncontrollably, "and the better armed with information you are the better your decisions may be. I want you well armed. I am an observer, but I have observed that which makes me believe in the potential of the keys even when the others do not."

"What have you seen? What do you know?" I asked for what seemed the millionth time. Despite his words, No-Thing was slow to share the knowledge I really wanted: How could I save myself?

"I heard orders from the Dead God's chief general, a command to find the keys else they were certain to fail. I heard your name spoken, Eva. Your soul will open the door for them. They say 'but she must not be allowed to close it first.'"

"So, it can be closed. I don't suppose they said how?"

"No."

Sandy, red-faced but under control now, flew up and hovered, looking me in the eyes. "The others won't give you a real chance to find out, so delay giving them the relic."

"That should be simple, as I don't know the first thing about it and certainly not how to find it."

"You need to appear more confident than that," she warned. "Your life depends on it. All our lives. I'm with No-Thing on this and believe it's possible for you to close Him out. The others are trusting in the Compact we brokered, but I do not have faith in it. Rules are broken all the time. Try to make a little bit of progress towards finding the relic but focus on stopping the Dead God."

I threw up my hands. "I still don't understand any better what to do. Some useful information please?"

"I know nothing more about the keys," No-Thing said, "but the Dead God's general might."

"Who is that?"

"Lili of Solheim."

My mother. She was alive, as Erick had said. Why did hope flare in me? I wanted to see her. Not just to ask how she could have sacrificed me, her own daughter, to the Dead God but also ... to see her face. To know what my mother looked like.

"Then I'll find a way to question her," I said. I often made bold statements with no idea how to achieve them. No-Thing and Sandy didn't seem to notice how impossible it sounded. Maybe because they were Impossibles themselves. "And the relic?" I added. "Why does Harbinger need me to find it?"

Neither answered my question.

"Either you or Ilsa would do," Sandy finally said. "It's your bloodline. Your father and all his family before him were keepers of the relic in Old Solheim. They protected it for millennia. Neither Harbinger nor any of the others could touch it with a keeper watching over it. The keeper must hand it over willingly, and believe me, your ancestors were good at seeing past trickery to keep a firm grip on it. Only now, it's no longer in their possession, lost beneath the sea here, along with other treasures stolen during the fall of Solheim. Harbinger believes you can go below and retrieve it, that your bloodline can claim it, and that you can be tricked or threatened into handing it over."

"And then he'll kill me, right?" I said.

"Of course."

"Aren't there any good guys?" I asked aloud.

"There's you," Sandy said, cheerfully.

That didn't reassure me, as I knew I was far from a paragon of virtue.

I was as quiet as Ilsa as we made our way back into the castle. Sandy and No-Thing didn't bother locking us in the tower again. They showed us to the kitchen, pointed out the salted pork and barrels of beans and other items in the larder, and left us to fend for ourselves.

My cooking was a comedy of errors. Ilsa stepped in to fix the stew I was making, still creepily silent, despite my attempts to draw her out.

Finally, I said, "Come on. I thought you were tough. You can't be that scared? Sure, things look dire, but we have a few Unmentionables on our side. We'll convince them we're more useful alive, and then we'll find a way to stop the Dead God."

"You keep assuming that's what I want," she hissed.

I stopped and stared at her. When I could speak again, I said, "Don't you understand? It's not natural for Death to walk the land. It's not about conquering the world; He will end the world. Gypsum and the others who serve Him may live, somewhere else, but everything and everyone here will die. No more High-crowne, the only home we've ever known. No more—"

"—You still haven't said a thing to change my mind. Solhans will live. I will live. What else is there, sister?"

Acid burned through that last word. I'd never seen such hate in her eyes before. Then it dawned on me.

"You can't be jealous? Mother left me behind in Solheim to die, an infant sacrificial bride to the God of Death. Is that the fate you wished you'd had? If Morgan hadn't come back for me...."

She raised her nose and scrunched her face. "This stew smells disgusting. Eat it yourself." And she stormed out of the kitchen.

I put out the fire in the stove but added another log to the fireplace, as its orange light was the only thing pushing back deep shadows in the huge kitchen.

I sat down at a long, wooden table meant for a dozen cooks and servers, now empty, and played with my dinner, letting the brownish liquid dribble out of my spoon again and again.

I felt as alone as I would be when the whole world was dead. Maybe Ilsa was right, and it would feel the same for me as now. Maybe it made no difference, life or death.

If you had a soul that was.

The Unmentionables would ensure that no part of us survived, not even our ghosts, unless we appeased them. I doubted even then we could be saved.

I threw the wooden spoon across the room and splattered brown liquid down the far wall.

Forget about me and Ilsa. I would not be the one who let every human, goblin, dwarf or Avian I'd ever known be dragged to the halls of the dead. What had been the point of it all? The striving, the clinging to life by the fingernails ... all of history for what? So, I could end everything?

No.

I thought of my nephew. Little Viktor deserved to grow up. I wanted to see what Bell would invent next, wanted to argue with the goblin doctor and with Nanny even. I wanted ... and that is what made me alive: wanting to keep on wanting.

I wiped the tears that had seeped unbidden from my eyes, picked up the spoon and washed it with water from a barrel before sitting back down and eating the stew so heartily it could have been the finest ever produced by a chef. When I was done, I leaned back and smiled, watching the flames in the fireplace dance and cast shifting shadows across the wall.

"That's the spirit," an unseen someone whispered.

"No-Thing?" I said, sitting up.

The voice hadn't sounded like his. It rasped, with a twinkle of delight I'd never heard from the invisible creature.

One of the shadows by the fire turned and walked in front of the flames, obscuring them. I saw a hunched shape with feathers sticking up from its back and horns on its head. Its legs were bent like a dog's or a wolf's, but the profile of its face was human. A red glowing eye, like a bit of trapped fire, looked at me. More fire filled its face as it smiled. It stepped toward me but remained only a shadow.

"Who are you?" I asked. "I didn't see you earlier with the other Unmentionables."

"You guess rightly that I am one of them, or was. Long ago. Until they kicked me out. Or did I leave? Details become fuzzy over the eons."

"Why did they kick you out?" Adrenaline made me stand, and my mind raced furiously. There was something decidedly dangerous about this creature, like all the others, but the thought of someone even the

Unmentionables didn't want, someone expelled from their councils, made me particularly jumpy.

"I cared not for their petty manipulations," he said, and my racing heart slowed a little. The creature smiled as it spoke, and it was hard to tell if it was lying or simply thought the whole world amusing. He leaned in, confidentially, and added, "My jokes were funnier than theirs."

"Why are you here now, talking to me?"

"You don't want my company?"

"I didn't say that. Only ... an introduction would be polite. I'm Eva, and you are?"

"Oh, I know who you are. When first I saw your face, you were a squalling little brat, laying on that cold white stone. The tears and wails haunt me now. I do not like squalling children. My ears are too sensitive. Something had to be done."

"What do you mean?"

"I had no idea when I sent that blade master in the right direction to find you that his saving you would cause such a fuss. Well, I may have guessed a bit. It did sound like fun to spoil the climax of a ritual ten long centuries in the making." He giggled, and it was like a hyena's laugh.

"You sent Morgan to save me?"

"He was on his way. I only helped. That's what I do. A little nudge here and there. Sometimes a help. Sometimes a hindrance is a help. And sometimes a hindrance is simply pleasure. For me that is. I do love to laugh, and there was nothing so funny as the look on your mother's face when she went to offer you up and there was nothing there. Other sacrifices were made, but still not enough. What a wonderful mess of things. You are still making such a wonderful mess of things, and I'm so glad I stopped you wailing. Although, you do need a nudge from time to time. All mortals do. It's for their own good I say. And so funny."

"You're the Trickster," I said, having finally reconciled the black ink drawings I'd seen in books with the real thing standing in front of me. The Trickster liked to cause trouble. There were tales of him fooling the Lightbringer into granting fire to primitives or getting Love and Wisdom to war with one another over a misunderstanding. "Wait a minute," I began, "You're a...."

"A god? A useless term that. Immortal? Perhaps. Able and willing to play with the fates of mortals? Oh yes. I think that is the best definition of a god. Else you'd be like a bored old Primal or the first ones. I have no idea how they spend their days and don't care to know. Give me life and death. Give me the end of the world."

"I'm going to stop it," I said, determined.

"That's right. I couldn't remember which I was hoping for now. I do so forget which game I'm playing."

"The game is not so fun when you're one of the pieces."

"Yes, it is. I was once like you. Well...." He looked at my chest and then at his. "Not exactly. Sometimes, I wish I could go back," he said, wistful.

"Why don't you?"

"Done is done." He capered about the room like a faun. "But tell Harbinger not to walk my path. Keep away from the First Soul. It's mine now, and I'll leave it lying where I like. It's none of Harbinger's business. You'll pass along the message?"

"Yes, but...?"

And the Trickster jumped into the flames and vanished, another giggle drifting through the air on the sparks and cloud of smoke he'd stirred up in the giant fireplace.

"But what should I do now?" I asked the emptiness.

I didn't think the Trickster cared.

I turned back to wash my bowl, when he suddenly reappeared beside me, leaning in like an old friend.

"You may want the First Soul for yourself. You may want it very much, for it was used to bring the Dead God here, and it will be needed to send Him back again. You against Harbinger. Can't wait to see that." There was a hungry, dangerous sound to his words, a stark contrast to his earlier glee, and I felt a chill before he vanished again.

I remembered the muscled vampire with his stag horns and predatory gaze. All the Unmentionables, even that creepy spider and Olyve with her hidden depths of darkness, deferred to him. He was one of the evil things drawn here to Faellion, the most frightening of frightening things I suspected.

He looked like a pushover to me. The game was on.

5   MUD AND WATER

Nothing like facing the loss of everything you held dear to motivate. It was the middle of the night, but I'd lost time trapped in Sandy's bubble somewhere between this world and the fairy lands. I was wide awake and not wanting to waste any more time, so I went looking for Olyve. Dragon godmothers had to be good for something.

"Olyvandra!" I called from the nearest balcony. The empty castle was a maze, but my night vision allowed me to find my way without a torch. Now that both moons had risen, the landscape outside was even clearer to see, the starry sky alight with a soft blue glow.

A dark form banked, blocking out the stars. The dragon's silhouette crossed the largest moon before coming to perch on the railing beside me. The sandstone cracked beneath her weight.

"Alright, Olyve," I said. "I've learned all Sandy and No-Thing know, which is nothing useful. You seem like a smart dragon lady. You tell me what I'm missing. What do I need to do to defeat the Dead God? How do I use a key and a relic?"

"If I knew, I would tell you," Olyve said, her dragon voice booming. Her golden scales rippled and turned into the golden locks of the small elf girl she pretended to be most of the time. She climbed down from the railing, her delicate satin slippers making a small sound as she did so. The broken railing crumbled and fell to the ground far below, the damage already done.

"Perhaps," she continued in a child's voice, "Ulric knows more about the keys. He was an Asheen, one of the Nine, and he is a friend."

"I'm not so sure about that." Then again, he might be easier to talk to than my mother.

"Nevertheless, you might compel answers from him. As for the relic, it is surrounded by beings drawn to the dark, and even we Unmentionables hesitate to go beneath the waves. Those creatures may let you pass, as you have a claim to the treasure, a legitimacy that we lack. I care not how you achieve it, but you must retrieve it, for it is one thing our number agrees on.

That and your extermination should you fail at any step."

Olyve might just be more frightening than Harbinger.

"I thought you were my godmother. Can't you talk to them, convince them to help instead of threaten? I know Harbinger wants the relic to become a god, but isn't defeating the one already destroying the world a bigger priority? We're all on the same side."

"No. We do not take sides and have no loyalty but to each other. It is our cardinal rule, not to fight among ourselves. If we did, the consequences would be terrible. You are on your own, Eva. You can rely on no one."

"Not the pep talk I was hoping for."

"It is a hard but vital lesson. You are a necromancer. Born for this. The only one who can decide your fate is you."

"I'm not a necromancer." Or was that the old me talking? I'd done some things I wasn't proud of lately. I certainly hadn't paid enough attention to Nanny's lessons to say I was trained.

Most assumed necromancy was raising the dead, but it was about that which endures beyond death. The soul. I had seen ghosts, rarely, but never learned to call them to me as necromancers usually did. Nanny told tales of raising corpses in her youth, reanimating them with a chained soul, and she might have been able to do it. But since the coming of the god, no one left dead bodies lying around to practice on. Before the market bombing that is. I'd seen plenty then, their souls harvested. I didn't like being stuck watching helplessly like that.

"Teach me more. I want to learn."

"Teach?" Olyve said, incredulous. "Death is not my skill."

"It's mine," I said. "Thane told me so himself. He said I should embrace my gift. I could end the world as easily as save it. Easier even. All I have to do is surrender. Help me do the right thing."

"I'm not sure I can. All I can do is stop you, my dear." The words seemed out of place with her high voice, but it was scarier because of that contrast. I was reminded of the dragon who hid beneath her girlish face. "Make no mistake, for I, like all the others, am here to judge you. I'm surprised you've swayed No-Thing to your side. Few know that Harbinger wants the artifact to become a god. He must trust you greatly."

"No-Thing didn't tell me, the Trickster did."

Olyve snapped back into her true form like the snap of a sheet being folded, her elf form wavering and shifting into a looming dragon with an angry snarl on its huge mouth. This time walls cracked, and I took several steps back, afraid the roof would come down on me.

"The Trickster. He was here? When?" she demanded to know.

"Not long ago. In the kitchen fireplace."

From Olyve's reaction, I didn't think it wise to say more, how he'd watched over me when I was an infant. Perhaps my whole life.

"Trickster will make it more difficult to retrieve the First Soul. He and Harbinger have forever been at odds."

"Why do you defer to Harbinger so much? He's just a vampire. You're a dragon for gods' sakes." Before I'd met real werewolves recently, not to mention gods, I probably never would have said 'just' a vampire, but perspective changes things.

"He was once a vampire, yes, as we were all once many things before becoming an Unmentionable. All of us are unique, powerful specimens of our kind. Survivors." She flexed her talons, and I got the distinct sense she was picturing all the animals and people skewered on them in her lifetime. "When everyone else has died around you, you begin to realize either you have a knack for living or a knack for bringing death to those you love. That 'vampire' is neither fully alive nor one to worry about love. He exists, and he has existed for a long time. The first predator. His knack is death itself. Like you.

"Only, he is far more experienced about it and lacks any weakness like self-doubt or compassion. Of all of us, Harbinger is the most ruthless. Even the Dead God, who must shepherd the souls of the departed between worlds, to punishment and reward, through the Forge of Fate, even He is more compassionate. He must be, for He has purpose. Harbinger has no purpose. That makes him dangerous," Olyve warned.

"I need the First Soul too," I said, "to shut out the Dead God. Trickster told me. So, I will have to face … or run away from Harbinger." After Olyve's little speech, running away sounded like a better plan than my usual ones.

"That is not good news. You cannot trust the Trickster, but it makes sense you would need the relic, as I'm sure the Solhan Nine included it in all their rituals. But there is no running from Harbinger, and fighting would be … unwise. Trickery always worked for Harbinger's nemesis. You must be crafty."

"Not my strong point."

"I cannot teach you guile any more than I can teach you necromancy." She seemed deep in thought, even though it was hard to tell with a dragon, her gaze straying to the moons. "I have one lesson I can teach."

She plucked me up, her yellow claws like a cage, and dangled me over the broken railing. Black rocks beckoned and ocean roiled beneath me. I screamed and scratched at her like a kitten.

She placed me back on the balcony and smirked, her dragon lips curling up on one side. "You must learn to ignore unwarranted fear."

"Fear of falling to my death is not unwarranted."

"Isn't it? When Death loves you?"

"Thane, not Death, although that whole split personality confuses me. Not to mention the whole thing is disturbing, so let's not go there."

When my heartbeat slowed, I added. "Wait a minute. Was that the one lesson? No secrets of the universe or tips for killing a vampire?"

"No. The lesson is this: learn to recognize your true enemies. I would not let you fall. Even so, there will be times when you know a true enemy has you caged, and the fear chills you to utter immobility. Here is an extra lesson free of charge: you must learn to deal with fear."

"I deal with it all the time, usually by charging head on. Nothing like the need to survive to hone the mind when you need it."

"You cannot rely on luck. Harbinger could rip out your throat before you blinked let alone opened your mouth to speak. You must learn to plan."

"That's another lesson you slipped in. Why don't you go ahead and teach me about magic now?"

"Alright. Again: You must face fear, swallow fear until there is nothing but pure intent remaining. Magical mastery does not depend on the memorization of spells, nor—in the case of beings such as you and I who do not use spells—raw strength of will. It is about focused intent, which begins with a focused mind."

"When you even say the word 'focus' my mind wanders." I thought about the time I'd drained a troll's life. "What about desire? Emotion? Instinct? Those things seem to work for me."

"Raw need can summon great power, but focused intent is required to make best use of it."

"Focus," I repeated. "Okay. That's all? There must be more to it than that?"

"Some use the words of spells, effigies, or charms to direct their will, but most rely on others' will already caged within such tokens. We have only this blank canvas before us. All was once plucked from the Void, and all is shapeable and re-shapeable with practice."

I reached out my senses and felt a few scurrying crabs, insects in the trees, sandflies and schools of fish close to the shore.

"There's not a lot of souls here for me to work with," I said. "And that seems to be what I do, manipulate souls."

"You have never done any other kind of magic? Usually the barriers between disciplines are only barriers of the mind. Of course, soul magic, true necromancy such as yours, is not the usual sort of magic, and few can accomplish it. Perhaps you are limited and have no other skills?"

"I have pushed people back with my will and some other things." I knew I sounded defensive, but I didn't like the label 'limited'.

"The difference between those who heal wounds and those who shape worlds from the Void is only a small one. Not even I can shape worlds, of course, for those with such skill are gods. But as Trickster knows, it is a short journey from here to there, especially if you cheat."

"Cheat?" I liked the sound of that.

"The First Soul is a cheat for would-be gods. Like a charm to an unschooled practitioner. It is borrowed focus. Trickster has learned more in his own right and no longer depends on the relic, but that was not the case when he first stole it from across the Void and brought it here to learn its secrets. Harbinger saw and began to covet the relic's power."

She shifted a bit of broken balustrade with the tip of one claw. It looked like a pebble next to her, but it was big enough to crush my foot, so I dodged when she almost rolled it over me. When it came to rest, she said, "Move this with your will then. You said you have done it before."

I tried; I really did. From focus to sheer anger. In the end, I kicked the rock and hurt my toe. Not even that shifted it.

"I don't understand," I said. "I can't seem to do it here. I've been able to command souls, to pull them out of bodies or squeeze them tight so they are confined, unable to shift … I've stopped a cave in for gods' sakes! Why can't I do this?"

"You're not seeing what's right in front of you."

"It's a rock."

"Look deeper."

"There's nothing deeper. Rock and more rock. A spark, maybe, but certainly not a soul."

"I'm not talking about souls. I'm talking about the Void stuff."

"Now that's just stupid. How can the Void have stuff? It wouldn't be a void then."

"Look."

"I can't."

"Then Harbinger will kill you." Olyve sounded like the fact didn't affect her one way or another.

Nothing like a bit of fear to motivate me.

I tried to 'see' what she was talking about. My soul sense had started coming to me easily, but this was like straining to see something hidden behind a mountain. Then I saw the mountain.

"Oh."

I sent my perception into the stone. It was heavy; it existed; it was a weight in the world, a bit of that thick, heavy blackness of the Void. Now that I knew what I was looking for, it was obvious.

"Oh. It's everywhere," I marveled, looking around me with new eyes. The world was gluggy. The air, the moonlight even, it was heavy. We were embedded in something like mud, gummed together. Sand or wind or water appeared different but were really the same.

"It doesn't shift about as easily as souls," I said, absently.

"Like a potter grows skilled in shaping clay, you can gain skill in shaping matter. Have you held clay?" she asked.

"It's thick and heavy too."

"Exactly. At first, you can barely scrape into it with your fingers, and must mold it slowly. Eventually, you learn to water it down, to set it spinning on a wheel, to more finely craft it."

"What's the equivalent of water? How do I get that?" Call me lazy.

"It was only an analogy. Water is power, and for the gods, molding our world is like shaping liquid clay, perhaps easier even. But we are not gods. You must do it the hard way."

"Oh." Why did I think it would be easy?

I tried. Again. But it's quite unnatural to do anything to a stone without touching it. It twitched, I think, before I gave up, frustrated and cursing, all hope of 'focus' impossible.

"It's ... something," Olyve said. "Nothing, actually. How can someone be so strong, yet so inept?"

"I think I prefer 'limited' to 'inept'." So, I wasn't the most talented pupil.

"Howsoever you manage it, and from all appearances without magic, you must make some attempt to recover the relic. Many of us, especially those who mistrust talk of 'keys', believe it alone can save us in the end. We Unmentionables will survive, no matter the cost," Olyve said.

"Is there a deadline?" The 'dead' part of that word made far more sense to me now.

"We will all have a say. No time is set, and many of my compatriots lose track of ages, but we are fast running out of ages. The Dead God's armies took the Fortress of Mages yesterday."

"No." I was shocked. The Fortress was legendary, the site of the greatest battles ever fought, the best human warlocks standing against a god ... were they all dead?

"Now that it has fallen, the enemy marches on the goblins to the south of us and pushes into old Darrub, where there is nothing but scattered tribes to face His hordes. Soon, only the Three Kingdoms will remain. On that day, the Compact will be broken. It is being chipped at even now, but it is certain to break when the Dead God chafes too much at it."

"Won't the other gods do something? No-Thing said—" I began.

"Lightbringer, Fortune, all the Elder gods are beyond our understanding. I fear that, even together, they cannot compel a Primal like Death to obey the Compact forever, and they merely wait for the storm to pass. The Dead God was summoned here, marking this world for annihilation. He will not leave until that task is achieved."

I'd always grumbled about Highcrowne winters, rude elves, Nanny's cooking. It all seemed precious now.

"What next then?"

"*Next* is the relic. Face the denizens of the depths and discover where it lies beneath the waves."

"Aren't the keys more important? You could take me back to Highcrowne, I could wrest some answers out of Ulric." I didn't enjoy the thought of facing my uncle, but he was a familiar foe.

"No," Olyve said, shifting form. She shook her tiny elf head to emphasize the point, but I kept picturing the dragon in her place. It must be an aftereffect of so much concentration. I could actually see where the majority of her bulk, her true form, was hidden in the folds of Void stuff.

"Why, no?"

"You need the First Soul. Trickster gave you that hint, and for all we know, the relic may be one of the keys. More importantly, we Unmentionables will feel safer knowing it is within reach, and you will be safer if it is under your control." Seemed Olyve wasn't keen to hand it over to Harbinger. Maybe she wanted the power for herself. Maybe they all wanted it and weren't willing to share, no matter their cardinal rule about getting along with one another.

"Will I be a god if I find it?" I asked, hesitant. I wasn't sure I could handle that. On first thought, it sounded fantastic, but then what? Politics between Primals and Elders, rules and betrayal…. The fairy had the right idea: stay out of it all unless the fate of the world was at stake.

"No," Olyve said in that curt, condescending way of hers. She looked at the broken stone that had bested me. "You will most certainly not be a god. It is a cheat for those almost there, not some miraculous object that could transform mere mortals. Else your whole family would be gods.”

“That makes sense.” Okay, I was a bit disappointed.

Then all her talking finally sunk in. “Wait,” I said. “Beneath the sea?”

“It is dangerous. The Denizens of the Deep can be deadly at the best of times, let alone when frenzied by the presence of the relic.”

“Go beneath the water hunting for it? Under the water. You know I can’t swim, right?” Not to mention the ‘denizens’, but first terrifying thought first.

“I don’t think you need to worry about swimming when underwater. It’s breathing that’s the trouble.”

“Breathing?” I grumbled.

She transformed once again and flew off, before I could cajole any more help out of her.

I stood alone on the broken sandstone balcony, looking down at the crashing waves—facing ‘unwarranted’ fear—dizzy and ready to throw up, but I soon had the answer.

Ilsa.

I found my sister easily. I’d never believed in that connection between twins, the finishing of each other’s sentences was just coincidence, but I wondered if there wasn't some truth to it when I let my feet guide me, and I found her on the roof next to the prison tower.

She was looking out to sea, towards Highcrowne or Solheim. I suspected Solheim, as the ancient city and the lurking god drew me too. Maybe we were more alike than I wanted to admit.

"Ilsa," I began sweetly. If she could manipulate, so could I. "I regret all of this, for both our sakes. Tell me more of the time we were friends. I'd like to remember."

"What do you want?" She sounded annoyed. I supposed there was no manipulating a master manipulator.

"Your charms. Not your 'Sugar' this and 'Sugar' that kind of charms that seem to work on besotted men and the social climbers you call friends, but the kind you craft from charcoal and embroidered thread. We need to retrieve that relic, or our souls will be destroyed. I need your help to go searching for it off the coast. And, as mentioned, I can't swim let alone breathe underwater."

"Our souls," she repeated, her tone haunted. "You hold all that is of value to me. You know that? It feels like the greatest part of me is missing. My ambition, my power, my dreams. All I have left is the faintest memory of them. You are crueler than I have ever been."

"At least I'm not a remorseless killer," I shot back. "You've had that mark on your hand since we were children." I pointed to the star-shaped scar on the webbing between her thumb and forefinger. Nanny had explained to me the Solhan custom of not leaving enemies alive, and when I first had to kill in self-defense she offered me the mark. I refused, ashamed of what I'd done. Ilsa had had the mark as long as I could remember.

"Killing is a mercy. Better than leaving someone in this state," she said. "And I never ended so many lives as after you took mine, *Sugar*. I tried to steal souls as you did, to no effect. It restored me for a time, but the stolen power always went away, returned to those it belonged to, even though they resided in the halls of the dead, it was theirs again. I have nothing. All I can think about, all I can hope, is that when you are dead, what you took from me will be returned."

"Who did you murder?" I asked. I was disgusted talking to her. I needed her, and a part of me didn't want to know all she'd done. I wouldn't be able to keep talking to her. But another part of me needed to know, so I could add them to the tally I was responsible for. She killed because of what I had done to her. Their deaths were on me. I should know their names.

She shrugged. "It doesn't matter. Refugees, travelers. The forgotten. I don't want to be forgotten. I will help you retrieve the relic, placate the

Unmentionables ... but then I will kill you and consign your name to the dust alongside those unfortunates."

Ilsa's bargain didn't sound enticing. "You can try to kill me," I warned, "but I won't make it easy for you."

6 Truce

There was little I understood as Ilsa worked. I helped her fetch cloth, thread, scissors, and needles from a castle storeroom, but afterwards, all I could do was watch her sew.

She fashioned a new dress out of golden silk. Her stitches to bind the larger pieces together were hasty and not pretty, but she took her time on the fine embroidery around the waist and neckline. I saw arcane symbols shaped from golden thread. I only knew half of them and not well enough to understand how they would behave when linked together. The dress she was making could be meant to kill me for all I knew.

"That one is yours. I want pants," I told her when I realized this would take all day. "I'll find us weapons and something to eat."

She snickered as I headed for the door.

"What?" I asked, exasperated. She was forever sniping at me with looks, a carefully placed word here or there, sighs and laughs she kept to herself. I didn't know why I kept asking to be let in on the joke.

"Weapons?" she replied this time. "We'll have our magic to protect us, sister dear, and that is all. Have you ever tried to wield a sword underwater?"

"And you have? Never mind. Daggers then, something. My magic isn't the reliable kind. You take your needle and embroider them to death, and I'll bring iron and silver. That should cover most dark creatures I'm aware of."

I found the armory. It was useful having a recently abandoned castle to ransack for whatever we needed. I liked the weight of a spiked iron mace but knew it wouldn't be practical. An iron stiletto would have to do. I was disappointed by the lack of silver swords, but the fleeing elves probably thought they'd need them to deal with the evil drawn to their island. They didn't know Harbinger. So, I went hunting for the dining cutlery.

I found a library instead. The books were too tempting to resist. Most were local histories, handmade and hand bound, but there was a section of the newer, machine printed books you could find in Highcrowne.

Viktor's shop, my bookshop technically, although it had never felt like mine and was more Kali's, carried the rarer, old fashioned kinds with leather covers and embossed lettering. They were works of art in their own right, but it was these cheap mass productions that drew me.

I wondered if they had the latest Elf Butler mystery? I loved them because they were told from the point of view of an amateur detective who spent his days as a butler, overlooked by the elf aristocracy, until he could swoop in and solve the crime. Who stole the sapphire broach? Who killed Duchess Celia's pet wyvern? That sort of thing.

I felt guilty even contemplating taking time to read a chapter or two, but it was a thrilling kind of guilty. I spotted what I was looking for, and my hand reached out for the white spine. I heard a noise, and I spun, bringing my new dagger to bear.

I wished I had my Ashur, but I hadn't remembered to ask Olyve for my family sword. I'm sure she'd taken it. The Unmentionables hadn't allowed us weapons, and there was no telling if they'd let me keep the dagger, but I needed something to defend myself with when I went relic hunting—and library browsing.

"Hello?" I called.

There was no answer. Shelves encircled the huge chamber, but the middle space was empty. In the center was a shadow that crept across the wood floor where no shadow should be. It was rat-shaped, with a snout, tail and the distinctive outline of claws and teeth. It made my hairs stand on end, and I was starting to realize why the castle was empty. I grabbed my book and hurried off.

It could have been Trickster or an Unmentionable stalking me. Or something else. Best I look busy. And find some silver.

I stopped in the dining room on my way back and rifled through drawers. The knives were dull, so I chose a silver serving wedge with a sharp edge. "It's knife-like," I said, justifying the choice to myself and whoever might be listening in.

I returned to find Ilsa had made shorts out of gauzy white cloth. That was not what I meant by pants. I did not like showing my legs, as I'd been forced to do since we'd cut our dresses for rope. It was unseemly and chilly.

"You have to make the top shorter and the pants longer," I said.

She smiled, and I realized this was another of her petty tricks.

"I've already finished the spells, and it would be a waste to redo them," she said. "How about I lengthen the top, add a solid underdress. Blue do you think? You love sky blue." Now she was sounding sweet. It made my hairs stand on end all over again.

I furrowed my brow. I'd filled Ilsa in on some of the things I'd learned about the First Soul, but not about Trickster, nor Harbinger's plans for the relic, not to mention how powerful it was. Actually, I'd told her nothing. Still, I worried she was being too helpful. I'd be watching her.

"I don't know what's down there, but there's a reason they're sending us expendable types to fetch it," I said. "Not to mention the fact this castle wouldn't be abandoned if a pod of friendly dolphins had moved in. I don't want to be half naked on top of being almost defenseless."

She nodded, once again unnerving me with her lack of argument.

I didn't read, as I'd been tempted, and instead tried to turn those shorts into pants. I did my best to attach some darker tubes of cloth that would hide my legs, but Ilsa was done before I could finish.

"Let's go. It's ready." She held up my new dress, and it definitely was a dress now. "That will come right off," she added, tearing away the extensions I'd worked hard to add to the lower half. Were trousers or riding pants really so difficult for her to tolerate? Little torments. That was Ilsa.

I noticed orange light streaming through the window, which made Ilsa's golden gown look spectacular. Of course, she got the nicer one.

"The day is nearly over," I said. "We should wait until tomorrow."

"It won't matter beneath the water. If we need to go deep, there'll be no light anyway."

I felt queasy. Trapped beneath tons of water, surrounded by deadly creatures, and at the mercy of my sister's spells for survival. This was the point in a case when I realized how stupid my plans always were. Problem was, I couldn't think of anything better.

"Fine." I stripped out of the rags of my old dress and put the new one on. It fit perfectly, of course. Ilsa and I were the same size. The sky blue, silk dress and gauzy top looked great together, and I even had comfortable shorts, if not pants, to wear beneath.

I felt the runes embroidered around the waist and neckline. They seemed harmless, but I didn't know enough about my magical sense to fully trust it.

"How do these work?" I asked.

"Invoke the symbols with your blood. You do know how to do that?" she asked, like I was a child.

"Yes."

"Then the rest is easy. Walk beneath the water as you would on land. If you need to rise up or float to the surface, run your finger across the runes. Do that again when you wish to drop down again."

"How did you learn all this?" I asked, impressed.

"With effort. You should try it some time." She wrinkled up her nose at me and set off, her ability to be sweet having obviously reached its limit.

I followed, hefting the iron dagger and the silver almost-knife I'd found. I was woefully unprepared for what lay ahead. I'd always been the brash one, more confident in my sword skills than my studies, but that needed to change.

Olyve and Ilsa weren't the first people to point out how poor a student I was. Magic would be nice to have now. I needed to face the Denizens of the Deep, whoever they were, not to mention Harbinger, and I couldn't help but think of that cheat, the First Soul, lying somewhere below. It wouldn't make me a god, but it certainly wouldn't hurt to get my hands on it as quick as I could?

The breeze blew my hair back, and I breathed deeply. There was something familiar about the sea, although I could have sworn I'd never been before. Perhaps as a child, and I forgot?

Ilsa marched into the waves without a backward glance. She was far too eager. She definitely wanted to get her hands on the First Soul too.

It would be a race.

I left my boots on the beach and ran after her, stumbling in loose sand, before being pushed around by the waves. I remembered to invoke the runes before I got too deep, using the dagger to prick my finger.

I'd learned magic at my uncle's knee, Morgan's actually. Ulric had servants for everything, even raising and educating his wards, Ilsa, Viktor, and I.

Hard to believe, but I'd been a dutiful child, until I didn't want to be anymore. Perhaps it was Viktor who rebelled first, and I followed him, or perhaps it was that nudge Trickster took credit for? All I knew was, one day I didn't care about pleasing Uncle Ulric any-more. Solhan necromancy was our inheritance, and he hated that I turned away from it, but some of the things Nanny began to teach turned my stomach. I stopped paying attention to magic, hoping it would forget about me too, but that wasn't to be. There is no running from who you are. Viktor taught me that after he died.

I held my breath and ducked down to test Ilsa's handiwork before trusting my life to it. The water was a beautiful, cerulean blue and so much calmer than the waves above. A small school of white fish raced past me. I twisted around, hair and dress swirling as I moved, feeling the water pressing against my eyes. I finally exhaled and opened my mouth. It was hard forcing myself to breathe water, and I prepared to choke as soon as the liquid hit my lungs, but it didn't.

I was breathing regular air, and the water never passed my lips. I said something, and air bubbles floated to the surface. I couldn't hear myself too well, the words muffled by a whooshing, gurgling sound from the waves.

Ilsa was ahead of me, her golden dress floating around her and lending her an ethereal quality that didn't match her disposition. She disappeared into the darker depths, and I hurried to catch up, my legs moving in slow motion through the water. The knives in my hands felt like toys, all my limbs lightened and buoyed. I reached out with both arms and pushed back, trying to propel myself forward, but my top half got ahead of my lower half, and I was swimming. A sad approximation of it, anyway.

It was too dark to see Ilsa or much of anything. The golden orange of sunset faded from the world above. Ahead of me was murky gray. I swam on, relieved when my dress began to glow in the dark. It put off a blue-tinged light all around. I still couldn't see Ilsa, but then I stopped worrying about following her. She didn't know where to go any more than I did.

I reached out with my senses: Souls surrounded me. The sparks of fish and fields of kelp, and larger souls too. Dark, menacing souls that reminded me of Olyve, ominous beasts swimming the oceans instead of the skies. They were deeper, many smaller souls clustered around them. The small souls were hungry, aching for power or vengeance.

That way.

I gripped an iron hilt in one hand and a silver handle in the other and felt how the salt sea fought them. The water ate at the iron, not caring that rusting it to nothing would take an age. The silver was more immune to the sea's attacks, its purifying spark burning away a dark miasma that had threaded its way through the water like a spill of evil. Iron and silver. They were as unwelcome here as I was.

More fish passed me, some coming in close, attracted to the light I put off. A few nibbled delicately at my elbows, startling me.

Forms lurked at the edge of my light. I felt their souls even if I couldn't see them. My goosebumps had goosebumps.

"Ilsa?" I called into the dark, my words stolen away by the press of water all around.

The reply was an iron trident flying at me from the dark.

Sharp tines were at my neck. In a panic, I wedged my knives between the tines and pushed back, so the weapon was no longer pressing into my skin. The trident spun, ripping the iron dagger from my left hand, but I held onto the silver server, the most useless of the two, and raised it again when the trident darted back towards me. I struggled to hold the attacking weapon an arm's length, and I sensed even greater strength in whoever wielded it. They were playing with me.

"Show yourself," I said.

Long, dark hair and pale skin made me think it was Ilsa at first, but the strange woman was naked from the waist up. Black scales covered her lower half, and instead of legs, she had a snake tail that ended in three large fins. The fins opened and closed like the lace fans elvish women fluttered about in Highcrowne's short summer. A mermaid.

If Unmentionables were the horror stories of my childhood, mermaids were the joke. Who could be afraid of mermaids? With their underwater castles, shell jewelry, and long hair that they spent all day combing on the rocks ... hardly the stuff of nightmares. But this one was armed.

"You trespass in the waters of The Many," she said. "Explain yourself well, or I label you a beast, spit you and carry you before our queen as tonight's unspeaking feast." Her powerful voice vibrated around me, and I felt as much as heard it.

"Oh, yes. You eat people." I shuddered, remembering the old stories now. An interesting fact Morgan shared in passing could be a lot scarier in reality. "I'm sorry. Don't spit me. Please." My words were snatched away by the water, so I hoped she heard.

"We have long held peace with the land dwellers, but that truce grows more difficult," she said, which didn't reassure me. "All but the smallest, simplest creatures have been driven away, and those who now linger here have vile-tasting flesh. Poisonous and difficult to prepare. We have grown ravenous."

I was even less reassured. I hated Ilsa, but some kind of back up, any back up, would be good about now.

"The Many will not surrender these waters," she continued. "This is our territory. Fought and died for many generations over. If our surrender is what you seek, then go now before I make real my threat and break our bargain with the land dwellers."

I let out a breath. Nanny and Ilsa threatened my life all the time, and sometimes they were joking. Mere threats weren't enough to scare me off; I considered them a leaping off point for discussions.

"I could use your help. I'm not here to break the treaty," I said, allowing her to believe I was protected by it. If she knew I was from Highcrowne, or could recognize I was a human instead of an elf, I might be in trouble, but to her I must seem close enough. Anything without fins would be a land dweller to a mermaid.

"To bargain then? It has been a long time since traders brought worthless wares, asking for our pearls. But now … we would trade all our treasures for the plainest foods." She did look gaunt and hungry, her chin and cheekbones too sharp.

Actually … I felt for my belt pouch. It was a small, leather bag I always had tied to my waist. It carried my house keys, fire sparker and other necessary junk, but I'd added a jar of preserved pears from the castle larder while hunting for silverware. Not that I'd thought I'd be able to eat underwater. I'd grabbed it for extra weight to help me sink and in case I climbed out again far from the castle and needed dinner handy.

"You can have this," I said, holding out the jar. "I don't want treasure in trade. All I want is information."

Her eyes were wide as she opened the jar, pear juice floating out and saltwater pouring in before she hastily resealed it. She lapped at the juice floating in the water around her. I could tell from how fast her tongue darted that she relished the sugar.

"So much better than the poisoned clams and seaweed in our gardens. I would take it all for myself, but … I should bring you before our queen. She can best decide what information you should have, and it is her privilege to claim first choice of gifts."

"If you help me, I can bring many more gifts later," I promised.

"Then come." She swam off, and I lost sight of her.

The hungry souls around pressed in, so I hurried to catch up.

Where was Ilsa? I wondered if the mermaids had already taken her captive. I hoped so. Nothing was more frightening than the knowledge there was a monster in your room—or in this case, a homicidal sister bent on murdering you—and being unable to find it under the bed or any of the usual places. She had to be somewhere.

The mermaid came back for me. She could have stolen the pears, and there was nothing I could do about it. I was glad to see she was trustworthy.

"I am Eva," I said. "Who are you, Great Warrior?" Flattery worked in every culture.

"Hashiva. Here, let me help you."

Told you flattery worked.

She strapped her trident to her back and gripped my shoulders in both hands. When she started swimming, I thought more than my collarbone would break this time. She was fast, and the water put up so much resistance it felt like I was being dragged through one solid wall after another.

I was dazed when we reached our destination. It took me a moment to orient myself, and I swung my arms, testing to make sure I was still in one piece.

When I got my bearings, I opened my mouth in awe. We were at the edge of a city that looked like a giant, underwater sandcastle. The structure wasn't sand, as that would fall apart, but made of sandstone blocks, like the castle of the 'land dwellers', the joins between blocks hidden by decorative shells and stones. The entire surface was covered in luminous patches of lichen, so it glowed in the deep dark. I had never seen anything like it before, and it was less silly looking than I first imagined the home of mermaids to be.

"You are not allowed in our city without permission," Hashiva said, "so you must remain here until I return. Do not wander into the kelp forest or away from the city lights, as they are the only protection." With a flick of her tail and a swirl of bubbles, she was gone.

"Protection? Against what?" I called after her. "Hashiva?"

She didn't seem to hear me.

I fidgeted, digging my bare foot into the sea floor. There were a few loose stones and shells, bits of broken wood, but mostly sand. Even the forbidden kelp forest I spied not too far away was looking thin, the flesh of the plants white and sickly. I didn't know much about farming, and even less about undersea farming, but I could tell nothing would grow here. The place was sterilized. Was the First Soul responsible for this 'taint' as she had called it?

Dark shapes pressed at the edge of the light. Large shapes. I took an involuntary step towards the mer-castle. Moving closer meant disobeying Hashiva, but I couldn't help myself.

Two rays of light, like full sunlight, hit me from the deep, and I covered my eyes with my arm, blinded. I took another step toward the castle.

"Hey!" I said. "Can you tone that down a bit?"

The light dimmed.

"Thanks." I blinked, but the sea at the edge of the mer-lands now looked pure black, aside from the yellow circles seared into my retinas.

"Who's there?" I sensed a soul, but it was like nothing else I'd run across. It was almost as though the ocean itself was standing in front of me, a being vast and uncontainable.

"Are you an Elder or baby god?" I asked, trying to remember the terminology. I'd run across one already since I'd been here, so it wasn't a stretch to think this creature could be something like Trickster. Or even Trickster. It was being awful annoying, just sitting there, menacing me. I should have been scared, but, really, there's no difference between a god, a knife in a dark alley, or a disease—all of them can kill you. You feel just as powerless against each one, until you learn how to defend yourself. My usual defense was to go on the offense.

"If it's you, O Laughing One," I said, annoyance coloring my tone, "can you help a little? You're the one who wants to keep Harbinger from getting the relic, so help me find it. Do some interfering. Please."

A glowing mouth appeared in the darkness, fiery like Trickster's, but this one was ringed with rows and rows of serrated teeth that appeared orange against the deeper red of the mouth. White light shot out from two tiny slits above that frightening orifice, and I realized they were eyelids. The sun-bright light I'd seen before was contained by them. The creature had its eyes closed, but one blink and his gaze would sear my eyeballs again.

Its voice made the ground shake. "The First Soul is poison," it said. "I would see all contaminated by it devoured and cleansed. Leave this place while you can. While you are uncorrupted, Solhan."

The sand beneath my feet shifted, knocking me to my knees. A massive tail, wide as a castle tower, coiled across the seabed in front of me.

The monster's eyes opened again, but he was looking away from me this time, so the light illuminated the area where we stood. The creature was massive, yet somehow sleek and graceful, despite its bulk. I would have thought it a dragon, with its interlocked scales like shields woven together, except for the gracefulness of its arms and hind limbs. They were long and delicate, as were the many necks emanating from the point where its thick, main neck met its body. I called them necks, because tiny heads were attached to each one, but the heads were eyeless and featureless, sporting only rings of sharp teeth as dangerous looking as those in the main mouth. A few heads reached back for me blindly, snapping as it swam away. Its spine was covered in long tubular growths, pale as some of the sea creatures that clung to rocks. All I could see before it vanished into the dark was that flowing white mane.

When the churning water settled, I took a breath, suddenly realizing I'd been holding it. I was stunned until Hashiva found me.

She took one look at my expression and then darted over to trace her fingers across the marks in the sand the creature had left behind.

"The trail of Leviathan," she said. "He has never ventured so close to our city before. Come away from here now. Come with me."

She didn't wait for me to attempt movement on my own but grabbed me by the shoulders again and hauled me to her castle.

The castle had roofs made of stone and bronze. We didn't enter through a window or side door but through a bronze-ringed entrance in the middle of the main roof. It looked like it was kept open most of the time but could be shut with a gate when needed.

When my feet touched down again, it was on a surface of solid sandstone. I was in a great hall. Mermaids ringed the periphery, leaving most of the floor empty, except for a few open nets where piles of fish, seaweed, and clams lay like you might find at the fish market. Only, in Highcrowne the fish market was limited to river fare, such as mud lobsters and freshwater fish much smaller than these.

At one end of the chamber, the recipient of these offerings sat on a throne carved from a single, giant piece of coral. It fit her form perfectly, allowing her long fish tail to nestle within smoothed grooves, while her human, upper portion leaned against what resembled a chair back with arm supports, even though underwater her arms floated ever so slightly above the coral seat. This mermaid was less human-looking than Hashiva though. Her skin was black as her scales, her eyes large and fishlike, and her hair pale and tubular like Leviathan's, only shorter. I think I said as much aloud, but I was still stunned, so I couldn't be sure exactly what I'd said.

"This land dweller drew Leviathan here? And now you bring her into Our court! I should have your flesh torn apart, Hashiva, and given to the poor and hungry at the edges of Our Realm."

This must be the Queen of the Mermaids. I wasn't off to a good start.

"The land dweller brought an offering of food and a promise of more." Hashiva laid the jar of pears at the queen's feet. It looked insignificant compared to the piles of seafood all around, but the queen's fierce, inhuman gaze softened nonetheless.

"It is uncontaminated?"

"Yes. And ever so sweet," Hashiva said. She removed a morsel using a scallop shell fork, careful not to lose anything from the jar, and gave it to her queen, who chewed thoughtfully.

I really didn't think sweet pears was a good enough argument to keep me alive, but maybe I was harder to please than other people.

The mer-queen smiled and asked me, "How much more can you bring?"

I thought about the castle larder I'd seen. "If you don't mind apples, cherries, asparagus ... if you're not picky it be pears, then I can bring about a hundred jars. If only pears, I saw about twenty."

The queen swooned. "Bring it all," she ordered. "And we will do all in our power to help find what you seek. What is it you seek?"

"My name is Eva, and you are?"

"Queen Yesbeth." Mermaids didn't have the same taboos about real names as fairies did.

"I'm looking for the thing that is poisoning these lands. I need the First Soul. It's a gem I hear. I don't know much more about it."

"Then you are already too late," Yesbeth said. "Leviathan has taken it and built a nest around it. We have tried to retrieve it and expunge it from our waters, for we sense its unnaturalness, but the beast devours my warriors as easily as a whale swallows the sea."

That didn't sound good, not the nest and not the devouring.

I realized then that Leviathan terrified me. I'm not sure why—death was death—but he did. He'd been polite, but I sensed the inhumanness of his soul. Arguing with him, fighting him, would be futile. What's more, he seemed ready to judge any who stood against him, even more sternly than Unmentionables judged.

All I had to do was look into the gaunt, starving faces of the mermaids around me, think of the inexorable tide of the Dead God's approach, imagine Highcrowne and those I loved blown out like a candle flame ... those imaginings overwhelmed fear. They made me angry.

"I'll find a way to retrieve it," I said. "In the meantime, why don't you and your people leave this place? I can bring the castle's supplies, but it would be easier for you to flee."

"This is our territory. Ours alone, and we will defend it to the end. Our neighbors defend their territories with equal ferocity." I translated that to mean going anyplace else would start a war against other mer-folk, one they would lose.

"This First Soul, as you call it," the queen continued, "it has lain unnoticed in a shipwreck for years until the tendrils of its subtle poison spread far. Many of Our people are as ill as the fish we can no longer eat. It is Our duty to make these waters safe and pure again. We will aid you against Leviathan."

"I appreciate your offer." That's what I said aloud, but I didn't think a tribe of skinny mermaids would be much use. Leviathan kept even the Unmentionables at bay. I would need Olyve's help, if I could convince her.

Of course, Olyve was nowhere to be found when I crawled onto land about dawn, sore from struggling through heavy water. My muscles ached, even my lungs, probably from the weight of the water. I wished I could say I'd been sleeping in the mermaid castle, and I may have dozed off a few times, but most of the evening was spent listening to the queen and her councilors debate and discard strategy after strategy for dealing with Leviathan. I didn't have anything to add, wanting to keep the dragon card up my sleeve, but I was happy when they finally settled on the terms of our agreement.

I'd won out in the end by keeping my mouth shut for once. I got Hashiva and an army to help me against Leviathan to use as I saw fit, in exchange for the castle's food. A sweet deal really.

"Olyve! Sandy! Anyone?" I shouted again, but there was no response.

Hashiva and her mermaid friends waited beyond the edge of the surf, looking more starved and desperate than the seagulls, so I climbed up to the castle alone to start fulfilling my bargain with them.

It was several hours later, after I'd transferred most of the crates, that someone finally showed.

"I've found it," I told Olyve. She was in her elf form and looked at me strangely when she came to investigate the jars of preserved food I was hauling down to the beach. On my own, I should point out again.

Ilsa was long gone. The merfolk had not seen her, and there was no sign of her as I searched the castle stores. I suspected she'd run for it, as her first impulse had been on hearing we'd be judged by the Unmentionables. I didn't tell Olyve she was missing. I'd stolen her soul and, for that crushing guilt, I could at least give her a head start.

"The relic?" Olyve asked.

"No, pears. Of course the relic. Why else do you think I'm bribing a tribe of mermaids?"

"Then if you want to live long enough to discover how the keys work, give it to me for protection. Harbinger will kill you for it," she reminded me.

"He's going to kill me one way or another, if I let him. But I haven't laid hands on it yet. I need your help. A distraction."

I was also a bit suspicious about Olyve's offer. She wasn't trying to become a god too was she? I'd learned my lesson and no longer trusted anyone. I mean anyone.

"I am not allowed to help you," she said.

"I thought you were willing to help hide it a second ago? Never mind. You obviously don't care as much about saving the world as you do about playing by Harbinger's rules." I was goading her, but she wasn't as impulsive or angry as me. Her expression remained calm.

"The rules are ancient beyond imagining and belong to no one, let alone Harbinger. The Unmentionables wait in the anteroom of eternity. All of us seek something more, and none dare risk what could be ours."

"Harbinger isn't afraid to risk. Except when it comes to facing Leviathan. Looks like he left the hard part to me."

"Leviathan has it?"

"From your expression I see you've heard of him."

"'Iron he treats like straw and bronze like broken wood,'" Olyve quoted. "I have indeed heard of Leviathan, for he was created alongside the Primals."

I dropped the crate I was carrying, the bottles rattling, and I grazed a toe. I hopped around a few times, cursing under my breath.

"A Primal?" I echoed. "Like the Dead God? How can he even be in this world?"

"Leviathan was born with this world, not summoned into it. He's not a Primal, exactly. More ... a pet. Nevertheless, he is a child of Mater. Not even Harbinger would dare face him."

"Can you kill Leviathan?" I could tell from her expression the answer was 'no'. "Or teach me more magic?" That question garnered me an equally stony response.

How was I to defeat something like Leviathan? It was impossible. With my brute force, head on approach that was. I needed to be crafty. I tried to think like the craftiest people I knew.

"What about the Void?" I said. "The goblin doctor told me there are openings all around us. He uses them to travel about. We could find one and shove Leviathan into it."

Olyve took a step back, and I knew I'd shocked her for once. "A tear in the Void? Such things are dangerous."

"Worse than Leviathan?" I pressed.

"He would never be drawn into one. He is an animal, but an intelligent one and knows where all the doorways are. It is impossible."

"What if we create a new tear and push him in?"

"Create one? The power required ... I could not do it alone."

"What do you need?"

"No. What if something else comes through? While we would not be summoning as the Solhans did, we'd be opening a door that anything nearby could step through."

"Shove the monster through, wash our hands, seal it up and be done," I said. "Easy as cake." Or was it pie? I liked cake more.

"Opening a door into the Void may be possible with focused power, and it would not hurt to have the First Soul at hand to call upon to do it, but sealing it up again? I've no idea how to do that."

Before I could fret too much over her objections, I got back into physical labor. I dragged the crate through the surf until it was sunk deep enough for the mermaids to come fetch. I spotted their tails in the water thrashing excitedly. Only a half dozen more boxes to go.

"Did you hear me?" Olyve said. "The risk is too great."

"No, it's not." My hair was dripping wet, with sweat as much as seawater, and I pulled it out of my eyes. "I need the First Soul to stop the Dead God. Another doorway into the Void, when there are already hundreds from what I hear, is unimportant compared to that. If you're too scared to do it, teach me how. I can learn."

I meant it. I looked at her expectantly, eager to be taught for once and determined to stay focused this time. I was sick of relying on others. I had power, and I wanted to use it.

"Very well," she said. "Let the consequences be on you."

7 HARD TRUTHS

The consequences were more hours—after I'd already spent hours lugging the food for my bargain with the mermaids out to sea with no help from Olyve—of listening, watching, trying and failing, until ... I managed to dry my clothes with magic. Of course, they could have dried naturally by then.

"I have never encountered a poorer student," Olyve said, shaking her head. "There's no choice but to aid you myself."

I didn't like it any more than she did. I wished I didn't need anyone. I was always relying on Bell or the goblin doctor for brains, Jorg the grall or Duane's goons, whichever happened to be nearby, for brawn, while all I managed was to find trouble.

Maybe that was my real skill? Convincing others to help, to do something about a situation that needed changing, when they'd just as soon sit around all day feeling powerful?

"I want my Ashur back," I told Olyve. "At least I know how to wield a blade."

"It is useless against Leviathan."

"I don't care. I want it." I had the silver serving wedge, but I'd rather die with a sword in hand. It was more dignified.

"Here," Olyve said. She pulled the sword from thin air, but while my 'focus' lacked, my magic sight had grown. I saw how she withdrew the weapon from the same fold in the Void in which she stored her dragon form.

She had explained folds, saying they were nothing like rips, more like pockets where mass from our reality could be stored. What we needed to do to trap Leviathan was different. We needed to cut the fabric of reality and make a tear big enough that the creature fell through from this world into the Void. Hopefully, he'd get lost there and not come back again, but there was no guarantee. Of course, I didn't hear Olyve coming up with anything better.

"Thanks," I said, taking my mother's sword. The handle, made of some ancestor's bone, should have repulsed me, but I found its carved shape comfortable in my hand. The serrated blade was even older than the handle, ancient and re-forged many times, passed down for centuries to the eldest in the female line.

Traditionalists like my uncle might not let women own property or run businesses, but even they expected a lady to defend herself from harm and kill her enemies. It was a warped Solhan view of things, and I was as used to it as I was the macabre weapon in my hand. It was home.

Olyve looked at me strangely. "You are unlike most Solhans ... except when you hold that. I sense you have killed with it and made it yours."

Had the Trickster made me unlike other Solhans? He'd hinted at needing to nudge me. Well, he'd failed the day I had to defend myself against Jhenna and steal her life before she stole mine. I hadn't taken her soul at least; I hadn't known how to do that then, but I sensed a lingering remnant on the blade. Along with countless other remnants from before my time.

"This too is yours," Olyve said, returning the fluff of white feather I'd thought stored safely in my belt pouch. "Avian artifacts such as this are rare. Keep a firm hold on it."

I frowned, before putting the feather into the oiled pouch at my waist. When had she stolen that? I hung the sword strap so the weapon could be drawn from my back.

"I'm ready to go against Leviathan," I said.

"When was the last time you slept?" she asked, sounding like my godmother again.

"I don't know. Sandy threw off my internal clock."

"See to such mundane things, regain your strength, and we will face Leviathan in the morning."

"I prefer not to wait."

"I prefer not to die, child. I will ask the help of the others in the meantime, those I can trust. It is critical I have assistance. The instant you lay your hands on the First Soul, the vampire's sights will be on you, and he will not rest until the relic is his. We must escape his long reach, and I cannot do that, nor face the beast, alone."

Good to know even Olyve needed help from time to time.

"How long did it take you to learn how to fold the Void, all of that? Am I really that slow a learner?" I asked.

"Yes, you are. It was long ago for me and hard to remember." She thought for a moment. "Yes, it did take some time. I was still a child when I learned, a fledgling in my mother's nest, but we dragons remain children a century, so it could have been decades."

I didn't feel so bad now.

I ate as she asked, and then I found a place in the castle to nap away the afternoon heat, all the time wondering where Ilsa was. At least, I knew my twin couldn't have stolen the relic, not with Leviathan guarding it.

Ilsa's soul was too dim for me to feel it easily, even when she was in the same room with me, so I didn't think I could track her that way. There was another, stronger soul I was familiar with, however. One from which I needed answers, and I thought of Uncle Ulric as I fell asleep.

I reached out to him in my dreams, and I was suddenly standing in his study, the leather chairs and polished desk reflecting candlelight. Such meagre illumination seemed unnecessary, as his soul was bright in its own right.

My uncle sat at his desk; the candle burned low from working through the night. He was always hard working, but I often wondered what he did, with his ledgers and books. Surely it didn't take all night to count his ill-gotten wealth or judge which neighbors hadn't paid on time and would need a visit from Duane or his other thugs the next day?

"Extortion is beneath my notice," he said to me.

Had I spoken my thoughts aloud?

"All thoughts are spoken on a dream walk," he explained, "as long as they are clear enough as words and not jumbled with emotion or images. I could have taught you this, Eva, taught you many things if only you had let me."

"I never wanted to be like you."

"Yet you are, despite being a woman. I never had children of my own, but you and Viktor made me proud."

"What about Ilsa?"

"She is … flawed. Too hungry for power, not realizing the cost it brings. I was like her when I was young, before we summoned the Dead God. My brother, your father, was the voice of reason to me. He convinced me to turn aside from that path. Perhaps you can convince her?"

"I'm not here to talk about Ilsa," I said. I felt time slipping by in the dream, just as the clock on his wall ticked annoyingly. Besides, I wasn't so sure my sister would ever listen to me, or that I knew what to tell her. Power drew me as well, like the force in Solheim that called to me to come and surrender, to let the world die and be done with it.

"Why didn't you at least tell me about my mother?" I asked. "Why didn't you warn me about Thane?"

"I don't know who Thane is. I don't know as much as you'd like. Your mother was high priestess of the rite, the rest of the Nine blinded by her promises until the end, when we realized what we had done. I knew you and Ilsa were important, and I tried always to protect you. This was your soul jar." He indicated a small vase among dozens on his shelves. I recalled seeing that sky blue one at my coming of age ceremony. I shivered.

"*My* soul jar?"

"I protected the greatest portion of your soul within it for many years, until it was time to return it to you.

My people also watched over you in Highcrowne, and I even had dwarves in my employ when you were in Gernwold. I've done all I can, all you've let me."

I was well aware of Duane's goons shadowing me, but I hadn't known they'd been there by my uncle's order. My whole past was different than I thought, but right now I had to focus on the future.

"I plan to face Leviathan and retrieve the First Soul from the bottom of the sea. What can you tell me about that?" I asked.

"You're in Faellion?" He seemed surprised. I must have eluded his watchers some time ago. Probably when the dirigible crashed, or when Gypsum pulled me through a doorway in the Void. I was on my own now.

"How do you know where the First Soul is?" I asked.

"Because I stole it. Your father told me to. Klaus distracted Lili so we could all escape. I took a ship and as much of the treasury as I could, determined to get us all far away and safe. To return and fight another day."

My father. Uncle had never spoken of him or told me so much before. Perhaps this was all wishful thinking, a dream.

"It's not."

I ignored his mental intrusion and asked an easier question than what I really wanted to know. "So, all your wealth comes from the Solhan treasury?"

"No, that treasure was lost along with the First Soul. We did not think of sanctuary in Highcrowne back then, besides the city would have been impossible to reach. The Wall has no gate and is opened for no one, let alone those of us fleeing the fall of Solheim.

"I steered our ship to the other side of the continent, as far west as I could, but a storm destroyed our vessel and nearly killed us all. You and Ilsa were infants, Morgan and Nanny watching out for you both, while Viktor tried to be a man. He oared our little rowboat after that, whenever I or the others needed to rest, and we found a safe shore. For a time, we dwelled in the Elf Lands. I searched for the Soul but never found it. The elves grew more troublesome to outsiders, so Highcrowne is where we settled."

"I don't remember any of that. Other than ... the sea feels familiar. So, I was here, on this same island with its sandstone castle when I was a child?"

"Ismerkel," Uncle smiled, knowingly. "Yes, that is where we lived in Faellion. You've found it then. Good. The First Soul should be yours. I could not be trusted with it anyway."

"I don't think I want it either. Somehow, its poisoning the waters and the mermaids have nothing to eat. Did it do the same thing to Solheim?"

"The sea is closer to the Void than the land, more changeable, and sometimes it reflects the nature of things more literally. The First Soul poisoned our Solhan minds with a blinding lust for power, but this literal poison you've seen is but a manifestation of its unharnessed power. Klaus is dead, he died helping us escape, and I felt it then when I carried the First Soul on our ship—the object lost its keeper and was freed. It summoned the storm, and the ship was tossed about so much, I had no opportunity to claim the stone again. I think it was trying to escape. Beware of it now, for it will try to escape you too. That or kill you. The First Soul shuns all masters, and only our line, of all the great Solhan necromancers, has had any success at controlling it. Though you might say, even we too failed."

My father was dead.

"One more thing trying to kill me. Great. As though Harbinger and Leviathan weren't enough," I said.

"Harbinger?" Uncle stood up and paced the floor behind his desk.

"You've heard the name?"

"I thought you were better off where you are. But Harbinger? That creature has fed on our kind since before we were thinking beings, and why even such as I remain wary of the night. Highcrowne has become unsafe. With the Matriarchy in shambles, the Avians silent, Fharen rules unquestioned and his distaste for humans has turned to.... Let us say, I hoped you would not see what has become of our city. With Harbinger in Faellion, however, you will be safer here. I can protect you."

I felt my heart pounding, but it wasn't my dream heart; it was the one in my chest where I slept in the castle. It made me aware of my body, and I felt my grip on the conversation fading. I was terrified for my friends. Had they even made it back after the dirigible crash? What exactly was happening in Highcrowne? I had so many questions, but I couldn't speak anymore. I reached out to my uncle, and I could see through my arm. I was nothing but a ghost in this place, my soul quickly being pulled back into my body.

Ulric noticed me fading as well. He looked me in the eyes and commanded, "Come back to Highcrowne."

I gasped and woke up in bed, coughing and choking. I was so cold, wracked with shivers, my teeth chattering uncontrollably. It felt as though my soul had left my body to die, cold and empty, and now that I was back, I carried the chill of the grave with me and would never be warm again. I wrapped the blanket around me, over my head too, and stumbled to the embers of the fire. I shivered in front of the coals, my teeth clacking so loudly it sounded like hammering.

Someone tossed more blankets over me, and arms wrapped around me. The warmth of another person worked. It seemed I could not make my own heat, but after borrowed warmth crept in, the shivers stopped, and I began to feel hot and feverish instead. I threw off the arms and the blanket and turned to see Sandy there.

"Thank you," I told her.

She shifted uncomfortably and wedged herself in the farthest corner of the room. "I'm not one for hugging or touching," she said, "so I hope you appreciate it."

"Thank you, again," I repeated.

"You looked near death. What happened?" she asked.

"A 'dream walk' my uncle called it."

"Not a good dream obviously."

"It was educational. My uncle has never told me so much before in my life. Or maybe … I wasn't listening before."

"Did he tell you that it was stupid to face Leviathan? Or maybe he told you an easier way to kill yourself might be to leap off the castle tower?"

"No. Ulric didn't bat an eyelash at mention of Leviathan, but Harbinger had him worried."

"Then he's as loony as you. I can't believe you talked Olyve into this insanity. Or that she talked me into it!"

"What has she asked you to do?"

"Help you escape as soon as you have the relic. I like that part, escaping, but it's the whole confronting Leviathan in his nest part that I don't like."

"Maybe we can lure him away from it?" I said. "He found me before, told me he was eating up all the poison in the waters, so he can't be guarding it constantly."

"Oh, he'll be guarding it. The moment he senses anyone draw near, he'll be wary. I say we let

Leviathan and the Dead God fight things out. Sure, the Dead God will obliterate everything on land before he heads to the sea and they come face to face, and Leviathan is likely to lose, so the seas will die too. But most of us can hide out in the fairy lands until the world restores itself in a few millennia. I'll even bring you along. How does that sound?"

"I can't let others die to save myself," I said. I sounded like a stupid paladin, like Conrad in his shining armor, but I meant it.

"Oh phooey," Sandy said with mingled frustration and defeat. "Why does saving the world have to be so hard? Fine, we'll follow Olyve's plan."

"Which is?" She hadn't shared anything with me. "Will she tear a hole in the Void like I suggested?" My plan hadn't really gotten much further than that.

"Yes, another stupid, stupid thing to do, but the person I really feel sorry for is No-Thing. His job is to push Leviathan in. He's bound to fall in himself."

"Oh, no."

"Don't worry. The Void is practically home to him but having Leviathan as a roommate will not be pleasant. I hope No-Thing finds his way back this century. His kind moves slowly when not travelling about in the material he animates."

"That's what I hear."

It was full dark outside the narrow window of the room I'd borrowed. The dream walk must have taken longer than I realized.

"Is it time to go?" I asked.

"Yes." Sandy frowned.

I don't know why I'd been so impatient, because now I felt a lead ball in my stomach. This was really happening.

8 MAKING WAVES

I followed Sandy down to the beach where Olyve and No-Thing waited. She was in her elf girl form, and he was now constructed of seaweed, shells, and other flotsam. How strange to have no real body— or no real soul for that matter? I had no concept of what No-Thing truly was, and like anything that boggled the mind so deeply, I preferred not to think about him. They were engrossed in conversation but stopped abruptly when we drew near.

"No-Thing thinks it's a stupid plan too, doesn't he?" I asked.

"I am old beyond reckoning and have heard no better idea to deal with a beast like Leviathan stand-ing between one and one's goal," No-Thing said. "Of course, most do not consider facing such ancients except for we Unmentionables and Miss Eva Thorne."

I couldn't be sure if he was just calling me stupid in a nicer way or not, but he'd included himself in the stupid pile also.

"Where is your sister?" Olyve asked.

I'd covered for Ilsa as long as I could.

"I have no idea. If she's smart, she's back in Highcrowne already. All it takes is a fast airship from the elf capital. That's just across the water on the mainland isn't it? If she's stupid, in her own power-hungry way, she's hiding, and she'll try to steal the First Soul from us as soon as we've defeated Leviathan. I can't tell you what she'll do."

Olyve nodded. "We will deal with her later then. Sandy!"

The fairy had wandered down the beach, immersed in gathering stones from the shore. The folded hem of her dress was full of them. She lumbered slowly back to us.

"What are you doing?" Olyve asked.

"We fairies have hollow bones. I don't sink, so I'll need these," she said.

Olyve sighed and waved her hand. A moment later the stones had transformed into a heavy belt about Sandy's waist.

"Oh," the fairy said. "That's much better." She waded in without waiting for the rest of us. A bubble formed around her head, its edges silvered by moonlight, just before she submerged.

No-Thing vanished into the waves next, literally becoming them, while Olyve turned dragon and flew high into the air before diving into the deeper water.

I thought about running back to Highcrowne too just then. Instead, I sighed and walked into the deep. I held my breath, not sure if Ilsa's stitching would hold two days in a row, but the enchantments were intact, and I soon found myself breathing normally beneath the waves.

Hashiva was there to show me the way. Sandy was waiting too, so we three made our way to Leviathan's lair. Olyve and No-Thing had vanished, and I hoped they'd show when needed.

My night vision worked poorly underwater, even with the added light my dress put off, but then Sandy unleashed her fairy glow, and I could see further than ever before. The poisoning was frighteningly clear. The rocks and sand were coated black, dead fish scattered across the seabed, and I saw an octopus stuck. It struggled weakly, so I grabbed a muscular tentacle and gave a tug to free the creature. It swam away, leaving a cloud of black residue behind.

Poison touched my skin, and I glimpsed the First Soul. It was a soul alright. I could see it with my magical sense, but where my uncle's soul was bright, this one was darkness. Where the light of a powerful soul would illuminate, this one obscured. It was the opposite of every soul I had ever encountered, even the Dead God's. It was ... disturbing.

The poison all around us, which blackened the sand and kelp and fish, it was merely the radiance of the dark soul. Its aura seeped out from its resting place somewhere ahead.

"What if I don't claim the First Soul?" I asked, fearing what would happen to me when I touched the relic. How had my father endured this? I was at the farthest edge of its 'radiance' and already it was too gruesome to bear.

"I don't know," Sandy said, shrugging. "Why are you asking me?"

I hadn't been, but it was better than admitting I talked to myself. A lot.

I stayed quiet as we made our way into the murkier depths, the First Soul's poison growing thicker. Hashiva put a wooden mask over her mouth to filter it, and Sandy's air bubble protected her, but I felt it touching my lips and face. Ilsa's enchantment kept it from filling my lungs, but I was bathed in the First Soul. As I grew more aware of it, it grew more aware of me.

Leviathan was aware too. When we reached the creature's nest, he was there waiting for us. The 'nest' was really a hollow dug out of the seabed. Leviathan had pushed silt and coral aside until he lay on solid bedrock. Mountains of sand and the treasures of sunken ships had been raised up around him. We climbed over silt and gold, all coated with black residue, until we reached the apex and looked down on the beast.

His massive body was coiled around and around like a snake's, his forelimbs cradling a clear gem the size of my hand. It was like a grain of sand next to his bulk. If the relic was a diamond it would be worth a kingdom, but it was no gem. Its surface was clear of the muck it had created around us, but I could see its darkness with my soul sight. It was like two images layered over one another. When I closed one eye, I saw only what Sandy and the others must see: a beautiful treasure, small and delicate, grasped in the enormity of Leviathan's form. With the other eye, I saw a massive black soul, pulsing and angry at being contained. Leviathan had wrapped his own equally large soul around it, the beast's shining bright and glorious. He was trying to smother the ill effects of the relic, but they were too insidious and pervasive, creeping out through the edges.

"It's my job to deal with that thing," I told Leviathan, as I bought time for Olyve and No-Thing to get the plan into motion. I had no idea how long it would take to create a tear in the Void, or how I was supposed to lure Leviathan to it.

Sandy hissed with fright when I started talking and ducked below the top of the sand mountain we'd climbed, before the creature could spot her. Hashiva swam the edge, moving behind Leviathan's coiled form, for what purpose I didn't know.

"What you're doing isn't working," I added. "You can see that. Souls are the province of my people. My father contained the First Soul and so can I. Give it to me."

"It was never contained," Leviathan rumbled, his voice shaking the ground so that I struggled to keep my feet. "Only harnessed. Look what it did to your people. It is too corrupt and flawed to do any good for this world. It is madness to think otherwise."

"You're right. But it can help undo a greater madness," I argued. "I need it to send the Dead God back where He belongs. After that, we can talk about how to deal with it once and for all. Perhaps return it to the place Trickster stole it from?"

"He or others will merely take it again. If I cannot contain the Soul, I must find a way to destroy it. I can trust no one else." His sun bright eyes were on me, and I had to look away.

"No," I said, panicked. "Help me to stop the Dead God then. You care for this world, else you wouldn't be doing this, so you must stop him too. Either let me or act yourself."

"I care not for the world or its denizens. Only water," Leviathan said. "Let this realm wither, as all must in time, as long as the waters remain mine and uncorrupted. I cannot fight all the battles of all the worlds, nor do I care to."

The blinding gaze of the creature darted to the side, illuminating the ground, and I noted footprints in the sand. Leviathan saw something I couldn't. Then the sand impaled by that light shifted and moved until the roughly man-shaped figure of No-Thing stood there.

Leviathan laughed. It was a disturbing sound, somewhere between the surge of surf and the scraping of metal over stone.

"You are trespassing here, Voidwalker. I care not for your kind any more than I care for this corrupt soul." The great beast lunged, and I was surprised to see him move so fast. One moment, he was coiled up and ready to sleep eons away, and then the next instant he'd swallowed the sand that had been No-Thing.

Time to go. This conversation was over. I saw those footprints again, running, and guessed No-Thing had gotten away. He knew Olyve's plan, the dragon unwilling to share much with me, so I followed them, hoping No-Thing knew what to do next. Leviathan followed us.

The creature was so fast I didn't make it far. The chase was over in a heartbeat. He had me then, long fingers encircled me, and I'm certain he could have crushed me if he wanted. Leviathan's flesh was strange, rubbery and boneless, but strong, as though a giant octopus held me.

I saw the First Soul clasped in his other hand, but his chest was as wide as an ocean galleon, so I had no hope of reaching it while I was caught. I struggled, of course, but I might as well have hit him with my feather, if I'd been able to reach it. My arms were pinned. Then a dragon mouth clamped over the beast's arm and bit in deep. It looked like a poodle nibbling on a gladiator, but still Leviathan released me to focus on the one with teeth.

I had teeth too and gritted them as I swam toward the relic. The dress was making me sink, but I remembered Ilsa's instructions and ran my fingers over the runes at the waist until I felt myself floating. Sheets of Leviathan's white, tubular hair were all around me, and I grabbed hold of them to propel myself towards his other hand. When I got there, a small, blind head came whipping around to bite me.

I struck with my iron dagger; my reflexes were always pretty good in the heat of a fight, and I plunged the blade upwards with enough force to pin the jaw to the top part of the mouth, like a toothpick sticking a sandwich together. It wouldn't hold for long, but it bought me seconds.

I grabbed the First Soul in both hands and instantly regretted it. The noxious mass of it crawled inside me, poisoning me far quicker and more thoroughly that it had poisoned the waters all around. I spit it out, so to speak, but bits of it were stuck fast, and I couldn't dislodge them.

It tried to merge with me, to takeover if I let it. I fought for control, fought harder than I have ever fought, because this was me at stake. I'd managed to steal Erick's soul back from the Halls of the Dead and subdue the restless souls of werewolves to smother their transformation—but this was an internal battle like nothing I'd experienced before, and it happened in an instant. Either my soul would be mine hereafter, or it wouldn't. Something else laid claim to it. This must be what it meant to be a keeper, like my father. He had done it and so could I.

I am Eva, I said, trying to hold onto my identity.

What does that mean? It asked.

I was stupid, angry and brash at times, the worst of my Solhan nature, but I was also more than that. I could love. I loved little Viktor and my friends, Morgan, and even Nanny. I'd have killed her long ago if I didn't love her. I don't know why that is the emotion I reached for, but somehow, I knew it was the only one that could save me.

I know how to love the unlovable, I answered.

I tried to love the First Soul in that instant, as much as I loved the noxious Nanny. As much as I loved Ilsa. I disliked my sister, hated her even, but at the same time there was a connection that transcended everything. She and the First Soul were alike in my mind. No matter what she or it had done, no matter how many others were killed because of their nature—I loved my sister, and so it was a simple thing to love the First Soul in the same way. Without condition.

It felt the truth of what I offered, and it quieted. At least, it stopped trying to consume me. We had a truce.

Now, on with the rest of the plan, which was equally ill conceived.

I pushed with my feet but couldn't free the gem from Leviathan's grasp. Mermaids distracted the multitude of heads that sprouted from Leviathan's shoulders as we fought, and two great fists made of stone and sand pounded into Leviathan like an invisible boxer, No-Thing at work most likely. Olyve's ferocious bites kept the beast's main head and sun-bright eyes focused on her.

"Hashiva," I called and indicated the head I'd temporarily put out of action. The mermaid nodded and shoved her trident into the next one that came for me.

I pulled my Ashur, as well as the silver server, and wedged both into the space around the gem. I cut with the Ashur while I pushed outward with the silverware, at the same time asking the First Soul for a little help. A moment later, the relic was free, and I held it in my hand.

Leviathan made a sound of pure rage. I started swimming, not even taking time to re-sheathe my Ashur. Terror made me move faster than I'd thought possible, but Leviathan cast off dragon, Voidwalker, and an army of mermaids like annoying gnats in order to chase me.

I saw it then, the tear in the Void Olyve was supposed to have created earlier. She was forming it right in front of me. This was why Olyve hadn't told me the whole plan—I was the bait!

I held tight to the First Soul, the pear-shaped gem pulling me along, as though it too wanted to escape Leviathan. I headed for the tear, knowing it was my only chance. It was a big one, bigger than the only other one I'd encountered at least. That door to the Void had had room for one or two people to pass through at a time, but this was big enough for Leviathan. I could see the infinite blackness beyond. It looked like a big place to get lost in.

I veered to the side, trying to avoid falling through the opening myself. Leviathan turned too, but it was then that No-Thing came at him. All the mountains of sand and coral from Leviathan's nest were transformed into a giant fist that slammed into the beast and pushed him into the Void.

"No," Leviathan called, and a tentacle shot out and wrapped around my arm. "I will not go without it."

He meant to drag me and the gem in with him. I summoned all my will to swim free, but it was useless. I was at the threshold to the Void now. Leviathan and the bulk of No-Thing had already gone in.

My head went through. I sensed the Dead God then, lurking in the Void. He sensed me too, and I panicked. I swung my Ashur at the tentacle holding me, putting my terror and desperation behind the blow. It wouldn't have worked if the First Soul hadn't helped. I felt it wanting to escape, felt the power it lent me at the instant I struck, and I cleaved through the thick appendage.

Leviathan screamed with rage as he fell into darkness. I backpedaled, an effort somewhere between swimming and moving by sheer will alone.

I felt the Dead God's desire to reach me, but He was trapped. I realized that was why He hadn't come through the portal near the Wall when first I saw him. His true form was stuck somewhere between Solheim and the Void. That meant all this world had experienced of Him, all His armies and the power I sensed now reaching for me, all of this was merely the tips of His fingers, stretching and straining to affect the things around Him.

I understood now why He had created Thane, a broken fragment to give Him freedom. I also understood why the world would end if the ritual was completed. He wouldn't be trapped anymore, and we'd feel His fist rather than His fingertips. His full power would be unleashed.

I was transfixed by the light of the Dead God's soul. He was far off, but still it was a struggle to look away. I'd been reading Him, learning things I desperately wanted to know, but He was reading me too. He'd almost learned that Thane had betrayed him.

I swam hard, treating the Void like water, but it was easier than water to manipulate. It was pure power.

"Close it!" I told Olyve when I was back through. The dragon was there, bleeding and haggard from her battle.

"I can't," she said. Her jaws snapped with fury, gobbling up a swarm of squid that were being pulled into the Void—Olyve was a stress eater—but she spat them out again. Their poisoned flesh must taste awful for her to pass up a meal.

I knew Leviathan would find his way back, and the Dead God's reaching fingertips would find me, searching my mind as I'd searched His. This had been an insane plan, and I wished Olyve had tried harder to talk me out of it.

"Use this," I told her, and I held out the First Soul.

Olyve reached for it, but the First Soul lashed her with a whip of shadow and pushed her back. She held her talon, the wound clearly painful. Despite our truce, the relic had a mind of its own. There wasn't time to convince it to play nicely with my friends. It was up to me.

I didn't know what I was doing, but I called upon the soul in my hand for aid and reached out to seal the rip Olyve had created.

The water around me was shaped from the Void so long ago it rebelled against returning there, resulting in a sharp border where ocean ended and nothingness began. I felt along that border, cajoling the water itself to aid me, but it refused, so I turned to the pure Void stuff. It was raw, but infinitely powerful. This was why everyone said I was wrong to call it nothingness. The Void was everything. The potential for all things.

Leviathan was swimming back. The Dead God crept closer. I smelled cinnamon now, felt Him calling to me, swore I heard my name.

"Eva!" It was Olyve shouting at me, her voice muffled by the water around us. "I will help."

I could sense what Olyve was doing, basically trying to undo what she had done, like stitching a tear in fabric, but it was all wrong. The raw power of the Void did not want to be sealed up again. It was like trying to contain a form that was now too big to fit. I knew that feeling well after having visited Gypsum in the rose gardens of Highcrowne and indulging in too many pastries.

The First Soul whispered to me of another way. Not with words so much as intuition. If the Void was all things, and matter came from it originally, then new matter could be crafted from it as well.

I reached for the Void stuff in the blackness beyond and pulled it tight to the breach, more and more of it, tighter and tighter, until it became dense. First, it became light—I was blinded in that moment and had to shut my eyes as I worked—and then it became air. I forced it tighter, until it became water. The matter I had created felt like a scab over a wound, fragile and flaking, and the First Soul nudged me again. I felt what was needed now. The bulk of the Void wedged into the opening had become 'fabric', so to speak. I curled it inward, toward us, a rush of hot water coming at us, and then sealed the edges between our reality and the Void. We dared not leave the tiniest gap behind. When we were done, there was nothing but a bit of newborn ocean around us to mark what had happened.

"Perhaps you are not so poor a student after all," Olyve said, gasping. Her part in the magic had required real effort, while I felt refreshed.

I looked at the gem in my hand. "I cheated."

The gem disappeared from my open palm.

"What?" I said, dismayed. I looked around, wondering if I'd dropped it, and spotted those footprints in the sand, running. Bare feet, about the size of my own had created them. Ilsa.

"Stop her!" I called. Sandy had emerged from wherever she'd been hiding to watch the final act of the battle, and she was standing close enough to head Ilsa off. "She's invisible. She stole the relic."

I ran after, but the dress Ilsa made turned on me. I felt heavier and heavier, until finally I lay crushed against the seabed. It stopped producing air as well, and I held my breath as I struggled. I cut at the dress with my Ashur, working from the neckline down, until it peeled off me. I was naked but I didn't care. I even dropped the Ashur as I fought my way to the surface. Hashiva grabbed me. We were deep, and she propelled me up and up. I felt relieved enough to think about more than survival for a moment and looked down to see Sandy had her arms around something invisible. Then she too vanished.

I sucked in air when we reached the surface. I swallowed water and coughed it out, coughed so hard I almost threw up. I couldn't swim, so Hashiva kept hold of me, directing me toward land. Olyve shot out of the water behind me, hurtling up toward the sky. Where was she going?

Hashiva deposited me on the beach and said, "I will hunt for the invisible one," before diving back into the depths.

I sat there, choking and gasping. I tried to stand, but my rubbery legs wouldn't support me.

Ilsa. I should have known. But invisibility? She was more skilled than I'd ever imagined.

A shadow loomed. I looked up and up, across dark boots, leathery cape, and then masses of white muscle, a chiseled jaw, an intense gaze set beneath a strong brow, long black hair, and, finally, a crown of antlers.

Harbinger.

I held out my hand. "Care to help me stand?"

9 SUSPICIONS

If I hadn't just faced Leviathan, not to mention the blight of the First Soul and the yawning chasm of darkness that was the Void itself, I would have found Harbinger impressive. Come to think of it, he still was. The masculine force of him made it seem a mountain stood before me rather than a man, but I think my brain just couldn't soak it in entirely. I was full up on menacing evil.

"I sense an ebbing of the dark," he said. Whatever that meant. "What have you done?"

"I've been hunting for the relic everyone told me so much about." I didn't mention how little they'd actually said, or that I'd held it only moments ago.

He took my hand finally. It was like electricity where he touched me, and he used the barest tips of his strong fingers. I think I was compelled to stand, hypnotized almost, and it had nothing to do with him physically helping me.

I shook it off. I was acutely aware of being naked, except for my belt pouch, but he wasn't looking at me. His gaze was on the ocean over my shoulder. Either that or the artery pulsing in my throat.

"Where is it?" I knew he meant the relic.

"I'm not sure," I said, and I wasn't lying. I think he would have detected a lie, maybe from a quickening of my pulse or some other animal sense.

Despite the stag horns on him, he was no docile creature of the forest. I thought it must be some ancient camouflage. I could more easily picture him crouched in a dark wood at sunset, lying in wait for human hunters foolish enough to come too near him. That's probably what fed him, and then he went to their widows in the village at midnight to toy with them and play at passion until he drained them too of blood by morning.

I was sensing his soul. That's how I knew these things, and he reacted to that, finally looking me in the eyes and cutting off the contact between us. At least I cut it off, because that gaze was so frightening, full of memories of blood and death and strife he had caused, with pleasure, over the eons.

"Olyve was helping me," I said, reminding him I had a scary godmother on my side. Sort of on my side. At least I thought she might be.

He continued to look at me like something to devour, and as disturbing as his gaze was, I felt a wave of desire. I fought it, knowing this was his power.

I could see why he wanted the relic. There was shared poison in each of them, but where the First Soul longed to be loved and accepted, Harbinger longed only for more poison, more blood, more and more until his endless desire was finally satiated, if it ever could be. I was doing it again, reading him, and he fought me again.

We were fencing with our wills, and I was too tired to keep it up.

I looked away. "Yes, Olyve will be here any moment, and we'll get back to it. I just...." I looked down at myself. "I lost my clothes down there. The sea is a strange place. I'm headed to the castle to get something else to wear. See you around."

I started walking, but a cold white hand clamped down on my shoulder.

"Do not toy with me."

"I'm not a toy-er. I'm a do-er, so let me get back to doing. I'll get my hands on the First Soul, and then we'll have something more to talk about." I knew he wanted it, and he knew I knew he wanted it, so there was no point in playing games.

"Say, should you even be out in the day? You're kinda smoking wherever that cape doesn't cover you," I said.

The sun peeked over the horizon, and I realized that's what Harbinger was watching, along with my artery. The hand he'd grabbed me with smoked in the sunlight, and I saw waves of heat coming off it. He quickly retracted it, hiding burnt flesh beneath his cloak.

"Careful, or you will feel my passion in more than memory," he said. Every word he spoke was seductive, but I knew he didn't mean 'sex' when he said 'passion': he meant 'blood-letting' and so I shivered.

Before I could come up with a witty comeback, even something pathetic, along the lines of 'go get it yourself if you're so tough', he was gone. There was the snap of leather, and then he was flying, like a giant bat, to vanish in the dark cave further along the beach where I'd first met the gathering of Unmentionables.

I wasn't to be given a moment's peace, unfortunately. As soon as Harbinger retreated, his cronies immediately took his place.

The blue demon with her sweeping horns and bony wings was followed by the gaunt man. They walked toward me from the cave, the woman raising her hand to shield her eyes from the sunlight. She didn't like it but tolerated it better than the vampire. What was worse was the spider that skittered with blinding speed behind them. It scurried over sand dunes and rocks, the light giving it more energy than it could bear, so it ran around unnecessarily, circling the approaching pair then darting to me.

I huddled in on myself, covering my nakedness and making myself small against the ground. The spider stirred up sand as it darted around, dry, sharp limbs touching me. It scrambled over me at one point, and I hunkered lower. It stopped, standing on top of me, and I sensed its desire to inject venom, to turn the flesh beneath my skin to jelly and suck it all up in a feast of liquefied organs.

I gagged.

I dialed down my soul sense, as it was freaking me out more than helping. I stood, giving the spider a shove. I would never have touched the creature with my bare hands if not driven by revulsion. I sent the creature sprawling.

"Keep that thing away from me," I told the newcomers.

"Erenes does not like being called a 'thing'," the gaunt man said.

The spider righted itself and circled me, its many black eyes hungry. "I do not," it said, its soft voice punctuated with mandible clicks.

"Enough," the blue demon ordered, her voice as harsh and angry as ever. I had not expected her to be my ally—and I was right. She came up to me and slapped me so hard I went flying, leaving me crumpled on the ground.

The demon stood over me and smiled, all jagged teeth in blue gums. She kicked me once, and all the breath left me. I really wish I had my sword.

"Now that you are reminded what a pathetically weak creature you are," she said, "perhaps you will listen when I speak. You are not our equal, so do not address us as such. You live at our whim and will die at it, be sure. Your usefulness buys you time only. Enjoy that time, swim in the sea and lay in the sun, but do not play with power. Harbinger wants the relic, and so he shall have it. If you are quick and helpful about it, he may allow you time to prove some other usefulness, to demonstrate you are this 'key' or whatever nonsense No-Thing blabbers on about. The moment you stand there and say 'no', or are for one instant anything but useful, your soul will be consumed. Keep that in mind. Now go."

"I've not had my turn," the gaunt man said. "For it is I who shall do the consuming, and I may not wish her to be useful. What if I encourage her to disobey, so that I might feast?"

I might be the only one here who could control souls, but I now knew how the Unmentionables could keep me from the Dead God. The gaunt man was a ravager, a ghoul that fed on souls instead of flesh. Solhans spoke of them with disgust. If nothing was a more precious resource than souls, then the creatures who shredded and devoured them were considered the most wasteful. Solhans had hunted them to extinction.

This one must be a survivor, like the other Unmentionables. The toughest, most dangerous example of his kind.

"Say my name, ravager. It's Thorne. My grandfather was famous for eradicating ghouls like you. Looks like he missed one, so it's up to me to finish things."

I felt for his soul, sifting through it for clues as to how to make good on my threat. It was unremarkable, really. Not black and blighted as the First Soul, nor bright as my uncle's. You might never guess what he was by looking at him. His mother named him Drasben before he ate her soul. I felt how hungry he'd been, how her milk failed to nourish him, how nothing that passed his lips was ever nourishment enough.

"Stop talking now," he said.

I'd just gotten started. "You are gaunt because you are hungry. I sense that hunger, along with the knowledge there is nothing around that can satisfy it. You can't allow yourself to satisfy it, anyway, for that would make enemies of your Unmentionable friends. They care for their own souls as well as the balance of the world. So, you must wait for them to unleash you on a chosen victim."

"That's you." He snapped his teeth.

"I don't think so," I said. "The Unmentionables need me more than I need them. I don't need any of you, in fact. All I need is for you to get out of my way."

I stood, still rubbery from the battle with Leviathan as well as from the whack the blue demon had given me.

Shevic growled. "Stay down, meat."

"I can't find what I'm looking for on my ass. Like I said, get out of my way." I pushed past them, trudging along the water's edge and looking out to sea for any sign of Olyve.

Shevic and Drasben grumbled but did not stop me. Some Unmentionables were clearly stronger than others. I'd hesitate to push Harbinger around, but these ones, as scary as they were, were weak. Take Drasben, a faded light on his way out of existence. If he faced me alone in a dark alley, that light would be extinguished real quick. When he and the others returned to the cave, I let out my breath. I wouldn't be going in there again. Especially for some trumped up judgement that would end in me being sacrificed to the ravager.

"Olyve! Sandy! ...Hashiva?" I called.

There was no reply, only the sound of surf and the occasional calling bird.

Sandy probably had Ilsa trapped in a bubble between this world and the fairyland, and the other two were searching ocean and sky fruitlessly. Who knew when Sandy would remember time passed more quickly out here? I finally gave up waiting and headed for the castle to find some clothes.

Of course Ilsa couldn't be trusted. Of course Ilsa had sewn invisibility into her dress and sabotaged mine so it would try to drown me. I truly was not surprised by any of it. I hadn't known how she would betray me, but I knew it would happen. The question was, what was I going to do about it?

I couldn't let anyone else have the relic, for one thing. Not even Sandy or Olyve. I had to make my own way out of here and go after them. Find Ilsa. Somehow.

I washed in fresh well water before donning squire's clothing, which I found in the room I'd slept in before. Then I headed for the docks. You didn't need to swim if you had a boat.

But where to? I tried my soul sense. The black miasma the First Soul put off should have been easy to spot, but I felt nothing. Fairy bubble. Had to be.

Then a song popped into my mind as I made my way out of the castle. I remembered hearing it when I was young. Maybe Nanny had sung it to me?

Darkest night, darkest soul.

To me must come your woe.

Forget me, lest I forget all.

Bow to me as I bow low.

Darkest soul, drink of me.

Be quenched. Be whole.

Lovely. Creepy Solhan words of course, but as I spoke them in my mind, I suddenly knew what they were. A plea to the First Soul. My connection to it shivered to life. I could feel the relic across miles, across sea and the hungry gazes of those who wished to possess it. It was far from here already. I had to go after it now.

There was a harbor on the far side of the island. Most of the ships were gone, taken when the place was abandoned, but several remained, probably because they were too small to be of use. I hoped one was seaworthy enough to get me to the mainland. I had my newfound connection to the relic to guide me in the right direction, but I wasn't sure how far I had to go. I avoided anything with a sail, as I was lacking in all nautical skills, and found something large enough to carry a small barrel of water with me, but not so large it would take more than one person to row.

I set off before I could talk myself out of it—or remember that I couldn't swim. If a storm came, like the one that sunk my uncle's ship decades ago, I'd be dead for sure. Best not to think about it. I was fairly good at not thinking.

By the time I was out of sight of land, and my hands were raw and pulsing with pain from using the wooden oars, I decided 'not thinking' was a bad trait to have. I wrapped my hands in cloth and kept going, stopping every once in a while to look behind me.

Whoever thought up the concept of a boat you steered backwards was an idiot.

The sea around Faellion was calm, but that didn't mean it was without waves. I was bounced about, sliding this way and that, as I fought to stay on course. I felt the relic on the move, and so I adjusted direction again and again.

I'd rowed half the day, taking breaks from time to time to guzzle water. The sunlight beat down without any shade. I had a borrowed hood and that was all, but the cloak it was attached to made me overheat more, so I stripped down to my undergarments and tied a lighter shirt around my head to keep the sun off and the sweat out of my eyes.

My stomach, arms, and shoulders were all killing me by the time I heard the sea bird. I hadn't looked behind me for some time, and when I did excitement shot through me. I saw land.

I rowed harder, but then a gust of wind almost overturned my boat. It was followed by a massive wave that managed what the wind hadn't. I was under, my sore arms flailing about blindly, until I smacked up against the edge of the overturned boat. Something gave me a boost from below, and I wondered if my mermaid friends were following me. I grabbed hold of the wood with my fingernails, digging in and scratching my way up the side like a cat would in a similar situation. My head was out of the water at least.

I saw Olyve in her dragon form floating beside me. Most of her bulk was underwater except for those massive, cream-colored eyes and the cavernous nostrils she was breathing through. Her head came up a bit more, causing another wave, and I nearly lost my grip on the boat. A moment later she became the small elf girl, and with a wave of her hand, the rowboat righted itself, dragging me along with it. Soaking wet, I sat on the seat. My oars, provisions and barrel of water still bobbing about in the water around us.

She climbed into the boat, nearly capsizing it again, and sat opposite me.

"Are you trying to kill me?" I asked her.

"Of course not. You're so small, I forget sometimes. Here, you'll need this I think." She reached out a hand and summoned the floating barrel back into the boat, and my Ashur appeared again as well. Trust my dragon godmother to keep track of it for me.

I was especially happy to see the water, still stoppered and unharmed, so I took another drink, relishing it more than a glass of good whisky. Not that I could ever afford the good stuff.

When I was hydrated and my heart stopped racing from the near drowning, I registered what she'd said. "Wait a minute. Can't you fly me to shore? I'd rather not row anymore." I held up my bloody hands. They stung when a breeze penetrated the wrappings.

She healed them instantly. Did I mention it was great to have a godmother?

"That's the elf capital over there," she said, pointing at the shoreline, reluctant to even look at it. "Enough spears, not to mention the ballistae on the castle walls that are akin to giant crossbows, will kill me. I dare not approach, not even in disguise. They have mages wherever they don't have dragon hunters. The battle with Leviathan weakened me. I prefer not be spitted or served on a plate, howsoever elves prefer to eat their delicacies."

"They'd eat you?"

"Perhaps with a nice sauce. Elves enjoy killing dragons and many other things. Why do you think there are so few of us?"

"Then why risk being here at all? I know you and Sandy didn't catch Ilsa. I can sense the First Soul."

"Good. Then you'll be able to retrieve it."

"I saw Harbinger. He knows something's up, but I don't think he can sense the relic as clearly as I can. Can't you give me a little push towards the shore, so I have a head start?"

"No, but I can give you some information. The fairy, Sandy as you call her, has vanished along with Ilsa. She must have helped her escape and I know not why. It would be unwise for her to defy Harbinger—or me. What's more, Lili of Solheim is in the capital treating with the Elf King even as we speak."

"What?" The Sandy part didn't shock me, as I had no idea how the fairy thought, but the fact my mother was so near could not be a coincidence. "Does she know we're here? Or do you think she's come for the relic as well? Why, after all these years? And how—if she's the Dead God's chief general—can she be allowed in Elf Lands?"

"It's a parlay, that's how she can be here. She is not restrained by the Compact, only the Dead God is. She could bring any mundane army into the Three Kingdoms and we'd have nothing but our own soldiers to intervene. Until now, she has not had an army that could threaten as, as the Risen hordes are forbidden here."

"What do you mean, until now?"

"The dwarves have joined her. She now has control of the largest army in the Three Kingdoms, and there is nothing but elves and Avian magic to stand in her way. She has come to ask for the Elf King's surrender. Such news travels fast."

"What? When?" I spluttered. "I destroyed King Rutgard's body and the wolf crown. I thought that ended their plan?"

"No, they retrieved the crown. Queen Gypsum wears it now, and the werewolves walk about openly. Gernwold is their seat of power and all are gathering there before turning on Highcrowne."

"Gypsum...?" Had this been what my 'friend' had wanted all along? To be queen? "How could everything have turned so sour so quickly?" I asked.

"Such is the nature of war. But we still have time to stop the Dead God. While the dwarf armies are gathering, their citizens are confused and in disarray. Lili is seeking capitulation through diplomacy, which means she does not yet have forces in place to obtain it."

"Then, even if I stop the Dead God, how does that help the Three Kingdoms?" I asked. "If the dwarves have turned on us, we're lost."

"Without the Dead God, they have no reason to fight. They serve Him. Dwarves might want an empire of their own as well. Who knows? But such mundane wars come and go and are of little consequence in the scheme of things. It is only the end of all things we must worry about, not who rules these kingdoms."

Trust Olyve to have a bird's eye perspective on things. Of course, it wasn't a human view, or even a compassionate one.

I started rowing. The boat was heavier, so I told Olyve to get off. "If you won't help, you might as well leave. I have a lot to do before I can rest. The relic is only the first step."

"Yes, much lies ahead of you. Another bit of advice before you go: Avoid your mother at all costs. You will feel compelled to catch a glimpse of her, but do not succumb to such weakness. I knew her well before you were born. She is dangerous."

"I'm aware of that."

"She is your greatest enemy."

"Even more than the Dead God?"

"Yes, for she birthed you only to summon Him here. It is her will He obeys. She is the one who wishes us all destroyed, so that she can be the immortal queen of a dead world. She is mad."

Maybe that's where Ilsa and I got it from. We two certainly weren't the most stable sticks in the barrel. Or rungs on the ladder. Whatever. I was terrible at sayings.

"I'll remember," I assured her. "Now get off."

She wasn't done giving instructions. "Once you recover the relic, leave the Elf Lands as quickly as you can, but avoid the dwarves of course. Highcrowne with its protections of Avian magic will be the only safe place. I will meet you there."

Ulric too had told me to go to Highcrowne, and it didn't sound all that safe. Still, I nodded, and Olyve launched herself into the air before she transformed. Her wingbeats nearly capsized me again, but I managed to stay upright. I watched her fly out to sea.

Olyve had said to stay away from Lili, but according to No-Thing, my mother knew how to undo the ritual that had summoned the Dead God. It was convenient she was so near. I wondered if that was where Ilsa was taking the First Soul? Did she know our mother would be here? Had she summoned her? While I was busy helping mermaids, had Ilsa been plotting this? I wouldn't be surprised. She was resourceful, in an evil kind of way.

The part that really hurt was thinking Ilsa knew how to contact our mother. That they had spoken before this, and Ilsa never told me.

Well, I would find a way to speak to Lili now. And get answers.

I put the oars back in their locks and heaved, determined to get to the elf capital. I'd figure out how to sneak into a political parlay between the Elf King and the Dead God's representative when I got there. Of course, I should put some thought into blending in, difficult when the city was composed entirely of elves at least a head shorter than me.

I was deep in thought, so it took me a moment to realize I was spinning in a circle and not getting anywhere. One oar was working but the other was stuck fast. It wasn't the lock; the oar was caught on something under the water. I tried to pull it free, bracing with my legs. Something greenish was down there. Seaweed? Then the oar pulled back with such force I lost my balance and tumbled over the side. Again. I really needed to learn to swim.

Between panicked coughs and flailing limbs, I caught a glimpse of a merman who lifted me up in his arms until my head was well above water. When I could breathe easily again, he remained under the water, hiding from me. I could understand why.

Female mermaids looked fairly human up top. They were once known for luring sailors and ships to their deaths and stealing their cargo, so that camouflage likely came in handy. Mermen, however, had never relied on lures. They were warriors and hunters, and since they didn't need to be pretty, they weren't.

"It's alright," I said. "You obviously want to talk to me, else you wouldn't be here, so I'll need to see your lips move. Show me your face."

The merman rose up, its powerful fishtail swirling the water below my feet. Impressive chest muscles were revealed, all covered with green scales, and a head that looked like a carp's, with huge lips and funny looking whiskers hanging down like a rubber mustache. Spiky fins along his jawbone were folded back adding to the impression of a balding, green man with strange facial hair. His eyes were black and huge, and they didn't blink. It was unnerving being stared at that way.

"Go on," I said.

"Eva," the merman croaked.

It knew my name. I must be famous among the creatures of the sea for battling Leviathan. Or maybe Hashiva had told him. It seemed to be struggling to speak, so I waited patiently.

Finally, its voice started working, and it said, "The Dead God knows where you are. He has been searching, and He sent me to fetch you, but I will not bring you back to Him. He and I are no longer one. I have been thinking about our kiss, Eva ... I won't give you to Him. You are mine."

Shivers went up my spine. I grabbed the edge of the boat and climbed out of his arms. When I was onboard, I drew my Ashur and leveled the blade.

"No, I won't be His, but I'm not 'yours' either, Thane. I'm not anyone's. The only reason I didn't kill you before was because you had Conrad's body. I don't know this merman, and while I might feel sad for him when I kill you, I happen to know mer-creatures do not live in family units, so I won't be making any orphans at least."

"You won't kill me."

"And why not?"

"I felt your soul when you kissed me. Beings such as you and I know souls, don't we? Tell me a soul can lie."

I couldn't, but …. "It can be tricked, manipulated, be-spelled. My mother 'married' me to the Dead God before I had any say in the matter, and I cannot trust anything I feel for you. I have no idea what was done to me."

His fish mouth opened and closed like he was trying to breathe, and he ducked beneath the water. He emerged a moment later, glistening wet.

"This form is a strange one," he said. "I have never been in anything so alien. The world below is glorious, but the world above burns this skin and makes each moment spent in it uncomfortable. I must find a new body soon, if I am to lead you overland and away from danger."

"Did you hear anything I just said? Stay away from me or I will kill you."

"You told me once I must win your heart, so that is what I will do. I will prove to you that I am not the Dead God anymore. I am Thane, and my wishes are not His. My only wish is to know life, with you."

"When I said you needed to win me, I was speaking generally of the way love works. Wooing and all. I didn't say you had a chance. You've already gone way overboard with the creep factor, manipulating me, lying to me, abducting me! And now this...."

"Do you not believe that people can change? That everyone deserves second chances?" he asked.

I thought of Ilsa and was about to say 'no', but then I thought about all the stupid mistakes I'd made, and I hoped I was forgiven those. I hoped that there was always a chance to learn and become someone new. Someone you'd be proud to be.

I sighed. "Fine, you have a clean slate. But go far away and stay there. When I'm done dealing with everything I have to deal with, the world is saved, the Dead God banished, and if I'm in a good mood ... I might not kill you."

"You need me to stop Him. Only I know how to get past the armies that surround Solheim, to penetrate the ancient chambers and reach the entrance to the Void where He is trapped. You see, it is more than Him wanting to push into this realm. He has been summoned to a particular place and time, and the summoning must be completed for Him to enter. There are rules. Without your soul, the way is closed to Him. He is trapped half in and half out, in agony, and He must escape before He can go anywhere else."

It was good to know the rip we'd made into the Void to stop Leviathan couldn't have let the Dead God through. Of course, none of us had realized that at the time. Another one of those stupid things I'd like to move on from. I'd have to start a list.

Thane dipped his merman form again, and when he emerged, he looked like an excited puppy, certain he had pleased me.

"You are not the only one who can help me," I said, trying to deflate his enthusiasm. "Lili of Solheim has all the answers I seek, and I'm going after her."

"You can't. She would kill you to complete the ritual."

"Do you know how to turn the 'key' and 'shut the door'? To expel the Dead God instead of letting him in?"

"No. I do not even know if the Dead God knows. It is powerful magic that compels Him to this place."

"Well, Lili knows how to undo the ritual. She's the only one who does. I need her more than I need you." I started rowing, done sharing my plan with the enemy. Of course, Thane could have drowned me, and the Dead God would have won, so he might believe what he was saying. I didn't know how long his puppy love desire to keep me alive would hold out, though, and it was best not to wait around to find out.

I lost sight of him, until I was close to the harbor, the masts of the tall ships like a forest of naked trees. He emerged again and said, "Then I will help you reach Lili, as you ask." And he disappeared beneath the water.

"I didn't ask you for anything!" I said, certain he wasn't listening.

I moored the rowboat at the end of the dock and got a few strange looks from the sailors. I ignored them, as I walked along the pier towards solid ground. No more ocean for me.

Of course, now I was in the elf capital, which was probably the one place worse. Not that it was ugly or anything. The docks alone were made of the palest wood, intricately carved with flowers and bas reliefs of elvish sea battles, all perfectly protected from the wear and tear of wind and sea by enchantments. The boats were unearthly, as though built from gossamer wings. But I could see through that gossamer to the rows of slaves chained to the oars. I supposed elves could have enchanted the boats to drift along by themselves, but why would they when they had humans to subjugate? It was all part of the fun to them.

If Highcrowne was like a layer cake resting on a pile of garbage, this place was like a rotting corpse smothered in yummy frosting. Beautiful on the outside, but not tasty. Far from tasty. No amount of glamour or artistry could hide the evil at its core.

That skyline was something, though. The sun was high, and I gawked at a horizon made entirely of crystal towers that glinted in the golden light. Some were milky, white, or rose quartz, while others were pure and clear enough to scatter the light into rainbows that dazzled the eye and crisscrossed the lower city with ribbons of color instead of shadow. I think I must have stood for a full minute with my mouth open.

"Slave," someone said, and it wasn't until she touched my shoulder, I knew the elf was speaking to me.

My first instinct was to say, 'do I look like a slave to you?' and draw my Ashur. The serrated blade against her neck would correct her of her delusion. However, I reminded myself this was the Elf Capital, called Illul Faellion, which meant 'Bones of the Defeated Fae', and it was rumored to be built on the bones of Sandy's people. A mass grave of the conquered. Why obliterate an entire species? Because they were not elves.

Sure, that was olden times and elves had become more progressive—snooty instead of genocidal—but there was a deep-rooted arrogance and superiority in them that made them want to dominate what they called 'lesser' species. Humans among them. While slavery was curtailed by the influence of the Avians and dwarven Matriarchy, here in the Elf Lands there was no one to enforce those rules.

The docks teemed with human slaves, and there were plenty of their masters around, not to mention soldiers watching from the gates to the city. I was the only human here that was free. I wouldn't stay that way for long if I went around threatening elves.

I smiled as I turned to look at the speaker. She stank, as most elves do, and I couldn't help pinching my nose shut. The cloying odor of cheap perfume mixed with rancid sweat made my stomach turn, and my stomach was already feeling delicate from the rolling, heaving waves I'd crossed to get here. The elf was a sailor, judging by her loose-legged pants and soft-soled shoes, but her coat was finely embroidered, and I guessed she was either a sea merchant or some officer on a ship. Elves treated everyone else badly, but at least their women were free, able to take on any profession they liked.

"Yes, ma'am?" I said, sounding as sweet as Ilsa managed when she was being disarming, although a bit nasally with my nose pinched.

"You can't leave that there, cluttering up the place," she said, pointing to the rowboat I'd left at the end of the dock. "Whose ship does it belong to, any-way? I see none moored out deeper in the harbor."

"Not a ship, my lady." I was really pouring on the subservient tone. "I've rowed all the way from Ismerkel. The island is abandoned, consumed by some ill fate. I hope not disease. Are there others from the island here, have you heard? So, I might join them?"

The moment I mentioned disease, the sailor paled and took several steps back. "There's none from there I know. Go to the citadel and ask the guards."

She vanished back to her ship, and the rest of the dock soon cleared after a wave of whispers crossed it. No sailor would take chances with illness, which could devastate the whole crew when confined in a small space. It was a relief to open my nose again.

I grabbed a nearby sack and tossed it over my shoulder. It looked huge but was light, probably wool from the dwarf lands, and I strolled merrily up to the city gate. Now was when I needed a new story, as mention of disease might get me quarantined.

I noted the name of the ship I'd stolen the wool from, the letters written in enchanted golden fire (did I mention elves were ostentatious?) and quickly concocted an elaborate tale about having lost sight of my master. "I need directions to the warehou—" I began, but I was waved through the gate before I could say more. Slaves were invisible.

I used my anonymity to make my way through the merchant quarter. Where Highcrowne streets would be choked with smoking, clanking miniature locomotives and other contraptions imported from the South,

Faellion was older, more traditional. None of the buildings seemed younger than five hundred years or so, and slave-drawn carriages were the main mode of transport, not that there weren't plenty of people on foot.

I saw more types of elves than I'd ever seen before. Highcrowne elves were usually wealthy merchants or nobles with golden skin, but here there were even shorter varieties with caramel, sallow, or cream-colored skin. They didn't look to be as wealthy, judging by their wardrobe, but their expressions were equally somber. The lack of smiling faces could sour anyone's mood, not that mine wasn't sour enough from enduring sore muscles and the sight of so many strangers. I had no friends here.

The city was not as large as Highcrowne, nor the wares for sale as diverse, but there was more fresh fruit and vegetables on offer. It got my stomach rumbling to see bananas and pineapples, when apples and plums were the best I could usually get. Other foodstuffs made my stomach somersault a different direction. The huge, fatty jollups harvested from the higher altitudes and laying like lumps of raw blubber on the tables was bad enough, but then I spotted the 'delicacies' section of the market, where humanoid pixies were packed into cages. Live food. The dried and hanging grall meat wasn't so alive, and neither was the human jerky. I shuddered. There were laws, but when did that ever stop poachers and the bizarrely wealthy who could afford their evil harvests?

It smelled too. The food, the people ... all in a thick miasma of afternoon heat. Walls and buildings blocked the sea breezes, and people pressed in from all sides. I was mesmerized by the contrasts of beauty and horror so far beyond my experiences in Highcrowne and Gernwold, and I knew I was standing and staring like a country bumpkin. An uncomfortable, angry one.

There were a lot of elves, and even more human slaves. Almost nothing else. No free humans either. They were all vacant-eyed and branded, a lot of bare flesh exposed in the heat, so I could see the magical marks on their arms that kept them pacified. A few goblin mercenaries, disarmed before entering the city, marched grumpily about, but there was not one dwarf and certainly no Avians—although they were never seen in Highcrowne either—but it was the lack of dwarves that was unnerving.

Dwarves had children faster than I could count to ten and were always swarming everywhere, doing all the skilled jobs and leaving no need for slaves. Elves liked cowed servants better, but even so there should be a dwarf or two. I remembered what Olyve had said about the dwarves now being our enemies. A hollow feeling formed in my stomach, which quickly grew heavy with guilt. Gypsum had done this somehow, and I hadn't stopped her.

Time to do something stupid. I wanted to start with the marketplace, maybe the entire elf lands, shake some sense and humanity into them all, but I wasn't an army, and armies were never much good for making sense of things anyway. What I could do was talk to the mother who wanted to kill me. Like I said, stupid, but that was me in a nutshell.

I didn't know where Lili of Solheim was, but I was certain it wasn't here. Most likely the palace if she was meeting the Elf King. Last I'd seen Fharen, he'd been fleeing a crashing dirigible, but it would have been easy for him to catch another one. Ilsa and I had been confined on the island for weeks, trapped halfway between here and the fairylands for most of it, but so much had happened in the outside world, it might as well have been a century.

I found a dodgy dealer at the edge of the quarter, a human running a dozing old elf's shop, and traded my stolen wool for coin. I then used the coin to buy fancy clothes more appropriate to a royal slave. I couldn't afford silk, but I got fine linen and slippers to match, which I changed into at the public bath house. The slave's bath house that was, not the elves'. It was still marble and opulent. Elves thought bathing was bad for your health, but they didn't seem to mind endangering the lesser ranks.

I'd hidden my sword behind the bale of wool before, but now I used it as a walking stick, which it was meant to resemble. I pretended to browse the stalls and eyed the entrance to the inner city, gated and flanked by alert soldiers. It didn't look as easy to get through there as it had been to pass the outer gate.

"You need to have the right papers, or blend into a retinue that does," a voice beside me said. It was an elf man, a middle-aged one in a plain robe, his golden hair fading to white in quite a few places. "I want to help you, Eva."

"Thane," I said, grinding my teeth. He could look like a friend, a merman or a stranger, but I knew who he was by the way he said my name. Intimately. It affected me too, sending an electric shiver along my nerves. I didn't like being affected by spells, rituals and god powers beyond my control. I didn't like it a lot. "I don't want your help. Besides, I had figured the retinue thing out myself. I'm waiting for a big enough group to sneak into."

"You'll need someone to vouch for you. The other slaves may or may not say anything, but their master will recognize a new face among them. I will take over a royal. It will be simple then to go where we need."

"Can you hop into anyone's body?" I asked, disturbed to think no one was safe.

"Only those whose resistance has been weakened by poison or illness or who have been deliberately opened to me through ritual. Conrad's initiation was how I took him. Others here have been initiated into the Dead God's service." He showed me the old elf's wrist, and I saw a fresh tattoo hidden behind his bracelets. It was the winged skull.

"His servants are growing in number," Thane continued. "They seek reward or mercy, reprieve from what is coming, but the Dead God will treat all equally in the Halls of Death. If such as this one knew that, they would not be so eager to give up. The Halls are not the same as living and are no substitute for the flesh."

"You're sounding like quite an expert for having only been walking the world ... how long have you been in human bodies?" I asked, as mesmerized by Thane's macabre existence as I was by the horrors of the market. "Come to think of it, do you even have a body of your own?"

"No. I came into being after you were taken from Solheim. I was sent to find you. I am as old as you are."

"But you never had a childhood?" Why was I asking? I supposed I was curious to know how Thane worked.

"No," he said in such a way that I wondered if he could miss something he had no experience of. Maybe he understood everything he wasn't from the memories of those he took over. He had certainly known everything about Conrad, even managed to copy most of his mannerisms, so maybe he knew what it was to be a child and a human, even though he was nothing of the sort. I still couldn't entirely get my head around what he was. A soul? Bodiless. Wandering wherever he was bid. It sounded like purgatory.

The marketplace was so crowded and noisy, I stood closer to him to avoid shouting. "Why didn't you kill me when first found me in Highcrowne? Why all the subterfuge, using Erick's body, getting me to … lying to me. Why bother?"

"Your soul was protected," he said, as though I should know this. "Ulric was the most powerful of the Nine, aside from Lili, and he guarded you and Ilsa always. It was not until you came of age that most of his protections were dispelled. The spells would not work on the strong willed, and a person's will, their soul, does not mature and bond firmly with the flesh until they reach their twentieth year."

"That's why Ulric called me back to Highcrowne for my coming of age ceremony. He had to rely on other protections after that," I said. That's why Duane's goons were always following me. I had so misunderstood my uncle's oppressive presence in my life. But if he had ever deigned to tell me…. He had treated me like a child, and so I'd behaved like one.

"Even so," Thane added, "I needed to both defeat Ulric and win your love to make you vulnerable. No simple task."

"You didn't win my love. I had a moment of … feeling for Erick."

"A moment is all it took. And I was Erick then."

I froze, realizing my real weakness. First Erick and then Conrad: the common factor was Thane. He had possessed them both. Seemed I kept falling for Thane over and over again. Was there any chance of resisting? Maybe if he kept inhabiting merman and smelly elves, but even so.... I took a step back, feeling awkward, wondering if I could trust myself around him at all.

Thane noticed my discomfort, but he continued, saying, "When you were finally vulnerable, we needed you as bait to capture Ulric's power. Lili demanded all the souls of the Nine be given to her, so Erick and I were sent to hunt them down. When it came to the last, to your uncle, we had to achieve that task before I could send you to the Halls of Death."

By now, I had pulled him behind the market stall, continuing our whispered conversation away from prying eyes.

"You thought you had killed me. And you did kill Viktor. I haven't forgotten," I said.

"Viktor was not me. It was Erick, and he regretted it. As for you, Eva ... I knew you were meant to rule alongside the Dead God, with me, that your destiny awaited. That's why, even though I hesitated, I obeyed. But I've changed. You said I have a clean slate."

"In theory. In reality, some things are hard to forgive. And I keep wondering if you are merely trying to lure me into some new trap. Maybe there's something else you need from me now? Like the First Soul?"

"No—" he began, but I didn't let him finish.

I lifted my Ashur cane and hit him with the steel ball at the end. It was built to be a head knocker, and it worked. Thane, or at least the elf's body he'd been inhabiting, was out cold.

10 LIES

I didn't kill Thane because I didn't want to be a killer, the type who took lives without reason or caring. There was no point, anyway. Thane would move on to the next idiot with a Dead God tattoo, and I'm sure there were plenty. Why did people think Death could be bargained with?

I noted the elf I'd clobbered had robes far finer than mine, if a bit austere. He could be useful for something. I'm glad he was smaller and lighter than me, as I slung him over my shoulder and hobbled up to the main gate, the Ashur a cane once more.

"Help me," I called out to the gate guards as I approached. "My master has been attacked by thieves."

They didn't stir from their position, until one finally twitched his gaze when I drew close enough to be his problem. There was recognition. "It's the priest of Fortune," the guard said, coming to take the man out of my arms. "Where was he attacked?"

"Over there," I pointed vaguely into the depths of the marketplace.

Priest of Fortune, huh? I'd never have guessed. Then again, I never attended the temples. I'd imagined Fortune's followers to be worshippers of gold and material things, but I supposed fortune was also another name for fate, and we all knew what a pain in the ass they could be. Apparently, the priest had tired of it as well, which is why he secretly switched allegiance to the Dead God. It was a bad sign if not even the priesthood could keep their faith.

One of the guards ran off in the direction I'd pointed but returned a short time later shaking his head. "I alerted the market guardhouse," he said.

The elf who had taken the priest from me told his compatriot, "I'll take him to the hall of healers." He marched into the inner city, and I followed because no one stopped me.

Easier than I thought. After they left me at the hall of healers, I had time to scout around and found there was yet another set of gates to penetrate before reaching the palace. They weren't even open and looked as fortified as the Central City in Highcrowne, lots of black-garbed Eleven Elite Protectorate standing around, or EEPs as I liked to call them.

I sighed. Not so easy. I found a shadowed corner within sight of the gates and sat, thinking. I could glue on some ears and not bathe for a month? Even so, I was too tall for an elf. If I could do reliable magic, I'd fly over the wall. Old fashioned cat burglary come nightfall might be the way to go, but there were a lot of EEPs, and I wasn't a professional. Was the palace even where I'd find Lili? Maybe I should wait for her to leave and ambush her on the way out? Was she taking dirigible or ship? Travelling overland?

I sighed louder and hunched lower in the dark corner. I was growing morose, and hungry, as I thought out and rejected plan after plan. I was always too brash. Maybe Thane's idea had been a good one. Too late now.

I could feel the First Soul near, but I wasn't sure if it was in the palace or even in the city, as it was a vague sense and not one you could plot a course by.

I also needed a way to compel answers from Lili. The relic could work as a bargaining chip, if my mother wanted it badly enough. Not that I would give it to her, but she didn't know that. First, I had to get it back. How was Ilsa moving about the city? I'm sure elf mages would detect her invisibility enchantment, and she'd have as difficult a time as me.

Come to think of it, Olyve should have detected her enchanted dress as well. I was unskilled, but she wasn't. Had she known Ilsa was hiding under the water with us? Had she let her take the First Soul?

Too much thinking wasn't good for me. It made me paranoid. Not that I didn't have plenty of reasons to be wary, but that wouldn't help right now. What I needed ... was a bit of good fortune.

I headed back to the hall of healers and found the priest I'd left awake and staring at me. He seemed alert—the healer mages must have done their job—but more importantly, I couldn't see Thane behind his eyes. I suddenly worried the priest would turn me in for bashing him, but even if he could remember what happened, I'd hit him from behind. He couldn't know it was me. Nevertheless, I was prepared to run if he pointed an accusatory finger.

"I remember you from the marketplace," he said.

Uh, oh. Time to run? Instead, I sat down beside him and took his hand, saying loudly, as you do with crazy people, "I was there because I'm your slave. You must have been hit hard, Master."

I smiled and shrugged, catching the eye of the nurses nearby. They didn't seem interested in our exchange, so I toned it down a bit. "What exactly do you remember?" I whispered.

"A divine presence. I was blessed, as I have never been blessed in all my years bent low before Fortune's wheel. I chose rightly when I took this mark." He showed me the winged skull, but I quickly covered it up.

"You don't want to go flashing that about," I said.

"Why not? I shall proselytize and proclaim the true faith loudly for all to hear!" His voice echoed through the huge chamber, and a few groggy patients turned our way.

"Quiet," I hissed.

I put a hand over his mouth and looked sheepishly at our audience. When the gazes turned away again, I removed my hand and said, "Our Lord has other plans for you."

That got his attention. I felt dirty pretending to be a follower, but I'd heard the way Ilsa said 'Our Lord' enough times, with that tone full of desire, that I could manage a fair imitation. The priest believed me. What's more, he remembered more than I thought he had.

"You are special to Him," he said. "I shall be your devoted servant, as I am His. Ask anything of me. Take my life, send me to the bosom of sweet death to dwell in His Halls for all eternity—"

"None of that," I said hastily. Then I remembered my role and added, "There will be no reward until you have earned it. Are you recovered enough to leave this place and help me?"

"Yes, yes. I could walk across coals."

"Once again, not necessary right now. Let's just head back to your temple. You have a private office where I can talk more freely?"

"I will not return there, to blindness and idleness at the feet of uncaring Fate."

"It's required," I insisted. "Your current position is of use to Our Lord."

"Of course. That is why I have been chosen. Come." He climbed to his feet with a bit of help. The nurses wanted him back in bed to be sure of his full recovery, but he waved them away, and they relented.

He kept an arm around my shoulder and told me where to go, waving off concerned clergy when we reached Fortune's temple, which wasn't too far away. We headed straight to his office at the back of the massive building.

I paused for a moment to stare up at the huge, wooden wheel that was suspended above the center of the temple hall like a chandelier. It had eight spokes and spun slowly, never stopping. Usually, I saw the symbol displayed vertically to show the up and down of the wheel, but this one was horizontal. I asked about it.

"It is to represent the fact that Fate is neither good nor bad, they simply are," the priest said. "Such tiring nonsense. I seek truth now, not the endless repetition of what can never be known. We all find truth in death, do we not? Tell me it shall be my reward?"

"Sure."

"I have served in this temple for eighty out of my ninety years, have seen treasures beyond imagining cross the altar, but never before has a promised treasure shined so brightly as the reprieve Our Lord offers."

I'd hit a ninety-year-old? Maybe we should have stayed at the healers' longer. Then again, elves lived twice as long as humans, so my earlier calculation of him being middle-aged was right. He sounded like he had a death wish, though, so I doubted he'd make it to two hundred.

We were in his office now, with the door tightly shut, and I said, "Have you heard that an emissary of the Dead God is here? Lili of Solheim?"

"Yes, she arrived yesterday. I hoped fervently to catch a glimpse when her procession traversed the city, but I could not get close enough. It was a popular sight. Too long has there been no face for the dreaded enemy in the South. For me of course, He is no longer my enemy but my savior."

"So, she came overland?"

"By airship, with dwarven and ... other companions. People have been talking and describing it all in such detail, I almost imagine I was there."

"Good. Where is Lili now?"

"In the palace, awaiting the arrival of King Fharen. He was summoned from Highcrowne the moment she arrived and should be here soon."

"I need you to get me in into the palace then. I must meet with Lili."

"Surely, if you tell them you are part of her retinue…?"

"No. I have a secret mission," I lied. I was learning to do it well, although not as good as my 'friends'. "I need to find something, a gem, that was brought here. I need to retrieve it before I meet her, and there can be no connection between us if I'm caught."

"I see. I see." He sat and contemplated. After a while, he said, "I am a lowly priest, revered only by the worshippers at this temple, as the nobles have their own private clerics. However, I do know one who we might entreat to gain entry to her rooms in the palace. I will send a message at once."

"Great. In the meantime, is there something I can eat?"

He scribbled a note and sent it off with an acolyte, before asking another to bring us some cheese and wine. I avoided the wine but could not resist the cheese. So what if it gave me a few more curves than Ilsa?

"Thank you," I told the priest when my stomach stopped growling. "You know, I haven't asked you your name, and you haven't asked me mine."

"I know yours. It is Eva. It was forever in the thoughts of the holy presence that inhabited me. I feel too insignificant to force mine upon you, but now that you have asked, it is Aylon."

"You seem unlike any elf I've known, Aylon. You haven't raised your nose at me once."

"I'd like to say I would always have treated you with respect, even if I had not known of your holy nature, as Fortune teaches all are crushed equally beneath their wheel, and of course all are equal in Death's Halls. The truth, however, is that I am no different from any other elf. Since birth, long before we are taught religion, we are taught to value ourselves and our culture above all others. From our mother's lap and from our first schoolmaster to our last, we are taught the world is overrun by lesser creatures who would destroy us if given the chance.

"Humans of course fall into this category, as they have spread like a plague across the world. Short-lived and short-sighted. Even our allies within the Kingdoms, the dwarves, are not excluded from our distrust, because their numbers grow even more quickly, like rats, confined to borders too small for them, and they tumble over into ours, encroaching on our ancient lands. Not an elf I encounter conversationally does not believe the Dead God's arrival is anything less than a blessing. He destroys only the human kingdoms, and now that the dwarves have turned sides, we have excuse to war with them and diminish their numbers."

"The Dead God will not stop at humanity," I warned. But then I remembered the role I was playing, good little servant of the god, like my sister, so I shut my mouth before I started lecturing. Instead, I changed the subject to the other aspect of his words that bothered me. I found them enlightening—and disturbing. "So, you would hate me if not for my connection to the god, and there really is an elf conspiracy to not only enslave humanity but wipe us from existence?"

"You are Solhan, my child, which is a different category entirely from human, so I would not go so far as that. Your kind and the Avians are our ancient brethren, and not so fecund, so to say, as the humans with whom you share a resemblance. We would never wipe your kind from existence, but we do believe it is only right that we rule now, as your empire has waned and ours is on the rise.

"King Fharen would be more popular among the people if he stayed true to his promises of seeing elf kind gain prominence among the Three Kingdoms, but instead he talks of opposing the Dead God. I and a few wise souls believe this is but a ploy to exterminate the dwarves and humans in open warfare, as we all seek, but many believe his focus should be here. Let the Dead God do His work and leave us out of it. That is why the king's nephew, Prince Gallan, is more popular among the common elves, and I suspect the nobles, although, as I have said, I do not often meet with such as them." The priest finished his explanation with a smile. As though elven plans for genocide were perfectly normal.

I was glad he was so forthright with me, but it worried me how no other elf I'd known was. They were all in on the conspiracy from the way he spoke. Then again, that could be his slant on things—he did end up selling his soul to the Dead God, so he wasn't the nicest person to begin with.

I didn't know what to say after the priests' racist spiel, and so I gave him a frozen smile. Finally, I said, "Now, how am I to get into the palace?"

"Here." He gave me an acolyte's robe. "Wear this. You cannot pass as a slave with anyone paying attention, for your gaze is too direct and your words too outspoken."

He made it sound like a failing.

When I had the robe on, I saw my ragged knees hanging out the bottom. "I'm a bit tall to be an elf," I pointed out. "I don't think I can hunch the whole time." I tried crouching down and walking, but after a few steps, my already sore back muscles were really hurting, so I stood up again.

"You look ludicrous. I meant a glamour of course." He passed his hand across my body, starting from the top of my head and working his way down, muttering some spell under his breath. It made me uncomfortable, but I tried hard not to move until it was complete.

"There," he said when he finished. He indicated the mirror on his wall. "See for yourself."

I saw and was impressed. I was a snooty elf acolyte now. A boy a bit younger than my real age, pimply faced, but with his brow already furrowed and nose scrunched up in distaste.

"Acolytes of Fortune are normally forbidden glamours until they are initiated," he said. "It is to teach them to accept fate and the looks they were given at birth. Few outside our temple would find your use of a disguise suspicious, however."

"I thought glamours were only meant to make you prettier. So, an elf can look like anyone they want? Isn't that dangerous? Anyone could be impersonated."

"We learn to recognize voices, and our mage guards can see through any disguise. It has long been our way, so we think nothing of it. Here, you look weary from your journeys and can rest while we wait for a reply to my message." He indicated a hard bench. I supposed Fortune didn't allow comfort either.

"Who did you write?" I asked.

"Duchess Ula, King Fharen's great aunt. She has no political power but offers a means for us to gain entry to the palace. My mentor was her lover. I said I'd like to bring her some trinkets of his, now that he has passed away. It was some months ago that he died, but it could have taken time to put affairs in order. I hope it is believable enough."

"Her lover? Wasn't he a priest?"

He shrugged. "We are not worshippers of Sorrow. His are the only priests required to abstain from all things joyful. As you can guess, few flock to him, and I do not even believe there is a temple in this city."

A god for everything. If only there was one who'd help me. Seemed none of them did anything useful, or like Trickster, had a self-centered view of things. I didn't think we needed any more like that, and certainly not Harbinger.

I sat while the priest worked, the uncomfortable seat he'd given me accentuating the pain from sore muscles. I fidgeted and found my thoughts straying to the First Soul. After I got hold of it and stopped the Dead God, what then? Would I take up my father's old job as keeper? What did that mean? Would I need to spend forever hiding it from everyone who wanted to be a god or do terrible things? It sounded like a worse gig than being a priest of Sorrow.

I didn't like thinking too far ahead, because the future terrified me. It was a relief when we got a message later. I'd fallen asleep somehow, and I crashed to the floor when the messenger entered.

"She has invited me to her chambers tonight," Aylon said, reading the note. "Let us prepare at once."

I was as prepared as I could be, but he took some time donning his best robes. He gathered some 'trinkets', most encrusted with gems and gold—where the association between 'Fortune' and 'fortune' came from—and placed them in a treasure chest. It was my job to carry it.

Aylon didn't introduce me to the other acolytes, and they didn't ask about me, which was just as well. I was already lying to the priest and would confuse myself if I had a cover story to juggle beneath my cover story. It had been a long day. And it wasn't over yet.

Another acolyte came with us, and she kicked the back of my leg whenever I slouched. Which I was doing a lot by the time we made it past all the checkpoints. I wanted to kick her back but was afraid I'd spill the treasure I carried. The glamour the priest cast went unnoticed as we passed the innermost gates.

A dirigible was moored above us, not as large as *The Mathésis*, which I'd helped crash, but it was almost as gaudy. From the emblem on the side, I guessed it was the Elf King's personal ship. My pace quickened, so I was soon nudging Aylon in the back to hurry him up.

I didn't know if the First Soul was calling me or if it was the desire for answers; all I knew was I was running out of time. If the King was here, he could meet with Lili and she could be gone again before I ever caught sight of her. Not that I expected the wheels of politics to turn so quickly, but it was better to act now before other people went around changing the game. King Fharen, from my brief experience, was an unpredictable player.

Once inside the elven palace, I didn't gawk. If you've seen Highcrowne's palace, all others pale in comparison. We had an escort all the way to Duchess Ula's door. Our EEP watchers didn't relax until the noble confirmed our visit.

"Shoo now and let them in," she said. The lady spoke from across the room, where she was ensconced in a comfortable chair with lots of blankets embroidered with golden threads, while her maid held the door open for us.

The maid was a human slave, and I smiled at her, instinctively trying to make a connection, but she paid no attention to me. She, like all the other slaves I'd seen in the city, were marked, branded by a magic which took away all will, leaving a mindless automaton behind. In fact, I'd met automatons with more personality.

While the maid saw to the priest, sitting him near the duchess and leaving us acolytes standing around, I peeked out the front door. The two EEPs were still there, waiting. I gave a little smile and wave, saying, "Hello," before I hurriedly shut the door again. My voice was my own, and I hoped they mistook it for a boy's rather than a woman's.

I took the small treasure chest to Aylon and whispered in his ear, "I really need to get out of here now. Is there a back way?"

"Oh, dear," he said aloud. "It seems my acolyte is not well. If your maid could show him to the facilities?"

The duchess rang a little bell she had beside her, despite the maid standing attentively nearby, and said, "Off with him. Show him where to go. Now, Aylon, it has been such a long time. I'm so sorry to hear of your master's passing...." She laid a comforting hand on his knee, and I did a double take at the expression on her face. Wasn't she a bit old for that sort of thing?

The maid led me to a bathroom with indoor plumbing. The toilet was a hole in the ground, but the sink worked, the height of modernity. I washed my hands and face and made a few retching sounds as the water ran. I peeked out, but the maid had been called for some other task, so I slunk out of the small chamber and went looking for a back door.

The royal apartments were rooms within the main palace. Nobility had as many rooms as their rank warranted, and the duchess had quite a suite. The place had a lived-in stink to it, and most items were worn and threadbare, like the faded finery of my own home. The maid didn't keep things too tidy, and there was only the one servant. Aylon was wise to bring Fortune's 'trinkets' along, as I suspected the duchess had little of value anymore besides her title. Hopefully, the priest could keep her occupied—all evening if he had to. I was sure the EEPs had done a head count of acolytes, and they would not be happy when we didn't all come out again.

I found another exit, after much searching, and it led into the servants' section of the palace. I saw maids and butlers scurrying between a noisy kitchen somewhere down the corridor and other nobles' apartments whose backdoors were spaced all along the passageway. I picked a direction at random, or more exactly let my desire to find the First Soul help me pick a direction, and I headed left. When the passageway turned abruptly where I didn't want to go, I took a breath and stepped through a door into a strange apartment.

A maid stood there, staring at me. It took me a few frantic seconds to disentangle my Ashur from beneath my acolyte robes and ready it for some head knocking.

The poor maid, significantly younger than the last one but equally vacant-eyed, stood there for a few moments staring, and I couldn't do it.

She finally said, "Are you expected? Should I inform my mistress?"

I sighed and leaned on the Ashur. "No need. I'm lost and only passing through. Can you show me the way to the front door?"

"This way." She set off at a sedate walk, and I followed, peeking around door frames, expecting EEP soldiers to be lying in wait. Instead, there were only more servants, all focused on their tasks and ignoring me. It was even more disturbing than being in Bell's workshop, with all the machines clattering about their inhuman business. These people were not machines.

Humans should not be here. Highcrowne law allowed only heredity slaves—slaves born of other slaves—to be bought and sold in the Three Kingdoms, but I knew full well King Fharen and likely most other elves disobeyed that rule. There were more humans in Faellion than I had expected, all with slave marks, none free, and I suspected they were illegally enslaved refugees. I'd seen it before.

I wanted to help every one of them, figure a way to go around removing slave marks, and see how the elves enjoyed their slaves when they weren't cowed by magic. But there was no point trying until the Dead God was defeated, only then would these people have lands to return to. I was learning you sometimes had to deal with the big things first, else you were only tossing people from the pan into the fire.

I was nearly to the front door, proud of my restraint and happy for the stroke of luck so far, when I spotted an elf girl with black hair standing in the parlor, maids removing her travelling cloak and hat. She stared at me without recognition, but I recognized her.

"Hilja?" I said, without thinking. I could have kicked myself. My voice was disturbingly high in the echoing chamber. I didn't sound like a boy, and the princess scowled.

Courting the Enemy

Last I'd seen Hilja, she'd been escaping *The Mathésis*. She'd been there with Duane. Their affair was the scandal of the court I heard, but it certainly wasn't Duane who stepped up behind her and turned her for a deep welcome kiss. It was some elf royal, all golden and perfect with glamour. When they finished their kiss, they both looked at me, and I realized I was rooted to the spot.

"Who are you?" the man asked. "Another ragamuffin my foolish Hilja picked up on her travels?"

Ragamuffin? I didn't like his attitude toward me or the princess. What was she doing kissing him back anyway? I put a hand on my hip, ready to start lecturing them both, and said, "My name is E—" before Hilja cut me off.

"His name is Everett, and yes he's a project of mine. I must see to him at once, and when we are both properly presentable, I will find you again, my darling."

She gave him another kiss before marching up to me, taking me by the arm, and hauling me into a room that looked like nothing more than a giant closet with racks of clothes, mirrors, and a few couches. She shoved me into a seat—she was stronger than she looked—and crossed her arms.

"Miss Eva Thorne," she said. "I am surprised to find you here. Your companions despaired of ever seeing you again. Mister Rose told me a grim tale of enduring beasts and battles, all after you survived that horrible crash. I'm so glad to see you are alright. You can remove that glamour around me."

"I don't know how. The main thing is...." I paused. "Mister Rose? You mean Duane is alright?" I sunk deeper into the couch. "Bell and the others? Did they all make it back?" I asked.

"All but you and Miss Gypsum."

"Conrad?"

"I'm not sure who that is. Duane never mentioned him." She seemed to notice the shock of the past weeks catching up to me and sat down beside me, putting a hand on my shoulder.

"And you never mentioned this man here in your apartments," I said, removing her hand. I felt indignant for Duane's sake. "Who is he?"

"Prince Gallan of the Northern Glades, an old title. It's all pre-arranged you know. That's how these things work when you're a princess. It's a state duty, you understand. Not that he's un-handsome in any way, a fine match really, it's just his hobbies and mine clash quite a bit. Otherwise, I think we should be quite happy. He's impatient for intimacy, as I'm sure you noticed, but I shall await a proper wedding. I only need a few more years to plan it."

I'd had enough of weddings ever since the guests all turned into werewolves at my friend's, Karolyne's, ceremony. Not that I thought Hilja would invite me to hers. What I was hoping she would do was help me with my current problem, so I kept my mouth shut about arranged marriages—I had more experience with those than I wanted—nor did I tear into her about deceiving Duane. Play nice, Eva.

"I wish I had more time to chat," I said, lying, "but I'm hunting for two very important things that are somewhere here in the palace."

"A scavenger hunt? I love those!" she clapped her hands together excitedly and did a little jump. "Oh. Wait. You mean you're on a 'case'. I do recall Duane telling me you believe you are a detective. Sounds fascinating."

"Not really. Unless you like mortal peril. Anyway, I see that you've just arrived, so I assume you came on the same dirigible from Highcrowne as your father?"

"Correct. I see why you're a detective." There wasn't any sarcasm in her tone, which felt strange. No one else took me seriously.

"That wasn't a hard one," I said. "Navigating this palace is. Do you know when your father is meeting the Dead God's representative? And where she's staying?" If Ilsa was bringing our mother the First Soul, then she'd be headed there too, if she wasn't there already. First order of business was to get that gem back. Then I'd have something to leverage with my mother. "And does Lili have any bodyguards with her? What kind of resistance would I be up against?"

"You're not thinking about derailing peace negotiations?" she asked, appalled. "My father has made a sacred vow. He dies if Lili dies and vice versa. It was the terms of the truce, and I can't allow you to endanger my father."

"I won't," I lied again. "I merely want a chance to see my mother, to speak with her uninterrupted."

"What's your mother got to do with this?"

"She's the representative."

Hilja seemed smart, but she was giving me a blank look now. I assumed everyone knew, but it was stupid to assume.

"Lili of Solheim is my mother," I said.

"Then you're a princess, like me!" Hilja hugged me, welcoming me to the club. "How wonderful to have an equal here. I've had enough of ladies in waiting, duchess this and baroness that, all wanting something from me or my father, of course. How refreshing to speak to someone who wants nothing from me."

I wouldn't say that. Nor would I point out it had been a long time since Solheim was an empire, and they didn't have princesses anymore. Thank the gods. Even the thought made me shudder. Nothing was more useless than royalty, not that I told Hilja that.

I covered my reaction with a concerned expression. "What's more, my mother and I were separated when I was an infant. I haven't seen her since. You understand why I must know where she is?"

"How sad! Of course, I will help you, Eva. I will find out where she is at once. And the other thing you were hunting? What is it?"

I didn't want to explain about the First Soul, so I said, "My sister, Ilsa. She's here somewhere, looking for our mother also, but I must speak to her first. It's urgent."

By 'speak', I meant hit her over the head and take the relic from her.

"Such a heartbreaking story, two sisters seeking to reconcile with their long-lost mother, now Queen of the Dead, and convince her to broker a true peace between the Three Kingdoms, all while sharing some dark secret one sister must not let the other speak. Perhaps it is an admonishment? Ilsa is angry at your abandonment and would say something unwise at a time like this? Is that it?" She was clearly fishing for more.

"No. Secrets are secrets, Hilja." I stayed tight-lipped, and she squirmed with excitement.

"Stay here while I discover the information you seek." Hilja took a gown off a rack. It looked to have never been worn and was encrusted in shiny things wherever it wasn't thick with tulle. When she handed it to me, I gave another shudder. "Wear this," she insisted. "You must dress appropriately when first you see your mother after so long. And take off that hideous glamour."

"I can't. A friend put it on me."

"I can't remove another's personal enchantment. Can you find your friend?" Hilja really didn't like my disguise for some reason.

"I don't want to go back there, even if I could find the way. But I have an idea." I took the Avian feather from the oiled pouch at my waist and held it up. Before I spoke the spell, I paused a moment and asked, "Won't it be dangerous if I go about the palace looking like myself?"

"Nonsense. You'll be with me and perfectly safe. Hurry it up."

Against my better judgment, I obeyed. I liked being anonymous, but then again, when Fortune's priests were done visiting the duchess, the EEPs would be looking for my current disguise, so it might be better to hide behind my own face. I lifted the feather to my eyes and said, " *Yusha Kalal.* "

The room shimmered and a few gowns lost their sparkle, turning into to dreary rags. The rest was unchanged, including Hilja—she was still annoyingly beautiful—and I looked down at my own hands again. I packed the feather away, while Hilja grumbled about the fake dresses the spell had revealed.

"How long will you be?" I asked, when Hilja headed for the door. The closet was grand, but it was still a closet with no other exits. I felt imprisoned already.

"Not long," she said. "Wait right here."

I nodded and smiled and did no such thing. As soon as she was gone, I donned the simplest dress she had, which was still quite gem-encrusted, made sure my carry pouch and Ashur were secure beneath the Acolyte's robe I wore over it, and headed out after Hilja. Her servants by the door seemed startled but didn't stop me leaving.

I followed her at a distance through the palace corridors, trying to maintain the vacant gaze the marked slaves had, until I came to a section barricaded by EEPs. They let Hilja through, but I lurked in a side passage and waited.

I was untrusting of people these days, with good reason, and while I believed the elf princess wanted to help me, I wasn't too sure her version of 'help' didn't mean alerting her father to the danger I represented to the negotiations and having me imprisoned by his personal guard. You could never be too sure.

"I know where she is," a slave said, making me jump.

The girl had snuck up beside me through some hidden passage I presumed; the place seemed riddled with them for servants' use. This slave, however, was not vacant-eyed and likely no slave at all. My hand went to my Ashur.

"Please don't hit me again," Thane said. "I'm trying to help. I know where Ilsa is."

That made me pause.

"Where?" I'd brain him, her, whatever you called a portion of the Dead God hiding in a body of the opposite sex, later, after I had the information. I assumed it was a trap, but those usually required bait, so Ilsa might actually be there.

"I'll show you."

"Tell me," I insisted.

"No. You'll knock me out again."

I took my hand off the sword. I was being a bit too obvious and needed to wait for a better time. "Fine. Lead the way."

"I know you, Eva, and you don't give in that easily. I'm watching you." Thane, the slave he was inhabiting anyway, led me into the secret passage she'd come out of, glancing back warily from time to time. I kept my hand away from my weapon.

I felt more relaxed jammed in the passageway with busy servants, like termites in the walls, and could afford a bit of time to check out whatever trap he'd laid for me. Did I mention 'suspicious' was my new middle name?

"You don't give up easily, either," I said after a while. "I told you to go far away from me, and here you are in a girl. What is she, nine or ten? It's creepy. Don't tell me she's a follower of the Dead God too?"

"No, but her soul is subdued by the slave mark, and she has no ability to resist. I chose her because she has access to the place we want to be."

"We. Why do people say that? You can't know what 'we' want, only what you want, and I'm not trusting you. Clean slate and all, you are the Dead God." I whispered that part, not that I thought the slaves around us would notice, but because I felt strange saying it too loudly. "And how you can turn against yourself—very weird once again—for supposed 'love' does my head in. You don't know anything about love."

"Neither do you."

Touché. He was wrong, though. "I love plenty of people. It's romantic love I've sworn off. It's more trouble than it's worth."

"No. Love compels one onward, gives one hope that they can be the person they should be. Such love transcends flesh and time and sorrow. It is the point of everything."

He'd taken up verbal sparring and armed himself with eloquence. How was I to compete with that?

We threaded our way through a bewildering maze of corridors in silence, after I failed to come up with a worthy comeback. If his plan had been to get me lost, he was succeeding. I wondered if I shouldn't have waited for Hilja. A two-timing elf princess had to be trustworthy? Right? More than a god suffering from split personality, surely?

Don't trust anyone, I reminded myself. When we stopped outside a door and Thane reached for the handle, I drew my Ashur and pointed it at his neck. It felt wrong threatening the life of a child, but I didn't intend to use the blade. It was more a visual statement to aid my argument, since I lacked eloquence.

"What's inside?" I asked, hoping I'd recognize the lie when I heard it.

"Ilsa."

I did feel the weight of the First Soul nearby, drawing me in, and when I closed one eye, I could see black tendrils of it reaching out to me from under the door. He wasn't lying about the prize being near.

"I meant, what else is inside? An army?" There was no way it could be this easy.

"Guards, most certainly, but you have a sword. Your mother, but you said you wanted to find her. What you seek is inside."

It was a well-baited trap. What choice did I have? At least I could enter it my way.

"Sorry, slave girl," I said, as I thumped Thane upside the head again.

He tried to dodge this time, but he wasn't fast enough, or at least the thin girl he was inhabiting wasn't. I dragged her unconscious form into a shadowed corner, where bags of linen to be washed were stacked, and hid her there. I felt the raised brand of the slave mark on her arm and wondered for a moment if I could remove it. She didn't deserve to have her soul enslaved, her body invaded. No one did.

I put my palm over the scar and felt for her squirming soul. It didn't struggle much anymore, tired from fighting. I stopped. I wasn't sure I could do it, and if I did, she'd be terrified. I remembered Kali's reaction when Erick had freed her. The elf capital was not a good place for a human to be, and I had no surety of getting myself out, let alone a frightened girl. It wasn't fair to put her life in danger.

I made a silent vow then, one of those little promises to myself I hesitated to make because I knew I'd have to follow up. I vowed to come back one day and make sure all humans in the Three Kingdoms were free, hereditary slave or not.

I had no idea how I'd pull that one off, but I'd have to. I'd never be able to sleep again thinking of these corridors of vacant-eyed drones serving their aristocratic masters, being bred to produce vacant-eyed children who served as well, one generation to the next. In some ways, the Dead God's hordes were less frightening.

I stood up and took a deep breath.

Ilsa and my mother. This would be interesting.

I stepped through the door, sword raised and ready for a fight, but saw only more servants. There were quite a few of them standing around, white-gloved hands folded as they waited for a summons.

"What are you doing?" I asked, curious to see them idle like this.

An older man wearing a butler's uniform turned his vacant gaze on me. "What do you require, madam?"

He was disappointedly bland in comparison to the Elf Butler who featured in the mysteries I loved. Probably because he was a human slave, and those stories were just stories. Nothing in real life was so pleasant or tidily bound into a few pages of text.

"I'd like to know why all these servants are here?" I said.

"Our master has commanded it. He requested privacy."

"And who is your master?"

"Our master."

End of the conversation reached already.

"Where are the guards and how many are there?" I asked, hoping that line of questioning would be more fruitful.

"Eight, two stationed at each doorway to the central chamber. They too were ordered not to listen," the butler said.

Interesting. Seemed Thane had led me to the official 'peace' negotiations. I felt the First Soul nearby as well, and it was close, its power beckoning.

"Thanks," I said, before I crept forward through the apartments.

Once out of the servants' section, which with its marble countertops and polished floors hadn't been anything to look down your nose at, the main apartments screamed opulence. There were gold and silver threads in the rich tapestries on the walls, the elegant cushions and chairs. The floor was marble, the furnishings polished wood and gilt with real gold, the chandeliers sparkling with crystal.

I felt underdressed, so I shook off the acolyte's robe to reveal Hilja's gown. Maybe it would give the guards pause if they spotted me. I was as Solhan-looking as it was possible to be: tall, pale to my very irises, with black hair like the Void to provide contrast. Hopefully they'd assume I was with Lili, drawn Ashur or not, and try not to kill me.

I'd try not to kill them either. It wasn't good for your soul.

Two guards stood at the end of the hall blocking my way. They weren't ordinary soldiers but EEPs in black uniforms, shiny black boots, and carefully canted berets. They hadn't spotted me, and I planned my approach. I could duck from one doorway to the next. Perhaps there were doors connecting the side rooms I could use to get closer? But the First Soul was nearby, and it seemed to goad me with confidence. I felt like taking a more direct approach.

I sheathed my Ashur, transferring the hilt to my right hand, and it became a walking cane again. I strode forward, not using the cane for support but as a drumbeat against the marble floors, heralding my approach. They were at full attention now, their own swords crossed in front of me to bar the way.

"Let me pass," I said when I reached the doors, my tone as arrogant as Ilsa's.

One of them shifted his gaze to the other and said, "Isn't she inside already? I swore I saw her."

"I was, now let me back in," I insisted.

"No one gets through," the other one said. "Use the door you exited by; they'd know if you're to be allowed back in."

Trust elves, and EEPs in particular, to be sticklers for the rules. Had no one told them there were no rules in war? It certainly wasn't peacetime yet.

I swung my Ashur at the one who'd looked away. I was so fast it was a blur. His jawbone popped, and he was down on the floor, moaning groggily. The other one swung his sword, and I blocked it with the sheath. He opened his mouth to shout a warning to the other six guards who must be somewhere around the corner, out of sight, when the First Soul whispered to me, telling me what to do.

I reached out for Void stuff, feeling it in the air the EEP breathed, and I thickened it so that he choked and coughed, unable to draw breath. He turned red, doubled over, and I had time to line up a perfect strike. He was out cold, and I finished off the groggy one with a similar blow. I checked to make sure both were still alive, not that I could do anything if they weren't, but knocking someone out was always risky. I could easily have another death on my conscious, and I already had more than I wanted.

That trick with the air was effective. I hoped I could do it again. Maybe I could suck the air out of the room? It would make things simpler.

I took a deep breath, flung the doors open and stepped inside. Any notion of 'focus' or using magic was impossible: I was transfixed by the strange tableau before me.

The first thing I noticed was Gypsum, my old friend, with the wolf crown on her head. She seemed startled by my entrance, and I'm sure that was a guilty expression on her face when she realized it was me. She should feel guilty. I didn't have time to give her my full attention, however, because there was so much to take in.

Beside Gypsum stood another dwarf I didn't recognize, his exposed skin covered in elaborate scars that likely made some pattern if more flesh was visible. I didn't want to see more flesh, because it was gray and dead. He was Risen.

The other two Risen were in more advanced stages of decay. Solhans I think, but it was hard to tell, as all I had to go on was black hair. The man wasn't as far gone as the woman; he still had masses of muscle, that combined with his height, which was substantial, made him appear as brutish as a shaved bear. A bear who'd been nicked a few times during the shaving process, because chunks of flesh were missing, abscesses from wounds which never healed properly.

Risen were immortal, as long as their flesh was intact that was. The Dead God controlled and preserved them, but not perfectly. He didn't seem to care about looks, only that they could move about and fight. The woman's appearance made that frightfully clear.

She was little more than a skeleton, half her ribcage missing, the skin clinging to the bones of her face and arms like leather. Her dress was new, though, some black and silver creation cut artfully to accentuate her bony hips, shoulders and shriveled cleavage, as well as reveal her gaping midriff. And she was flirting with me. Her thin lips, heavy with red lipstick, blew me a kiss. I did a double take and shuddered.

I knew the Compact forbade them in the Three Kingdoms, so these couldn't be Risen. Parlay or no parlay, it would be a clear breach. Then again, these ones had too much character, too much life behind the eyes. Every corpse controlled by the Dead God I'd ever seen had a mad, feral glint. Either that or a distant gaze, depending on whether it was being drawn to Solheim or intent on killing me. I'd experienced the latter a bit too often. No, these creatures were conscious, I could sense it. They weren't Risen at all— they were undead necromancers, powerful enough to weld their own souls to their flesh. Liches. Another Solhan fairy tale. I'd seen plenty of them come true of late, so these didn't surprise me too much.

They weren't even the only disturbing things in the scene before me.

My nemesis—although he didn't know or care I hated him—King Fharen was there. The floor had liquefied in one spot, capturing his feet, and a tendril of it had reached up to encircle his arms, so it seemed he was held captive by giant, marble hands. Ilsa was pinned too, her elbows wrapped in bronze twisted off from the massive candelabra beside her. The person responsible stood opposite them, the First Soul in her hand. I couldn't see her well through the dark cloud of the active soul, but I knew immediately who it was— my mother, Lili. The relic lent her power, allowing her to bend the matter in the room to her will and to hold her captives in place.

"This is an interesting way to negotiate peace," I said, finally overcoming my shock enough to speak. "I mean capitulation. Looks effective."

The First Soul was turned on me then, but I was its keeper now. It knew me, called to me, and I fed it calming thoughts, unconditional love. Everything that was alien and desirable to me, I gave to it, knowing we craved the same things. We too were equally lost.

The blackness ebbed, and I could see my mother for the first time. She wore a dark gown in an ancient fashion, all ruffled and hipped with wireframe petticoats. Her hair was up, like Ilsa's, her hair dark as ours, but the similarities ended there. Her face was past white; it was gray and bloodless, a shriveled husk of mummified flesh. Her eyes were milky, but she gazed on me with something beyond ordinary sight.

"You," she said, and it was amazing how much disappointment a mother could infuse in one word.

12   Taking Sides

"Take the relic from her," King Fharen ordered, his mouth free of the marble gag now that the animated hands were no longer shifting to hold his squirming form. He acted like I was one of his loyal subjects, or even capable of doing what he wanted.

I needed the First Soul, and I needed answers, but I had no idea how to get either from Lili. My mother looked at me with that pitiless, inhuman face of hers, and I was as rooted in place as Ilsa and the king.

"What happened to you?" I asked, wanting to know more than anything at that moment. "Is this what the Dead God will do to me?"

She scoffed. "You should be so fortunate, child of mine. I will rule eternal over the living, while you rule the Halls of the Dead. You should thank me for what I've given you, but do not be jealous if I chose the better bargain for myself."

"You look dead. How is that better?"

"To be eternal, you can be neither alive nor dead but something more. My reward, however, is not complete, and it shall not be until the bargain is fully met. Hand over your soul to Our Lord, darling, and let us be done with all this nonsense. I need no kingly servants," she glanced at Fharen wrapped in marble, "when you complete your purpose." She beckoned me closer, arms wide like a loving mother, but in the hand that did not hold the relic was a flash of silver, a small dagger ready to strike. She was so brazen about it.

"I'm quite good at disappointing family, or so Uncle tells me, and I'm not sorry to disappoint you," I said.

"Then I'll come to you." She stepped toward me, and I drew the Ashur. She paused at sight of the weapon that had once been hers.

"Cut off her head, Eva," Ilsa called from the sidelines, cheering me on for once.

"I thought you were on her side?" I said.

"By my command, do not kill her," King Fharen interjected. "We are under a flag of truce, and I am sworn."

Hilja had mentioned that vow. It meant something to elves, as sworn truces were rare and powerful magic that, if the terms were violated, would result in the death of the oath breaker. But it wasn't my oath, and I didn't care if Fharen died.

I raised the Ashur and used it to knock the dagger out of her grip. She reached out, and what I could only call the essence of death came for me. A dread chill skulked forward, cloaked in unnatural shadow. Where it touched my wrist, my flesh froze. The Ashur fell from my suddenly limp hand. I clutched the lifeless appendage to me and backpedaled across the room, trying to get away.

Gypsum gasped and took a step forward, like she truly cared. The necromancers surrounding her stayed immobile, however, showing no more interest in me than an insect, besides the flirty one that was. I was in too much agony to care about any of them at the moment. My wrist was frozen, the pain excruciating. I struggled to dodge, fighting through the pain, and that shadow reached for me again.

All four sets of double doors around us burst open and Protectorate soldiers poured in, robed mages close behind them. An EEP threw himself between me and the reaching shadow.

"Eva," the strange elf said familiarly, before he screamed from the creature's touch.

It was a terrible scream. I didn't think Thane had much experience with pain, other than the knocks over the head I'd given him lately and that one time I killed the body he was inhabiting…. Maybe I was being too hard on him. The cold in my hand was unbearable. It ripped away all memory of warmth or life, and that's what I felt from the barest touch. What must Thane, in his newest stolen body, be feeling?

"Stop this, Lili," Thane said through gritted teeth. "I command it."

My mother didn't seem to hear, or she didn't choose to recognize Thane's authority, because the shadow kept wrapping itself around him like a python until he stopped breathing, his eyes wide with shock. It came for me again.

A wall of fire appeared then, the heat as unbearable as the cold had been, and I shielded my face with my good arm. The elven mages had encircled Lili with fire, forcing the dread shadow to pause and turn back in defense of its master.

"Don't harm her," King Fharen repeated.

Fharen spoke something in elvish under his breath and made a magical gesture that ended in a clenched fist. I couldn't see what effect his spell had, except Lili tore her baleful gaze from me and seemed to finally notice the army of elves that had surrounded her. It was hard to recognize expressions on her shriveled face, but I thought she looked annoyed.

She shouted at me over the roar of the fire, saying, "I will find you again, my darling." She clapped her hands together, the First Soul caught between them, and then she and her allies vanished.

I'd seen Ulric teleport once before, but I guessed it wasn't a common trick, because the elves around me looked dumbfounded.

"It's not possible," one said.

The ring of fire faded, and mages reached out to touch the empty spaces that Gypsum, the liches, and my mother had once occupied. Some chanted spells under their breaths, casting about for any sign of them, as if they were merely invisible.

"They're gone," I said, dismally. My mother had taken the First Soul and the answers I needed with her.

"Seize the Solhan," Fharen ordered, and I realized he was talking about me.

EEPs grabbed my arms, while some of the mages managed to transform the marble holding Fharen prisoner into water. He stood, soaked. Ilsa had to cough and remind him to arrange for her release as well.

Fharen looked at her then back at me and said, "Take both of them to my private chambers and set a guard. I will question them shortly."

"Hey," Ilsa protested. "I brought it to you. How dare you—?"

"—Silence," Fharen said, cutting her off. It was clear he didn't want to discuss anything in front of so many underlings.

Ilsa and I were restrained, arms behind our backs, my Ashur taken from the ground where it had fallen, and we were dragged into another, nearby section of the palace.

"Seems familiar," I told her when we were locked inside a room. "No windows to climb out this time."

"Oh, shut up," Ilsa said. "If only you'd killed her, but you can't do anything right, can you? I suppose you hesitated out of filial love?"

"I hesitated because I had my hand frozen off." From the wrist down it was turning the same dead gray as Lili's and the necromancers' flesh. The pain was terrible but dulling a bit. I didn't know if that was a good thing. "You did see that shadow creature, right?"

She *humphed* but didn't critique the fight further. It always looked easier from the sidelines.

I'd spun a convincing argument, but the truth was Ilsa might be right. Had I hesitated? I knew Lili had every intention of murdering me so she could gain power, yet I had knocked her dagger aside and stood there when I could have easily struck with the Ashur again and chopped her head off, as Ilsa had, so grizzly, asked. But ... I couldn't kill my own mother.

I didn't say that aloud. My twin would only see it as weakness. Besides, there were other, more rational, reasons for keeping Lili alive. For one thing, I had no idea how to expel the Dead God without her.

Ilsa quieted. After a few moments, though, I couldn't resist poking the sleeping serpent and asked, "How did you get caught by her, anyway? And why did you give her the First Soul to begin with? That was stupid."

"I didn't give it to her. Alright, I planned to give it to her, but when we finally met, I saw how little regard she has for me. I gave it to Fharen for safekeeping. He promised me a crown in exchange, which I did not turn down, and the thing is useless to me anyway. It lies inert in my hands, taunting me."

"So, you weren't going to give it to the Dead God yourself?"

"I was ... undecided. Our Lord does not seek it, only our mother wanted it, as far as she told me in my visions. They began after you stole my soul, by the way, my one comfort. The relic serves no purpose to Him or to me. In the end, Fharen makes convincing promises."

"I don't see a crown on your head now."

"That fool couldn't hold onto the relic. He tried to compel Lili to submit to him, and she turned the situation around faster than you could blink. She has real power." There was a note of awe in her voice.

"Doubting your chosen side?" I said.

"I'm on my own side, always."

"I haven't forgotten it. How did you convince Sandy to help you escape? I didn't think she took sides either."

"That stupid fairy wants only to deny Harbinger the power he seeks. I think she believes you and I are interchangeable; at least she cannot tell us apart. She did not care which of us took the First Soul."

"Harbinger can fetch it from Lili if he wants it then." I laughed at the thought of letting the bad guys deal with each other. How could Harbinger be worse than my mother? He wanted to be a dark god with a thirst for blood, but she wanted to kill everyone.... Equally bad. Okay, I had to get the gem, because I couldn't leave it to either one of them.

"Untie me," I said, and Ilsa hesitated for only an instant before turning herself so we were back to back. She worked at my bonds, and when I was free, I undid her.

"You trusted me pretty quickly. I could easily have left you tied up," I said.

"You are predictable, Sugar. Always playing nice, or at least trying to. You put on a better glamour than an elf."

I didn't comment. From her, that was almost a compliment, even though it hurt me to think I lived behind a façade. It wasn't true. I was not evil covered with a veneer of good like her. Evil and good were never so clear cut. They churned together inside me, like mermaids and Leviathan battling in the depths.

I felt the First Soul nearby, and I suspected Lili had not teleported far. Perhaps in the palace. If I got out of here soon, I might be able to track her down.

Then what? I asked myself. I hadn't done too well against her the first time. And now I was down one sword arm.

I peeked out the door and spotted a squad of EEPs outside.

"Let's find another way," I said. We began searching the walls for a hidden servants' entrance, anything. In the meantime, I armed myself with a golden torch from the wall sconce, and Ilsa grabbed a candelabra.

When Fharen entered the room, three of his personal bodyguard behind him, and shut the door, Ilsa set the makeshift weapon down like she'd merely been cleaning it.

"Darling," she said, "I think this charade has gone on long enough. I can't believe you had them tie me up."

"Tell me what game you are playing, Ilsa," the king said. "And you ... what was your name again?"

"Eva." I put the torch behind my back. "We met on *The Mathésis*. I saw you naked." You self-absorbed ass.

"And you broke the mood, I recall. Now, I don't care which of you speaks, but tell me all you know about Lili of Solheim and the relic. Why did she want it—and you, Eva—so badly." It wasn't a question; it was a royal command. I think it surprised him when I didn't obey.

I had no time for interrogations. The First Soul felt nearby. I said, "We have to go after the relic. Now. Lili will do terrible things with it." I didn't want to say how desperately I needed it myself. Then again, Fharen had once spoken of opposing the Dead God, had even forsaken Highcrowne's neutrality in the war, so he might understand. I added, "And it will help us defeat the Dead God."

"Us? I think I can manage that on my own." Fharen reached into his waistcoat and pulled out the First Soul.

I could sense it, but it felt farther away than it was, obscured by elvish glamour, the black tendrils of its soul smudged to gray in my magical sight.

I took a step toward it, and he put it away again.

"That's mine," I said. "Give it back."

"I was under the impression it was mine." He looked at Ilsa.

She blushed. "Eva is its 'keeper' or some such thing. It was hard to overhear every conversation clearly, no matter how small that island was. I did overhear how much Harbinger wanted it, so I assume you're prepared to deal with him when he comes for it? Better than you managed with my mother?" By the end of her lecture, she had turned her tone to a familiar condescension. Nice to know not even the King of the Elves was spared her ire.

"I'm here to ask the questions, by any means required. Guards," Fharen called, despite the fact the EEPs were right behind him, "make sure they are both properly bound this time."

"What?" Ilsa guffawed.

The EEPs came forward, two forcing her arms behind her back again and one for me. I felt a bit disappointed I wasn't seen as the greater threat. Probably because one of my hands wasn't working.

As the EEP bound my wrists tighter and tighter with enchanted knots until it seemed my flesh would be sliced through, I gritted my teeth and tried sweet logic.

"There is no need for this. I'm happy to tell you anything. My mother, Lili, needs me dead, whether dead by accident or EEP abuse," I said, trying to pull away, the pain extreme in the one wrist that wasn't already deadened and blackening. "Stop this."

"Forgive me if I prefer to believe confessions extracted by pain rather than patriotic devotion to the Crowns," Fharen said. "Though I should say 'Crown'," he added.

"I wouldn't say that with an Avian in earshot." I hissed. I struggled with the too-tight bindings, both physically and with my magical sense. They were enchanted with a spell etched into the threads of the woven cuffs, strength and impregnability. They were glamoured and hidden from my magical sight like the First Soul.

"These are impressive bindings," I added. "And they are killing me, so I hope you believe me when I say that killing me is the last thing you want to do. The moment I am dead, by any means, my soul goes to the Dead God, completing the ritual Lili used to summon Him here. When that happens, He will no longer be stuck in the threshold between worlds but free to step through fully. A Primal whose sole purpose is death and the harvesting of souls. Lili wants a lifeless world to rule over in undeath, and you could easily give it to her. Help me instead."

"And the gem?" he asked, brow furrowed in thought, as though he might believe me.

"I need the relic to stop Him, to reverse the ritual. It's as simple as that. Help me for your own sake, for the sake of everything."

Ilsa too strained at her bonds, gasping with pain. She said, "Listen to Eva. She's too stupid to lie. She's throwing herself on the mercy of your goodness, my love. Not realizing you don't have any."

"I do have self-interest and intelligence enough to know truth when I hear it. Even though her lips are so similar to yours, my Ilsa, I have never seen such pearls on your own."

Fharen turned to his guards. "Release Eva, that one on the right, and summon a mage to tend her wounds. Keep her alive at all costs," he added.

"And me?" Ilsa purred, turning to show him how the bonds were cutting off her circulation, her hands white and her wrists purple.

"Are you useful to me in anyway?" Fharen asked, his tone implying he expected her to produce no reason.

"She's useful to me," I said. "I need her soul to help reverse the ritual too. It's complicated." I didn't say I had already taken the greatest part of her soul.

His face soured, sensing my lie of omission. That or not liking the word 'complicated'. Few liked that word, me included.

"Your defense of your sister sounds half-hearted, but it is unnecessary anyway. Her life is not in danger." Ilsa smiled triumphantly, until he added, "Take her to the dungeon. I've grown weary of her, and now I have the other sister to get to know."

I liked that even less than Ilsa did. She was dragged off, spitting and cursing in the most unladylike manner, and it gave me a bit of fun to see her so instantly unnerved. Fharen didn't know my sister, though, and he had just made a big mistake.

I didn't like that lecherous gleam in the Elf King's eye, either.

Another figure stood in the doorway, stepping aside ever so slightly to allow Ilsa and her captors through. He was massive for an elf, taller than most, more muscled, and had an impressive ability to look down on what was happening around him. It was Hilja's fiancé, Prince Gallan, who I'd glimpsed briefly when I was disguised as an acolyte. He didn't recognize me, of course, but Hilja did. Her diminutive form was hidden behind his. After the EEPs departed, they both stormed into the room.

"How dare you treat Eva like this, father," Hilja said.

At the same time her fiancé demanded, "I want to know what has happened to the peace negotiations. I hear troubling whispers."

"I am the king," Fharen said, "and these are my chambers. Neither of you were summoned."

I thought that would have sent them running, but they ignored him and came further into the room anyway. Hilja's fiancé met Fharen's gaze and did not back down.

"The peace negotiations affect us all, My King," Gallan said. "I speak for the other lords on this matter. We have all been waiting for the emissary to be presented, to face our questions, and instead I hear you have driven her away unilaterally."

"She threatened my life."

"After you threatened her. I was informed of your attack on her. How dare you?"

"You have spies among my personal guard now? How dare you, Prince Gallan. Leave my presence at once." Fharen pointed at the door, but I wasn't sure it was his commanding tone so much as the half a dozen EEPs who marched into the room after hearing his raised voice, and the mage with them, that got through to the elf.

"Come, Hilja." Gallan took the princess's arm and dragged her out. She looked annoyed, glaring at the hand on her arm, but before she vanished from sight, she gave me an encouraging smile and mouthed something that looked like 'I'll be back, Eva'.

King Fharen stood for a time after they left, a brewing storm glowering at the empty doorway. After a while, he gestured at me and ordered his soldiers, "Tend her and keep her under guard." He left too, and I wondered if he needed to go do some explaining to the other lords.

EEPs peeled off to follow him, but two remained behind with me, plus the mage who'd removed my bonds and was now examining my frozen wrist.

"This is bad," the mage clucked.

"It feels worse than it looks," I said.

He didn't answer me but stayed focused on my wound. I'd seen that sort of disinterested elf, or human even, come into my brother's bookshop looking for obscure texts and more concerned with whatever thoughts occupied their head than noticing the world around them. At least the EEP soldiers paid attention to me, looking at me like a thief ready to steal the silverware. I did have a tendency to do that, but purely for defensive purposes.

"Don't any of you think it's a bad idea to make peace with the Dead God?" I asked loudly. They could ignore me, or the elephant in the room, but surely even the common elf had an opinion on the subject?

The EEPs twitched, flinching away from my confronting stare, but it was the mage who spoke. "The world is falling to pieces," he said. "If we do not broker peace, how will we, the Ageless, survive it? To avoid Death's embrace is desirable at all costs, I should believe."

I'd been in His embrace, Thane's at least, and it was far from undesirable. It was dangerously seductive. I shook off the memory and laughed. That unnerved them. People often told me I shouldn't laugh. It was a melodic, haunting sound that carried warning instead of mirth.

"Ageless?" I said. "I've heard elves call themselves that before, usually those glamoured up to the eyeballs to hide their true age. A short reprieve, a truce ... nothing is as eternal as death. He will come for you. He may come for you last, but He will come."

I must have sounded pretty ominous—I was using my ghost story voice, which usually had Little Viktor shivering and Nanny heckling—because it worked on the EEPs. I saw them shiver. They almost jumped out of their armor when the door opened again.

It was Hilja.

"Are you alright? Is there anything I can do?" she asked, hovering over the mage who was studying my arm academically rather than doing anything to treat it.

"Gallan had a pretty firm hold on you," I said. "Maybe your wrist could use some tending too." I indicated where Hilja's was red and bruising.

She put the arm behind her and shook her head at me, as though I was stepping on dangerous ground, and she needed to warn me off. I stepped harder.

"Do the Ageless let the Elf King's only child be treated that way?" I asked the mage. "Is that part of the bargain for peace? Will they soon be shackling Hilja outside the dragon's lair as in ancient times, an offering for the dark forces beyond your comprehension?"

"You are schooled in elvish history," the mage noted.

Actually, Olyve had mentioned it, when she'd been hungry and hankering for the days when elves kindly delivered her lunch rather than trying to kill her when she went hunting for it. I didn't mention the true source of my knowledge.

"Oh, stop." Hilja rolled her eyes. "Mister Rose said you could be melodramatic. Gallan is simply unaware of his own strength. Please see to my wrist when you are done with hers, good mage." She revealed her arm again, pretending not to be ashamed of it. Her defense of Gallan made me dislike him even more.

"A simple task." The mage ran a hand over her wrist. When he was done, the bruising was gone. "Your damage is far more amenable to magic than hers. I cannot for the life of me see how to restore an essentially lifeless hunk of flesh. There may be nothing for it but to hack it off and ensure a prosthetic is attached cleanly. Do you prefer a hook or wooden fingers?" he asked me.

"Neither." I snatched my arm back. The realm of lifeless things was precisely the domain of necromancers, like me. "I'll figure something out myself."

"King Fharen instructed me—" the mage began, but Hilja cut him off.

"—Why don't you think on another solution for a bit longer," Hilja said. "I'm sure my father meant for you to make her whole again if you could. In the meantime, I'll look after her in my apartments. That dress is ruined already, so we must find another. I've so wanted a sister." She smiled as she took my shoulder, fingering the fabric of the dress I'd borrowed from her and torn and burnt in the fight. The EEPs soured at her calling me 'sister', and I shrunk back as well. This could get ugly, especially if she was anything like my real sister.

"We have orders," an EEP said, "and can't let her out of our sight."

"You can guard her as easily in my care. Come along, Eva."

There must be some respect for the princess, for they obeyed and allowed her to lead me away. I thought I might have a shot at sneaking out through the servants' halls, but the EEP guards and the mage shadowed us every step of the way.

In Hilja's quarters, I was plied with wine and conversation, as I tried on yet more dresses from the princess's wardrobe. I poked my head out the door, looking for a chance to run for it, but the guards were still there. Hilja prattled away the whole time.

"It's so wonderful having you here, Eva. And Ilsa in the dungeon. She may look like you, but she was always so ... rude. I have to say it. Not very kind at all. I mean, if she were an elf such behavior could be understood, but for a non-elf to consider it? Presumptuous and rude I say. You're not like that at all. You're so friendly and approachable."

That's not how I thought of myself. Then again, she had elves for comparison.

"I wonder if father will let me keep you here, in my apartment?" she added, suddenly looking around like she could set up a dog bed for me in the corner of the wardrobe. Just lovely.

I wasn't anyone's pet, and I wasn't as frivolously concerned about what I was wearing as I was about getting my hand back. I stared at the lifeless thing and sensed nothing within it. It was like a rock, and my soul had retreated from it. At least it didn't hurt anymore.

"Perhaps a glove?" Hilja suggested. "Satin, not the lace. We'll choose a color when we find the right gown."

"That's not why I'm staring at it. Can you give me a moment's peace to concentrate?" I said, raising my voice. I might not be Ilsa, but I was as Solhan as her, and the tone of my command made Hilja freeze mid gesture.

The frightened look on her face was awful. Like I'd stepped on a kitten's tail. I wanted to apologize and warm my voice, tell her I appreciated her help, but I couldn't. I was as angered by her fear as I was by my trapped state.

"Why do you jump when I raise my voice?" I said, raising it more to demonstrate her reaction. "How many bruises have you had mended by mages?"

"I usually use an enchanted compress. It works well. I have no idea why you're suddenly being so impolite. Perhaps you've been switched for Ilsa." She turned her back on me and pretended to search her wardrobe.

"It's Gallan, isn't it? Why are you marrying such a bastard?"

"He's a prince. Definitely not a bastard, as his parentage is well documented."

"You know what I mean."

"I'm afraid I do not. You said you need privacy to concentrate, so I will leave you now. Call for me when you are ready—and in a better mood." Hilja scurried out the door, and I felt like I'd kicked the kitten after stepping on its tail.

How could a smart girl be so stupid? I had enough things to worry about, so I didn't know why I let Hilja's domestic troubles consume me. Maybe it was because there was something disconcerting in the resonance of her soul. Something out of tune that needed to be corrected. She wasn't as bad off as the marked slaves all around, but the princess was a bit of a slave herself, and that bothered me. Lots of little injustices bothered me, and I tended to attack them head on. That method wouldn't work for Hilja; I'd only scare her off again. I needed to find a gentler approach. It didn't come naturally, but I'd try when next I had a chance.

Thinking about it, perhaps a gentler approach would work on my hand as well? I'd been thinking along the lines of transforming stone to flesh with brute force magic, but it wasn't working, no matter how much I concentrated. I lacked that kind of skill. What I was good with was souls.

I sent a tendril of my soul into the lifeless hand, a small spark. I felt another spark ignite, the green fire of power that dwelled inside me. The ball of green light rekindled itself in my dead palm, and I moved my fingers. The gray hand and lower arm looked like something pulled out of a grave, but it functioned normally again.

It was definitely something. 'Limited,' I think not. Take that Olyve!

13 WELCOME TO THE PARTY

I stuck my head out the door, glaring at the EEPs keeping me hostage, and called for Hilja. She came, hesitant, and I smiled, beckoning her into her own wardrobe.

"I'm sorry," I said, not being clear about what.

I wasn't sorry for pointing out that Gallan was a bastard, but I was trying to be gentle, and it was working. She relaxed.

Before she could speak, and start prattling again, I said, "I can't stay here forever. I need the relic your father took from Lili. It's mine actually, and I could use your help to get it back."

"Oh, no. When father wants something, father gets it. I understand it's yours, but that really doesn't matter. He takes plenty of things that belong to other people all the time and no one can stop him. It's called Royal Privilege. I'm quite a subscriber to that. Where would the world be without it?"

"Weren't you telling me once how awful it was that people like Duane and other humans were forced into a life of thievery? That your father and elf society mistreated them? Well, I'm being forced to robbery here too." I was already wondering how I might use the servants' corridors to sneak into the king's chambers. I'm sure the EEPs would try to stop me, but there had to be some way to get past them and reach the First Soul? Perhaps during shift change? I slept terribly these days and could stay up all night if I had to.

"I do believe that!" Hilja insisted. "In Mister Rose's case, anyway. He's far too handsome to be a common street urchin. It's a shame. That's why I'm also a member of the People's Party and the Progressive Party."

"Parties? What are you talking about? Like a get together with drinks?"

"Usually tea. Can't have a proper Party without tea," she said.

Even more confusing. I paused, trying to come up with a convincing argument that wouldn't add more fuel to her chatter fire, when two new EEPs opened the door to the wardrobe and marched in. It was a big wardrobe with plenty of room for marching.

"How dare you," Hilja bristled. "Get out at once."

King Fharen followed them.

"Oh, father," Hilja said, relaxing. "It's just you. What is it?"

"Isn't Eva dressed yet?"

"We were working on it. These things take time."

"Hurry it up. The seneschal can assist." Fharen indicated a shorter, brown elf who came in behind him. The newcomer had fiery, passionate eyes but wore the robes of a servant.

"Not Ernest, father. He's such a bore. No offense, Ernest."

"None taken, milady. Of course, I will have to mention this dismissive attitude of the lower ranks at the next People's Party meeting."

"Oh, yes," Fharen smiled, and it seemed out of place on his features. "Do tell us more about the People again."

"The People are the workers, the proletariat, those who contribute to our food, our clothing, all the necessities of life—or at least the ones who direct the slaves to procure these items for us, such as myself. They are the only important members of society. The clergy, the monarchy, the military, all must be servants of the People, to maintain functioning of the machine, not to direct the machine, for the machine is the People. In fact, a truly autonomous machine is possible and no monarchy needed at all, if only the proletariat can come together, united, as comrades."

"Wonderful," Fharen chuckled, tears of mirth at the corner of his eyes he had to wipe away. "I never tire of you, Ernest. Always good for a laugh. Well I must get back to grinding the gears of the machine and all that. Please make sure Miss Thorne here is ready for the evening. And remember any misstep on her part will mean you pay the price, Ernest. I'd far rather cut off your head that hers."

"Of course, sir," the Seneschal said calmly, but the fire in his eyes flared a bit with suppressed fury. He certainly wasn't being subtle about it, but the king didn't seem to care.

When Fharen and his guards were gone, Hilja resumed her prattling. "Of course, petit fours are wonderful to have at a Party meeting too. Aren't they, Ernest?"

"If only the People's Party had petit fours, we'd be taken more seriously. Sandwiches, however, is where I believe the future lies. A more robust meal to get the digestive system churning along with the cogs of thought to stoke the boilers of change. Not pastrami, though. That clogs the arteries and the channels of progress. Perhaps a refreshing cucumber sandwich?" The Seneschal flicked expertly through Hilja's wardrobe as he spoke, clearly more familiar with her garments than she was, and pulled out a blood red gown that suited me perfectly.

"I've had enough of that color," I said, shuddering. "And does it have to be a dress? And what's all this about dinner anyway? Is it cucumber sandwiches or tea or what?" I was confused and not afraid to show it. But Fharen was still in the palace, the relic in his inner pocket, and if I had to wear a gown to get to be in the same room with him long enough to retrieve it, I would. Reluctantly.

"Poor, ignorant human," Ernest said, "the princess and I were discussing Party food, a serious matter that. I will invite you to our next People's Party meeting so you might understand its import. You, of course, cannot join in the discussions as you're not people, being human, but you may find it enlightening. In the meantime, the king has requested your presence at dinner this evening. I presume in a seat rather than on the plate, thus the request to clothe you. Perhaps blue? I think your black hair would contrast beautifully with a sapphire shade."

"No, no, no," Hilja said, taking the blue dress from him. "Her skin is far too pale. Try dark orange. Here."

It was a good color. I went behind the folded screen to change and was happy to see it was short enough and the skirt flared enough not to hinder movement. It was probably short because it was made for Hilja, but I didn't mind. It did bother me that the waist was tighter than I'd like. Surely tinned pears couldn't have added too much to my waistline? Hilja noted the tightness when I showed it to her.

"Hmm, we must do something about that. Ernest," she said.

"Of course, my lady. I will get a slave to let it out a bit." Ernest turned to the nearest slave to pass down the order. He didn't look to be all that essential of a worker in the scheme of things, at least from where I was standing.

"You'll have to take it off again," he told me. "You must bathe as well. You are far too odiferous for one of your race and rank."

I recalled that elves chose not to bathe due to health reasons as well as a sign of superiority, the more superior the smellier. It was a privilege to sniff them, apparently, and royals didn't want to go around smelling lesser folk. Seemed the seneschal spouted egalitarianism in one breath and social stratification in the other.

"Didn't the king want this hurried up?" I asked.

"You cannot hurry dinner preparations," Ernest said before he stepped outside and clapped. Slaves swarmed around him, and he set them tasks in a series of efficiently barked orders.

In moments, they had my measurements, the gown was being altered, and I was in a hot bath, screened off from Ernest by a folding divider, thank the gods. I was self-conscious about having so many onlookers. The female slaves scrubbing me were unnerving enough.

"Don't you have any privacy?" I asked Hilja.

"What?" she said, looking around for what I was talking about. "The servants? Ignore them. They're like furniture. It's those Elven Protectorate who infuriate me. Barging in wherever and whenever. Make sure you wash her hair, thoroughly," the last bit directed at the slave who was tackling my seaweed-encrusted locks. I thought Hilja stank pretty bad, but if she was curling up her nose at me, I must be particularly foul. I blamed the underwater residue the First Soul had left behind on Ismerkel.

"They are not furniture," I argued. I tried to catch the eye of one of the slaves buzzing around us to get them on my side, but they were all marked. "You've turned them from thinking beings to your servants, often from birth, and it's monstrous. Don't you see that?"

"It's terrible, I know," Hilja said. "But how are we to exist without servants? How are we to maintain Royal Privilege? There'd be anarchy."

"Free them, pay them. It's not about what's easiest for you. They aren't yours," I said, feeling really uncomfortable now. I'd allowed myself to enjoy the royal treatment, and it was seductive, but it was also wrong. I stood up and dried myself off, pushing the reaching hands away, and dressed myself.

"It is a seneschal's job to see to the slaves. You would take away my purpose?" Ernest asked me, appalled.

"I'm sure a savvy elf like you can find a new job," I said.

"Perhaps the Upside Down Party is a better affiliation for you than the People's," Ernest said, lip curled.

"What is all this about Parties?" I asked, exasperated.

"It's how Faellion works," Hilja explained. "The nobles, and some who oppose the nobility, like Ernest here, form a Party where like-minded elves can discuss how to achieve their mutual goals. With the right connections and right rhetoric, an influential noble might be drawn to your cause. In which case, they may be able to sway the House of Lords, who in turn will make suggestions to my father, which he might follow. It's a bit of an uncertain process, but it works. I think."

"Has any Party actually swayed Fharen?" I asked, realizing this was a devious way to keep his opponents busy.

"Well..." Hilja said, thinking.

"We live in hope," Ernest finished. "You do sound more and more like the Upside Down Party. They really aren't a proper Party, as they don't even have tea. They're anarchists who would topple the entire system."

"Definitely my kind of people. Can you point me to them?" I said, only half joking. A bit of toppling might allow me to get back what belonged to me. Fharen had fooled my mother with his illusions, so I needed to be extra wary that whatever I was stealing back was the real relic. Fharen being distracted by political unrest wouldn't hurt.

"No," Ernest and Hilja said at once. Then Ernest continued, "You must attend dinner and be on your best behavior, else the king will have my head. Meaning no longer attached to my body."

"No one knows who the Upside Down Party members are or where they meet anyway," Hilja added. "They plaster propaganda on the streets, stealing books from father's library and reprinting them for the people to read, freeing slaves. Real anarchists."

"And they're elves?" I asked, suddenly wondering if they weren't. I'd never met an elf friendly to humans. Hilja and Ernest were as good as it got. The priest who'd helped me didn't remotely count, as he hated humans and was trying to help the Dead God exterminate them.

"Let us save such disturbing discussions for another time," Ernest said, indicating I should turn around. He clapped again, and a slave was soon lacing up the back of the gown. I tried to shoo them off and do it myself, but the fastenings were impossible to reach without help.

The seneschal sighed and said, "There. You will have a proper dinner with the king, no talk of the Upside Downs, and agree to whatever he asks of you. For my sake."

"Whatever he asks of me? What's that likely to be?"

Hilja looked away and began rummaging for a gown for herself.

Ernest blushed, but when I didn't lower my questioning eyebrow, he said, "King Fharen was quite fond of your sister. You are identical. And although she has fallen out of favor, I am sure he could grow to be quite fond of you as well. If you also achieve his purposes."

"I'm not achieving anyone's purposes but my own, and I've had quite enough of fondness of late. No fondness, Ernest. You hear me? If any fondness starts, I am out of there." I'd far rather risk being killed as an intruder to retrieve the Soul than come by it using Ilsa's methods. I was only going to dinner to stake out the place and bide my time until dark, when I might have a better chance of stealing it.

"Few oppose King Fharen and live," Ernest warned in a whisper.

"Tell me which few do," I whispered back. "Those are the people I want to meet."

"My fiancé for one," Hilja said, not caring to whisper. She'd obviously heard us clearly enough anyway. "He is leader of the Peace Party and Elven Triumph Party. They and others are vocally opposed to father's warmongering. They believe we must make peace with the Dead God, sooner rather than later if we are to gain from it. They forced father to this meeting with Lili of Solheim, but I think he is happy it went sour. Now father can proceed with the attack on Solheim he has long dreamed of. Prince Gallan and his fellows, however, are not happy. They will have something more to say about this."

Sounded like her fiancé's compatriots weren't any better to get in bed with (figuratively speaking!) than Fharen was. Weren't there any good guys? Actually, Fharen's plan to attack Solheim sounded pretty good, I just couldn't stand the human-hating slime personally.

"What will your fiancé..." I tried not to betray my distaste for Prince Gallan when I said the word, but I must have slipped up, because Hilja frowned "...and his friends do now that my mother has vanished and the peace talks are derailed?" I asked Hilja.

"I'm not sure," she said, thoughtful. "There's a lot of grumbling among the nobles. I may have to get married in a secret ceremony soon. I hate that. No reason to wear the nice dress if no one can see it."

"Why would you do that?"

"In case Prince Gallan seizes control of the House of Lords. I must make sure I'm either the daughter of, or married to, whoever is effectively ruling the elf lands."

"Aren't you the shrewd one," I said. Hilja had seemed idealistic and naïve to me, and I still thought her so, but also a bit calculating. Is that why she put up with Gallan?

Hilja needed more time to get dressed, so it was Seneschal Ernest who escorted me to dinner, along with the EEPs. They made me feel uncomfortably hemmed in, and I was unable to case the joint as much as I'd have liked.

A slave walked past us, head down. He was indistinguishable from the others streaming past, until he suddenly looked into my eyes, another's gaze peering out of those orbs, and said, "Eva," before dropping his head back down again.

Thane was lurking around still, jumping bodies again. I felt even more hemmed in now.

A few moments later, another slave passed and did the same thing. This time saying, "I must speak..."

By the time a dozen had tossed a few separate words at me, only when close enough for me to hear and not the seneschal or the EEPs, did I string together the full message: "Eva, I must speak with you tonight. You are in danger. Lili is coming."

It was an ominous message, but nothing I didn't already know. I wouldn't heed it anyway. The fact Thane could leap from slave to slave, his will overtaking theirs, made me reluctant to follow his counsel.

My plan was my own: Get the First Soul by whatever means necessary, short of sleeping with Fharen, *yuck*, and then leave this city for Highcrowne first chance I got. Maybe I'd trust Uncle Ulric to help me. Maybe. But at least in Highcrowne I had other friends, people like Bell and Karolyne and Kali. Maybe I couldn't trust them either, but it was a place to start. I'd hide the soul from Olyve even, and then I'd expel the Dead God from this world.

The plan was a bit fuzzy, but my plans always were.

Not until I saw the intimate dinner arrangements in Fharen's apartments, no grand banquet hall, only a table set for six, with glistening crystal illuminated by flickering candlelight, did I start to worry about part one of my plan.

Fharen was already there, and he stood, holding out a hand. "Sit beside me, Eva."

I would not bed him. Ever. But it looked like he had other ideas, judging by the charming way he was behaving.

"What do you want from me?" I blurted out.

"I believe I asked you to take a seat for dinner."

"You know what I'm talking about. You send Ilsa to the dungeon and put me in the palace. One sister can't fulfill your ambitions for Solheim, so you think the other can. What are your ambitions? What do you want from me?" I needed to set the ground rules right away.

"Very well. I want an empire. Can you give me that?"

"Can you give me my relic?"

"Call the relic by its name. I've heard of the First Soul. I know what it can do. Why would I give it back?"

"You said you want an empire. The first step is to depose the god who now controls it."

I hoped that would entice him, but it seemed to frighten him off, based on how quickly he looked away. He was ambitious but skittish. He was building an army to take against Solheim but was afraid to face the god. What was the army for then? To help him feel safer?

"Let us not discuss politics at dinner," Fharen said. "This is a friendly gathering."

I didn't like the emphasis he put on 'friendly'.

"I know wooing when I see it, King Fharen. There'll be no wooing."

"Should I simply take what I want then? I am not so barbaric." Despite his words, his gaze flashed with barbarism.

He wanted an empire, but I wasn't the person to give it to him.

"You should have stuck with Ilsa," I said. "You'll gain no political advantage from marrying me. I'm already married."

"A pity. I must kill the man then."

"I wish you would. But you'll need to give me the First Soul before you can. The Dead God is my husband."

The King blanched. "What do you mean?"

"I mean it's all part of the ritual that brought Him here. Did you think you could forget about Him? What was your plan? Sue for peace with Lili, threaten with an army, marry a princess and be done with it? This is a whole different kind of war than you're used to."

Fharen turned contemplative. Obviously Ilsa hadn't told him everything, but then again, I hadn't told Ilsa everything either.

When servants opened the door to usher in more guests, the king looked to them, almost relieved, until he spotted Gallan. The two political rivals stared daggers at one another, before the prince took his seat diagonally opposite me and the Elf King.

"I thought this was a 'friendly' gathering," I said, unable to help myself. They ignored my comment in silence.

The other guest who arrived with Gallan was unknown to me. He was an older elf with a hard cast to him, a scar along his weathered cheek, meaning he wore no glamour or chose one that added to his fearsomeness. His skin was darkly tanned, making me think of a shriveled orange left out all summer to dry in the Highcrowne markets because no one could afford to buy oranges.

"Good evening," the man said, nodding first to the king and then to me ever so slightly, before he took the seat at the head of the table. He must have already said hello to Gallan, for he ignored the prince and reached for a bread roll, buttering it heavily and then smashing the whole thing into his mouth. He chewed with loud smacks and gurgles, clearly starved. With an appetite like that I had no idea how he remained so thin and wiry.

Hilja arrived and sat beside me. Voices soon filled the room, her voice at least. "Oh, Doctor, so good to see you've joined us this evening. Eva, have you met Doctor Heltune?"

"No," I said. "How do you do?" I managed to be civil, remembering the torturous debutante training I'd tried *not* to learn in my formative years.

The newcomer grunted and waved, before focusing on the roast goose that a servant laid in the center of the table. He ripped off its head and chewed the exposed meat along the neck.

"The doctor travelled by airship with us from Highcrowne, didn't he father? What a lovely trip this time, unlike that unfortunate affair with *The Mathésis.* You should have seen how grand that vessel was, Doctor Heltune, but it was an ill-fated voyage...." Hilja didn't leave Fharen enough room in the conversation to reply, not that it looked like he was listening. He divided his time between glaring at Gallan and gazing at my neckline, while he nibbled at roast spatchcock and apricots.

I looked at the one that had arrived on my plate and thought it too small a bird to eat. The mound of jollup fat next to it was even less enticing. I spent my time eying Fharen's suit pocket instead.

Was the First Soul in there, or hidden in his rooms? I could feel it vaguely, but it was impossible to tell how near or far away it was. How had the king managed such a glamour? The relic seemed so powerful and uncontainable, but then again, my father had protected it in Solheim for decades. His ancestors had protected it even longer. The way the soul had called evil to it in Ismerkel was unusual, because the relic had been exposed, without a keeper, or else all things seeking power would descend on whoever had it and overwhelm them.

"How do you think you can keep the First Soul?" I suddenly asked Fharen. "Lili will return when she realizes she's been fooled. Others will come too."

"Who better to protect it? You?" He smirked.

"I'm its keeper, and I think I'm beginning to understand what that means. I think your glamour works on my mind and the minds of those near you, but its range does not extend across the world, does it? Without me near, the relic will be exposed, unleashing hell on you, King Fharen."

His eyes widened, considering what I'd said. I must have been right about the glamour. He tried to recover, but there was a tremor in his voice when he shot back, "Then you must always be near."

"Not a chance."

"…The doctor's work is fascinating," Hilja continued, not caring that Fharen and I weren't paying attention. "He has been to many exotic locales, to the farthest tip of Darrub, and has even seen Solheim itself. Solheim! Before the war of course. I insisted he join us his first evening back in Faellion. You don't mind, Eva? This is your first honor as well, and I do hope you don't think we're overshadowing it with another special guest? Eva?"

I tore my glare away from Fharen. "Not feeling overshadowed at all," I reassured her. Of course, that changed a moment later when yet one more person arrived.

"Good evening." The man removed his cloak, handing it to a servant and stepping into the candlelight. Shadow and darkness came with him. A familiar dread feeling.

"Ah, Count Bram. Good to see you after so long," Fharen said, rising to greet the noble and looking relieved to turn from the distressing conversation I'd forced on him.

The elf was handsome, with rich, dark curls and a direct gaze that put Fharen to shame. He too looked at my neckline, but only briefly, and I was sure it was my bare neck more than my cleavage. He bowed to the king and Princess Hilja before taking the seat across from me. He settled, steepling his fingers and looking over them at me in such a comfortable manner, it seemed he intended to watch me all through dinner.

Evidently, no one else saw Count Bram as I did: the darkness shrouding him, an extension of soul not contained by the glamour he wore. That soul was familiar.

Harbinger.

Despite the missing antlers and the added elf ears, as well as the glamour that made him shorter and golden skinned, I'd recognize him anywhere. I could see his soul. I could also see the bloodlust in his eyes, something more predatory than the elven arrogance Fharen possessed.

Fharen chatted with him like an old friend. "I need my allies at court these days." The Elf King cast a glance at Hilja and her fiancé. Did he distrust Hilja as well? How interesting.

Golden goblets were on a platter, and the king took one, filling it from a carafe. He offered it to Harbinger, "Some refreshment, Count, after your long journey?"

Harbinger held up a hand. "I do not drink ... wine."

"Oh, we don't drink wine either," Fharen chuckled. "That is very servant class. You are ever so amusing with your foreign ways. This is pixie blood."

"I'll have some then." Harbinger took from the proffered goblet and drank. He was thirsty. I noticed the soul shadows around him quiet and sink closer to his body.

Pixie blood? I was glad I hadn't taken a sip. I also had a sudden urge to free pixies, wherever they were. In the kitchen perhaps, being drained? Human slaves to free, pixies, the First Soul to liberate ... not to mention getting myself, and possibly Ilsa, out of here. I needed to get busy. Where were the anarchists when you needed them? I did have Harbinger. He was obviously after the same thing I was, but that could be used to my advantage. I decided to stir things up a bit.

"So, Hilja tells me there is a Peace Party with a lot of pull here in Faellion. What party do you belong to, Count Bram?"

"The War Party," Fharen answered for him.

"And you're foreign, I heard the king say?" I continued hammering Harbinger with questions, ignoring the Elf King for the moment.

"Yes, from the northern mountains."

"Isn't that traditionally Avian territory?"

"My kind … elves have resided there for generations." Harbinger might be correct about the elves, but he meant vampires like him.

"So Fharen must cast his net far afield to find allies," I mused. "If you are a compatriot of his, a member of the War Party, then perhaps you can tell me what makes him want war? What makes him so confident? Is it Fharen's 'secret' army of slaves? I stopped him from abducting the poor refugees in Highcrowne, but plenty more pour across the border from the South every day. I'm sure he has intercepted many, not to mention the hereditary slaves he has access to."

"They do not work so well as the freshly branded," Fharen said, untroubled by my accusations. It was true then, and he was not the least bit afraid to admit to illegally enslaving people.

"Work so well for what? What makes you believe this army can stand against the Dead God's legions," I asked, "or the separatist dwarves for that matter? You've seen what a few werewolves can do, Fharen. What happens when Gypsum uses the crown to turn thousands upon thousands of dwarves into an army of those creatures? You did know the Dwarf King's crown can do that, didn't you?"

"I do not believe his slave army will succeed, nor would I call King Fharen confident," Harbinger said, truthfully.

Fharen looked shocked by Harbinger's lack of faith. He shifted in his seat and shot a warning glare at first Count Bram and then Prince Gallan, who was smiling a vicious smile just then. Hilja chattered while Doctor Heltune continued to chew noisily.

"Not that I think the Peace Party has the right of it either," I added. "You can't surrender. You can't fight and win. Maybe you should try something else, Fharen? Give back what belongs to me and let me try."

Fharen felt the First Soul hidden in his inner pocket, and I thrilled, knowing for certain where it was. Of course, as I also suspected would happen, Harbinger shifted his intense gaze from me to the king. The vampire's expression was more dangerous than anything Gallan could manage.

Harbinger remained still, probably wondering if he should tear out the Elf King's throat then and there.

Of course, he might have been biding his time because he knew he needed the soul's keeper, that's me, to get it to obey, so his gaze met mine again.

If he could have hypnotized me to his will, he would have.

The same didn't hold for everyone else. Harbinger waved a hand, saying, "Silence." And that's exactly what he got. Hilja halted mid-monologue, the doctor mid-chew. Gallan's and Fharen's opposing glowers were frozen in place. Not even the guards standing at the periphery twitched.

"Impressive," I said. How often had I longed for a similar power at family gatherings?

The vampire's gaze settled on my neck again. Some men were so single-minded. "You retrieved it from Leviathan and are proving your worth, but I am not yet convinced you are useful enough. Give me the First Soul."

I looked at Fharen's jacket. Was it really there? I couldn't be sure, and even if it was, I couldn't take it without Harbinger going after me next. Better he stayed focused on Fharen for the time being. It would give me time to think of a way to get what I wanted and get out of here.

"No," I said. "I am not groping the Elf King here at dinner. Let's act civilized. Besides, I need assurances. My soul protected and the Unmentionables off my back, in exchange for the relic."

"I cannot make such promises, even if I were inclined. The ancient order is not mine to command. Yet."

"And neither is the First Soul. Give me time to negotiate with it on your behalf. It's a soul, a living thing, and it doesn't do whatever I say. I need time to convince it." And time to stall, I thought.

Harbinger frowned. He made even that expression seem sensuous. "My life is eternal but not my patience."

I shrugged. Tell it to someone who cared.

He passed a hand before the Elf King's eyes, saying, "Convince her to make the relic serve us." And Fharen suddenly inhaled.

The whole room awoke, once more filled with the chattering, chewing, silverware-clanking sounds of dinner. The silence of a moment before was all the more eerie in comparison. They all seemed oblivious to the frozen moment and the time they'd lost. However, the fury drained from the king's features, and he turned his baleful gaze from Gallan to me.

"I prefer to wield such weapons as the relic myself, rather than entrust them to a mere girl. If you will all excuse me, I have lost my appetite. Do continue without me." Fharen stood up and dropped his napkin on his plate.

Everyone but Harbinger and I bowed to the king as he left. Gallan looked triumphant, knowing his political rival had been verbally sparred into retreat. The chewing doctor eyed us with an expression somehow both curious and disinterested. Only Hilja looked pained for her father, but she did not follow him.

The Elf King stopped at the door and whispered into the ear of the guard standing there. Before the guests sat back down again, the EEP came forward and grabbed my arm. Hilja gasped with shock. I pulled away instinctively, but more EEPs descended and dragged me from the table.

"My apologies once again," Fharen called to the diners before he joined the soldiers dragging me down the hall.

"This is not the friendly kind of dinner I thought it would be," I told Fharen. "No dessert?"

"I will get my desserts when you are racked, my dear. There is plenty a skilled torturer can do to you without releasing your soul to the Dead God. You might beg for release, but I shall not grant it."

"What did I say?" I asked, innocent. I really had expected more political squabbling and innuendo. I had to remember these were elves who liked to torture first and ask questions later.

"It is what I hope you will say that matters," Fharen said. "I have listened to your reasoning and now see how important the First Soul is. In my hands. You will tell me how to wield it, how to defeat the Dead God. I will not leave power such as this to anyone else."

Oh, crap. Another fine mess I'd gotten myself into. Would Fharen believe me when I said I didn't know anything? Probably not.

14   Guess Who's Coming to Prison

I've been in a fair few prison cells in my life. Okay, two, and one of those was a tower, but I had to say the palace dungeon in the elf capital was more impressive than most. It wasn't clean by any means—blood and gore had stained the stone permanent shades of brown, black, and purple—but it was roomy and well equipped. I didn't recognize half of the torture implements. Some were enchanted though; I could tell that much. While low-ceilinged, it was wide, with arches and alcoves everywhere, not to mention whole corridors of prison cells I'd glimpsed coming in. Ilsa must be in one of those.

"The rack is a new experience," I said, as an EEP strapped me onto the table. It was angled upward so the blood wouldn't rush to my head. How considerate. I thought Fharen was bluffing, else I would have struggled more. Time to call him out.

"You have an interesting way of charming women," I said.

"What I failed to grasp before was how important the First Soul is. You may not be necessary at all. Dispensable, really. Your main value right now lies in telling me what I need to know. How do I use the relic to defeat the Dead God?"

"You can't kill me. I warned you what would happen."

"And I told you there are things worse than death that I can do to you."

"Like dinner? That was pretty agonizing. The meal, certainly, but the company especially. You do know who Count Bram is don't you?"

"You suspect he's more than my staunchest ally?"

I was about to tell him 'a lot more' but stopped myself. It might be better to keep a few cards up my sleeve for later.

"I've decided talking isn't for me," I said. "I'd be rewarding your rude behavior. Set me free, put the First Soul into my hands where it belongs, and then I'll share with you."

"You will speak on my terms. Think on it. The torturer will arrive soon, once he's finished his supper.

In the meantime, I'll arrange for another prisoner to keep you company, one who can impress upon you how important it is to answer questions when asked." Fharen eyed my cleavage one last time before turning away.

As soon as the king and his guards disappeared, I wrestled with my restraints. The leather was strong. No breaking out of them with my sheer impressive strength alone, and I sensed they were enchanted to resist magical manipulation. Not that I was good at magic, but I'd try something as soon as my heart stopped hammering and I could focus. It wasn't long before an EEP returned, and I had to lay placid again. The forced inaction helped calm my mind, and I could imagine turning the wood of the rack into sand. I could imagine it, but I wasn't sure how to do it.

I thought the prisoner they'd bring to taunt me was Ilsa, so I was surprised when they rolled out a cage with a man inside. He was smeared with filth and caked with blood. His wounds were infected: red, swollen, and spreading tendrils through the skin. He would die soon if not healed, and I didn't mean with a few bandages. He needed serious healing of the miraculous sort.

The EEPs left us alone, and the quiet was unnerving. Only the man's breathing filled the silence, that and the distant drip of water. Dungeons always had to be damp for some reason. Maybe because they were underground?

The man swayed, dangling from the shackles on his wrists and bumping against the sides of the cage. I was uncomfortable with my mute prison mate and didn't know how to start the conversation. *Enjoying Faellion?* Came to mind, but it didn't seem right to joke with someone who looked so abject and miserable. Humor allowed me to deal with a lot of things, that and anger, but this man's state made my chest hurt, and I felt nothing but sympathy. I tried to turn that emotion into something more useful, like outrage. No one should be treated like that. When I got my hands on the First Soul, I'd show Fharen what misery felt like.

The prisoner's circular pendulum motions finally slowed and left him face to face with me, a few feet between us. I glimpsed eyes, wide and glistening white among all the grunginess. They were bloodshot, one infected as well, oozing yellow gunk. It's because of all that it took me so long to recognize him.

"Conrad?" I said, heart in my throat.

"Eva," he croaked.

I wasn't thinking clearly, so the first thing that came out of my mouth was, "What are you doing here?"

It took him a few moments to reply, as he tried to wet his dried and cracking lips. His voice sounded like it had been dragged over hot coals, like other portions of his anatomy, when he said, "Answering questions."

All right. I was getting us out of here no matter what.

I summoned the green glow into my hands, but this far from Solheim it was weak, nothing like the wolves' claws I'd managed when close to the wall. I had fury behind me though, so I struggled harder against the restraints, and I sent the glow into them, trying to disintegrate the straps, anything. The spells imbued into the leather were too effective. The green glow settled back into the palms of my hands, one white and one dead gray. Useless.

I needed to try something else. I relaxed, observing the Void stuff around me. I must have looked calmer than I felt, because Conrad said, "That's right. Don't fight, Eva. Give them whatever they want. There's no point you suffering as I have."

Now I couldn't focus at all. The defeat in Conrad's tone was horrifying. "No," I said. "Don't say things like that. What did they want from you anyway? Why did you resist them so much?"

"I didn't, but I didn't have the answers they were looking for. They didn't believe me."

I could only imagine what Conrad had gone through. Actually, I might not have to imagine it soon. "I don't know anything either!"

"It won't save you."

I didn't want to think about that right now. Fortunately, there were plenty of other thoughts to distract me. "How did Fharen even capture you? Last I saw you were with Gypsum, or Thane was, on the other side of the wall. I thought for sure I'd never see you again. Do you remember any of that?"

"All of it."

"Oh. I'm so sorry I kissed ... you. Thane, I mean." Was that a lie? The problem when I tried to calm my mind to do magic was that I saw into it more than I liked.

"It doesn't matter," Conrad said. "Nothing matters."

"Fharen thinks you must know what Thane knows. I ran across a priest possessed by him recently, and he learned some things."

"Surface thoughts only. Not what Fharen needs: he wants the Dead God's strategies, weaknesses, all of it." Conrad shifted and whimpered, as though my questioning reminded him of the torturer's questioning, and he was feeling the pain all over again.

"I'm sorry," I repeated.

"I'm sorry too. I've hurt him so terribly. It's all my fault." There was a different note to his voice, and my spine stiffened. It wasn't Conrad anymore.

"Thane?" I said.

He nodded weakly, moaning more from the torture wounds than Conrad had. Thane wasn't used to suffering, not when it was so easy to jump into a new body and walk away.

"Get out of him, now!" I hissed, angrier than I'd ever been. "You've caused him enough pain."

"It was never my intention. I took him back to Highcrowne to set him free. If I hadn't acted, he would have been enslaved to our legions. I was unaware Fharen's spies had learned he was involved with what happened on the dirigible. I left him where I thought he would be safe. I swear it."

"You should never have taken Conrad over in the first place. Go away. You and the Dead God both. Go away and never come back. Leave us alone!" I screamed.

His head dropped, like I'd struck him physically, hard enough to knock him out. "Eva," he whispered.

"Thane? Is that you?" Before Conrad spoke, I already knew the answer. I could see souls.

"Disappointed?" Conrad asked.

"I just want to know who I'm talking to." I was turning into such a liar.

Thane was gone. I could feel the absence of him so strongly, I suddenly realized he was usually near me, unseen, bodiless. So, this is what it felt like without him?

"He is sorry," Conrad said.

"Don't you start. You've got that weird condition prisoners get when they've been kept too long or broken. You're not broken. Don't defend the people who hurt you," I ordered.

"You shouldn't have scared Thane away. King Fharen wants answers only he has. I'm so tired. I just want to give them to him."

So that was it. Conrad had willingly invited Thane in. And I'd been the lure. Thane followed me everywhere, and Conrad knew that, had likely said as much under torture. Had this been Fharen's plan from the moment he captured me?

"Don't surrender," I warned. "I don't know how it works, but Thane could take you over entirely for all we know. Let him in again, and there might not be any *you* left."

"I'm more afraid there will be."

Enough wallowing. Time to call him on it.

"So, you've been tortured, so you've been enslaved. So has Kali and too many others. This suicidal depression isn't you, Conrad."

"You don't know me," he shot back.

I'd thought the same about him often enough. He didn't see me as anything other than the femme fatale, the damsel in distress. And I didn't know him as anything other than shining Guardsman, protector of Highcrowne.

"Enlighten me. We have time. You know how long elves take to eat dinner."

"You don't know what I've done, Eva. You wouldn't like me anymore."

"I'm not liking you much right now."

"I started wanting only the rule of law, but then the law ... the law asked terrible things of me, and I obeyed. While I was helping you find your brother's murderer, I was helping my superiors track whoever was illegally freeing slaves. They were quite pleased when the Solhan you killed was one and the same person."

He paused, gauging my reaction, but I didn't even blink. I knew slavery was legal, no matter how wrong that was, and I knew Conrad was a guard. He would obey the law. "You haven't shocked me yet."

"I would have turned Kali into them, when I learned she was no school friend of yours, but there was already a deposition and papers on file exonerating her. I had no need to do my duty, and the worst part of it was I felt guilty about that. I knew the law had been broken, and I'd let it be."

Okay. Now I was a bit angry. Sweet little Kali? Really?

"You look at me with shock in your eyes, but this is who I am, Eva. I obey my king. Highcrowne is my home, the only refuge for us, and I am loyal to it. I bow to Fharen and Calka and Rutgard. But Rutgard is no more. You saw to that. I watched in dismay as you consigned a Crown to the Void. Thane possessed me then, and I was powerless to stop you. I would die at Fharen's hands now, if that was his will, or give him the answers he seeks, but you sent Thane away and made me a traitor again."

"A traitor? You have been done a number on."

"I ... care for you, Eva. But duty and honor are callings. You must understand that? Something greater than ourselves. We sacrifice our lives for it, and our loves if need be."

"I've never found anything worth sacrificing love for." I shook my head. "You're really scaring me. Let's get out of here, get you healed. Then you'll start talking sense. I know a priest, maybe others in this city who would help...."

"No. Call Thane back. Or let me die. I'm so tired."

I would not allow Conrad to give up, no matter how much he begged. If magic was useless, I'd try something else. "Is anyone there?" I shouted.

"Just us prisoners," Ilsa's voice didn't lose its sharpness despite the corridor it travelled down.

"Could you hear us?" I asked, self-conscious.

"Why yes, and I did so enjoy that little drama between you and the idiot guardsman. You're both highly entertaining. It was hard not to laugh."

"Why didn't you call out? Beg Fharen to release you when he was here?"

"There's no use screaming in a torture room, Sugar. The walls are used to it."

"Have you been screaming? What have they done to you?" I asked.

"Other than giving me damp straw and gelatinous, inedible food? Nothing, really. I think Fharen loves me. The softie."

"He hasn't asked you about the First Soul?"

"Of course, and I told him all I knew. Why wouldn't I?"

"Well telling him everything doesn't seem to be good enough. Else I wouldn't be here."

"But you lied to Fharen and you lied to Conrad just now. You haven't revealed everything, have you, Eva? I know you and, while you are pathetically simple, you're also stubborn."

I thought of the things Olyve and Trickster had told me, about the Soul being a shortcut to godhood. There was no way I was telling Fharen about that. And Ilsa was being a bit too nice.

"You're in on this," I said. "Fharen thinks I'll tell you or Conrad whatever I'm hiding. He doesn't understand me very well then. Besides, I'm not hiding anything. I have no idea how the First Soul works, only that I need it. You do know me, right? How I just blunder along until I figure it out. Fharen needs to release me—and Conrad—so I can start blundering."

"You give me too much credit, Sugar. Fharen is an untrustworthy ally. If he has marked you for torture, I will be next."

She was trying to make me feel sorry for her. It was working a little, so I pointed out: "You should never have given him the relic to begin with."

"A slight miscalculation." There was self-recrimination in her tone. That was a new one.

Conrad was silent now too. Maybe they'd finally give me some peace, so I could figure a way out of here.

I closed my eyes, trying to calm my mind—not easy with everything Conrad had thrown at me—but it was all I had right now. So, the straps were enchanted and impervious? What about the wooden rack I laid on? I reached out my senses. Ah ha! The wood was vulnerable. I opened my eyes. Now....

A shadow moved across the ceiling. The hairs along my arms rose up, and I stopped mid thought.

"What is that?" I asked. Conrad was in a cage and Ilsa in another cell, so I was the only one who could see it.

I watched the shadow get blacker and thicker and drop to the floor like a fog settling in a valley. It was a black mist, exactly like the one that had carried the scary Unmentionables to the meeting in the cave the other night.

The aura of Harbinger's soul was familiarly distasteful by now, so I was not surprised when the fog solidified into the vampire, in all his horned glory. I preferred this, the rawness of his true form, to the overly coiffed handsomeness of his elf disguise.

"Good evening," he whispered, like we were old lovers. He had the animal seductiveness turned up to high as well. His dark eyes smoldering, hypnotic. His bare muscles flexed as he reached out for me. One clawed fingertip followed the curve of my jaw down along the line of my neck until it rested against the base of my throat.

"How I long to taste you, but that must wait until you give me what I seek," he said. "The First Soul. Now. Only you, Eva, can subdue it to my will. You will give it to me." I could tell he'd turned the hypnotism to full power this time. No holding back anything, not to maintain a glamour or silence a dinner party. All his substantial focus was on me.

"No," I said. Maybe the torturer would show up soon and save me from this seductive drivel.

He stared blankly at me, shocked that the whole smoldering gaze thing hadn't worked.

"You must do what I say."

"No," I repeated. I was immune, and it was obviously killing him. Even a day spent among elves and locked in prison could have its moments of joy.

"She'll never help you," Ilsa called. "But I will if you get me out of here. I was the one who stole the relic from her and brought it here. You don't need her."

Harbinger bared his fangs, and his expression turned hungry. I knew then he wanted to rip my throat out, and he lunged. His teeth were in my skin, their sharp sting like a jolt of electricity. There was no pleasure in it, only pain and a sudden hammering of my heart, a primal fear that this was it. To be eaten. An animal. Prey.

He pulled back with a snarl, two small droplets of blood glistening on the white tips of his eye teeth, and smiled.

"I will save you for later. When I am a god, I will chain you to my throne, at my feet, and drain a bit of you each night after sunset and before sunrise. Over and over until you are spent. Then you may be of some use to me."

Harbinger pulled his cloak across his body and became black mist. The miasma rolled across the floor and down the corridor toward Ilsa.

Conrad held his breath like me, but the quiet was disturbed by the sound of tearing metal. I heard the cell door clang against the stone floor, and I knew Ilsa was free even before I saw her, cradled in Harbinger's arms. He carried her past me without looking at me again, but Ilsa smiled and gave a little wave.

Harbinger tossed Ilsa over one shoulder and tore apart the stone wall and the soil beyond as though he were tearing cobwebs from his path. Moonlight beamed down through the destruction he'd created. He shot upward with Ilsa, vanishing into the night.

"That was a bit impressive too," I said, after the dust settled.

"There is your door to freedom," Conrad said. "Take it."

"I'm still a bit tied up here." I'd have to change that.

I concentrated; nothing like fear to focus me. I heard footsteps echoing down corridors. The commotion in the dungeon had not gone unnoticed. I stilled my racing thoughts and heart, and for one clear moment, I had it.

I wedged my mind in that place, like a foot in the door to something wider. It was pinching, crushing me out, but I grabbed enough serene control to transform the wood of the rack I was tied to into sand. Like the sand of the beach that touched the waters where I'd found the First Soul. It heard me think of it and helped, reaching out its dark tendrils, searching through Fharen's castle for my call, until it found me. I could see its taint as a stain on my soul sight. It disintegrated the wood around me. I crashed to the floor and then shook off sand as I stood.

"Now, to get you out of there," I told Conrad. His cage was locked. I tried to turn the latch into sand as well, but the door was shut on my focus. It didn't help that there were footsteps drawing closer.

"Go, Eva," Conrad said. "Save yourself."

"You don't want to hand me over to your king?"

"No."

"I'm not leaving you." I grabbed one of the many deadly instruments from a nearby table, something long and sharp, and turned around to face whatever was coming.

It was Hilja and a serving maid. The princess had my Ashur. I took it from her in a fast, disarming action and dropped the torture implement, brandishing the sword instead.

"Where are the prison guards? Are they coming?" I steeled myself for the army of EEPs soon to flood over us.

"No one. They were all fast asleep when we walked past."

Harbinger.

"This one told me where you were," Hilja continued, indicating the servant, but the slave was already hurrying away. I caught a direct gaze and knew right away it was Thane. I'd felt his presence before that. I knew what that feeling was now. Excitement, a pull, or more a desire, to turn towards sunlight. If I were a tree it would be a like that, but with me it was more turning toward something vast and endless, like a dark chasm where you couldn't see the bottom until you hit. Hit hard. Best to avoid that attraction.

The servant housing Thane was gone, and it took me a moment to register Hilja was still talking.

"...will be tearing apart the grounds in no time, with all that ruckus," she said. "Oh my, that hole in the wall is large. Howsoever did you make it? Not the way to go, though. My, no. Far too obvious. You must learn a touch of subtlety. Let us go back while they all sleep. Back up the stairs. I know where to hide you."

"Your closet?"

"What? No. A place my father never goes."

"You're here to rescue me? Why would you do that?" Asking her to lead me to my own mother was one thing, but this was something else.

"I thought we were friends."

I didn't want any more friends, but I didn't tell her that.

"We have to free Conrad first." I picked up the iron spike again and hammered at the lock, metallic bangs echoing through the dungeon and hurting my ears.

"Wait," Hilja said between blows. She waved a key in front of my face. I stopped hammering.

"My, you are noisy when escaping. I have the key. How do you think I got in here?"

"You said the guards were asleep."

"And the door locked. Quite the mystery. It wasn't you?"

I debated about mentioning Harbinger. First things first. "Get Conrad out and get us to safety."

"You have the perfect commanding tone for a princess. We must induct you into the Party first chance we get. I hate being the only member." She opened the lock, and Conrad spilled out like a sack of potatoes. Hilja sidestepped and held her wrists limply. "How awful. What a stench."

"Can you stand?" I asked Conrad, as I took his hand. He did smell awful. I didn't let that stop me from putting his arm around my shoulder. I couldn't support his full weight, but after a moment, he was standing.

"Leave me," he whispered into my ear.

"Not again. I couldn't live with myself. Now get walking. For me."

Conrad obeyed like a good soldier.

Hilja led the way up the stairs. The fallen guards were stirring, so we walked faster, Conrad groaning at the effort.

We ducked into a side passage as booted footsteps filled the hall. They marched past and down the stairs. Hilja opened a hidden door into the servants' hallways and sighed when we were inside.

"They'll never find us here," she said.

"What? EEPs never search the hidden passageways right beside the dungeons? It's the first place they'll look!"

"No, the entrance here is not known, and these corridors are blocked off from the others. No one comes in here."

Now that she mentioned it, the place was cobwebbed and dusty. Wall sconces were burning, however. I pointed them out and said, "Looks like someone does."

"I mean, only the Triumph Party frequents these corridors. The membership is select. And secret. No one knows I'm a member. How fun!" She gave a little squeal of joy before leading us deeper into the hidden area, obviously enjoying the cloak and dagger.

Once again, I thought about taking a different route when Hilja wasn't looking. I didn't trust her, especially with the silly princess routine interspersed with moments of shrewdness. I remembered those marching boots, however, and decided it wouldn't hurt to wait for the search to die down, plus someone in this Triumph Party might be able to help Conrad. His blood was poisoned. It explained the smell and the waves of heat pouring off his skin. His talk of wanting to die was all due to the fever, I was sure. Torture changed people, not that I knew anyone who had gone through what Conrad had, but I'd heard stories. Maybe they could heal his mind too.

"Are any mages members of this secret Party?" I asked.

"My yes, quite a few. We cannot hope to overthrow my father without defeating the court mages."

"Overthrow your father?" I was all for seeing Fharen dead, or imprisoned and tortured like Conrad, but it also mattered who replaced him. "Who will wear the crown instead? You?"

"I could, I suppose. Sounds a bit tedious I must admit. No, the plan is for my husband to have the honors. He has so many friends in high places that we depend on for this to work. It's only fair he wears the target, I mean crown. Not that father ever wears a crown, but you know what I mean. Gallan and I will be married in a quick little ceremony later tonight. Another little secret. After father dragged you away from the dinner table this evening, we had to skip dessert and start scheming. What is father up to?"

Elf politics was absolutely insane. Countless Parties, betrayals and double betrayals... They were playing games with people's lives; spoiled children who would get us all killed.

"Focus on what's important here," I said, speaking slowly. "Me. Conrad. Out of here now."

"I'm working on it. But there are proper ways and means to every end. You are safe here with me." She took my arm.

The moment Hilja led me to the inner sanctum, and I got a look at Prince Gallan—a real look where he wasn't distracted by Fharen or didn't know I was important—I knew something darker lurked within. Call it my soul sense, but I knew exactly why he liked this hidey hole so near the dungeon. That's why he had a key too. He liked to go inside, have a turn or two on the prisoners. Many of the prison guards worked for him and could keep quiet, although his victims did not. Some of Conrad's worse wounds, the mental ones, were his handiwork. Conrad shivered beside me at sight of him. Gallan....

"Eva?" Hilja said again. I'd been so lost seeing into Gallan's soul I'd forgotten to notice his lips were moving and he'd been talking. That was the risk of all this inner seeing crap. You lost sight of the world around you and the danger too.

"Yes? I'm sorry. The ordeal. Is there a place Conrad and I can sit and recover?" I hoped the weak girl speak would galvanize Hilja, and it did.

"Business can wait, my love," she told Gallan, although her voice had dropped down a few levels in its commanding timbre. He frightened her too. "Let's get them settled, and I'm sure Eva will gladly help us."

That's what they'd been talking about. I knew for sure I did not want to help Gallan.

He waved us off, and Hilja found a bed for Conrad. After she left to fetch a mage, I sat down beside Conrad and held his hand. He fell fast asleep. The infection was worsening. He'd gone from feverish babbling—which is what I considered his dungeon confessions—to intermittent moments of consciousness. I couldn't wait around for Hilja to fetch a healer. I'd find one myself.

The hideout consisted of disused servants' corridors as far as I could tell. Not as fancy as I was expecting for a group conspiring against the king. I crept around and spotted a Protectorate soldier. He was guarding a blank wall, so I assumed that was an exit. Good to know. He spotted me too, and I ducked back into the infirmary.

Gallan had EEPs on his side, prison guards, and royalty. No wonder he thought he was king already. I'd detected that in his presence as well, hovering above the malignant desires at his core, a megalomaniacal wish for power that reminded me of my mother's. He'd be happy to see all the Three Kingdoms crushed beneath the Dead God's might, as long as he ruled over the corpse-strewn fields. I shuddered. Why did I always see the sicko's souls, like Harbinger's and Gallan's, more clearly than everyone else's? And why were they always after power?

My heart hammered. I didn't know where to go to find help for Conrad. I suspected we were merely in a different prison than before, with different captors.

I wished I'd gone through the hole in the wall Harbinger had made. Now everything was worse. I wasn't the only one hunting the relic anymore. Harbinger and Ilsa were after the First Soul, and they were ahead of me. I couldn't let them get it.

Once Conrad was healed, I'd find a way out of here. That was the plan. Of course, nothing ever went according to plan.

15 NEVER WHAT IT SEEMS

A healer found us, but it wasn't a mage. It was Doctor Heltune, from dinner. I looked to see if there was a mage behind him—I'd had a taste of mundane doctoring, and it was frightening—but he was alone. Perhaps his doctorate was in theoretical studies, and he was here to bore Conrad to sleep before the operation? Poor Conrad was already out cold, so there was no need. The infection in his blood was worsening.

"Don't tell me Hilja sent you? Is this part of the palace tour or something?" I suspected, since he was a special guest at dinner, he was either Hilja's or Gallan's ally, but it never hurt to prod for more information. You never know what you might get. Heltune did not disappoint.

"Miss Eva Thorne. It's me," he said.

"Do I know you?" While I hate to admit most elves looked alike to me, probably because they all wore the same fashionable glamours to hide their bulging bellies and unwashed skin, Heltune's rough appearance would have stood out. I was sure I'd never seen him before.

"Oh, yes. The disguise. Give me a moment." He lifted up his shirt, something I did not want to see, as it was all hairy beneath, and revealed a device belted to his stomach. It was a copper box with ivory dials and tubes containing the glowing goo the Avian's cooked up to magically fuel the poorly designed gadgets in use around Highcrowne. After he fiddled with it a bit, I suddenly noticed the doctor was green. And a goblin.

"Doctor Ghunnan?" I said, surprised.

"At your service. Er, well, not exactly. On the Emperor's service to be more accurate, although I am not averse to helping a young lady from time to time while on a mission. There has to be some perks to being a spy." He winked.

"Your legs. They're working. And what are you doing wearing elvish glamour? I thought you didn't have magic. Or didn't believe in it. Whatever."

"This is not magic. It is a device of my own design that bends and alters light around the wearer, thus camouflaging them with an image projection of my choosing, one etched on brass wheels deep within the mechanism. The etching was the tricky part I tell you. My Doctor Heltune persona is far uglier than I hoped, not that all elves aren't ugly to goblins, but this one was particularly hideous. Nothing for it but to embrace the rugged image. The deceit, I find, makes me quite famished. I could have eaten the entire table at dinner. Legs and all."

"Speaking of your legs?"

"Oh, those. After my student, Katherine, graduated, although 'ran off' is perhaps the correct term, I found myself quite indisposed. Then, of course, I remembered the mechanical legs I'd been working on for some time. Seemed all they required was some of this green lubricant, which I haven't quite figured out, although I'm sure I will understand its properties soon. And here I am." He lowered his trousers—another thing I didn't want to see—and showed me the mechanical legs he meant. He'd made them twice as long as his own, atrophied versions, which I glimpsed strapped tightly inside the metal casing. That's how he was elf height.

"Wait a minute. You had these already and didn't really need that poor girl, Katherine, to carry you?"

"Apparently not. However, my Doctor Ghunnan persona is well known for his debilitated condition. It has helped me evade suspicion on more than one occasion, my dear. And, once deep undercover, Imperial training dictates one must not slip up."

I laughed then. A kind of mad laugh that made the goblin raise a large, gray eyebrow in concern.

When I could catch my breath, I said, "I'm fine. Don't worry about me. Simply dealing with yet more falsehoods I didn't see through, yet one more betrayal in a long, long list of betrayals. I'm fine."

"I hope you don't think I've betrayed you?"

"You did already. Remember? You called in your goblin commandos and Miss Kissel tried to kill me and my friends?"

"Yes. That. Terribly sorry. No hard feelings?"

"You did help in the end. So, sure. All forgiven." I'd forgiven Thane hadn't I? Hadn't I? "Clean slates all around."

"Oh, good show. Now back on with the disguise in case someone comes in. I did break cover for you, my dear, so I hope you appreciate the gesture."

"In context, yes I do. Thank you very much, Doctor, for not lying to me again."

He fiddled with his gizmo for some time and finally had to hit the pump to get it circulating the Avian goo. The image snapped back into place, and the rangy old elf with his scared face was looking at me.

"You do know that green stuff powering your machines is magic, don't you?" I asked.

"Nonsense. It's a lubricating hydraulic fluid. Necessary, of course, as the device won't function without it for some reason, but certainly nothing mystical."

"Uh, huh." I found it was impossible to educate anyone educated. "So, tell me, what brings you to Faellion? Insurrection? Intrigue? Assassination perhaps?"

"Can I choose all of the above? Actually, no. This little alliance between my government and the Triumph Party may be part of my official assignment, but something far more personal brings me here."

He wasn't winking at me again behind his disguise, was he? I backed up a bit just in case, before I said, "Whatever do you mean? Pray tell?"

"Vampires."

"Vampires? Like Harbinger?"

"You've heard of him!" He grabbed my arms, and I realized I hadn't backed up far enough. "What do you know?"

"I ... I," I stammered, feeling like I was in the middle of an examination, and tried to remember what I knew, mostly from browsing books in Viktor's bookshop. "...Vampires are half-dead creatures who rely on the blood of the living to survive. Their souls are chained to a master vampire in exchange for his power, power to obfuscate and befuddle, seduce and devour, and to change forms at will." Okay, that bit I'd definitely read somewhere, but the goblin had me off balance. When I was thinking again, I added, "Harbinger is the Master of all master vampires, I think. The oldest anyway. He has antlers and a primitive cast to his raw features that harkens to a more primitive past for humanity."

He hugged me then, and I gave him a moment before I started extracting arms. His elf disguise even felt real to the touch.

"Thank you, my dear. You have confirmed my suspicion that this creature can be found here. You have seen him, have you not?"

"Uh, yes." I didn't add that I'd seen him not half an hour ago breaking Ilsa out of prison. "Why are you looking for him?" I was looking for him too, or more accurately, looking to avoid him and grab the First Soul from Fharen before he did. The goblin doctor might complicate things for me. Not that they weren't already complicated.

"I've been hunting him for some time. A rumor here, a sighting there. Call it a hobby of mine. He has almost supernatural abilities to avoid detection and capture," the goblin said. I should start thinking of him as Doctor Heltune to avoid mistakes later.

"He is supernatural. He's a vam-pire." I enunciated the term slowly. "I've seen him turn into black mist for gods' sake."

"This so-called vampire is, I believe, a rare species that predates even Solhans on this world. A proto-Solhan, a primitive ancestor, now extinct but for this one specimen. Many primitives drink blood. Goblins drink blood. Nothing yummier when mixed with some warm milk fresh from the cow's udder, as my mother used to make." He looked wistful, remembering for a moment.

"Why are you interested in proto-Solhans?" I prodded.

"My plague research."

"You're still doing that? It wasn't simply part of your 'cover' in Highcrowne?"

"Oh no, I find the best deceits are based on truths. In fact, I see my duties for the Emperor as a convenient way of pursing my scientific endeavors as well. I am still quite concerned about this plague. You have heard that the affected hordes of humans in the South are now making their way into the goblin swamps? We are well fortified, our great cities hidden; nevertheless, danger is upon us. I must find a way to mitigate this madness that has consumed them. Or perhaps an ancient virus that could kill them all off? Either way, I'm sure it would put a stop to this trouble."

"How thoughtful of you." I wasn't worried for the hordes of the Dead God's army, since they were dead already, but there was no use explaining that to the goblin—Doctor Heltune—again. "Harbinger won't be any help to you."

"I will make that judgement when I find and examine the elusive creature. This so-called vampire is famously good at hiding. I'll give him that."

"He'll eat you if you corner him."

"I will not be frightened off by superstitious fables."

"Why can't you accept that there are vampires and that they like to eat people? You were there when werewolves attacked, when the god was speaking to us out of that rift between the worlds? You remember all that, don't you?"

"Hallucinogens. I've concluded that the airships' larder was contaminated with an insidious hallucinogenic fungus. I've encountered it from time to time. Have yet to isolate and study it, but it's there. Perhaps if I had a bigger microscope? Or perhaps it was gas leaking from the malfunctioning balloon? So difficult to adequately study past occurrences when compromised. We were quite off our rockers, my dear!"

"Someone was. Or is," I said, drolly. "This has been fun, Doctor, really. But will someone heal Conrad before he dies of blood poisoning?"

"I'm at your service."

"Go and remind Hilja to send a mage."

"Mage? Oh, my poor dear. You must have a hallucinogenic fungus infection endemic to your person. Perhaps on your feet? They are a bit smelly."

"Hey."

"I'm perfectly capable of dealing with this," he said, as he examined Conrad more closely, but he trailed off mid-sentence. The elf face curled its lip in disgust and the eyes bulged a bit. "Oh my, this is quite advanced. Nothing for it but to drain all of the infected blood. Purge it from his system with a spigot system, perhaps, as leeches will not do it fast enough."

"Doesn't he need his blood?"

"Yes. There is that. Well, I have found the chemical miasmas produced by some molds and fungi seem to have some success against infections such as this, directly attacking the invading creatures, which I have named 'organisms viewable only with magnification through a microscope'."

"Shouldn't you call them micro-organisms?"

"I like that. Catchy."

"Well, treat him them, with chemical miasmas or whatever. Just no leeches. That's what gives doctors a bad name."

"I'm afraid my limited success has been with external wounds, surface infections, where I can directly apply the mold with a poultice. This is too deeply rooted into his body. I'm afraid there's nothing I can do." He hung his head sadly.

I gave an exasperated exhale and marched out to find Hilja. She said the Triumph Party had powerful mages in its employ, and I was determined to find one. What I found, first, however, was my babysitter.

Ernest, the elven seneschal Fharen had set to watch over me, was tied up in a nearby room, a gag in his mouth. I removed it, which was probably a mistake.

"There you are!" he said, as though I'd been hiding from him. "You must return to the dungeon at once. The guards are looking for you, and for me! I'm responsible for your good behavior. Don't you have any compassion?"

"Not enough to chain myself to the rack and allow people to torture me. We're safe here. For now. Why has Hilja tied you up? Wait. Never mind. I understand completely. If I undo your bonds, you'll run back to Fharen, right?"

He nodded. "But you must come with me. Else I am the scapegoat. The sacrificial beast, as all workers are sacrificed on the wheel of progress, broken by the machine and spit out in tiny chunks."

"What machine are you talking about?" I hadn't understood a thing Ernest said since I met him. Tea and sandwiches and machines that turned people into bite-sized meat? I really hoped it wasn't what I was thinking.

"The machine is the status quo. The inequities of power...."

I held up my hand. "Stop. I really don't have time. Let me know when you're ready to be rescued. In the meantime, I have to save Conrad's life." I put the gag back on him and ran out before I could succumb to a twinge of guilt.

What did a mage look like anyway? Most wore robes, but so did seneschals, priests, and nobles. I wandered the corridors of the Triumph Party's secret headquarters and grabbed every robed person I saw, asking, "Are you a mage?"

There were invariably widened eyes and rapid shakes of the head to indicate 'no'. Where were they hiding them? I know I came across as a mad woman, but I had a long to-do list, and I could feel Harbinger and Ilsa stalking the First Soul while I was wasting time.

Finally, I found the foul heart of the place. Gallan's inner sanctum, and I found out why Hilja hadn't yet returned with a mage as she'd promised.

The princess was crying, the tears diluting the blood trickling from her lip. As soon as I walked in, I knew what I'd missed. Gallan had struck her. I put a hand on my Ashur, but Hilja shook her head, frightened of what I would do. I didn't pull the blade, but I kept my hand there.

"Here she is," Gallan said. He had a hand on his own sword hilt as he sneered at me. "I've tired of waiting and so has Fharen's people. They are searching everywhere and are likely to find us. I need answers from you now, woman. Or should I say, the harlot of the hour? I do find it strange to look into Ilsa's eyes yet see a different soul peering from them. Yours is weak as water, weak as a woman's tears."

"Don't mistake the fact that I have a soul with being any less tough than Ilsa. I stole hers by the way. Her soul is in here too. Careful around me, Prince, or I might just add yours to the tally."

It was an empty threat, as I had no idea how to steal his soul. I'd gotten Ilsa's because Erick had already set up an elaborate ritual that I'd merely tapped into it. There was that moment with Reginald, though, when I was connected to him and started draining him. I didn't think Gallan would open himself to me so readily. Oh, and the troll. I tried to forget about the troll. Still, Thane had been there, egging me on, and I knew it hadn't been all my own doing. I would never....

Gallan laughed. "As I thought. Weakness and hesitation. Drop your weapon."

"No."

I hadn't seen Gallan's pet EEPs in the shadowed corner of the room. They caught me by surprise and snatched the Ashur from me. They went for my arms next, but I dodged and put my back to a wall.

Hilja's tears threw me off more than anything. "Do something," I told her. "Tell these EEPs to arrest Gallan, not me. You're the princess."

"No," she said, wiping at the tears. "He's to be my husband, and when my father is dead, he'll be king. I must obey my king. Royal Privilege, you know."

Her tears turned to sobs, and I wanted to slap her too. As it was, I settled for slapping away the EEP who reached for me. I summoned green fire from my palms, inadequate looking compared to what I'd managed before, but it made the elf pause.

"Gather a mage to subdue her," Gallan ordered. Seemed he was hesitant too. Elves had magic to their very bones, but it was all glamours and sleight of hand, more show than substance. Only a few could control more than their looks.

"I haven't spotted one anywhere," I said. "Seems they're in short supply, and you'll have to face me yourself. You'll find I don't cry so easily. In fact, let me show you what blood and tears taste like."

I lashed out with what would have been long, deadly claws of green fire when I faced wolves, but was now a thin whip of power, muted by distance from Solheim ... or the absence of Thane. I didn't know which was more frightening, that the Dead God or his offspring gave me my magic, 'limited' as it was.

A year ago, I'd have said I didn't want power, but now that I'd had a taste, I knew what I was missing. Especially when I'd tasted what I could do with the First Soul, but it took far too much concentration and time, neither of which I had right now. Effortless power would have been far simpler.

While my attack was pathetic by my standards, it had the effect of a real whip, striking the elf prince's pretty face, slicing through glamour and cutting the real skin beneath. I saw blood before his glamour closed over again, making him appear unhurt. It was not what I'd been going for, but they didn't know that. It reinforced their belief I was a mage, and it kept them a few paces away.

Gallan touched the spot that I knew was bleeding, even if no one else could see it. An EEP took off in pursuit of magical backup, which left just two bad guys to face down.

"And you are a bad guy, aren't you Gallan?" I said aloud. "Not *the* bad guy, but another one. One of many. Seems the whole world is full of them, whether they spend their time eradicating nations, torturing dungeon denizens, or simply bullying the weak." Hilja looked at me when I said that, and I knew she understood I was talking about his treatment of her. "Why do you creeps always come out of the woodwork when times get tough? Easier prey to be had?"

"You're not the prey I want," Gallan said. I knew he was biding time with words now. Waiting for reinforcements. "King Fharen is my target, and I want to understand what he needs from you. Tell me about this relic you were discussing, and you can go."

"I don't believe that. You forget my magic, prince. It allows me to see into your soul, and I know what lurks there. Most people are difficult to read anything from; they're complex, but you and others ... your soul is so blackened it's like a bad stink in the room."

I stepped forward, and the prince took a step back, but I wasn't unleashing more green fire. I rolled and grabbed my sword from the EEP who held it loosely in one hand. He had expected more magic, not such acrobatics, and I caught him off guard. I crouched and drew the weapon, cutting across the soldier's knee in one smooth stroke, severing tendon. He went down howling. I kicked him in the jaw to shut him up as I stood, but my eye was on Gallan.

My soul sense gave me flashes of his past, the glint of steel washed in blood. What part of him I should cut off in recompense for what he'd stolen from his victims, from people like Conrad? Then he suddenly crumpled.

Hilja had hit him from behind with a candlestick. Now that the room was empty of threats, I realized it was a beautifully appointed apartment, with embroidered tapestries, polished wood, and gilded candlesticks that must have good, solid, head-thumping pewter or bronze beneath the veneer of gold.

"You're not crying anymore," I noted.

Hilja's expression was twisted with hate, and she spat on Gallan's face, the spittle puddling up in the groove between his nose and eye. Unconscious, his glamour fell away, revealing the bleeding gash I'd given him as well as a myriad other scars. Seemed his other victims had fought too.

"He deserves to die," she said.

"I agree."

"No." She held up a hand. "You can't kill him."

I hadn't been planning to. I didn't like what killing did to me. Still, I was confused by her indecision. Did she hate him or not? "You just said—"

"—He's the only one keeping my father in check. One bad guy, as you'd say, to balance out another. If these two aren't fighting each other, my father can turn his full attention to Highcrowne, to enslaving humans, or as he truly desires, exterminating them. Go, now. Get out of here."

The princess's crocodile tears had dried, and I was glad she had a spine after all. Things were never what they seemed in my experience.

"Aren't you coming?" I asked.

"No. I'll say you used magic to levitate the candlestick or something. I still have work to do here. Find Doctor Heltune. He's in the third chamber down the hall to the right. He's a compatriot of mine and can help you."

"I know who he is and where he is," I said.

"Then go. I distracted the mages with duties elsewhere when I learned what Gallan planned to have them do to you." Anything Gallan had planned wouldn't be good. "I can't rescue you if you don't leave when I've made it easy."

I smiled. "Thank you."

I retraced my steps to where I'd left the goblin. Conrad was covered with leeches, and the doctor was sharpening a bone saw.

"What in the hell is that?" I asked, snatching the surgical implement from him. "And take those off. We're leaving."

I ripped leeches away, but none of them came willingly. They had an amazing amount of stretch in them, and when they did pry loose, they left a bloody pinprick behind in Conrad's already sallow flesh, before bending and trying to reattach themselves to my hand. I flicked each one across the room after that, the goblin dodging, as I may have been trying to hit him a bit.

"Where are we going?" the doctor asked.

"Out of here. Hilja said you could help."

"I do know an unguarded exit." He headed for the door.

"What about Conrad?"

"He's too large for me to carry. I may look like a burly elf, but I have my normal strength, I assure you." Only a goblin half an elf's size would consider an elf 'burly'.

"Carry an arm or whatever you can manage," I ordered. I grabbed Conrad and hefted him into a sitting position. He was flopping around unhelpfully, but I felt his heartbeat and knew he wasn't dead, despite the goblin's efforts. "Put that down," I told the doctor again when he went for the amputation saw. "I meant, carry an arm while still attached to his body."

"Oh, yes, of course. Limbs are difficult to reassemble." He lifted Conrad's arm while I took a shoulder. We managed to drag him to the door on his knees, but I was huffing and puffing.

"We need help," I said, and I dashed across the hall to where Seneschal Ernest was tied up.

"You've changed your mind?" he asked, after I removed his gag. "You'll go back to the king?"

"Sure," I half-lied. "Help me get Conrad out of here, and you can take me to King Fharen." I'd be meeting up with the king soon to steal back the First Soul, not turn myself in. Only, Ernest didn't need to know the details.

Ernest also didn't need to know the goblin was anything other than Doctor Heltune, and I didn't have time for introductions anyway.

The three of us managed to get Conrad into a secret passage within the secret Triumph Party headquarters. "Is this palace made up of anything but secret passages?" I asked no one in particular.

"They're the only ones I use," the doctor said.

"There is one main hall that runs the length and ends at the throne room," the seneschal pointed out. "All the royal apartments emanate from that central axis. I daresay only the most unimportant supplicants are forced to use that route, however."

"Maybe that's the way out then?" I said.

"No, I have a better way." The goblin tapped on a wall until something clicked, and it shifted aside to reveal a cobwebbed and musty smelling passage, the walls made of rough-hewn stone. "This route is as old as the primordial caves of the faerie, the first denizens of these lands, before elven invaders came."

"This has always been elvish land," Ernest said, offended.

"Shut up and help me with Conrad," I told him. "We all know elves wiped out the fairies, so stop spouting the party line. I don't want to be next on the list. Let's get moving."

"You know the revisionist tenets of the Elven History Reform Party?" he said.

"It was a guess."

I couldn't speak much after that, because even with Ernest helping, Conrad was heavy. Unconscious, he weighed as much as some men did in full armor. I've dragged my share of bodies around, so I knew.

The goblin pulled a lantern from somewhere and held it aloft, trying to read charcoal symbols on the walls as he led the way. He hadn't been helping much anyway, but I still grumbled. If the goblin had been a mage, we could have had Conrad healed and on his feet by now. Of course, if I were a real mage, I could have done it. I wasn't though, and I didn't think of myself as one. I knew just enough swordplay to get myself into trouble and just enough magic to get myself killed.

When we reached the end of the passage, the goblin tapped the wall again, and stones shifted aside. Sweat ran down my face in rivulets, and I mopped my brow so much I knew there was more water soaked into my sleeve than left in my body.

"Where are we?" I asked, after the goblin popped his head out the newly opened doorway and back in again.

"Near the forge."

That explained why it was so hot. Faellion was all jungle and desert and hot enough as it was, but for the heat to be warming these stone walls it had to be intense. There were no sounds of hammering, so I knew the goblin meant the magic forges. Elves used mages instead of blacksmiths to melt metals, pour them into molds, and refine them with spells.

"Is it safe?" I asked.

"It's probably safer in this passage for now. I'll make contact with my allies and return shortly."

"I'm not staying here," I said. "I need to find a healer for Conrad."

"I assure you, my dear, I will return with all the assistance we need." The goblin dashed off before I could ask him anything else.

"Can you lend me a glamour?" I asked Ernest. "I know a priest who might help as well."

"I'm not skilled enough to wield, let alone lend, glamours, my lady," he said.

Come to think of it, Ernest and his working-class brethren weren't as abhorrently beautiful as the other elves. Maybe none of them could do glamours? All part of the class divide.

"I can fetch a healer for you," he added.

"How do I know you won't fetch the king's guard?"

He paused, thinking. That probably had been his plan.

"It seems to me your desire to please the king and keep your head in exchange for mine is against the principals of your People's Party," I said.

"How so? I've already said you're not people."

I snarled at that but bit my tongue. When I could speak reasonably again, I said, "You want to smash the machine and raise the people above the ruling class?"

"Not above. Equal to."

"Whatever. There needs to be some machine smashing, first, right?"

"Agreed."

"And is not the monarchy the very gears of the machine. Or the handle or whatever. What kind of machine is it? Like a windmill or an auto-carriage?"

Ernest thought for a moment. "An auto-carriage. I like those."

"Something you don't like. We're smashing it, remember."

"Oh, yes. An automatic press then, like in the foundry here. It takes the raw, molten potential of the people and stamps it into a tool for work or a weapon for murder, dictated to by the molds of the bourgeois elite rather than the nature of the material itself. Pressed into form, oppressed and pounded...."

"Okay, I get it. Well then, to get freedom, you need to break the molds. Smash them to bits. And you know where they're made? Who orders whether you get a sickle or a sword out the other end? Fharen does.

He's the boss, the master, the head honcho, the dictator for life. He's trying to force me into a mold right now. The mold of prisoner, of tool for his own ends. He's doing the exact same thing to you. Fight back. Why not the mold of leader for you? I bet you'd make a great head honcho."

"Me?"

"Of course, you. Why not? You could lead all your people around, smashing molds. Set yourself up as a new mold-maker even. Ask each person who they want to be and help that dream take shape."

"Me? A mold-maker?" His eyes were alight, gazing into distant and far off possibilities. I had him now.

"I can help you. There's a reason Fharen wants to control me. It's because I can help you and the people."

"Really?"

"Why do you think Gallan is after me too? They want to keep the people oppressed. All you have to do is help me, and the factory is yours."

He stood up, headed for the way out.

"Not that factory out there. You can't do any smashing with those mages around melting metals and equally capable of vaporizing people. I mean the metaphorical factory of the future."

"I knew what you meant. Where is this priest you seek? I will fetch him."

Perfect. No demands to know exactly how I could give him the reigns or how much help I'd require. It seemed the fact Fharen and Gallan wanted me was all the evidence he needed that I was worth something.

I told him where to find Aylon in Fortune's temple and added, "Bring back water too. Lots of water." It was hot.

I hoped the goblin returned first, with reinforcements, in case Ernest decided to betray me.

I was alone with Conrad, waiting, like the helpless damsel. I hated that. I tried to use the time, formulating a backup plan in case I heard EEPs marching into grab me—I had a good one that involved running the other way—and practicing my magic. It was unreliable, and of course nothing happened. Even the green fire in my palms wouldn't spark. Maybe I wasn't terrified or angry enough right now, or maybe my racing thoughts were sabotaging me.

I couldn't heal Conrad. I couldn't even look at his wounds. That was the problem. They made me heartsick and reminded me I was to blame. Not Thane. Me. I attracted Death to me, literally, and everyone around me paid the price.

"Conrad," I said aloud, "if you ever wake up again, know I'm sorry. I will stay away from you from now on. Far away. You'll be safer if you find a nice human girl, or even a dwarf, as long as she's not a werewolf. Avoid Solhans though. We are a plague on this world. Me especially."

"Don't say that," he whispered. His eyes were closed, lips cracked, and the words quiet.

"So, you're not dead yet?"

"Feeling like it. You should let me go."

More of that defeatism. I couldn't stomach it. "Quit trying to take the easy way out. Life is crap, and it hurts. Deal with it." I didn't do comforting.

"Kiss me," he said.

"What?"

"Honor a dying man's wish."

"I won't let you die. Then, when I kiss you, and you survive, everything will be awkward, especially at your wedding to a nice dwarf girl."

"I can't marry a dwarf."

"Probably not. There's too few, and you'd be competing against mobs of desperate male dwarves. A sweet human girl, then, like Kali. Of course, she's taken, so I'll have to do some looking."

"I love you, Eva."

I hadn't wanted him to say that, not ever. I realized it the moment the words came out of his mouth, and I felt a terror so strong the green ball of magic in my right palm flared to life. I covered it, worried it might give us away to the foundry mages.

"Now, you're really delirious with fever," I half-joked. He was burning up, the infection consuming his body, so the fever was real, and this crazy talk from him could well be a symptom. "You can't love me.

You said it yourself: I don't know you. And you certainly don't know me. Not the real me."

That's why I was afraid.

Conrad had always been the golden knight to my barely chained dragon. Now that I'd met a dragon, I thought it an apt analogy.

He went quiet then, and I worried he had died. I felt his pulse, panic building, as it was hard to find and slow, but it was there.

I kissed him. A real kiss. One full of all the desire I'd felt for him since that day I'd first spotted him glinting in the sunlight. He deserved a kiss like that if he was going to die, and even if he didn't, I wanted to feel that dream. What if I did marry him, and we lived happily ever after? What if he accepted and understood all the dark places in my soul, and I wasn't alone anymore? What if ...?

He woke enough to kiss me back, and I could feel him putting all of himself into it, could feel his soul pushing at the bounds of his body, ready to break free, to join with me.

It wasn't enough.

It wasn't like that kiss on *The Mathésis*, the one that filled me with heat and eternity, nor the one in the Dead God's shrine where a soul as bright as the sun burned into me, an inferno I could never extinguish.

No, that had been someone else. It had been Thane.

Part of me wanted Conrad's soul still, but not to kiss. Part of me wanted it for something else. I pulled away and tried to force his soul back into his body with my will. It had threaded out of him and into me, so it was like pulling noodles out of your throat and squeezing them back into the bowl, pretending you hadn't eaten them.

"Eva," he said, reaching for me.

I had almost killed him, and he didn't even care.

"No, Conrad. Stop this. I don't love you. I will never love you. All I can do is consume and destroy you." I suddenly realized how the world looked to Harbinger, nothing but lives to consume, and I knew how he'd grown so calloused. "Stop wasting your energy on me and take a look at yourself. If you don't like what you see, fix it. Stay alive and fix it. But I can't help you anymore than you can help me. We're on our own, and that's the way it should be."

"Eva." He looked at me with a bit more fire in his eyes, shocked by my words. But they had to be spoken.

I turned my back on his outstretched arm and walked away. It hurt, but not as much as I thought it would. It was a relief, really, to close one door of possibility. Shut it for good. Otherwise, it would always be there, distracting me from what mattered— fixing the mess we Solhans had made of the world.

The passageway was too narrow for me to get as far from him as I wanted, so I went back the way we'd come, deeper into the tunnel, and I sat, staring into the darkness.

16 Seeing Clearly

I don't know how long I waited for Ernest and the goblin to return, but they arrived at almost the same time, for which I was glad. Ernest had the priest with him, rather than guards, for which I was doubly glad. And now Conrad wouldn't be vulnerable and alone with me, for which I was triply glad.

"Aylon," I said, welcoming the elf. "I hope your evening with Duchess Ula went better than my dinner with King Fharen?"

"I heard you were arrested, and I asked Our Lord for guidance. Thane instructed me to keep away from the palace, but I have been waiting, hoping to be summoned to your aid again. I never expected the summons to come from the king's own seneschal." He indicated Ernest.

Both the goblin and Ernest seemed confused by the mention of 'Our Lord' and 'Thane', but Conrad stirred. He knew who the priest was talking about, having been possessed, but he hadn't enjoyed it so much. I had to tread carefully to keep Aylon on my side, while not alerting the others we were dealing with a devotee of the Dead God.

"It's not I who need your help so much as my friend here. Conrad is with *us*," I said, trying to indicate to the priest that the other two weren't, and he should be more circumspect.

I think Aylon got the hint, because he paused, glancing at the others, before he knelt beside Conrad and examined him. He rose a few moments later, saying, "Leave him here with me, and I will summon my acolytes to carry him. You should flee, my lady, so you can accomplish your mission. I could not bear for anything to stand in your way."

Conrad grabbed the hem of my dress and shook his head. He was too weak for words now, and I felt bad. Maybe I should have left things at a kiss, with hope of something more? Then, if he died … No. Even if he died, it was better we be truthful with one another. He deserved that. And so did I.

I crouched low and whispered in his ear. "Play along with his beliefs. He too was possessed by Thane, but more importantly, he can help you. I can't."

"If he's made well enough to travel—although that would take 'magic' and we may be better off leaving him behind—my allies can help get him out of the city easily." The doctor eyed the priest, adding, "Are you sure you shouldn't entrust Mister Falconbridge to the hospital? I doubt any have my skill there, but it may give him a better chance of success than superstition."

"I will deliver him to the healer's hall," Aylon explained, "as I am no healer myself. But I can be sure we avoid all suspicion. How do I find you later?"

"We'll find you," the goblin said in a tone made all the more ominous by his rugged elf disguise.

"All right," I said, "it's a plan. Now, when will you introduce me to your 'friends', Doctor?" The First Soul was my objective, and I could use all the help I could get finding it.

"My allies have agreed to meet us in a safe location. I will bring you there now."

"I'm coming with you," Ernest said.

"Of course, you are," I said. Anyone who could get close to King Fharen and help steal back the Soul was indispensable. If I could convince the seneschal to be more of a rebel.

"I'm not sure my associates will be comfortable meeting so many new faces." The goblin shifted his belt, and his disguise wavered for a moment.

"Tell them to get comfortable, because I want him along. He is one of *the people*, and *the people* are the most crucial allies we have." I hoped I'd put the correct emphasis on 'the people', but Ernest beamed with importance, so I must have done it right. I was getting pretty good at dealing with insanity.

The goblin thought a moment and nodded. "My associates will definitely agree with that sentiment. Come."

I followed the goblin out into the searing heat of the elven forge. Its scale was impressive, but nothing compared to what I'd encountered in Gernwold, the dwarven capital, where I'd lived for some years. The dwarves had massive numbers and produced tools on an equally massive scale. But this wasn't that kind of forge. This was one geared for war, the molds rattling along the mechanized assembly line all carrying the shapes of swords, axes, and arrowheads.

When had elves become so reliant on the mechanized contraptions of the South? It was a bad sign when even the traditionalists had fallen victim to 'progress'. At least the metal poured into the molds was infused with spells; I could sense them. A more sensible approach to weapon manufacture if you asked me.

The vats suspended above the assembly line, whose liquid contents glowed orange, were etched with runes to keep the metal at the correct temperature. They levitated, unsuspended by chains, and poured a perfect measure of molten metal into each shape that passed below them. The goblin blithely ignored this demonstration of magic.

I spotted two mages at the far end of the chamber who were overseeing the refinement of the cast weapons. They wielded no hammers and had no iron to pound on, instead each newly created armament was suspended in midair and the rough edges of metal seemed to fall away like dust, leaving shining, sharp blades behind.

There were no slaves, which was a strange sight for Faellion.

"They are not allowed weapons," Ernest explained when I asked. "To touch one means their death." Obviously, the powers that be needed to keep their slaves from revolting, but weren't the slave marks enough? Seemed they were paranoid, these elves. Of course, Fharen was creating an army from slaves. Had the rules been bent? Were these weapons meant for them?

"If Fharen plans to attack Solheim, he must be confident in his army. Have you seen it?" I asked Ernest.

"Seen what?"

"The king's army. Where is it gathering? What are its numbers? Is it made entirely of human slaves?"

"I'm unable to share such secrets," he said, evasively, and I wondered if he even knew.

"I've seen it," the doctor said. "It is a wonder of biological innovation. I have no idea how they managed to fuse.... Well, I will arrange for you to admire it yourself, Eva, as words do not do it justice."

"It is an injustice, it's very existence," I said. "Best you don't show it to me."

"That may be unavoidable. If you seek King Fharen, that is where you will find him. He has left the city. Some say in search of a fugitive—you I presume—but my friends know he has had no choice but to abandon the search and call upon his army. Now that the Dead *God*'s," the doctor said the word with disdain, "emissary has left without a treaty signed, there is no option but war. Lili of Solheim did not receive an elven surrender, and so she is coming to take it by force."

"Then take me to Fharen straightaway." I wanted help, but if there was a chance he'd get killed in battle before I got what was mine, I didn't want to risk it.

"We need my associates, for while I might know where to find Fharen, they are the only ones who can get us there alive."

"Us? You keep saying that. Why are you helping me—" I almost said Doctor Ghunnan, but changed it in time to, "—Doctor Heltune?"

"I thought we were friends?"

I scowled. He was about as deceitful as most of my friends.

"Well, alright," he continued, "I presume that if I aid you, you will aid me in finally capturing this elusive Harbinger fellow. Let us strike the bargain now then."

"I don't think so." I preferred to avoid Harbinger and focus on what was more important.

"You can extract what you need from King Fharen without my help then? I shall go now." The goblin started walking back the way we'd come.

"Wait." I literally had to bite my tongue. I was on the run in the elven capital and needed all the help I could get. "Fine. If you and your friends help me retrieve the relic, I will help you with Harbinger. He's a menace that shouldn't be wandering the streets anyway. After I deal with the Dead God, that is. He is the priority."

"And if that maniacal conqueror kills you?"

"Then I'll tell you all I know about Harbinger in my dying breath. Better yet, help me defeat the god."

"I would once have said that is not in the Emperor's interests, but I daresay our foreign policy has changed in light of the recent invasion of our lands. It is a bargain then. Quid pro quo."

The goblin led Ernest and I out of the mostly empty foundry and into the harsh light of midday. He seemed confident in his elvish disguise, forgetting I didn't have one. I should have asked the priest for another glamour, but it was too late now.

"Give me your robe, Ernest," I hissed.

"No."

"You want to be a mold-maker or stay oppressed forever?"

He sighed and took off his outer robe. I was worried he was naked beneath, but he had on breeches and a tunic. In fact, they were far nicer than his seneschal robes, all silk and lace and embroidery. I raised an eyebrow at that. "Is that what 'the people' wear beneath their rags?"

"Certain rough appearances must be maintained. I happen to prefer the feel of silk against my skin instead of that burlap cowl of confinement, the emblem of my subjugation. You are welcome to it."

I didn't have a chance to change clothes, as the doctor continued inexorably on. I draped the robe over me as a hood and walked hunched like an old person to hide my height.

I thought our excursion would be over before it started, as the doctor did not seem to understand the concept of stealth, walking brazenly about. But maybe that's why it worked.

The tunnel had brought us to the inner city, where the market lay, as I could see it nearby. The foundry where we'd emerged was part of a cluster of factories, some producing perfumes, others cloth or ceramics. I called them factories, but while they had the frighteningly insidious technologies you'd find in Highcrowne, with workers all lined up along conveyor belts and machines fueled by Avian goo clanking away, they were different. All were magical factories, like the foundry. A mixture of enchantments, machines and slaves, with a central mage or two at the heart of each enterprise. Magic was dangerous, machines were annoying, and slavery was institutionalized evil. I didn't like any of it.

But the important thing was they were all being industrious and not paying attention to us as we made our way through the city. Soon, we reached a section of town where the streets were empty and so quiet not even the wind stirred. I found it unnerving, especially when the doctor led us to one of the pink, crystal spires Faellion was famed for.

"Your friends live in a mage's tower?" I asked, surprised the scientifically-minded doctor chose to associate with 'fakers' as he liked to call them.

"It is a meeting place only, and please don't call such fakers—" Told you. "—mages. Besides, you will see this particular tower is far more suited to my interests."

It was a big tower, not as needle-like as the others that dotted the city, and instead of tapering to a point, it ended in a dome. I was intrigued as we made our way up the circular staircase. Up and up for quite a while without any landings or rooms, until we reached the domed chamber at the top.

What I could only call a giant, bronze spyglass filled the chamber. It seemed to be aimed at the sky through a large opening that bisected the dome.

"What is this place?" I asked.

"The observatory," Ernest said.

"What does it observe? Clouds? Birds?" I thought a huge lens like that might be able to see all the way to Highcrowne if there weren't mountains in the way.

"It observes other worlds," the goblin said, awe in his voice as he stroked an instrument panel at the base. It consisted of levers, dials and graduated numbers etched onto the bronze.

"Like the ones through the portals you were telling me about?" Tears in the Void could create passageways. While we'd sent Leviathan into the space between, the goblin had once explained there were also doorways that led to worlds 'eerily similar' to our own.

"Not exactly," the doctor said. "Not like the doors. These worlds are far more alien and always above our heads, out of reach. No one ever looks up, else they would realize our moons and the stars are but the tiniest portion of the worlds in the universe beyond. This place is unused, for the elves look only at themselves and have no desire to see their miniscule place in the cosmos."

"Why do they have an observatory then?" I asked.

"Because it is a trophy, a treasure pillaged from old Darrub." The voice that spoke was familiar, but I drew my Ashur anyway.

A group I hoped were the goblin's 'friends' had come up the stairs behind us. They were all human. What's more, I recognized their leader, the one who had spoken.

He was a former goon of my uncle's, before he struck out on his own. Aguragas, Agura for short, but I liked to call him 'Gas' or 'Windbag'. He always had lots to say and none of it good. He was the reason Duane went bad to begin with: I blamed it all on him and his little assassination squad of Darrub refugees.

They say Darrub vanished in a day, but that was its monarchy, slaughtered at midnight by Unmentionables I now knew. The people lingered, torn apart by factions of opposing warlords, and the refugees spread to Highcrowne long before the Dead God sent more fleeing to the city.

Duane's ancestors were from a border kingdom of Darrub's, some vassal state that rebelled in the vacuum of power. They paid the price for that rebellion, at least Duane's parents had. Gas's family on the other hand were probably as close to royal as was left, their advisors, Viziers they called them.

Agura was my opposite, with black skin and white hair. He liked that, how I was destined to be his, his compliment. I hadn't seen him for years, and I'd forgotten all about him and his talk. He hadn't forgotten about me.

"Eva," he said.

I stiffened, wondering if it was Thane for a moment, but my name was spoken with a different sort of desire, one that was far less innocent. Strange I should consider Thane, Death incarnate, more innocent, but you didn't know Aguragas. He wasn't a nice man.

I gave him one of my good glares. "If I'd known you were a part of this, I would have said no."

"No to our aid, or to human freedom? You prefer I turn you into Fharen for the reward?" He smiled, like he looked forward to doing just that.

"If it will get me close enough to him to steal back what's mine, fine go ahead," I said.

"What did the Elf King steal from you that's so valuable?" Gas was intrigued, but he could stay that way.

"Nothing you can use, and nothing of any value to anyone. Ask the survivors of Ismerkel."

"Death is valuable. Extremely."

"This isn't a shining dagger you can use to slit someone's throat in the night. This is uncontrolled death best left to those like me who know Death after the fact rather than from being the cause of it."

"You were never aware of death when I knew you, Eva, or at least shied from it. I hear all that's changed. I hear you even took a life or three," Gas said.

"Where did you...?" I trailed off.

Gas had been one of my uncle's informants, and it looked like he still kept an eye on me. No detective work needed, though, as my killing of Erick and Jenna were public knowledge, investigated by the Highcrowne authorities, and I was officially cleared of any wrongdoing. Of course, in the Outskirts the authorities were my uncle's people, who would let me get away with murder like him, or guards like Conrad who didn't know me well enough to know I was not as innocent as I seemed. Gas had misjudged me as well. He didn't think I was innocent, though. He thought I was like him deep inside, a killer waiting to emerge. The fact was, I was somewhere in between.

I shut up then. I could spar with Gas all day, as he never ran out of air. I didn't have time for him and said as much.

"Will you help me or talk me to death? And what's your price? You don't shed a drop of blood without being paid for it."

"Is that what you want me to do? Shed blood for you, Eva?" He made it sound intimate, and I found myself wishing for Thane's voice instead—it was less creepy, despite it being the creepiest thing ever.

"I asked for a price. Name it or let me turn myself into Fharen for the reward. It's not a half bad plan. I escaped from his dungeon once and can do it again."

"He has no dungeon now. He's on the battlefield. Seems he angered some peace envoy and now war is coming to Faellion. I like that. War is good for business. So, I don't really need money, at least not what the aesthetic niece of minor gangster can gather."

So, my uncle was now a 'minor gangster' to him? Gas thought more highly of himself than ever.

"Then I have nothing to offer you, and we're done here. I'll see you around, Gas."

"Wait a minute. I said I don't want coin, but you know what I do want."

"Never going to happen." I almost gagged.

"You mistake me. And unduly flatter yourself. I didn't mean that. Faellion teems with marked concubines better schooled than you. You do, however, have a hold over The Black Rose."

"Duane?" He went by many names, and The Black Rose was my least favorite. It wasn't on my list only because of tackiness. I hated it the most because it was the name he'd gone by when Gas and him ran together. When Duane became a killer.

"I'm not as friendly with Duane as I used to be. Hilja has a tighter hold over him these days. She even got him to wear a suit."

"What I want from him only you can get for me. I want the life he owes me."

I paled. He wasn't? "I won't kill Duane." I wasn't a killer, but even if I were I could never....

"I didn't think you would—or could. Duane owes me a life still, and he's been reluctant to pay. I have a target for him. I get your property back, and you give him the coin." He handed me a gold coin with a name etched across the three faces of Highcrowne's monarchs. It said, 'Calka.'

"The Avian Queen? Why in the world do you want her dead?" I hadn't seen that coming. "You're a political assassin now?"

"It's always been political."

"Duane wouldn't do it even if I asked. It's suicide. Besides, the last thing Highcrowne needs is no one left to stand up to Fharen."

"I'll handle Fharen. You took out the Dwarf King—" I tried to protest, but in a way it was true. It had not been my intention. "—that leaves one Crown standing between us and human freedom."

The goblin and Ernest cleared their throats.

"Are you sure I should be hearing this?" the goblin asked.

"Human freedom?" Ernest said, sounding concerned.

"I meant The People's freedom," Gas told him and the goblin with a smile no one believed for a second.

"What you seem to be forgetting is the Dead God," I pointed out. "As they say, everyone finds freedom in death, so if that's what you're aiming for then keep standing in my way. I don't care about kings and queens or even bottom-feeding scum like you. All I care about is defeating Him."

"You are certainly more ambitious than I remembered you to be," Gas said with another smile, one I found far more disturbing than the last. "So, this is what the relic you seek is all about? Necromantic mumbo jumbo? I'll help you, but my price is the same. A life."

"No." I glared at the goblin for getting Gas involved in all of this.

"Defeating Death is worth a life, isn't it?"

"It's worth mine," I said, "but I'm not taking anyone else with me if I can help it, not Duane nor Calka, and I'd rather not give up mine either."

"Ambitious but just as naïve. Lives are already piling up in your wake, but never mind. We can barter later, when you realize what my help is worth. For now, let's call this a free sample. Fharen has your relic from Ismerkel in his possession at all times, but I've seen it. At least my 'eyes' have. It's not Solhan or anything like anything my spies have seen before. It looks like a diamond worth salivating over at first, but my people know the real thing, and this is something else. It makes you feel … powerful. The moment Fharen heard Lili of Solheim was coming back for a visit, this time with a dwarven army behind her, he didn't try to talk. He started rallying his new troops."

"A dwarven army?"

It was real now. They were coming. The Compact forbade the Dead God or His hordes entry to the Three Kingdoms, but my mother was circumventing the rules. Now that they—and I should say Gypsum—had the dwarf crown, they not only ruled Gernwold and the dwarven lands, but they had a means of commanding and producing more werewolves. It was more than a dwarven army, it was something undefeatable. And the Compact couldn't protect us from it. They were coming here, and nothing could protect us.

I must have looked shaky, because Ernest touched my shoulder. "What is it?"

"Let me think." I sat down on the observatory floor. The lens focused a ray of light peeking through the clouds into a blinding beam I had to shuffle away from.

Gas shook his head, putting a cover over the device. "Idiot elves don't know what to do with Darrub science."

I stood up again. "How do we get the relic from Fharen?" I asked. "Doctor Heltune said you could get me to Fharen's side. Is that included in your free sample?"

"My eyes could fetch it and bring it to you."

"They might be fetching an illusion. My ... Lili of Solheim was tricked, so your minion could be as well, and Fharen would know we were coming. No telling what he might do then. I will recognize the real relic when I touch it." At least I hoped so.

"I can get you there if you do exactly what I say." Gas seemed a bit too pleased at the thought.

"Not just me. I'm taking Doctor Heltune along."

"Why?" the goblin asked.

"Because it's a condition for my help with Harbinger, and despite the fact you've betrayed me before, I trust you more than I trust Gas. I don't want to be on my own in enemy territory."

"I'm coming as well," Ernest insisted.

"Fine," I agreed. "Three of us and Gas. You, Aguragas, and not your minions. I don't trust you, but I trust you'd never do anything to get yourself killed. Anyone else you'd send is expendable." I glanced at his associates, but they didn't batt an eyelash. They knew their value.

"I won't betray you. I'm waiting on a life, remember?"

"I don't trust anyone anymore," I said. Not the goblin or Ernest either, but there was safety in numbers.

"Very well. I had hoped it would be just the two of us," Gas said. "It will be difficult to get so many past Fharen's guards without notice, but I will try."

"I've got myself covered," Doctor Heltune patted his stomach, and I knew he meant his disguise. Ernest too should have an easy time of it. Gas and I were the ones who couldn't hide so well.

I wasn't sure I wanted to do this, but what choice was there? Who else could I trust to wield the First Soul? The relic was said to draw evil to it, and all the villains were coming out of the woodwork: Harbinger, Fharen, Gallan and Aguragas. Was I one of them? Called by its dark voice? I remembered what I'd almost done to Conrad, and I shuddered. There was no going back, only forward.

Gas and his people took us out of the city in a merchant caravan with no questions asked by the city guards. It was smooth and precise, and I understood why Gas thought his help was invaluable.

Once I got my hands on the First Soul, I'd dump Gas like the sack of garbage he was. I didn't know how the goblin had become entangled with hardened assassins or how Gas had gone from Highcrowne to the Upside Down Party, but I didn't really want their story. I was focused.

That made me all the more antsy as I paced the main hall of the country estate Gas had us holed up in. It belonged to a minor elf noble who was out of town. All marble, gold and silks, and even tackier than Fharen's palace. Doctor Heltune lounged, filling his face with grapes and jollups, washed down with some pixie blood and wine from time to time, and I gagged.

Ernest instinctively tried to order the house slaves around but was put off when none obeyed. They were all freed, the mark imprisoning them removed and replaced by a fake brand of burnt flesh and elven glamour. I saw a lot of stolen books around the place too, with the ex-slaves laying out type for the printing presses and carefully copying over the most inspiring and controversial passages.

Watching all of them, and me, was a gaggle of Gas's goons. They had clearly never been slaves, all burly muscle, bronze Darrub skin and the hard look of seasoned assassins.

"Your boss had better return soon," I told them, "or this arrangement is over. He said sunrise, and it's almost noon."

"He'll be here," said one with steely blue eyes. The color stood out against his dark skin, and I noticed he almost never blinked. Creepy.

"This was stupid," I grumbled for the tenth time. I'd made Conrad's freedom part of our bargain but had to upgrade the terms from free sample to 'I'll consider it'. I had Calka's death coin in my belt pouch, and it weighed like lead.

The metal gates in the courtyard screeched open, and I hurried out into the searing sunlight. The hot breeze sucked the air from my lungs, and I covered my eyes against the glare.

I was never complaining about Highcrowne winter again, because Faellion summer was ten times as inhospitable.

Aguragas rode in, his horse stopping to guzzle from the trough, and so he climbed down and left the beast to it. I didn't see anyone with him and was about to give him a good kick before I asked what went wrong, when two donkeys came through the gate. They'd been slow but hurried to join the horse at refreshment.

I recognized Fortune's priest, and the other one was Conrad. His carriage was unmistakable, erect and guard-like, as he climbed down. The main thing was he managed it by himself. He was healed.

I went to him. "You okay?"

"Do you care?" The look he gave me was cold enough to freeze the sweat dripping from my brow.

"Of course." I could tell he was in no mood for the 'I still want to be friends' talk, and I have to admit neither was I. I was not feeling friendly.

I turned to Gas and said, "Now for the rest. Get Conrad on the next ship to Highcrowne, and then we can stop lazing around here and get to work." Harbinger was after the relic too, and time was wasting.

"I don't need your help or your friends. I'm ready to go on my own, to where I'm wanted." Conrad climbed back onto his donkey.

"Don't be an idiot. Have a drink of water first," I said.

Conrad wouldn't even look at me, but when he tried to nudge the donkey it wouldn't move.

I laughed. I couldn't help it. "Not sure which of you will win this one. You two are equally stubborn."

I grabbed the pack I'd put together while Gas was busy fetching Conrad. It had supplies for what I was told would be half a day's journey. I didn't think I'd need much food, but I would need extra cushioning for the saddle—I hated horses—and the pack held a blanket and ointment. Lots of ointment.

I nudged the goblin, who still wore his elf disguise. He would not break cover for anyone but me, which was somewhat flattering. I told him and the seneschal, "Let's get moving."

Agura guzzled water from a goblet one of his flunkies brought out on a silver tray, before saying, "I'm ready whenever you are." He whispered instructions to his henchman, who then fetched fresh horses from the stables.

As I adjusted the saddle, I stood near the priest. He was transferring his things from the tired donkey still slurping at the trough. "Why didn't you stay at your temple, Aylon?" I asked.

"I wish to accompany my holy charge a while. He too was a vessel for Our Lord, and I feel a camaraderie I cannot explain. I wish to understand this experience better."

"Fine with me. Maybe you can keep him from doing anything else stupid."

Conrad was still trying to get the donkey to move. The priest nodded with understanding and went to help him transfer mounts. I was glad for the buffer. I didn't want to talk to Conrad any more than I had to, because it caused him pain. I was done with that. He was better off without me, and I could use fewer distractions. Things were complicated enough.

At the estate gate, we parted ways. One of Gas's people led Conrad and the priest in the direction of the river docks, and he did not give me a backward glance.

It hurt that Conrad could shut me out so quickly and completely. He must have felt I'd done the same to him. He wasn't aware of my internal arguments, the sleepless nights, where I was unable to shut my eyes on one day for fear of what the next day would bring. My cinnamon dreams. But when Conrad was gone, vanished into the next canyon, and I saw Gas's look of anticipation, the hurt feeling was quickly replaced with dread. What had I gotten myself into?

"Lead the way," I said, making sure Aguragas wouldn't be at my back.

Ernest and the doctor rode side by side at the rear, chatting about various machinery they'd seen, and I tuned them out. The journey gave me time to think. I wore a wide-brimmed hat and wiped sweat out of my eyes from time to time, clutching the saddle whenever I felt I might slip off, but it all became automatic.

With time to think came time to worry.

The impending attack by my mother and the dwarven army seemed to terrify me more than anyone else. Were they stupid? I supposed the doctor and the assassin could move on to another city, another kingdom, or even switch sides if the mood struck them. Nice being unencumbered with troublesome things like morals and loyalty.

I, on the other hand, feared for the human slaves about to be crushed by Lili's and Gypsum's forces. I even felt bad for the elves. They couldn't all be monsters. And none of them could redeem themselves

if they were dead. I meant what I'd said to Thane—
everyone deserved a second chance. I glanced at Gas.
Maybe even him.

But what if this was the beginning of the end?

With an army rampaging within the borders of the
Three Kingdoms, how could we stand together to
defeat the Dead God? I didn't think Avian magic was
enough. Naked and vulnerable, we would soon be taken
apart, 'defeated in detail', as the military types liked to
say.

I couldn't let that happen. I couldn't fight an army
or lead people into battle, but I could cause trouble. I
could undo what my mother had done and send the
Dead God back. The first step was the First Soul.

The sun was on the horizon by the time we neared
our prize. The oases, hidden in small canyons just
outside Illul Faellion, had given way to a wide, verdant
valley where a tributary of the Serpent's Ribbon ran.
The river plain was dotted with farmhouses, but the
fields had been devoured by the mass of troops now
encamped there, the crops stamped into mud.

We left Ernest with the horses, while the rest of us
crept forward for a closer look.

"How do we get the relic from Fharen?" I asked
Gas.

I hadn't spotted the Elf King yet, but a giant,
flowering plant with golden veins and silken petals
looked like a good place to start. The strange growth

was surrounded by EEPs, and Elven Protectorate usually meant royalty were nearby.

Dozens of the giant plants sprouted from the ruined farmlands. Maybe they were the crops? They were like nothing I'd seen before. Tents perhaps? People made strange shelters, like Avians who lived in nests or goblins in mud huts. Elves were accustomed to their creature comforts of golden slippers and lace cushions, and I'd never heard of them sleeping on flower petals, but maybe it was a new fad.

Something niggled for my attention, and I realized I hadn't seen any slaves, certainly not the new army of them Fharen had supposedly been creating. The soldiers dotting the plain in squads and regiments were all elvish. Horsemen, archers, swordsmen, glaive wielders and, of course, mages. Those were easy to spot with my soul sight, for they glowed as they worked; the power drawn to them left a halo around their souls.

The giant flower structures glowed with a similar radiance when I closed one eye and looked at them from the side. There was something magical happening.

I extended by senses and felt more souls gathering on the horizon, just on the other side of the valley. They were only a shadow to the naked eye, like a black fog creeping across the landscape. But I could sense who and what they were—dwarves. Not any dwarves. These were the sort who did not need axes and swords. The sort who could transform into creatures that moved in a blur to shred muscle and bone with equal ease. Gypsum's army.

I sensed her there. My friend ... alongside my mother. They must have had troops waiting near the border to bring them here so quickly. The peace negotiations had only been a means for Lili to assess her opponent, and she must have soon realized only decadent elves stood in her way. She could plunder the First Soul—or kill—as she desired. And I knew now all she desired from me, her eldest daughter, was death.

"That's your job," Gas said.

"What?" I'd been so lost in thought, I forgot I'd asked him a question.

"I said I would get you to Fharen's side. It's your job to get the relic you seek. We enter as slaves." He showed me a bundle of tattered clothing he'd brought along.

When we were changed, I said, "Ernest, stay here and guard my sword." I was reluctant to hand over my Ashur, but even disguised as a cane it would look out of place with a farm slave. "You can fetch help from the Upside Down Party if anything goes wrong. You should stay as well, Doctor Heltune." I didn't want to go in there alone with Gas, but it was important I had backup. No good if all of us were captured.

"I've infiltrated this camp before," the doctor said. "Rest assured, I can get you in smoothly, my dear."

"Where's 'there'? I don't see Fharen anywhere, nor the slaves. How can we expect to blend in when I see nothing but elves?" I asked.

"The humans are in there. They're all in there," the goblin assured me, gesturing at the fields.

"Those big flowers?" Agura asked. "They're what my eyes spoke of, but I had no idea. What are they?"

"I'd like to know myself," the doctor said. "From what I've seen previously, they are of keen interest to those of us who know how easily technology can change the nature of war."

"Then my interest is keen as well." Agura looked too eager, and it gave me pause.

"Change of plan," I told Gas. I pulled the coin with Calka's face on it out of my pouch and tossed it to the assassin. He caught it without even looking. "The deal is off. I'll try it the doctor's way first, especially if it spares the Avian Queen's life." I still remembered the feather she'd given me. Its ability to dispel magic had helped on more than one occasion.

"You swore."

"I lied."

"I like that you are embracing this wild side of yourself, Eva. It shall be fun. And I understand you don't want to be indebted to me, but you already are." Gas was smiling, but his smiles weren't the reassuring kind.

"You said I could have a free sample. The sample ends here." I turned my back on him and felt an itch between my shoulder blades. I hoped he didn't try to put a dagger there. "Come on," I told the doctor, hurrying away.

We made our way down into the valley, sliding on loose soil from time to time, and I had no idea how I would climb back up, especially if soldiers were chasing me. The river seemed like a possibility. I had learned how to row a boat.

"Look more vacant-eyed. Oh, and let me just fix…." The doctor said, as he rubbed more dirt on my shift.

In the end, my clothing looked like something not even a dog would sleep on. Next, he pulled a collar and leash from somewhere. I did not want to know why he carried those around. I looked, smelled and felt like a collared mutt, as I was led down into the thick of the elvish army.

I glanced back, and I could barely make out Ernest and the horses. Gas gave me a small salute, and I wondered what he meant by that. Was he ceding this match to me? I doubted it. There would be repercussions, but it was better to nip our working relationship in the bud now, as Gas had a tendency to get his hooks into you and never let go. I'd seen it happen.

We reached the outer picket, and Doctor Heltune was quite the sight. That eye patch, weathered skin, and scarred face was shocking to the glamoured elves who watched us approach from their cushioned chairs.

I supposed even guards couldn't be expected to be on their feet all day. It would be very un-elvish.

"I caught another wanderer. Let me through, as there may yet be time to include her," the doctor said.

"Oh, yes. She should be included," a blonde elf nodded, clearly pretending to be in the know.

One of the elves was standing instead of lounging. He was a muscled, hunter type, like those you sometimes saw in Highcrowne, keen to return to the glory days of elvish might and superiority.

"Let me see your papers," he barked.

I didn't have any papers. I did have a dagger tied high up on my thigh which could be useful at some point.

"Don't you know who he is?" the blonde guard asked arrogantly. "He's been at the king's table." Well, maybe he knew a few things. "Heltune has captured more slaves than any human hunter."

A famed 'human hunter'? What interesting depths the goblin had. I stiffened, wondering if Gas might not have been the better companion, but I was in an awkward position. Even speaking would draw attention to me, so I looked vacuous.

The doctor had papers. He handed them over, crumpled and stained, a good match for his rugged persona. The self-important EEP perused, looking for the smallest flaw, then handed them back with a sniff of dismissal.

"I'll take her from here," the soldier said, reaching for my leash.

Doctor Heltune clamped a hand like iron, in fact it had a metallic ring to it, onto the elf's wrist and said, "Back away. My prize, my reward."

"Then I'll escort—"

"—I know the way." The doctor pushed past the guards, grumbling, as he dragged me along behind him.

"Human hunter?" I hissed when we were out of ear-shot.

"Another cover," he whispered back.

"Capturing slaves part sounds real enough. I knew I couldn't trust you." I 'tripped', and when I regained my feet, I had my dagger at his crotch, where the goblin's would be anyway; it came up to the stomach on his magical disguise. "If you intend to hand me over, you'll be bringing in three less parts of your own."

"I am on your side. Your enemies are mine. Sometimes legends spread with little substance behind them." He leaned down and grabbed my shoulders, saying loud enough for onlookers to hear, "Stand up you mangy cur."

I stood but kept my dagger at his spine as we walked. He'd be even more crippled if he tried a double cross. As usual, the goblin's machinations made my head spin.

We neared a giant flower structure, where a squad of EEPs stood guard. I wanted to know more before we went in there. "You didn't need Gas for any of this, did you?" I whispered. "Why did you enlist him, and what are we walking into?"

"Gas likes to feel valuable, and I wanted him to witness the birth we're about to see with his own eyes. It will keep his side focused on our mutual interests."

"What is his side...?" I began, but then the 'birth' part I was about to ask about next became shockingly obvious.

The flower structure spasmed, its petals curling up and falling off, so that the surrounding elf soldiers ran for cover. A few were caught beneath the giant petals but managed to crawl out to safety. The goblin kept us at a distance.

"How did you know it would do that?" I asked.

"Wait. It's not over."

The green body of the flower swelled, looking like a rosehip, but with golden veins spreading through the flesh, the liquid inside pulsing and bubbling faster and faster. With my soul sense, I could see it glow brighter, until it was almost blinding, and then it burst.

I ducked instinctively, which was smart, as plant goo mixed with a golden liquid that smelled like honey covered me from head to foot, other than the small part of my body blocked by Doctor Heltune. He got the brunt of it, but he smiled.

"Wondrous," he said.

"You've seen this before?" I asked, shaking off goo. At least my skin was well moisturized.

"Once, in the experimental stages. Now, we witness the full culmination of King Fharen's vision. He has an intriguing imagination, but it his skill, or that of his subordinates, in the biological sciences that I wish to understand and one day emulate. What he has achieved boggles the mind."

What Fharen had 'achieved' was obvious moments later when the first person climbed out of the remains of the flower. Only ... it wasn't a person anymore.

The man was human once, but now he was infused with golden veins, his skin green and fibrous, plant tendrils shifting over his body and face. His eyes were gone, leaving empty sockets, black and cavernous. I watched with horror as a yellow flower bloomed inside. One bloom after another, until it was a creature that was looking at me and not a human at all. Even his soul ... no, his soul was in there still. Trapped, battling a glowing soul of ancient power. The plant was at war with the slave, and the plant was winning.

"By the gods," I said, feeling like I would throw up. "We have to set him free ... set them all free." More people were climbing out of the gore, thousands of them. Other flowers were bursting around the encampment as well, one after another. This was Fharen's new army?

"We are not here to set them free," the goblin said, bemused by my concern. "I believe the intention is they will free us from the shadow of the 'Dead God' as you like to call him. These armies are a match for his insane horde. I am completely in agreement with that plan, as is my Emperor, but we do like to take the long view. My concern is what Fharen will do with this army when he's done. Easy enough for him to defeat what remains of the known world and become but another conqueror. My job, my dear, is to find out how these things work and how to stop them. But only when the time is right."

"How they work? They are an abomination. The creation of some ancient creature long buried beneath layers of stone and sediment..." I could see it all from my contact with the plant's soul. It looked like many separate buds and flowers, thousands of separate slaves turned walking plant, but it was all one creature. "Fharen has awoken something he should not, for it is not his to control. Instead, this creature takes the marked souls of the enslaved and leashes them to it. They belong to it now, and only their plant master will they obey."

The goblin stared at me, mouth agape. I too was shocked by the unusual poetic lilt to my words, but I think it was the plant influencing me. I shook off my connection to it, for I felt that if it became aware of me, I would not enjoy the result.

"You surprise me as often as I surprise you, my dear," the goblin said. "Other than your primitive ideas of souls, rather than biochemical energy, I believe you are on to something. Where did you get your information?"

"I can't say." If he didn't believe in souls, he wouldn't believe in my ability to read them, and the plant's was so strong, like Harbinger's, it was almost impossible not to read. It was like the polar lights blazing across the horizon for all to see if they would only look to those far places.

Damn, being poetic again. I shivered.

"I see. You have your sources, I have mine. I must investigate this centrally controlling entity then. You may have discovered the key to taming these creatures when the time is right."

"You promised to take me to Fharen. All I care about right now is the relic." I cared about the slaves too, but one bad guy at a time. They were already piling up and outnumbering me: The Dead God, Harbinger, Fharen, the plant, Gas ... the list went on and on to the point I'd go mad if I thought about more than the next step I needed to take.

"Don't you want—?"

"—No. Fharen. Now."

"He will be overseeing the birth. He will recognize you."

"I'm counting on it."

Fharen's forces had tripled in size thanks to the 'births' from those monstrous flowers. I was disturbed by Fharen more than ever before, not because I knew he wanted to torture and use me, or because we were in the middle of an army that he might well turn on Highcrowne next. It was the nature of that army. He had done this, to people. I now understood how malevolent Fharen truly was.

For their part, the plant-enslaved humans had traded one evil, if recognizable, master for another sort of evil all together. An impersonal evil. Where before their identities were smothered by the mark their elvish masters placed on them, now even their inmost thoughts were another's. And that 'other' did not think as we did. The golden fluid running through their veins whispered of green places with endless sunlight, rich soil, and nothing that walked, flew, or crawled to eat their leaves or steal their fruit. The plant desired nothing but to clear away all things in the path of its growth. Lili's army was only the first obstacle to be destroyed.

Even before the doctor led me to Fharen's travelling palace, I knew we were in the right spot. I'd felt the controlling soul in the slaves grow stronger as we neared the structure. The heart of the plant was here. I could feel it. I didn't tell the goblin, not because I couldn't pinpoint its location, although I suspected it was somewhere underground, but because he would lose focus again. *One enemy at a time*, I repeated.

I took off the slave's collar and leash the goblin had given me and decided on a new tactic. "Fharen!" I called from across the sea of soldiers and courtiers that surrounded him.

His throne was perched on a large balcony that protruded like a gold-encrusted wart from the mobile palace. And it was a palace, despite being smaller than his usual one: Same opulent décor, silk hangings, carved alabaster and oak furniture. Only difference was the strong, steel walls instead of stone. The huge structure was carried on the back of a mechanical contraption the size of twenty wagons. Its metal treads were as tall as me and moved of their own accord, tearing into the soil as it crept forward like a guest trying to make a polite exit from a dull dinner party. Chimneys high above coughed and spluttered black smog so loudly no one at the far edges of the gathering could have heard me speak. I'm not sure Fharen did either, but he saw me, and with a gesture the engine shut off and everything went quiet.

"Ilsa's sister," he said. "Whatever your name was. And Doctor Heltune. Is it to you whom I owe the reward for her capture?"

"You owe me," I said. "I'm here of my own free will. I've changed my mind and want to help you unleash the full power of the First S—"

He cut me off before I could speak the relic's name. "Clean her up and bring her to my rooms."

The quiet ended then as the courtiers went back to their usual chatter. Let them think me another concubine. Doctor Heltune looked like he might battle the EEP soldiers who came for me.

I whispered, "Wait for me with Ernest. I will find you later. I will get out of here."

"Miss Thorne, I protest. As a gentleman, I cannot leave you."

"You have before and worse. Pretend you're the heartless slave hunter now if that makes you feel better. I will see you at midnight."

If I didn't have the First Soul by then, I wouldn't be coming back. The sun was nearly gone, so it didn't leave much time.

As EEP soldiers roughly dragged me, unnecessary roughness I might add, to the baths, I watched Fharen. He had no clue Hilja and Prince Gallan were plotting to take over his capital. He had even less of a clue about what he had just unleashed on the world.

New plant soldiers paraded before him, bowing, but I knew it was not to the king they showed deference but to the entity buried in the soil somewhere beneath his feet.

And growing larger on the horizon of a distant hill was the black fog of my mother's army.

17   A Clash of Leaf and Claw

Lili did not wait until dawn to attack.

I sat in Fharen's silken bedchamber, prettied up and pretty smelling. The servants had despaired at the dead, gray flesh of my left hand, which no amount of scrubbing could fix. They were even more disturbed when it moved—I had full control now with barely any concentration required—because it made a cracking sound like dried twigs. In the end they gave me long gloves that complemented the black lace negligée that barely covered my private parts. I had inherited Nanny's sense of decorum, and it took force of will to lounge in the bedchamber in such unseemly fashion. But I was ready to say whatever, maybe even do whatever, to get my hands on the First Soul.

I waited. And waited. Fharen didn't show. Just as I'd decided to break down the door keeping me here and go looking for him, I heard shouts.

"Get in here and wait." The commanding tone was that of an EEP, but the person who unbolted the door and walked in certainly wasn't.

"Aylon?" I said, surprised to see the priest of Fortune here of all places.

Seneschal Ernest was with him, and my first thought was, *Where in all the hells is my sword?*

"Lady Ilsa?" Ernest asked.

I felt uncomfortable with that mistake, but I did look like her now, dressed, or semi-dressed, to the nines and ready to beguile my way to what I wanted. I pulled out the shiv I'd made from a broken goblet as part of my Plan B—you don't want to know where I had that hidden—and said, "No. It's Eva. What's happening out there?"

"Bedlam," Ernest, said, shaking his head.

"It is Our Lord's coming." The priest smiled and looked like he expected me to be as excited as he was. "I hope I can be a suitable vessel."

"Vessel?" I barely got the word out before a roar of engine deafened us and the floor shifted. The mobile palace was on the move again. I stepped closer to Aylon so he could hear me over the rumbling machine. "Thane? Is that you?"

"Not as yet. I live in hope of serving again, mistress," Aylon said.

"No use waiting. We won't be seeing Thane," I said. I'd driven him away. Although, Thane might have had some useful information about what was happening out there now. At least that's how I explained the twinge of disappointment I felt.

"How were you captured?" I finally asked. "And where's Conrad?"

"I failed," the priest said, his excitement suddenly quashed. "I tried to keep them from taking him, but I was struck and left for dead." He turned around to show me the large, bloody scab on the back of his skull. He was lucky to be alive.

"Where's Conrad?" I repeated. I couldn't leave him in Fharen's dungeon again.

"Our guide turned on us."

Aguragas. Of course. He never planned to honor our bargain.

"I followed your route and found the seneschal. I felt I must inform you immediately, mistress," he added, like he expected punishment.

I was angry, but it was all my fault. "I'll have to deal with Conrad's kidnapping later. Gas will keep him alive as leverage." One villain at a time.

"And you?" I shot at Ernest, wondering what other bad news awaited. "Have you changed sides again? Are you loyal to Fharen or to your people?"

"I did not intend to stand outdoors all night watching the horses, not when there is a fine palace here. ...All we need do is clear it of imperialists and make way for the people!" He smiled. "I'm here to get you out." He pulled my Ashur from the folds of his robe, and I could have kissed him.

I did give him a hug after I dropped my shiv. I drew the ancient Solhan blade, and the sense of security it gave me is hard to explain. I was ready to take on whatever stood in my way.

"Where's Fharen?" I asked.

"Most likely in the command chamber atop this palace," Ernest said. "The Elven Protectorate are concerned with attack from without, so now is our opportunity to attack from within."

"Perfect distraction," I said. "Come on."

I took down the guard outside with a savage knock to the head with the hilt of my Ashur. I felt his soul laying there, vulnerable, and a pang of hunger gripped me. I reached out for it but pulled back. Somehow, despite the Compact, the presence of the Dead God was growing stronger, and with it my own power. My own thirst for souls.

I shook off the desire and kept moving, disabling EEP after EEP as we made our way towards the command area. Ernest and the priest got in a few good whacks as well.

The seneschal was right that most of the EEPs were looking outward for danger, literally. The elvish soldiers aimed crossbows and heavier armament, such as giant mangonels with enchanted arrows the size of javelins, through slits in the metal walls of the palace. They fired again and again, with an air of desperation.

I heard something like the scrabble of claws on a tin roof and knew Gypsum's werewolves had reached us. So much for Fharen's new army. I could have told you flowers didn't stand a chance against fang and claw. Then again, the scrabble of claws was followed by yelps and howls of pain, so maybe the plant slaves were putting up a fight.

"This way," Ernest said.

He led us up a spiral staircase to a domed chamber at the top of the mechanized palace. We crouched on the last steps, so as not to be seen, but I could see plenty. The dome curved from floor to ceiling and was crystal, or something like it, allowing us to observe the surrounding battlefield through it. In every direction was war.

The golden blood of the plant slaves sprayed from their wounds, and the red blood of dwarf turned werewolf lay in puddles around furry carcasses that bubbled as though coated with acid. I saw tendrils shoot out from a plant warrior that stopped a werewolf mid charge and left it a twitching heap in the bloody mud. The wolf's body swelled, bloated, and finally ruptured, oozing the acid the plant had injected into it.

The werewolves had penetrated Fharen's outer defenses in scores of places, elven sentinels no match for their preternatural speed, but there was a traditional war happening at the periphery.

Columns of armored dwarves, those not able to change form, perhaps, or those not yet converted by the dwarven crown Gypsum had stolen from the Void, marched on an outer ring of elven formations. The elves there remained disciplined, despite the wolf incursions behind them.

Fharen's forces dug in. Mages called up walls made of thorns or fire or ice, depending on their specialty, creating inward and outward facing defenses. They were fighting two fronts at once.

The werewolves, or whatever power commanded them, was aware the mages were the true danger. The attack on the mobile palace suddenly ceased, the wolves a blur as they seemed to almost vanish and reappear around the mage towers. The structures were on treads, like the palace, and equally fortified, the only difference being a sheltered platform at the top where mages stood to gain a clear view of the battle. Shields made of light deflected fire arrows shot from the dwarven lines. I noted no magic came from the dwarves to combat it. Mages were rare among their kind, but I didn't know why Lili held back. Perhaps the Compact curtailed some of her magic as well? If her power came from the Dead God, that might explain it.

The wolves were a formidable weapon though, and where they touched the mage shields, the magic fizzled. Their claws scrambled for purchase on the iron, but they failed to climb up to where the elves desperately cast ice and fire down on them, the magic turning to water around them. It was a stalemate. One quickly broken by conventional means.

Elven archers rained arrows on the wolves, not caring if they hit the plant slaves as well, but it was the plants who drove the wolves back from the mage's defenses. Catapults fired what looked like the after-birth of the giant flowers: chunks of pod that oozed golden liquid that now smelled of acid instead of honey. The golden missiles melted through armor or fur, and wherever they struck, rows of dwarves were decimated.

Lili's and Gypsum's forces had their own catapults, however, and they flung balls of flaming pitch or heavy stones at the defenders, crumbling the archers' formations. They must have gotten an idea from the elves, because they followed up with missiles made of their own creations. Wolves were shot at the mage towers, and this time their claws found purchase in the flesh of the mages themselves. Moments later, all the barriers they'd erected crumbled, and the dwarven army pressed in.

"Get us out of here!" I heard Fharen's order on the loudspeaker, and I had a sudden memory of *The*

Mathésis in chaos from the attack of only one wolf. There was an army of them out there.

The mobile palace jerked, nearly knocking me off my feet, and went into high gear. Only, we weren't headed away from Lili's lines but towards them.

"You're headed the wrong way," Fharen shouted. I heard his voice more clearly through the nearest speaker, but it was preceded by his real voice, coming from deeper within the domed chamber. I spotted him, ensconced on yet another throne, this one at the center of the room where he could see the battle outside and send instructions through the bullhorn positioned before him. His eyes were on Lili's army only, and he did not seem aware of us creeping up on him.

"They're inside!" the voice of the driver screeched through the speakers before abruptly cutting off. The palace, instead of offering safety, was slowly trundling toward the heart of the enemy.

The chaos in the command center was matched by the chaos without. Forces embraced in a maelstrom of fighting that was hard to follow. Spearmen, axe men and sword wielders clanged blade to armor and sometimes into soundless flesh. Horsemen harried the flanks, looking for a way to break the dwarf regiments' formations. It was pandemonium. And, far at the edge of the horizon, I saw a black banner with a white-winged skull. The symbol of the Dead God. My mother's banner.

EEPs spotted us on the staircase, so I couldn't waste time taking in the sights anymore. They closed on Ernest, the priest and me. I didn't know if I could count on any of the others in a fight, but I had my blade drawn, and I knew I could count on it.

I cut the first EEP that got too close, and the other three drew weapons and took a wary stance. The one I'd wounded had to use one hand to staunch the bleeding from his other, and so he had no hands to fight with. I liked that tactic, so I went for fingers and wrists, dancing between elvish blades as I did.

And I was hungry.

Could it have been the sight of that symbol out there on the battlefield that thrilled me? Did Lili carry the presence of the Dead God with her in some way? All I knew was, I felt strong and unstoppable. Two more EEPs lost minor body parts, and as they tried to staunch the blood—Ernest watching in horror and the priest of Fortune benevolently going to their aid—the final EEP backed toward Fharen.

Checkmate. Not that I was good at chess, but I could recognize a cornered king.

Fharen seemed not to have heard the clash of my steel over the sounds of battle outside. He was on his knees, whispering something frantically under his breath. The sight of Death's banner filled him with an entirely different feeling than it did me. He was terrified.

The battle was louder and closer, whole regiments of elves collapsing in on themselves as the force Lili and Gypsum brought to bear crushed them. Only the plant slaves held a circle around us, like poisoned ground where no weed could take root. But they hadn't stopped something from getting inside. I heard screams echo from metal walls. Something was coming up behind us.

There were twice as many unopened flowers dotting the landscape. If they had 'ripened', releasing their creations, the tide of battle might have turned. The elves could have won. But Lili had struck too fast, and most of the pods were immature. Fharen's new army of golden-blooded creatures were slowly rent apart one by one. Coordinated packs of wolves were as patient and unrelenting as any normal pack harrying a lone sheep. There were many packs and fewer plants. In the short time I'd fought to reach the Elf King, the fortunes on the battlefield outside had shifted dramatically.

I felt a pang for the human slaves who had suffered first at the hands of slavers, and then from Fharen's experiments. Now they endured the savaging of wolves. Not only had I not saved them, had not stopped their suffering—I was the cause of it. Lili was coming for me.

"Get up," I told the Elf King. "Stop your whimpering and do something to stop what's happening for once. Give me the First Soul."

I wanted to add, 'or I'll take it from your corpse', but that would be my least favorite part of me talking. The power I felt coursing through me could make me start thinking a bit like Gypsum or even Lili if I let it. The flutter of EEP souls fighting for their lives after being savaged by my blade were tempting enough, let alone the sea of souls outside ready to be harvested.

There was so much power all around me, but even a taste, even one death by my hand, would quickly turn into more than a taste. I would gorge myself on darkness and be unable to return, or even remember the light.

I took a deep breath, cleaned and put away my Ashur, then stood unarmed before Fharen.

Calmly, I repeated: "Give me the First Soul."

"Promise you'll save me from them," he demanded. Even begging on his knees, he demanded.

Something snarled nearby, and the EEPs I'd spared died behind me.

Ernest and the priest hovered at the edge of my vision, their gasps and terrified whimpers telling me all I needed to know about the werewolf advancing on us.

Fharen looked ready to plead some more, holding out his hands to me, a diamond-like gem resting in his cupped palms. "Don't say a word." I warned. I couldn't stomach the sound of his voice.

I reached for the black miasma, the cloud in my soul sight that told me the First Soul was in Fharen's hand. It was like feeling for a stone in the murky blackness of ocean silt, so hard to see the object for the darkness it shone on the world. I could tell it longed for me, for the sweet words of love and acceptance I would offer it, but I was so far away. So far.

It wasn't here at all.

"Where is it?" I hissed, drawing my blade once more. Another glamour. Another deception.

"I would never bring it here, to the thick of battle for Lili of Solheim to take," Fharen said, as though I were simple. "I gave it to my good and trusted friend for safekeeping. And even now I cannot fault Count Bram's counsel."

"You gave it to Harbinger?"

I was so furious my snarl was a match for that of the wolf. I sensed it leap, and I spun, lashing out with both Ashur and green claws of magic. In one strike, I cut off its head and tore out its soul.

It might have been a dwarf once. Maybe even someone I knew. I didn't look at the headless and naked corpse that fell at my feet to see if he possessed Reginald's eyes or Bert's permanent scowl, because I held his soul in my hand. I knew the dwarf's whole life, how he'd never left home before. How he'd never seen King Rutgard, but when Queen Gypsum came along the high street, her wolfish soldiers behind her, he felt a thrill like electricity. This is what it meant to be a dwarf. This was not a future in the mines or tending the children, this was what he was made for. Life and death and the open air. Sunshine and moonlight.

And now he was dead. The light of his soul warming the dead gray flesh of my hand. I wanted to swallow that light like I'd almost swallowed Conrad's. I wanted....

I flung the soul away from me like it was a physical thing. I sent the fake relic flying along with it. There was enough magical force behind the projectile that the dome shattered around us.

Ernest and Aylon overcame their shock enough to dive beneath Fharen's throne. The Elf King hunched over, face on the floor. I didn't even move. The glass disturbed me no more than spring rain.

Harbinger. And that foolish, foolish Fharen. Mesmerized, tricked.... But which fool was more foolish? Me of course.

My fury left me, and I suddenly felt spent. Drained.

Had I just killed a werewolf?

If not for the shattered crystal and the wind that tore through the chamber carrying the metal tang of steel, the blood and moans of those dying from the battle without, I might have thought it had all been a dream. So sudden, so ephemeral.

Poetry. Damn. I shut down my soul sense, so the plant master didn't come gunning for me too.

I'd come all this way. For nothing. Fury surged up again.

"I put this on," I indicated the negligée, even though Fharen wasn't looking at me. "Put myself in the middle of a war. All of it—so you could give the

First Soul to the one person who shouldn't have it? You tell me where Harbinger is, right now. Count Bram. Whatever you call the asshole who has my relic."

"Home. In his home, I assume." Fharen stammered. I raised my sword, and he pressed his forehead to the ground. His hand slipped in blood, and he muttered a desperate prayer over and over. "*Save me. Save me....*"

As much as I'd like to, I couldn't kill him.

"We're leaving," I said, a command in my tone that made Ernest stand to attention.

But the priest didn't stir. He gazed on the approaching army of dwarves and wolves with the same desire Harbinger had for my blood and his own power. I knew which side he was on.

"Stay here," I told him. "When you meet my mother, tell her hello from me. If she leaves you alive. And tell my friend ... tell Queen Gypsum she has another Crown to share her tea with now." I nudged Fharen with the tip of my boot, and the petrified elf toppled over as though he were truly petrified. His mouth gaped like a fish, his eyes staring at nothing, while a faint chant still streamed over his lips.

I saw what he had scratched into the wood and blood with manicured fingernails that were now cracked and broken. The winged skull symbol of the Dead God.

"Changing sides so soon?" I asked. "Or are you bargaining for your life? That's not Death's domain. I thought you were confident in your new army, in your Elven Protectorate, in your iron rule? Reap what you sow," I said it like a curse, and it was an old Solhan one Nanny had uttered from time to time.

I turned away, forgetting the king I had despised and blamed for all the ills of Highcrowne, seeing him now as the pathetic grasper he really was.

Then he said my name in a certain way: "Eva."

I froze. "Thane?"

Fharen stood, and it wasn't Fharen anymore. There were the same suave, blonde looks and gaudy clothing, the stench of perfume, but he changed when Thane possessed him. His cruel features lost their tightness and smiled in a way the elf had never managed. His eyes sparkled with new life, with a new soul.

"He's still in here," Thane assured me. "But his prayer to the Dead God found me instead. I will save his life and that of all the remaining elves I can. I can help you too."

"Let Fharen get the death he deserves. And I told you to stay away from me."

"I must make amends." Thane didn't wait for my next protest, because he must have known what I'd say.

He rushed past the awed priest and pushed Ernest out of the way to reach the bullhorn. "Pass down the order," he said over the loudspeaker. "Retreat to Illul Faellion. You will place yourself under the command of Princess Hilja alone and make your stand there. Go!"

The bullhorn must have been augmented by magic to reach the commanders in the field, for I saw even the most distant elf troops suddenly form up. They had renewed vigor as they formed defensive shells and slowly retreated toward the mobile palace. Archers and catapults renewed their efforts, covering the retreat of the foot soldiers, before they too slowly fell back.

"We should go now," Thane said. He had borrowed Fharen's tone of undisputed command.

"What are you doing?"

"Helping you in any way I can."

My stubborn reflex almost made me stay, but that was insane. I looked at the hated face of Fharen, golden skin and hair, cruel beauty, now transformed with a new expression and another soul burning behind his eyes. If I weren't still so angry with Thane, I might have said something else, it was hard not to when he looked at me that way, but all I did was nod.

"I will remain behind," the priest said, "and relay your message to Lili of Solheim as commanded."

"And you, Ernest?"

The seneschal picked up a fallen EEP's weapon. "My people are here. I will fight and help as best I can." He seemed frightened of the sword in his hand, but then a determined look settled over his features.

Humans weren't his people, and neither were Solhans. I nodded and said, "Save as many as you can. This war is far from over."

I set off down the stairs with Thane. He knew the maze-like corridors of the mobile palace as well as Fharen did. Only, it was no longer mobile. Its engines had stopped. Carnage everywhere. Few had survived after the werewolf penetrated the defenses. Once again, I thought of *The Mathésis* and remembered that feeling of being trapped.

I pushed Thane. "Go faster."

We exited through a trapdoor on the bottom level. Massive metal tracks and wheels hid us from view, but I saw the legs of the retreating elf forces. A blur smashed into one group, and soldiers fell. The werewolf paused long enough to tear out a soldier's throat, and it looked at me then with glowing silver eyes.

I reached out for its soul, as I'd practiced so many times with Reginald, and I molded it like clay, forcing it into a new shape. The wolf yelped as it was suddenly made dwarf again. He was so startled he had no time to defend himself from the elf soldiers who slaughtered him in revenge.

"I have horses in the hills west of here." I told Thane. "Count Bram's castle is in the mountains to the north. We skirt this army and go after him."

"As you command, Eva."

"Stop saying my name." I didn't know why it bothered me so much, but Fharen had never remembered it, and the way Thane spoke it was too intimate. "I'm only keeping you around as long as you're helpful."

I stood up and faced the next blur of werewolves who attacked. I shifted all three back at once, and they lay in the muddy battlefield helpless and naked.

"In fact, I'm not sure I need you," I added.

The standard regiments opened fire then and arrows rained down. Thane grabbed an EEPs shield and raised it over both our heads. Then he vanished.

I ducked, fearing the shield had vanished as well, but the rain of arrows continued to avoid us. I reached out and felt cloth, silk, and the hard shape of a flexed bicep.

"Nice trick," I said.

Invisible fingertips touched my cheek, and I flinched. I could see him then.

"We're both hidden now," he said. "I can be helpful."

I'd never noticed the flecks of green and purple in Fharen's eyes before. Thane's eyes now.

I tore a golden cloak from a dead soldier—the negligee was a bit chilly—and wrapped it around my shoulders.

"I might keep you around a little while longer. Keep up." I set off without a backward glance.

18   The Hunt

I'd like to say I ran the whole way, but stamina isn't one of my strengths. It was more a series of short sprints interspersed with gasps. Thane kept up. Damn him.

We reached the hill where I'd left the horses, expecting them to have run off, what with Ernest having abandoned his post, but the doctor was there waiting. He yelped when Thane dropped the invisibility glamour and we appeared out of what seemed like thin air.

"Miss Thorne?"

"For the millionth time, it was magic, a glamour," I told the goblin.

"Are you saying that explains the mysterious disappearance of your clothing? Why are you naked?"

I clutched the cloak tighter. "I'm not naked. It's lingerie. Give me my pack already."

Gas had outfitted us when we were in his camp, and I had a change of clothing in my saddle bags. Pants, thank the gods! I relished the soft silk on my legs. I didn't even complain about the tight white blouse cut for an elf. It was still more seemly than lace. While unbearably hot during the day, Faellion grew chilly at night, especially when you were 'naked'.

"Aren't you the least bit curious how we managed invisibility?" I asked the goblin.

"Fungus, my dear. Fungus."

"My feet are fine," I insisted.

Thane looked confused, but I wasn't about to explain. I gave the doctor a sour look and mounted up.

The first thing I realized once I was sitting a horse—and don't get me started about how awful smelling and uncomfortable the damn things are—was that I wasn't sure where to go. I could sense the direction of the First Soul now that Fharen's glamour over the fake one was dispelled. It was headed north, to the mountains, but there was a lot of north and a lot of mountains to search.

Perhaps my quid pro quo arrangement with the goblin could be even more useful to me.

"Seems we're now hunting the same creature," I told him, our horses walking sedately side by side as they awaited direction. "Harbinger now has what's mine. You will help me track him down. We must find his lair."

"Is that the Elf King astride Seneschal Ernest's horse, my lady?'

Seemed the goblin was reluctant to discuss his hobby in front of Fharen.

"No. He just looks like him. You've met Thane before, but you knew him as Conrad then. Thane, this is Doctor Ghunnan. Doctor, this is the Dead God—sort of."

"Hello again, Doctor," Thane said. "I'm glad you escaped the cave in. I found your lectures as we travelled quite engaging and look forward to this next journey."

The goblin blanched then shook his head, muttering "Fungus" again.

Thane. I seemed as drawn to thinking his name as he was to saying mine.

Thane had possessed King Fharen. Another Crown had fallen to the Dead God. Unless he was telling the truth, and he really was on my side? I realized I believed him now. Else I wouldn't have left him conscious or given him a horse. There'd been too many chances to kill me, and he hadn't taken any of them.

Believing Thane was something other than my arch enemy was one thing. Trusting him was another. And forgiving him something else again.

He looked at me, as though he knew I was thinking about him. "If it will make you more comfortable, I can drop the glamour Fharen usually maintains," Thane said.

Suddenly, the blonde locks were gone, replaced with pure black hair that was straight and long. His nose was sharper and his skin paler, although not as pale as mine. Fharen had Solhan blood I recalled, thus his interest in reclaiming the long-lost Solhan empire. Elves, however, were distasteful of 'impure' bloodlines, so Fharen never revealed his true lineage. I'd only learned of it when I caught him and Ilsa unaware in a private moment.

I wasn't entirely sure I was more comfortable with Thane in this guise, as I couldn't help remembering Fharen's nakedness in that moment.

The doctor shrugged. "Very well. Let us call this the start of a new mission, and so a change in appearance is not uncalled for." He deactivated the device at his waist and was all goblin again, no more elf disguise. He looked me squarely in the eyes and said, "I have absolutely no idea where we can find Harbinger."

"Something led you to Faellion. You told me so yourself, that you were using your 'duties' for the goblin emperor to help your plague research. Some clue must have drawn you?"

"It was actually the Elf King's experiments on the slaves that drew me, but I did catch many more rumors of Harbinger here than anywhere else. They were all nonsense about giant bat forms flying through the night, but from time to time a farmer would lose a whole crop of slaves. Like wolves prowling on the sheep, something here hunted and fed on humans. Mostly. From time to time an elf child disappeared and Harbinger was blamed. There was certainly no map to his lair in any of the legends."

"Well, Count Bram's residence is somewhere in those mountains, and I have an irresistible feeling the relic is headed there too."

"Count Bram. From dinner?" The goblin was discombobulated again. "What does he have to do with this?"

"He's Harbinger."

"This is wonderful! We have a chance to find this illusive proto-Solhan and get the answers I need."

"We're going to kill him." I said grinding my teeth, a bad habit I'd picked up of late.

"Oh, yes that's fine. All I need is a blood sample first. Or after."

We continued picking our way across the darkened landscape, the sounds of battle having died down and the ocean of campfires at our backs grew farther away.

I didn't want to stop until we were far from Lili's army. I couldn't count on Thane's glamour throwing them off our scent. He seemed to have acquired all Fharen's skill, but I couldn't rely on him for many reasons. My mother was too determined to kill me, and

Gypsum had an army of bloodhounds (or was it *werehounds?)* to help track me down.

Fortunately, the moons were bright enough to light the horses' way, and the goblin chattered so excitedly about our destination there was no sign he needed any sleep. I didn't. Anger fueled me.

"I can see into your soul. I know you don't want me here," Thane said.

"What I want doesn't matter. I'm starting to figure that out. There are more lives at stake right now. I need what Harbinger stole. With it I can set everything right."

"Lili cannot harm me. I will go back and delay her, buy you time." Thane turned his horse and was off before I could speak.

"Damn." I cantered after him and grabbed for his reigns. I almost fell off and swore again. "Stop already!"

"Why? I see now how I can be of most use—and stay away from you. I don't want to cause you more pain."

"Like I said, what I want doesn't matter. I need you to hide the doctor and me from Harbinger. He can supposedly sniff a blood trail from miles away, so I'm hoping your glamour and noxious elf perfume will prevent that."

"What makes you think the First Soul is the answer to all ills?" he asked.

"It … tells me things. Am I wrong? You said you didn't know how to send the Dead God back. Were you lying?"

"No, I don't know how. And it is a powerful artifact, so you may well be right. *It* may be right. But I have also heard tell of its corrupting influence. I worry for you, Eva."

He said my name in that certain way again, and I shivered.

"Don't." I turned back to join the goblin doctor who'd been steadily plodding along, talking about the life cycle of jollups without an audience. "You coming?" I prompted Thane.

He looked at me, looked into me more like it, for his gaze ignored my eyes and even my cleavage, which had been Fharen's favorite view before, and went deeper.

"You do need me," he said.

When he was alongside again, I shot, "I don't."

The goblin said, "…and, of course, you can't find them in Highcrowne anymore. The elves hunting for appetizers was one thing, but now with the survivors trying to fatten up and survive the coming winter, there's not a jollup left below zeppelin altitudes."

The doctor's ramblings sunk in, and I asked, "Who is eating all the jollups? Refugees?"

"Everyone. They starve the workers in the camps, so they'll climb, risking arrows, and snatch the low ones out of the air. I fear jollups in that region of the High Peaks may go extinct, and nowhere else do they have those distinct purple streaks around their periphery. A shame."

"Wait. Workers starving? Who is starving them and shooting arrows?"

"Elves. Haven't you heard a word?"

"No," I admitted. "Olyve, my godmother, told me that in the weeks I was gone everything has changed. And Uncle Ulric hinted ... he hinted at terrible things happening in Highcrowne."

"Indeed," the goblin said. "Poor jollups."

"Forget the blasted jollups. Tell me about the people."

"Well, after you pushed Rutgard into the Void between doorways—I do believe that memory is not too clouded by hallucinogenic mushroom spores—and vanished through the doorway yourself, the rest of us dug our way out and returned to a familiar Highcrowne. For a time. Duty called me elsewhere, and when next I passed through that city, things were much changed. Gypsum had declared herself Dwarf Queen and ruled from Gernwold, so that all remaining dwarves were either imprisoned as spies or fled to her banner."

"Bert and Reginald," I whispered.

"Probably in Fharen's work camp. He rounded up all the humans for his slave army and put the dwarves to work as slaves in their stead. Very topsy-turvy."

"What? All the humans?" My family? My friends? The whole Outskirts?

"Hyperbole. I apologize. No, not all. Some are still crucial workers, and many are in hiding or fled, but I daresay a fair score of them were earmarked for his new army. I followed those shipments here."

"We must free them," Thane said. "This troubles Eva greatly."

I didn't like him reading my soul … or trying to please me. But I was troubled. More than troubled, furious.

"It's too late, Your Majesty. I mean, Thane. Whatever your name is. Those people are changed irrevocably." The goblin shook his head with the same disappointment he'd expressed when telling us about the plight of jollups.

"You don't know that," I cut in. "You said you didn't know how the transformation worked."

"I do know that I captured a specimen from an early trial, and it perished when taken too far from its pod. Perhaps it was immature. Nevertheless, in the time it was alive, I could see no way to extract the plant from the person. They had become intermingled at the most fundamental level."

"Uncle was alive. I spoke to him in my dream," I said, grasping for hope. He was powerful and crafty, and if he was alive, he'd see to it that Viktor, Morgan, and Nanny were protected as well.

Duane too had an uncanny survival instinct. He would look out for Bell and Kali.

It was Karolyne I worried about the most. She tended to be in the thick of things.

All those people.... We had to find a way to save them, somehow. But...

One evil at a time, I reminded myself.

Like the slave girl I'd knocked unconscious in Faellion. Freeing the people transformed into plants would not help, not when they faced certain death from Lili's army or the Risen hordes. It was short-sighted. I was done with that. I would focus on the big picture and sort out the mess later.

The First Soul lay ahead. I needed to kick Harbinger's ass and get on with things.

"You want to redeem yourself?" I told Thane. "Then get me to Harbinger undetected. I don't need any more pointless chivalry. I need allies."

Thane hardened his lips. "I am that. But I know you, Eva. I have watched you all your life. This is not you."

"I'll forget how creepy that sounds and simply tell you that nobody knows me, not even me. Just try and keep up." I spurred my horse on.

I thought about leaving them both behind and facing Harbinger alone, but that was my old self talking. Time to be strategic, use the assets at hand, and come out victorious for once. But no sentimentality, no 'friends' like Gypsum.

There was no relying on enemies or allies. They could always surprise or disappoint. But I could count on me—as long as I was willing to face pain.

We travelled the whole night, pausing to gulp water from the river we followed into the hills. Dawn began with a gray light on the horizon, and with it, the smoke of soldiers' fires in the valley below became visible, hovering over the plain like a fog.

"Thane." I hated saying his name aloud. Not because I hated him, that would have been alright, but because of how intimate it felt. "Tell me what my mother will do with her army. You served her. Or did she serve you?"

"I was ... apart from Lili. Even from myself, the Dead God. You understand?"

I nodded. I was getting this 'Thane was the Dead God and yet not' stuff now. He was more like a grown up with vague memories of his childhood, a copy of the Dead God who had taken a different path. I would never have understood if I hadn't been peering into people's souls of late. I knew those people intimately, were them, and yet were not them. It was weird.

"I reported in from time to time, but most of my years were spent abroad, hunting down Lili's enemies to fulfill our pact, or waiting for Ulric to make a mistake. To leave you unprotected. Do I have to talk about this...?"

"I was there when you tried to kill me, so skip to the stuff about my mother."

"Lili was pitiless. She wanted you dead as soon as Ulric's protections were removed."

"When I was released from my soul jar?" I shivered at that image. I'd lived with my soul extracted ... explained all the restless confusion of my early years.

"Yes. Your death would release the Dead God, but she forgot that the pact involved a wedding and required an admission of love on your part. Which I obtained. As Erick."

"Hey, I didn't say I loved him, you. There was no vow. Besides what married couple is in love?"

"Pacts such as this have specific rules."

Unmentionables talked a lot about rules too. Should I learn them? Now, that really didn't sound like me.

"And I judged what you felt in your soul, not what crossed your lips," he added.

"You can do that?" Of course, he could. If I could, so could he. Why did that make me suddenly nervous? Best to change the subject.

"And my mother? Focus." I used a hurry up gesture, as my initial automatic foot tapping made the horse neigh, and I didn't want to be thrown.

"The point is, Lili is impatient for your death and her full reward. I am certain your mother will attack

Illul Faellion if she thinks there's any chance you are there."

"Do you think she can sense the First Soul is headed towards the mountains? Will she follow it and us?"

"I can vaguely sense its dark presence, so she may eventually. Yet, even if she and her servants pursue, the bulk of her army will remain here to ravage Faellion before moving on. I've known your mother long enough to know she wants everything and will not allow anything she desires to slip her grasp."

"So, my uncle is the nice one in the family?" Maybe even Ilsa had a charming disposition in comparison. "Well, if we keep moving, we may get the relic before she even senses it and follows. Let's hope for a head start." This time I did spur my horse, which tended to slip into a lazy walk when left to its own devices, and cantered along the dirt road we'd been following.

As the known dangers diminished with distance, the unknown dangers ahead loomed over me like the mountains. They were huge and jagged, volcanic formations grown atop an ancient range of eroded foothills that had once held Avian kind in vast numbers. Those birds were near extinct now, and their ancient lands claimed by elves and other invaders.

Thane hung back while I stayed alone in the front, until our destination drew nearer, at which point I slowed to ride alongside the goblin. His metal legs in the stirrups were bare and incongruous against the brown horseflesh.

"What else do you know about the vampire we're about to face?" I asked. The doctor had prattled the whole journey about one subject or another, me paying cursory attention and grunting from time to time, so he was shocked that I started a topic of conversation.

"You were the one who met him, my dear."

I'd seen into his soul too. "I know about Harbinger's desires and dreams, not his weaknesses. I assumed he's like any other vampire, but I've seen him do things I thought impossible. That black mist was impressive. Is he vulnerable to anything besides sunlight?" I recalled how much he avoided the sunshine on Ismerkel's beach. All my reading of horror tales hadn't been for naught. I knew daylight was probably the best weapon I had, but it didn't hurt to ask.

The goblin put on his thinking expression. "The legends vary. Burial at crossroads, buried face down with garlic in the mouth, decapitation, burning, hanging.... I think most means of killing will work on this so-called vampire, my dear. Garlic and daylight? I doubt they will be of much use. However, it may be an effective distraction to temporarily blind him with light while I collect my blood sample. Garlic in the eyes would sting as well."

"You're assuming you're right and he's just an ancient member of an extinct species. What if I'm right, and he's not that simple to kill?"

He laughed. "Oh, you do amuse me so. Believing in real vampires."

"There are real werewolves too. You saw them. Again."

"I find proximity to your endemic fungal spores highly entertaining. I hope I do not become addicted!"

"Humor me then. How do I best kill a vampire?"

"Very well. A 'vampire' would surely die if we destroy that which sustains it."

"Blood?"

"Precisely. Hypothetically speaking, as this is all nonsense of course. While the creature may be able to fast for long periods, if the blood within his person were contaminated, so to say, poisoned, then he must die."

"How do we feed him poisoned blood? What would poison him?"

"Is there any blood a vampire dare not devour?" the goblin asked.

"Dead blood," I said, knowing the answer immediately. "A vampire is what it eats. It needs living blood to live, and with dead blood it would be as a dead thing. Like one more in the ranks of the Dead God's army. Of course!"

"Glad to see you are pleased by the use of logic. You should try it more often, my dear. Now, for more mundane and less hypothetical concerns. How do we cross that wall?"

The road we'd been following along the river veered south, and the only path—although that was a generous term for the boulder-strewn goat trail—that led into the mountains was bisected by a stone construction. I assumed it was the wall the goblin spoke of. It looked like an ancient aqueduct to me, with two tiers of arches still intact. The river flowed beneath it, but there was a path leading through one arch.

"What are you talking about? It's not a wall." I rode up and indicated the path we should take.

The goblin shook his head and climbed down. He reached out and pounded on empty air. "It is solid brick my delusional young Solhan."

"You're the delusional one..." I began, but Thane cut in.

"It is a wall."

Was I crazy? Or the only sane person? I joined the goblin on the ground and went to step through the arch, when I hit an invisible barrier. It felt like a wall, but I saw a shimmer of green light. Then I noted the markings in the stone and the channels where thin lines of goo moved at glacial speed.

"It's Avian magic," I said.

Thane nodded. "Of course. Fharen's eyes cannot see it and neither can my soul sight. Thus, I am blind to it."

Why could I see it?

The goblin looked ready to head back.

"Wait. Give me a minute." I fished in my belt pouch and pulled out the Avian feather. Despite several underwater trips and battles, it looked none the worse for wear. I held it over my eyes and called out, "Yusha Kalal."

I saw the green shimmer vanish, but Thane and the goblin both went "Oh." Obviously the 'wall' had disappeared.

I smirked, vindicated, and led the way.

The river we'd been following narrowed but grew more turbulent as it rushed over rocks and crashed in waterfalls. The path too grew more difficult, steeper and rockier, until we had to dismount and guide the horses.

I was about to release them and worry about the escape plan later—I doubt horses would have helped when escaping a vengeful vampire, so a big part of the escape plan would be killing Harbinger before we could stroll out of here—when the path widened again.

We were in a valley, snow-capped mountains rising above us, meadows and fields of wheat stretching before us. I made out the distant outlines of one- and two-story buildings.

"A village?" I said.

The goblin adjusted his glasses, and I realized he had added an extra lens over one eye to magnify his sight. "Tumble down stone, weathered.... But the crops do look tended, so someone must dwell here."

"We should go around," Thane insisted.

"We don't know where we're going," I pointed out. "Maybe we can ask for directions."

I wasn't stupid enough to stroll down the main street, of course. We left the horses to graze and approached on foot. The goblin was obscured by the crops, but Thane and I had to crouch, slinking our way forward like predators.

The village was something from another time. Its worn buildings were almost as old as the Avian aqueduct. I spotted a few elves, so we were still in Fharen's kingdom, but there were no crystal towers. Nor were there mechanical contraptions like you'd see in Highcrowne, or magic for that matter. Water was drawn by hand from the central well, and the smithy rang with the sounds of metal on metal.

"Do you think they are criminals?" Thane asked. He pointed to a line of three young elves staked to poles in the center of the village, opposite the well. They hung their heads, resigned to their fate.

"Maybe. Or outsiders," I said. "This place looks like they've never even heard of machinery, and the lack of elven glamour to even give the place the illusion of tidiness is disturbing. Smells like fanatics on the fringe to me, certainly not a place welcoming to new ideas or newcomers."

"I will approach them to learn more." Thane stood, glamour in place and looking like Fharen all of a sudden, and only then did I realize I'd forgotten he was the Elf King. Thane could wear any body and mimic their behaviors perfectly when he wanted. It was disturbing to see.

"No," I said, pulling him back down into concealment. "I'd prefer we call on Doctor Heltune."

"Indeed. I have extensive experience in both anthropological observation and information extraction. One moment." The goblin fiddled with his belt device. It was several moments, and a few frustrated slaps to the device later, but soon the doctor was the rugged slave hunter again.

The goblin strode forward in his elf disguise, and he almost made it into town before he was spotted. He raised his arms in a gesture of surrender, but no one was aiming a weapon at him. They all scattered and hid inside the main barn, which seemed to serve as food storage and community center, or panicked and ducked into the nearest building. The goblin shrugged. He made his way to the staked-out prisoners. They weren't getting away at least.

The goblin spoke to them for some time, and a few of the braver locals peeked out of their hiding places. They ducked back in again when the doctor strode confidently down the main road to rejoin us.

"What did you find out?" I asked, dying of curiosity.

"We are in the right place. Harbinger is here. They are sacrifices for him."

"Sacrifices?"

"As best I could interpret, as my archaic elvish is a bit rusty. Their dialect is at least a thousand years old. I must tell my fellow professors with interest in linguistics about this backwards place. It is a dream. I, however, have a different dream: to finally bring my long-sought quarry to ground. The whole village is his. Harbinger's."

"What do you mean 'his'? As in part of Count Bram's lands?"

"No. They hold no delusions as to him being elven nobility. They know Harbinger as 'vampire' alone. Their superstitious dread is almost quaint, and I can well imagine the legends of Harbinger's preternatural powers might well have been spread by such simple folk as these. It explains much. Let us be on our way. I am in a hurry to finally see and study this specimen myself."

"Did they tell you where to hurry off to?"

"The one I spoke to warned us not to seek the castle on the mountain north of the village, as certain doom awaits, and none return alive from there. I do believe it is the very place we wish to go, indeed!"

"Lovely," I said, feeling the goblin's excitement was at odds with the prisoner's warning. I was not so keen to face Harbinger. All I wanted was the First Soul, and if we could steal it rather than fight for it, all the better. I needed a plan.

The trek across the valley took far too long, the sun lowering quickly with so many tall mountains crowding the horizon. We were losing the light, and we all knew it. We sprinted until the horses tired and were forced to trot or plod along after that. There was no sound but the tread of hooves, as we all considered what lay ahead.

It wasn't good when I had time to think, because it meant I had time to doubt.

How was I to fight Harbinger? Could I count on the power the First Soul might lend me when I was near enough to it? *Might* was the difficult word in that plan. Dead blood? Theories and stories. I hadn't even had time to craft wooden stakes or raid the villagers' gardens for garlic, probably because I believed they were nonsense too.

I was counting on the sun, as it was the only thing I'd seen hurt Harbinger. But there was still no sign of his castle and, assuming we could find it, we'd never make it before nightfall.

We stumbled along rocky paths and climbed up and up, eventually reaching the shore of a mountain lake. It was wide and still, its silver surface reflecting the pink clouds like a mirror.

Beautiful, and I didn't stop to soak in beauty often. Wow.

"We should camp here," the goblin said, his nose against the ground, inspecting some slime or algae that had caught his attention.

"Time is wasting," I said, impatient. Was that the outline of a castle, or a peculiarly shaped crag I saw in the distance?

"Do you want to face Harbinger in the night?" Thane asked.

I frowned, hating when I agreed with him. "Fine. But it's not safe in the middle of the trail either." The 'trail' was mostly overgrown grass, not even goats used it, but I didn't want to take any chances. I spotted some ruins that looked to be Avian, like the aqueduct and pointed. "Over there."

The ruin was half in the lake and half out, with a sheltered, windowless area where we could build a fire. I didn't need the light or the warmth. Even this high in the mountains it was balmy compared to Highcrowne, but the goblin was uncomfortable, shivering and complaining about not packing enough warm clothing.

"You want a fire, it's your responsibility," I told him. I could just picture him begging me to chop firewood with my Ashur, and that was not going to happen.

I dug out supplies and snacks from my bags, before setting the horses to graze on the cattails and tall grasses that bordered the ruin.

I went inside and tried to find a soft spot for my bedroll, but there were stones and insects everywhere I looked. Did I mention I'm not an outdoor person? Sure, Highcrowne bed bugs were nasty, but they were content in your mattress and wouldn't come crawling out often. I finally spotted a dais, raised above the overgrowth, that looked safe. There was no roof, but the clouds were high and wispy, reflecting the reds and purples of sunset, and unlikely to start spitting out rain.

From the dais I could see a stone dock, bordered by arches. The Avian structure may have been some sort of fancy boathouse or bath in its time. Hard to tell with so little of it remaining, but the overall effect was of nature framed with classical architecture. Picturesque. I didn't know why I was being plagued by notions of aesthetics, enjoying the dying day around me. Maybe because there could be other types of dying tomorrow when we went to face Harbinger.

I found some branches and started carving them into stakes with my Ashur. It felt like I was doing something at least. As pathetic as it was.

Thane set himself on the stone dock beside the lake to fish, and I did a double take. Seeing Fharen's form—the blonde elvish perfection in a silk brocade suit—with his pants rolled up and feet in the water, sporting a stick and a bait-less hook, was a strange sight. Thane was smiling, also strange.

I had an irresistible desire to know what had made him so happy, but I quashed the urge to speak to him. I couldn't trust myself around Thane.

I found the goblin, hoping to discuss more vampire-fighting theories. He had an ingenious sort of fire sparker with a small flame that instantly appeared whenever he pressed a button.

"A fire lighter like that could be useful against Harbinger," I said. "Any way we can make it bigger?"

"The fuel source is limited, and I do not have the materials at hand to refine more."

"Looks like magic to me. You're sure it's not powered by Avian goo? We could boost it if we find more in the ruins."

"It is not. If it were magic, and not a liquefied gas I personally purified from carbonaceous rock, I would have the campfire roaring already." He sparked flame after flame, but the wood wouldn't catch.

"You can build a contraption like that but can't build a fire? Here, allow me."

I grabbed some of the ubiquitous grass that was poking through cracks in the stone floor and added other small kindling, not to mention restructuring the entire stick setup he had. I waved away his offered flame and used my own fire sparker, which scratched metal against metal to generate a spark.

Once the kindling was burning well, I couldn't help asking, "You travel all around the Kingdoms and who knows where else without fire?"

"I'm usually accompanied by a student who deals with such mundane tasks. Or I stay at inns. Much more civilized."

"I see. Roughing it isn't for me either, but I'd freeze at home if I couldn't light a fireplace. Surely...?"

"I admit my theoretical understanding of fire creation falls short in practical application. Thus, the inns. And I have not been home to the warm goblin swamps in quite some time. We seldom need fires there."

"I'm missing home too. I feel like I've been away from Highcrowne far too long already. I was always itching to leave one day, but now I just want to go back."

"I daresay I would regret you being there and not here, Miss Thorne. You invariably ferret out the secrets I and my government most wish to know, and personally, I enjoy your company." The goblin adjusted his glasses and set about hunting for dinner in his pack, studiously avoiding my gaze.

"Did you say something nice to me?"

"I may have. Do not let my genuine, if modest, admiration deter you from doing that which you do best, Miss Thorne. I should not intervene in a controlled experiment, so to speak. I understand there are many variables beyond your control or mine, and we must compensate for them as best we may, and so I am here to offer whatever assistance you require. Nevertheless, I have every confidence that, left to your own devices, you will obtain the blood sample I seek as well as the relic you seek."

"So, you're saying you'll be my backup? Sweet. But I agree, I need to rely on the one thing I can control: Me."

"Perfectly summarized, my dear."

"But what if I can't control me, either?" Although we were far enough away from Thane's fishing spot, I lowered my voice. "Thane was ... betrothed to me. And I ... I need some advice, Doctor."

"Oh, my. I assumed a female family member has instructed you on such natural biological processes? However, I can provide diagrams or whatever is needed."

"I don't mean sex. I'm well versed in that. Not too well. I'm not a tramp. I mean ... it's more complicated than that. Thane says he wants me, but he's the Dead God. I feel so drawn to him I can't trust myself. Is it some spell placed on me at birth? All I know is I feel a physical pull whenever he says my name. And how I feel when he kisses me.... Is it a lie or is it true desire? How do I fight that? I don't even know why I asked him to come along. He's a weakness in judgement I can't afford to have."

"We are all weak in one way or another." He indicated the shriveled legs ensconced in a mechanized prosthetic. He unstrapped the device and breathed a relieved sigh. "Things would be much simpler if we were invincible. But where's the challenge in that?"

"I don't want a challenge. I want the people I care about safe. No wars or other-worldly, seductive evil to contend with. Peace and calm. That's me."

"Peace is but the gasp for breath between wars, my dear."

"That's depressing."

"But a truth based on an in-depth study of history and the motivations of allies and enemies, for every ally can be an enemy and vice versa. It all comes to pass over the eons of historical time."

"Not if Death wins. He calls my name, and when ... if I answer Him, this whole world could die. There will be no more eons."

"So, you would rather have never heard your name on Death's lips? Never felt what Thane makes you feel? You would rather you had never lived?" he asked.

I stopped, remembering how I had once considered such a thing long ago. Would the world be safer without me and Ilsa in it? Probably. Unless Lili had borne a different child to sacrifice, someone less stubborn than me.

"All I know is, fewer people would get hurt if they avoided me. If I ever get all this figured out and put things right, then I should return to abandoned Ismerkel and become a hermit."

"Here's a bit of knowledge my first wife gave me."

"You were married?"

"Many times. Each doomed by the siren call of a new mission for the Emperor, a new damsel to save or femme fatale to fence with.... Ah, the joys of my youth, which I do miss. As I do my wife. She once said, 'there's avoiding people, or someone in particular, because you know they are not right for you—and then there's avoiding real love because it's complicated and painful.' All real love is painful, Miss Thorne, because we know they will know us and make us face ourselves in their eyes. And because, one day, time and death will take them from us."

"Not death. Not if what you love is Death."

Is that how I felt? Was I drawn to Thane because he was unreal? Did I spurn Conrad because of his annoying need to treat me like a helpless woman, or because he was too human? What about the other humans who were too flawed for me? I tried not to think Duane's name, but an image of his face popped into my mind. The first time I ever saw blood on it. Was my soul any cleaner?

And thinking of souls, Thane's had burned like a thousand suns, drawing me into warmth and peace. Calm. That's what I felt when I had kissed him on the doorstep to the Void—all the passion and desire of life compressed into a moment of calm eternity.

I blinked and realized the doctor was staring into my eyes, studying me. He said, "I do not believe in Death or gods as literally as you do, my dear, but here is my advice, in your parlance: If you love Death, then life will take him from you. You cannot avoid pain. Not for anything worth your soul."

That was just the thing. My soul was the source of all confusion. How much easier to be without one?

"Thank you, Doctor. I'm not any less confused, but it was good to have someone listen."

"I'm afraid all this talk has worn me out. I am an old goblin now, and you a fresh young thing with a star-filled night ahead of you." The first stars were beginning to twinkle in a deep blue sky, as were a few tears in the corners of the doctor's eyes. Thinking of wives and times past must have stirred buried emotions. He wrapped himself in his bedroll and turned away to hide them from me. Seemed I'd made him recall something he regretted.

I didn't want any regrets.

I went and sat beside Thane. Both of us so quiet I could hear the lapping of water against the bank and the buzz of insects drawn to the crackling fire behind us.

"I can't let the world die," I finally said. "I will defeat the Dead God. Nothing else matters."

"And I will help you."

"How can you? How can I trust you?"

"Because I—"

"—Don't tell me you love me. I've heard that more than I like of late, and it doesn't mean anything."

"I was going to say, because I've seen you. Seen you care and fight and ... seen so much that I don't want *you* to end."

"You've said that before. You've been watching me my whole life, and that's just scary. You were waiting for a chance to woo and kill me. To complete the ritual and bring the Dead God fully into this world."

"It was what I was made for. But it's not who I've now chosen to be." He quieted until his words sunk in.

I'd been made for one thing too, to be a sacrifice, but it's not what I was choosing to be. Not by a long shot.

"It's still creepy."

"You have to understand light."

"Light?"

"Without it, there is only darkness. Like the night sky without stars. That is what my existence was, darkness. Endless nothingness. Before I ever inhabited a body and learned what life felt like, I was not alive. But one day, after I came into existence, the Dead God showed me you, told me what I was to do in that way souls speak to one another, but I can barely recall what He said. For I saw light. It was you, Eva. A candle in all that darkness. You were suddenly my whole world, the only thing I could see."

"It would have been a pretty dim light, because I'm not that great."

"But you are. Look." He passed his hand over the water, and it became a mirror for his memory.

I saw the moment where I stood on the stoop of Ulric's house, my hand on the door latch. It was a day like any other. I'd been back from boarding school long enough to have no excuses for being so lost and confused. I was working for Karolyne, but I had no wish to follow her path or the one my uncle was laying out before me. I had no idea what I wanted to do, where I wanted to go. My whole future was like the darkness Thane spoke about. I didn't even have a candle. Still, I took a breath and turned and walked away. I had no idea what I wanted, but I wanted something different. So, I moved in with Karolyne that day. I turned my back on my family, not for any one act, for I could cite a lifetime of acts that disturbed me. It was simply one moment in the snow when I suddenly decided to find out who I was.

And Thane had seen it. Somehow, he'd been there.

Half a dozen more images were spread over the surface showing me my best and worst moments. My blade dripping with Jhenna's blood, laughing with Karolyne and Gypsum as we sipped whisky and pointed at Juliette passed out on a stone bed.

How had he seen all of this? Then I noticed the viewer was not disembodied. There was an arm visible from time to time, a teacher's robe, a city guard's uniform, a refugee's tattered clothing. Thane had been all of them at one time or another, so near, and me so unaware. It would have given me chills all over again, made my stomach turn with terror ... if I couldn't sense Thane's soul so strongly.

He reacted to each memory with a powerful longing. He had wanted so much to share in the laugh or to comfort me when the hollow look set in my eyes after my first kill. He knew that I was meant for Death and a world beyond this one, that I should not dwell so much on the transient pain of life, but it was my very reaction to it all that made him begin to feel alive.

I could read him as clearly as I'd read Harbinger's grim history in his soul, but what I saw in Thane was an entirely different history.

Thane began to access the memories of the bodies he temporarily inhabited. He tapped into their feelings, and so he learned to feel. To fear, to hate, but most of all to love. It was that emotion he enjoyed best of all, and so he began to label his own feelings for me. And he did have feelings of his own, he realized. He worshiped his one candle in the vast darkness of eternity.

Knowing him, being him, it was hard to hate him. His soul tasted nothing like Harbinger's or Fharen's. Not like anyone's. There was no desire for power or to cause pain. Thane was innocent and pure in his way. And the way he looked at each moment of my life with the same purity and acceptance, the same love for me no matter what I had done.... It was like having the Lightbringer himself comfort and forgive you.

Thane had come to accept he would only see me from afar, that I would take his help, nothing else, and he was okay. His love for me did not change, or demand or crave more than the knowledge he could aid me in some small way. It was unconditional.

His fishing line tightened, and ripples disturbed the images. He pulled up a silver fish that sparkled in the firelight.

"Dinner," I said, not that I liked fish. I had my own supplies.

"I don't want to kill it. Only admire it." He removed the hook, smooth and un-barbed, and tossed the fish back in.

"Why were you fishing if you didn't want to catch anything? And why did it make you smile so?" I asked. I could have found the answer in his soul, but I didn't look for it. I wanted to hear him speak, like two ordinary people having a conversation. Not Death incarnate and Solhan necromancer, but Thane to Eva.

"Because I like waiting," he said, the smile still on his lips. "You know? That quiet time where something may or may not come to you, but it doesn't matter. You are happy simply being there. Waiting."

I kissed him then.

19 WHO I AM

It was just as amazing as the last time, when he had taken over Conrad and led me to the Dead God's shrine. He was still the bad guy then. I'd sensed turmoil within him and tried to distract him with a kiss, but I had been the one distracted. Consumed by it. A million suns of heat in one kiss.

This time, after we kissed, he laughed.

I pulled away. "What's so funny?"

"I could hear you and Doctor Ghunnan talking a little while ago. Now I know it's true. You love me too."

I punched him. "Do not. I said I loved Death."

"Now I'm jealous. Of myself."

"Don't be." I kissed him again, and it didn't matter that he looked like Fharen or smelled like perfume mingled with the sweat of travel and dirt of the road. When I closed my eyes, all I saw was the brilliant glow of his soul.

"I don't know why you ever thought you dwelled in darkness. You are the brightest light I have ever known," I said.

I was lost in his kiss again. In him. Our lights mingling and sharing things I dared not think or say aloud. It simply was. Being fully aware of who I was, of who he was, everything known and forgiven in one another. I knew how lost and alone he had been, why he clung to me like a moth to flame, but I was the moth too. I hungered for him, and I breathed him in. Took his soul into me like air, and it did not tear from his body because there was so much of it to give. I breathed it back out again and knew I could do this forever.

But what about the time I was wasting? What about...?

"Harbinger. I know," Thane voiced my thought. "But you can do nothing tonight but sleep."

"I don't plan to sleep." I kissed him deep, because the moment he spoke of Harbinger and all that lay ahead of us, I realized I wanted to forget it. For one night, I wanted this. Simply this.

"Eva," he said my name as we gasped for air, and the shiver it gave me was delicious.

"Thane," I said. "Thane, Thane, Thane." Always before I'd felt guilty when I spoke of him aloud, as though I was making something forbidden and invisible real. But now I let the desire I felt for him come out for all the world to hear.

"Your touch. To feel … This is all I've dreamed of since our first time together," he said, pressing hard against me.

"This is our first time together. The first time I've known it was you. And I want you." Part of me knew we had made love when he was in the guise of Erick, that his hands moved so expertly across my body because of all the knowledge he'd gleaned from his hosts, but I didn't care.

I disentangled myself from his grasp and stood. He watched with amazement as I took off my clothes, but what shocked him more was when I dived into the water.

I didn't care that I couldn't swim. I knew he would come for me.

He didn't even bother to get undressed. His arms encircled me, warming me in the cold water. He wrapped one leg around mine too, and fire travelled from his touch wherever naked flesh met, at ankle, neck and fingertips. He kissed me again, and then I was like a balloon of light, floating away into the night like a rising spark from the fire, up and up forever.

He pulled me to shore, and when he noticed me shiver from the cold stone, he lifted me into his lap. I straddled him, pulling off his damp shirt to reveal warm skin, but it was the heat of his soul pressing out from the flesh that contained him that warmed me. I pressed my naked breast against his chest, barely feeling the hairs that tickled, but I did feel his fingers. I gasped. I lost all patience then and reached into his pants, squeezing until he moaned.

"You said you wanted to feel this," I told him. "You told me once this is what made you want life. So live."

We made love on his bedroll beside the lake, not caring that our cries likely woke the goblin as well as scared the fish and night birds away.

When he looked exhausted and ready to sleep, I crawled towards my own bedroll on the dais, but he wouldn't let me go. He pulled me back into a new kiss. I scurried a little farther, and he crawled after me on hands and knees, stealing another soul-consuming kiss each time he caught me. Soon, I reached my destination, dry clothes and bedding, but I didn't make use of them. He was atop me, warming me, filling me with everything I desired, so I had no need to think about warmth or food or sleep. We were. That was all that mattered.

I woke in the night. Thane was sleeping, with his long, raven hair spread out like wings around him. My Thane. It was hard to envision the hated king in his features. They held an innocent repose, content, dreaming what I too had dreamt. Sweet cinnamon. I licked my lips and kissed him to taste it again.

He stirred, but I pulled away before he woke. For his sake. He could go until he killed the body he inhabited, so I let him recover. I slipped on my clothes and went to stand barefoot on the stone dock to admire the lake at night.

The jagged mountains surrounding us, covered with the even sharper outlines of pines like hairs along a giant's back, were as clear as daylight to me. Solhan night vision. A way of seeing shared by all creatures who dwelled in darkness.

But Thane had helped me see the world in a new way. The images of my past, good and bad, did not frighten or confuse when viewed through his eyes. Tarnished memories given a fresh polish. He made it all make sense.

I breathed deep. The air was fresh and new. None of the tang of Highcrowne offal, metal, or grease. For a moment, I couldn't remember why I should ever leave this spot.

"I thought you two would never finish." It was the fairy, Sandy, suddenly standing beside me, sparkles of glowing magic drifting from her as she appeared.

Faeries had sparkle magic! I couldn't help smiling stupidly.

She took a step closer, and I backed away, saying, "Don't touch me. I can't afford to lose more weeks trapped halfway to the fairy lands."

"If you insist. I come with a message you may not want that eavesdropping goblin to hear."

The doctor sounded like he was snoring, but then again, he was a spy. "Doctor Ghunnan doesn't believe in things like fairies, let alone Unmentionables, so whatever he hears he'll dismiss as delusion."

"Alright. First, you are Eva, correct?"

"Yes."

"Olyve made me swear to make sure this time."

"If I were Ilsa I could be lying."

"Good point. I did hear the elf calling your name loudly, however, so I'll trust you are telling the truth."

I blushed, thinking of being observed with Thane. Then again, that's what the Unmentionables were famed for: Watching. Judging. They could all go to hell.

"What do you want?" I pressed, suddenly impatient to have the fairy gone.

"We know what you intend. We're not the only ones who know, but Olyve said to tell you that she's done all she can to keep the other Unmentionables out of this. Our one rule is we cannot attack each other, but there is no requirement we defend one another. None will interfere when you face Harbinger."

"You sound like I should be grateful. The end of the world is at stake and still you play games and abide by rules that make no sense. Why can't you help?"

"Because it might turn out worse for everyone if we do. Anyway, I've passed on the message. Good luck."

"Stop. Can't you help even a little?"

"No. Oh, wait. I can tell you they are coming for you right now. Goodbye." She vanished again, popping away into a fairy bubble.

They?

Then I saw a ripple spread across the lake, as though something heavy had dropped into it. A white mist rolled out from the far shore too fast to be natural. I could see in the night almost as well as the day, but the depths of the lake were now hidden in mist and reflection. The hairs along my neck stood on end.

I ran back to my pack and grabbed my Ashur. I drew it and unceremoniously gave Thane a kick. A kiss would have been a nicer method to wake him, but I was practical above all else. "Something's coming," I said.

Thane's physical form was exhausted, but my words reached the core of him, and I saw him send a jolt of power through his body. He bolted awake and reached for his dagger. Thane shrouded the doctor and me with invisibility at the same time, but it did not deter those who could smell a drop of blood in an ocean. Within moments, we were surrounded by white mist that settled into shifting, writhing, naked forms as pale as the mist.

Hundreds of them.

The goblin doctor was awake, so he might have been listening in, but his eyes were squint shut as he searched for his spectacles. "What is it?"

"What's pale, fanged, and can cross a lake so fast the water may as well not even be there?"

"I like riddles! Let me see. A troll? A swamp spider? Oh, I know…"

"Vampires," I finished for him

I unleashed green whips of magic and lashed each creature that came near. Those hit felt not only their flesh shredded but their souls as well. They were half-dead already, and it took little effort to pry loose the souls clinging tenuously to their bodies. They pulled back before I could make sure they were more than half dead—or I pulled back. I may have hesitated because the sensation frightened me as much as it did them.

The goblin reacted quickly, grabbing a torch from the fire and waving it around to keep attackers at bay. The gaunt creatures cowered, covering their eyes. They were nothing like Harbinger. They were more like the vampires I was used to reading about. Feral, animal-like, their fangs and claws bared so they barely resembled the elven villagers they'd once been. But from their small size and pointed ears, I guessed that's what they had to be. This is where the sacrifices went.

I indicated Thane should drop the glamour of invisibility, as it wasn't working anyway. I swept my gaze across the huddled forms and said, "Where is Harbinger? I've come for him, not his pets."

More fog rolled across the water, and the sea of landed vampires parted for it. Out of the white smoke appeared three women of incredible beauty. These ones were not cowering.

Their aggressive stance roused the feral vampires, gave them courage, so I lashed out with my magic again, making them whimper once more. I struck one of the females as well, but she did not even wince. Her soul was buried deep inside her form, like a vein of gold locked in a mountain of quartz. I would not pry hers so easily lose.

The woman's eyes glowed like a predator's. I saw fangs, not registering much else before I swung my sword and cut off her head. The corpse reached for me and did not bleed. It finally toppled over when Thane knocked her legs out from under her. She was naked. The others were similarly under-dressed, but I supposed they did not mind the cold.

The goblin took a hit and went down, bleeding from long scratches that looked like they'd been made by a lion. I stood over him and cut off the vampire's reaching hands. Her claws were yellow and as long as a finger, so she needed the manicure. She hissed at me, and I was not impressed.

"I'd have thought Harbinger would choose brides with more wit and conversation skill to help him while away the centuries," I said. "No wonder Ilsa impresses, if you're what he has for comparison."

"Do not judge my sisters so harshly," a fourth female said as she emerged from beneath the lake.

She'd seen us slaughter her 'sisters' but her expression was impassive. Her red hair looked like blood where it fell over white shoulders and gray freckles. She wore a copper-colored gown that had seen better eons.

"They are hungry," she continued. "We're all hungry, but I'm here to invite you to join us for dinner. Come this way. And do return my sister's hands."

The goblin had staunched the bleeding from his shoulder and held them out, entranced by the twitching yellow claws. From the expression on his face, he must have been thinking the psychedelic fungus affecting him had taken his imaginings on a disturbing turn. I was disturbed too, especially when the vampire I'd dismembered pushed her bloodless stumps against the wrists and fused them to her again.

Hissing, growling brides reattached the first one's head. They were all whole once more.

I sheathed my useless sword and said, "I'm sure Harbinger understands if we prefer to rest out here this evening. We'll see him in the morning."

The redhead clucked her tongue. "That would be most sad for your friend. Conrad. I could say his name over and over. Conrad, sweet Conrad, whose blood is twice as sweet. We are allowed a few nibbles every hour, and with each sweet draw, our hunger grows rather than diminishes. We are ravenous now, and I fear your friend will not last the night."

That sounded about right. So much for the sunlight plan. I would have to act soon. Damn Conrad for getting caught again. Damn me for my sentimentality.

"Aguragas brought Conrad to you, I suppose. What did you give him in return?" I asked, buying time to think.

"Payment. Gold and gems and knowledge of certain things, things that mortals such as he believes are of great import. That was all the mercenary wanted, and your sister assured us of the usefulness of the bargain. I see from your reaction she was right."

"So Ilsa couldn't get the First Soul to work for you, and you think I will?"

"We hope you will. For everyone's sake, especially yours."

I leaned into Thane and said, "You and Doctor Ghunnan wait here for me. I'll see you when Harbinger and I complete negotiations.... Have faith in me," I whispered that last part in his ear, certain the vampires' keen hearing made whispering pointless, but we had a code that not even they could read. For when my lips touched his skin, our souls met, and he knew what I truly meant to say.

"I do," Thane answered, and I dared not give him the kiss I so longed to impart in farewell. I didn't want the brides to see how much I cared for him, else Conrad's life might be worthless, for they'd know they had another's to bargain with.

What I really told Thane, in that wordless way we shared, was I would find the First Soul and then face Harbinger if need be. *It was always meant to come down to him and me. I'm the relic's keeper now, and there are greater things at stake than my life or even Conrad's. I will find a way to win. I have to.*

And Thane told me, *I will follow you with fire, stakes and whatever else the goblin and I can find. I will tear down shutters or the walls themselves to bring sunlight into Harbinger's castle. Whatever it takes. We will kill Harbinger and defeat the Dead God together. We will always be together.*

I smiled, hoping his wordless promise was possible.

"By negotiations, I do hope you mean acquire a blood sample?" the goblin confirmed, having only heard my spoken words.

I ignored him and told the redhead. "Lead the way."

The brides and their feral spawn played at being frightening. Crawling all around me, licking my skin, but they were animals. The redhead noticed my disdain and, with a wave of her hand, sent them scurrying off, so we two walked to the edge of the lake like old friends.

"You must be Harbinger's first wife," I said. "How do you feel about Ilsa moving in?"

"Your twin will never be one of us. And I am far from his first, only his current favorite."

"I don't like sharing my men."

"Eternal life has its rewards, and whose marriage could be more full of love than ours? A shared love and lust for life. You do not understand."

I could see her soul, so I understood completely. "You're never alone now, are you? You love your sisters and your pain. I'm happy for you. All I want is what's mine."

"Conrad?"

"He's not mine, but I'll take him away from you. No, I want my relic. Harbinger and the rest of you don't have to die if you just give me what I want."

Her laughter was genuine, ringing through the mountains like a clear bell.

"You Solhans have ever been mad and swelled with a sense of your own power. You cannot kill the un-killable."

"Nothing is that. Not even Death. I have a bigger enemy. We have a bigger enemy. Can't we get along?"

"Hmm. No. Come along now."

The castle perched upon a distant ridge blocked out starlight and was more visible because of that absence.

"I can't climb a mountain," I said, pointing out the obvious geological barriers.

"I'll carry you," she said. "Put your arms around me."

I obeyed, reluctantly, and gagged at her fetid breath. Blood had rotted in there. Her body felt soft and cold, like hugging a snowdrift. She smiled beguilingly.

I had to say: "Surely this doesn't work when you hunt men? Unless you're mesmerizing them all?"

"I am a devoted wife. I do not hunt. I feed only on what scraps my husband gives me."

"Okay, now we're really at odds. I don't do the dutiful wife thing. Don't you have a mind of your own?"

"I know that my mind, as it is, lives because of another, so I must obey that other. You might fare better if you learn such appreciation."

"Oh, I appreciate being alive, but when my mother hatched me into the world and left me to be Death's bride, I lost all desire to submit out of gratitude. And it's good for you I have, else you and your 'Master' would be dead already."

"So, you are saying I owe greater devotion to you?"

"Well ... yeah. If that convinces you?"

"Umm ... No."

Shot down again. "Fine then. Let's go. Quickly."

And she was quick. My arms were nearly jerked out of their sockets when we set off. As awful as she smelled and felt, I clung tight. We flew across the surface of the lake in a fog, her body half material and half vapor, something between this world and the next. Like a wind, we blew through the branches of the pine forest, up the next cliff face, and in through an arched side door of Harbinger's castle. Fortunately, it had been left open, for while the vampire might have been able to vaporize herself completely and move through the cracks, I could not.

I should have taken in the sights more, but the trip was so fast, and my eyes clenched so tightly through most of it, that I barely saw a thing. I peeled myself off her and stood, trembling, staring down at granite tiles.

When the shock wore off, I said, "Werewolves have nothing on you." At least I'd managed to hold onto my stomach contents, unlike the time a werewolf had carried me. I'd been trying all the modes of travel of late: boat, horse, vampire ... I preferred walking.

"If you or Conrad run," she warned, "I will catch you before you can scream. Grant my husband's wishes, and you will survive. Perhaps even free. Disobey, and you will remain here for all eternity as our pet. My husband told me of your condition, the frailty of your life and how it must be protected from the Dead God. Perhaps the best protection is to lock your soul within your corpse?"

"Hmm ... No." It was my turn to say, but I didn't think she was listening. She'd told me the terms.

Harbinger would be a tough bargainer. What had Ilsa gotten us into?

When I saw Ilsa, I had that old, irresistible urge to slap her across the face. She was standing beside the velvet-clad throne that was the only decoration in an otherwise vast and empty hall. What had once been stained-glass windows were now bricked over and as dull as the rest of the place. Ilsa looked poised to sit down when someone wasn't looking, and I could imagine her mentally sizing up the castle for curtains, as well as devising ways to dispose of the matrimonial competition. Watch out redhead.

Ilsa was still alive. They hadn't turned her into a vampire. There was still time to save my sister. As stupid as that was, it was reassuring.

But the self-satisfied smirk Ilsa gave me reminded me again of what I hated most about her: She thought she was so clever. The only thing that stopped me from punching her was the seven-foot tall slab of vampiric muscle standing in the way.

"Harbinger," I said, smiling. "Here's the deal. I was the one who found the First Soul. It's mine. Give it back."

He stood there for several long, awkward moments until the full stupidity of my simplistic demand was evident to all in the room, especially me. I took a step back and saw Ilsa smirk again. Harbinger shifted ever so slightly on his feet to occupy my full view once more.

"Aren't you going to enquire about your lover?" he asked. "Come, I'll show him to you."

"He's not my lover, and I didn't ask about him." It probably wouldn't work, but I was hoping they'd focus on me instead of Conrad.

"Then I can let my brides finish draining him?"

Called my bluff.

"Look," I said. "You know what I want, I know what you want. How about we make a reasonable deal? Let me borrow the First Soul long enough to kill the Dead God, and then you can have it to become a god, and then I'll kill you too. Sound like a plan?"

"I'll fetch him," Ilsa said, smiling.

She paraded to an iron door positioned behind the throne and opened it, revealing a small cell that could easily have been a royal closet, before the castle became infested with vampires instead of rats. The rats had probably not survived long with so many blood-suckers around. Unlike the main hall, the cell was decorated, albeit with scratches and dried blood for wallpaper.

Conrad's naked form lay huddled on the floor, hugging himself for warmth, his skin pockmarked by dozens of small bites.

I turned my back.

I hoped Harbinger would think that meant I didn't care, but really I couldn't bear to look at him. I had to buy more time. Dawn was hours away.

I threw up my hands. "You offer me no good choice then. Deliver Conrad to my friends, and I will stay in his stead. I cannot hand over control of the relic to you. It doesn't work like that. It and I ... we are linked." It was part of me, and I was part of it, somehow. No matter how much I didn't want to be, that connection was there. And when I thought about the First Soul, I felt it. Nearby, but not in the room. Somewhere in the castle. "I can convince it to lend its power to you, to help you become Master of the Night or whatever it is you desire."

"I am Master of the Night."

"A god then. But not the only one. Trickster told me to tell you to keep your hands off his toys. He'll leave them laying wherever he pleases. So, beware stepping onto a bigger playground."

Harbinger's eyes flared, literally, glowing yellow.

His favorite wife whispered into his hear for quite a while, calming him, and I noted the jealousy in Ilsa's expression. She didn't like being excluded. By the time the redhead finished, Harbinger's eyes had settled into their usual creepy glow, and he smiled.

I didn't like it when the villains smiled like that.

"Warning noted," he said. "Now. Here are my terms. Your lover—"

"—he's not my—"

"—Your lover stays. You will want him nearby soon enough. And you, you I will make one of them." He indicated the naked brides, hovering at the edges of the room, hissing and squirming like serpents.

"You do know that's not what anyone would call a bargain?" I said, feeling my stomach turn.

"This was not the deal," Ilsa began, but he shot a look at her that made her take a step back. She was useful only as food now, and she must have finally realized how stupid she'd been.

"You will do my bidding, Eva, and in turn the First Soul will do mine." Harbinger spoke with the rich satisfaction I used when savoring a favorite dessert, but I caught the redhead's lips moving in sync and knew this had all been her idea. "You will be protected from the Dead God for all eternity," he continued, each word enunciated to melodramatic effect. "Half-dead, he can never have you. For you shall be mine."

I was sick of this 'mine' ownership talk. I'd finally broken Thane of such archaic thinking, but Harbinger, the first predator, was as old fashioned as they came.

"I'm not yours. I'm mine," I said, summoning green magic into my palms.

He was a blur and stood against me before I had time to blink. He loomed over me with his broad white shoulders, the yellow light of his eyes making his antlers glow like a crown of fire.

I didn't have a chance to strike or even scream before Harbinger was at my throat. No hypnotic gaze, just fierce, hungry eyes seared into my vision as he tore at my flesh.

The pain was sharp, the loss of blood even worse, and I grew weaker with every heartbeat. I thought of the Ashur strapped to my back, of the lives it had taken and hungered for, just as the vampire hungered for my blood. They were both equally sharp and cold and remorseless. But a sword was a useless weapon among creatures who could be cut into chunks and reassembled again. Power is what mattered. In the end, I clawed my hand and scratched at him like a cornered animal.

20 CROSSED LINES

Green fire arced from my hand, and Harbinger drew back with a gasp of pain. This cornered animal had claws.

I summoned more green fire, and he threw me off him. I went flying and hit stone so hard I thought I must have broken every bone in my body. I heard my skull crack, and then I wasn't aware of anything.

I woke in frigid darkness, not knowing where I was. Shivers wracked my body. My teeth were chattering, like the time I had dream walked, and I reached out for a blanket, anything.

I found something, or rather someone, else slightly warmer than I was. I wrapped myself around that warmth, soaking it up until the shivering subsided.

Only then could I think clearly enough to recognize the marble cell and Conrad, who I was wrapped tightly around. I had not only stolen his warmth, but his soul. He was dying.

I uncoiled myself, like a python releasing its grip, and tried desperately to push his soul back in his body as I'd done before.

He fought me. He wanted to die. His soul was like putty in my hands, and I more than knew his thoughts and memories. I knew everything.

I knew what he'd told me about serving the Crowns and enforcing slavery was true. I knew he loved me— and that he loved duty more.

None of that mattered.

"I will not kill, and I will especially not kill you, Conrad. No matter how much you want to give up. I can't. This will destroy me."

I pushed his soul back into his body as hard as I could, and it was like trying to put the yolk back into the crackling, fragile shell of a broken egg. He held onto life, but it was a feeble thing.

I remembered seeing the wounded after the marketplace bombing in Highcrowne, the souls hovering over the dead and dying. That's what Conrad was. Dying.

"No." Tears streamed down my face.

I hated crying. Every Solhan bone in my body told me it was weakness, but I couldn't help myself. Great, goopy sobs wracked me as badly as shivers had before.

I was a monster.

Not only Conrad, but everything, would die because of me.

"I'm weak. I've failed you. Failed everyone."

"You're not. You haven't," Conrad whispered, and I thrilled.

He wasn't dying. It would be okay.

But then I saw it—another soul.

So bright it seemed the sun had slipped into our cell. Part of it had reached inside of Conrad and made his lips move as you would a puppet. Thane.

There was another shape behind the light, the part of Thane unable to fit inside Conrad's dying form. I hadn't seen that looming shadow since I killed Erick, because Thane usually hid fully inside the person he possessed. This was his true form. Light and shadow. The brightness I saw with my soul sight was a contrast to the grim shade my eyes witnessed. Which was Thane? Did it matter? Not right now.

"Can you heal him? Please?" What had I done?

"I can't heal," he reminded me, speaking with Conrad's voice. "My power, the Dead God's, is over souls, but only to carry them to the land of the dead. I can dwell inside a body alongside another soul only so long as they live and grant permission, or are too vulnerable to resist. When Conrad's soul leaves, The Dead God's will enter in three days and imbue the corpse with His power. But Conrad will be elsewhere. I cannot change that. I'm sorry."

"But he's here. Right here. All you have to do is push the soul back inside."

"He is too weak to sustain it. And his soul ... He has been drained to the point of death. The blood loss."

"It's not my fault?" I don't know why that mattered so much, but it did, and I latched onto that. I had pulled his soul free, but only because it was already slipping away. It mattered.

"Don't blame yourself, Eva. But what you want is possible. With Solhan necromancy. With your power. Alive or dead, you can chain his soul to his body and have it do your bidding."

"No." I shook my head. I couldn't do that to Conrad.

"Doctor Ghunnan and Fharen—whom the goblin insisted on tying up before I left: that goblin is such a distrustful sceptic and calls me 'another personality'— they are still too far away. I came alone to help however I can, and now I see what I can do. Advise you. Think what a risen corpse under your command could do? Save yourself, Eva. Please." He was the one begging now.

I did think of it, of the destruction I'd seen risen corpses inflict, when powered by the Dead God at least. I doubted it would work the same for me. Nevertheless, I suddenly knew another way to defeat Harbinger.

But.

This was Conrad.

I couldn't....

Talk about going dark. This was dark, evil Solhan necromancy stuff the likes of which Bell and never imagined. Not even Ilsa had done anything so monstrous.

I almost waited too long. Thane was forced out of Conrad with a last rattle of breath. He hadn't even looked at me or said goodbye. He was simply dead.

But Conrad's soul had not gone far. It hovered over him, a small ball of white light next to the massive radiance of Thane. At least that's how it looked to my soul sight. While Thane's soul had a weight that created a gravity of its own, a gravity that drew me even now, Conrad's soul was like a white feather on the breeze. I saw it drifting away, and I snatched it from the air.

I held it in my hand, and I knew him. Deep down, he was a good man, no matter what he believed.

"I can free his soul again can't I? I don't want him enslaved to me. He deserves to find peace in the lands of the dead." When he was old and had lived a long life.

Thane was a shadowy specter with no body to control, but our souls had forged a connection. I knew I was seeing his true form, seeing the real him, which had always been there just out of sight. I'd opened my eyes so to speak. And now I opened my ears. I 'heard' Thane's true voice: warm, cinnamon thoughts whispered at the back of my mind.

"Of course, you can free him. You think you are weak, Eva..." the way he said my name always made me shiver, never more so than now, *"...but in this world you hold more power than I. You have power over both life and death, over all you dream. You are Solhan and this world is yours. What is your command?"*

I knew what Ilsa longed to feel in that moment and how Uncle must feel most days. I felt powerful, unstoppable, able to imagine and achieve almost anything. Gone was self-doubt and hesitation. In a flash, I was unrepentantly Eva.

I placed the white feather of Conrad's soul into his mouth and watched his corpse swallow it.

"Come back to me," I commanded. "You don't get to give up that easily."

His eyes opened, but he did not breath.

Thane was wrong when he said I could bring life. All I could manage was the semblance of it. With a sinking horror, I realized what I'd done.

"Sit up," I commanded, and Conrad sat up.

I didn't want to order his every movement, and the whole situation was beginning to freak me out. The everyday Eva was back, fear, doubt and all.

"Conrad?" I said.

"Yes."

"Can you be Conrad? I know your soul is in there. You're as pale as me now, and your heart doesn't beat anymore, but it is you. Please. Just be you."

"It ..." He struggled visibly, like his tongue was stuck, and then he said, "It takes effort. Mental effort. To say anything. To do. Anything."

"*He will grow more practiced at this,*" Thane said, "*but he needs your power, Eva. Feed it to him. Like any magic, it cannot be sustained without will and power. You defy the natural order, and that always comes with a price.*"

"It's magic. Okay." I summoned the green fire into my palms that had allowed me to defend myself from Harbinger and werewolves. The fire that was stronger than ever in Thane's presence, and I fed that energy into Conrad.

He jolted to his feet and then stood there, looking at his hands as though they were foreign to him.

"*I know that feeling,*" Thane said, and I sensed amusement in his tone.

I was more disturbed than amused. Once again, I wondered what I'd done.

"Are you ok now?" I asked him, and I felt stupid. He was dead. Of course he wasn't ok.

"I feel. I feel like things are less complicated," Conrad said. "I stand on a threshold, ready to set out on a journey to I know not where or when or how. But it does not matter. I am merely waiting."

I was instantly reminded of Thane sitting on the dock only a few hours before—waiting for me.

"*He waits for Death,*" Thane said, as though he'd read my mind. He'd probably read my soul. "*You have but three days before He comes, Eva. Use it wisely.*" Thane's whispered voice in my mind reminded me he could no longer control Conrad's mouth. I was doing that now. I was the monster.

"Three days? No." It was too short a time for Conrad. It wasn't fair.

"*Someone is coming,*" Thane warned. He had stretched out tendrils of shadow beneath the door and all over the room, the smoke-like extensions searching for danger.

"We need to get out of here. Is it day or night outside?"

"*Night,*" Thane answered, "*but close to dawn.*"

"I know what I must do," Conrad said, and he banged on the door. "I must get you out of here."

Oh, no. Of course, he'd do exactly as I commanded.

"Stop," I said, and he stopped. I wasn't enjoying this and found myself struggling to find the right words. I had to choose them carefully.

"*He is yours now,*" Thane said. "*Solhans once rose the dead for their armies alongside their wolves. Before they lost interest in conquering, and before the Dead God came along and stole all the dead from them. It seems unnatural to you, but it is something you will grow used to. At least you have learned to control the urge to feed. I instructed you to take the troll's life to save your own, and it unleashed a hunger in you, and I'm sorry.*"

"Is that something Solhans do too? Feed on souls?" I asked.

"Are you talking to me?" Conrad asked.

"No."

"*They do not,*" Thane said. "*That is Death's domain. The souls consumed fuel His, or your, or my power—confusing we three—but they are not gone. Consumed, they are transformed, stripped of all unnecessary things, so that they enter the lands of the dead naked. Reborn.*"

I relaxed then. I hadn't realized how much consuming the troll's soul had weighed on me. How much it had bothered me nearly eating Reginald's and Conrad's too. I would still be a monster in any normal person's eyes. What would Karo say when I told her all this? If I got a chance to tell her? At least I didn't feel so much like a monster inside.

Until I looked at Conrad again.

He was dead. The golden knight in shining armor was no more, would never be the same again. And it was all my fault.

Stop it, Eva, I told myself. Wallowing in guilt was a luxury I'd have to save for another day.

Time to start fixing whatever I could.

"Alright," I said, taking a deep breath. "I have a plan."

I was waiting for someone who knew my wacky plans to laugh at that, but neither Conrad nor Thane did. Both listened intently.

I decided not to say anything and got to work. I began by smearing the meagre blood from Conrad's wounds across my now healed neck.

Whatever part of Conrad's soul I'd devoured before restoring him had not only warmed me but saved my life. It fully healed whatever had broken when Harbinger threw me against the wall and sealed the gash in my throat. I owed Conrad more than I could ever repay.

I steeled myself and put my mouth over some vampire's bite mark and sucked until more blood came out of Conrad. I spit, disgusted by the metallic tang, but forced myself to draw more and smear it over my face and throat. I needed to make sure I looked the part.

"Lay down and play dead," I told Conrad.

He dropped like a sack of potatoes and looked as dead as he was. I should have told him to lay down more carefully, but could he really be hurt anymore?

Pain welled in my chest.

He'd never get to marry a sweet dwarf girl. Or me.

"*That's what you wanted?*" Thane said, and I'd forgotten he could read my soul as well as I read his.

Couldn't I mourn in peace?

"*I'm sorry. This is all my fault,*" Thane continued. "*I'm the one who brought him into this. I said I would make amends, and I failed.*"

"You don't get all the credit. Everything I touch is cursed. Best you go now, or I'll get you killed somehow too."

"I cannot die, for I do not live. Not like him or you. … And was that concern for me I heard in your voice?" That tone of amusement was back, and if he had a body, I'd strangle him. With Conrad lying there, it was like laughing at a funeral. Of course, trust Death incarnate to have a dark sense of humor.

"No. I was trying to get rid of you because I can't stand you right now."

"That's what I thought." There was still a smile in his tone.

"I mean it."

"You really want to face Harbinger alone?"

"All I have is me, and that's scary."

"I am yours. Conrad is yours. You have admirers dying to do anything for you." There was that dark comedy again when he said 'dying'. *"We are yours, so make use of us."*

"Look at what I've done. To Conrad … With you. Now the First Soul calls…" I sensed it within the walls, wanting to be unleashed again. "…I can't trust myself."

"I trust you."

"And I'm supposed to believe you? How do I know a soul as powerful as yours can't lie? My best friend betrayed me for power; my mother betrayed me for power; Ilsa too. My twin. There's no one I can trust, because you all want something from me."

"You're right. But it's not power I want, for I have it. All I want is you, Eva. And I will do whatever I must—even if that means leaving you to stand alone. I have faith in you. I have touched your soul like no one else has, and I know what you are capable of, even if you do not. Until we meet again." When he said the last, it felt like lips kissing the back of my neck. I shivered.

And then Thane was gone.

No.

I was alone with a dead man, and the cold lump in my chest was back. I hadn't realized it had faded when I argued with Thane, not until the pain returned. Now there was nothing to distract me. I sunk to my knees and let tears come.

I mourned for Conrad, even though he was there, listening. He could hear everything I whispered, everything I would have said over his grave, and so he knew. He knew I might have loved him if everything was different. If....

The door behind me opened, and I recognized the red-haired bride when she spoke. "To take the life of those we love is the gift of our kind. Consumed, their blood flowing into our mouths, swallowed deeply. They dwell inside us forever and free us from the restraints of life. Come. Join us."

She took my arm and helped me rise. She led me from the room, and I glanced back to see she had left the door to Conrad's cell open. They might come to dispose of him later, but for now he was free. And along with my goodbyes, I had whispered his instructions. He knew what I wanted him to do.

The brides sprawled across a giant bed in a lush chamber where the tapestries and velvet curtains were heavy with centuries of dust. I looked around for Harbinger, but there was no sign of him. Or Ilsa.

"What have you done with my sister?"

"You should ask what she has done with us. She has disturbed our balance, our world, seeking power she does not understand. You understand now, don't you? You have tasted blood, are one of us."

As I hoped, she thought I'd been turned. I didn't know what happened after I blacked out, how vampires initiated you into the club, but along with healing me, Conrad's soul must have helped me fight off that infection as well.

I thought my heartbeat might give me away, but then I looked down and noted all Conrad's blood smeared across my torso. The tales Nanny told always said the blood of the dead was a mirror to vampires, and they see only their own reflection in it.

I tried my best evil smile, surprised by how good I was at it, and said, "Yes. I understand, and that's why

I seek Ilsa. It's time I hunt her as she hunted me. This will be fun."

The head wife seemed to buy the glee in my eyes, only it wasn't about vengeance on Ilsa, as tempting as that was, but about having her lead me to wherever Harbinger had the First Soul. I felt it nearby, but as before 'nearby' could be anywhere in the massive and ancient castle. I hadn't spotted any pockets in Harbinger's suit—it was all sheer black cape and tight riding pants like some sex dream made manifest—so I knew he must have it secreted somewhere. Head wifey might guess something was up if I asked her, but Ilsa would know she was in trouble by now and all too willing to switch sides yet again.

"As much as I would relish watching the gore of a fledgling's first hunt," the wife said, "Harbinger has forbidden it."

I shook my head. "A shame, but I suppose that was Ilsa's bargain. Me for her claiming your place of honor as head wife. I suppose you knew you'd be supplanted one day?"

The wife's eyes narrowed. She looked back to where the harem of naked and feral lesser brides writhed on the dilapidated cushions, probably wondering if that would be her soon. She drew a moth-eaten curtain over the scene and opened the massive wooden door opposite. It led to a stone corridor.

"Our husband will visit soon," she said, "until then there is no reason to keep you from exploring your new home. I understand the most interesting sights can be found in the north tower."

Another tower. More stairs. Great. I hoped I wouldn't have to grapnel my way out of this one, but for wifey's sake I tried to look grateful. And hungry. "I'm sure I'll find exactly what I crave there."

I stalked out, but after I rounded a corner out of sight, I stood upright with a groan. My back ached. I couldn't keep up the vampire act. I was lucky she didn't notice the lack of teeth for one thing, so it was good to be out of there. I doubted she'd leave me unobserved for long, so I headed for the tower.

On the way I paused, feeling for my connection to Thane, soul to soul, and I knew he was nearby, but he kept his distance. I had lashed out at him with mistrust. I regretted it, regretted him withdrawing from me, yet I was glad he'd learned to give me space when I needed it. I sent a silent apology. He didn't respond, so I wasn't sure he heard.

I did feel a new soul connection when I reached out. Conrad. When I thought of it, I could see a silver thread connecting me to him, puppet master to puppet. It felt shameful, but I gave it a tug, checking on his whereabouts, and I knew he was where I told him to wait.

I climbed the stairs, huffing and puffing. I thought tower rooms were built for torture as much as dungeons were, just a different type of torture. I kept going until a barred gate blocked my way.

Ilsa was on the other side, face down on the floor in a pool of blood. I was too late.

The door was padlocked, but I'd learned a few things during my time as a detective, mostly when I was a pet detective breaking beloved companions out of cooking cages, so I found a rusty nail and got the lock open before I'd even stopped panting from my earlier exertion.

I hesitated before lifting Ilsa's head. It was eerie, like examining my own corpse. She was so pale. A Solhan was usually white as marble, but now she was ash-stained snow.

An ache filled me, squeezing my chest. There was no saving her this time. I'd failed. I'd have to tell Uncle I never even tried.

"Why? Why did you have to be so foolish, sister?"

I couldn't find the remnants of her soul on the best of days, so there was no restoring her, even for a time, as I'd done Conrad. No saying goodbye. I was all out of tears by now anyway. Numb.

I went to the tower window. It was more secure than our earlier prison, for I couldn't budge the bars. The sun was rising over the mountains, and I felt a lightening of the agony. The sun meant I could avenge her. I could stop Harbinger.

When I turned around, Ilsa was standing there. She smiled and it was all predator. She was one of them.

"Ilsa?"

"It's me, Sugar. So good of you to come calling." She was playing sweet, knowing that always unnerved me more than anything else she could do.

"You asked for this, didn't you?"

"Of course. And I have never felt more alive, more powerful. Not since you stole my soul. You did this to me."

"I'm sorry." Stealing her soul had unleashed a torrent of darkness in me I'd been unable to slow ever since. I was being pushed along to a place I never wanted to end up, but it seemed there was no fighting it.

"If you are sorry, then give me another soul in exchange. Give the relic to me." She held out her hand like I had it, but it was still secreted somewhere else

"What will you do with it, Ilsa?" I said, trying to be reasonable. "Only I can wield it, so let me. Let me stop the Dead God and afterwards we can discuss what you want. Maybe I can figure out how to undo this."

"I don't want it undone." She circled me, and the preternatural grace suited her. "You don't make deals, Sugar. At least not ones you intend to keep. The First Soul is power to do almost anything. Release control of it to me, tell it to obey me, and I will do with it what I want. Who says you alone can stop the Dead God? Why do you think you're so special? You would leave it at that too, wouldn't you? No ambition. Solheim could be rebuilt. I could have the world at my feet. Give me that, sister dear. You owe me."

I turned, trying to track her, but she was circling me so fast now it was a blur. Head spinning, I closed my eyes and told her, "No."

I wouldn't trade one evil for another, and my sister was evil. Maybe not to the degree of my mother, but evil was evil. Same reason I wouldn't trust the Solhan crown to anyone who wanted it, least of all my blood. Or even me.

When I opened my eyes, she was right there in front of me, staring into my pupils like she could see into my mind. Whatever she saw was an alien landscape to her, for she looked baffled.

"We will make you change your mind." The voice was rich, deep and familiar. Harbinger dropped from the high ceiling like a heavy shadow. He'd been watching us the whole time.

"Silence," he ordered, and I stood frozen, obeying.

He circled me, taking in my bloodstained clothes, pale skin, although nowhere near as pale as Ilsa's now, and frowned.

"You cannot fool me with peasant tricks," he said. "I know the scent of dead blood, although I know not how you managed a risen corpse when I have seen none but those yoked to the Dead God these past decades." He said 'decade' like I'd say 'minutes'.

I gave up my statue pose and shrugged. "I might as well stop pretending. Peasant tricks, you say? Maybe you'll appreciate this trick more."

I struck with a lash of green magic, encircling his neck and cutting Harbinger's flesh to the bone. The vampire's eyes went blood red. I felt his soul as I had on the island, exposed and full of ancient longing, dark deeds conducted in the shadow of night, and a hunger ... not unlike mine. Part of me hungered for the golden thread of soul within him, but it was buried deeper in the stone of his immortality than the brides' souls had been.

Unfortunately, my strike hadn't managed to remove his head either.

He moved so fast, I expected him to catch me unaware as before, but the sun was coming, and he was slower than usual. He passed me by and swept up Ilsa in one arm like a doll.

Ilsa laughed again, high and sweet, and said, "You want the First Soul? Join us in darkness."

Then she and Harbinger were gone, black wings screeching down the stair into a trap I was required to step into.

Ilsa was pushing me into a corner. A place I didn't want to go. Vampires could be killed. Sisters included. Hopefully it wouldn't come to that, because killing Ilsa was even worse than what I'd done to Conrad. It was the line I most feared to cross.

I sighed and followed them down the stairs and into darkness.

The redhead was waiting. "Harbinger is displeased."

"I'm afraid I wandered where I shouldn't have," I said.

The bride hung her head, and I knew she'd suffer for my actions. That was kind of the point. My sympathy for monsters only went so far, me included.

"He awaits you. Please him and your eternity can be a pleasurable one. Anger him and know torment."

"An eternity around you creatures would be torment." When I sensed Conrad nearby, I smiled and said, "But lead the way."

When we returned to the great hall, I thought Harbinger would be on his throne, but instead the stone seat had slid aside to reveal a narrow passageway that led deeper into the castle. This must be his inner lair and as far from daylight as it was possible to be.

I went down a spiral staircase, the redhead behind me, and stopped at the bottom to let my eyes adjust. The darkness was so pure not even my night vision was enough. I summoned the green glow in my palms and let its light illuminate the scene before me.

Harbinger had another throne mirroring the one above. He sat upon it, fighting weariness, while Ilsa was already asleep on a plinth, looking like the statue atop a sarcophagus, she was so still.

The lesser brides slunk across the floor on hands and knees before curling up at Harbinger's feet to sleep like dogs. Only Harbinger and the head wife remained conscious as day came to the world outside.

Fewer to fight. I grew more hopeful. I also felt the relic close enough to taste.

"Alright," I said. "Let me talk to the First Soul. I'll hand it over to you."

"I am not foolish. If I give it to you, you will run."

"Where to? Even all day on a fast horse would not be far enough, come nightfall you'd catch up to me. I bet you'd even be able to keep up with Olyve."

"She will not help you. None of them will."

"I know it."

He studied the acceptance in my gaze for quite some time before a satisfied smile curled one side of his wine-colored lips. "Very well."

He stood, nudging moaning brides aside, and walked to the wall. He pulled an unlit sconce and a section slid aside. I spotted chests spilling over with rubies and gold coins, alongside mannequins displaying ancient armor left to corrode. Harbinger emerged with the Soul in his hand. I knew it was real, because not only could I see its dark miasma drown out the little light available, I heard it clearly speak for the first time.

This and more can all be yours.

I held out my hand.

He hesitated. "No closer. Tell it to obey me. Speak now."

I glanced up at the ceiling. "Sun's up."

He looked. It made me giggle.

I smiled. "Want to see?"

Conrad, hidden from their sight by his very nature, reached out of the darkness and encircled the vampire with arms like a marble vice. The dead blood in him served as shield as well as a mirror, reflecting back all Harbinger's struggles. The vampire couldn't move or transform. I pried the relic from his cold hand.

The brides around the throne woke and screeched together in a single, ear-piercing voice. A moment later they went up in flames.

That hadn't been me.

I caught sight of Doctor Ghunnan then. He had come down the stair and held a metal tube which spouted flame. The stream of fire was unleashed on the next squirming bride, and she went up like dry grass, her cry vanishing from the chorus. They all went silent then. That was unnerving.

As was the horde of lesser vampires that spilled into the chamber from all sides.

The flamethrower moved across the room, killing everything in its path, and soon the heat was unbearable. I backed away, not caring how they died, but thrilling at the feel of the First Soul in my hand.

Thane was there then, wearing Fharen's body, and he summoned a fae light that pushed back the hordes around us.

"Eva," he said.

It felt like he'd shaken me awake. I looked at him, the glowing light of his soul, and it was the only thing that could compete with the relic in my hand.

"You came back," I said.

"I had faith you could do this alone, but why should you have to? You're not alone anymore." He smiled, and I felt a warmth inside that pushed the First Soul's darkness even further away.

It wasn't happy about that.

The goblins device stopped working. He shook it, backing toward Thane and I, and said, "Appears I've run out of that green lubricant. An excellent suggestion, Miss Thorne, using the residue from the Avian ruins. Seems that, when mixed with my own firelighter, the flammable properties are magnified exponentially. I must be more careful when working with the substance in future. Although it would be desirable to have a bit more currently."

The lesser vampires stayed down, but the brides the goblin had burnt slowly climbed to their feet. Their blackened skin crackled as they moved, and when they opened their eyes and mouths, ash poured out.

"Time to go," I said, inching toward the staircase.

"Did you get a blood sample?" the goblin doctor pressed.

"Not yet."

"When were you planning to?"

"This is a work in progress."

Conrad, I called silently, spurring him to move faster. He dragged Harbinger up the first step.

The vampire was not happy. He said, "Kill all but Eva."

The brides descended on us, ignoring Thane's light. The doctor went flying. I pulled my Ashur and recalled how useless it was against such creatures, but I had another weapon. Poison.

"Sorry," I said, wincing, as I slashed a long gash across Conrad's skin, but he didn't seem to notice. He continued to drag the struggling Harbinger a few inches at a time. No blood oozed from the wound I'd made, but I saw black liquid on my blade.

I cut the first bride who came too close, and she screamed. She retreated across the room, thrashing and choking before lying still.

"Serve me, Eva," Harbinger said, trying another tactic. "Gift the relic's power to me. Make me the god I have long deserved to be, and I will help you kill Death. You will reign at my side or claim the world for your own, whatever you desire. I can give you your desires."

Harbinger had turned on that mesmerizing stare and, combined with the wisps of clothing that revealed lots of rippling muscle, I could see why he thought the approach would work. I had to admit I felt a twinge in my nether regions, who wouldn't?

"If I don't want to be Death's bride, I certainly don't want to be yours," I said.

I stabbed Harbinger this time, just to shut him up. Where the dead blood on my blade mingled with his own there was a chemical reaction, like caustic soda in water, bubbling. Maybe I didn't need sunlight.

I swung my sword back for a better strike, but it caught on something. I looked down to see the goblin collecting a few drops of Harbinger's blood from the Ashur's serrated blade and depositing them into a glass phial.

The doctor looked up at me sheepishly. "Apologies, my dear. I'm quite finished. You may proceed with your duel."

He'd ruined my stride though, and Harbinger recovered. Fueled by fury and pain, the vampire threw off Conrad's arms. Not good. He transformed into a black cloud like the one that had carried judgment to me and Ilsa on Ismerkel.

I raised the First Soul above my head, and its obscuring light battled with Harbinger's darkness. The seething, turbulent smoke was pushed back, but white hands reached out blindly and squeezed my arm so tight it went instantly numb. I would have dropped the Soul if it hadn't been clenched in my deadened left hand. My fist froze like stone the moment my blood no longer flowed through it, and there was no prying the relic loose, as much as Harbinger's reaching hands tried. His stony fingers found my throat, instead, and began to squeeze.

Thane and Conrad futilely grappled the smoke, and even the goblin, phial of blood safely stowed away, attempted to defend me with a wooden stake that was useless without a solid heart to impale.

My vision faded as I struggled to breathe. Harbinger didn't snap my neck as I knew he could. He needed me alive, or at least half alive, to control the First Soul for him. He didn't need anything from the others, so he wrapped them in a suffocating blanket of night and said, "They will die if you do not submit."

I was not the submitting type. I called green fire to burn the disembodied hands strangling me. It hurt Harbinger, I could tell by the way the black fog contracted into serpentine coils wrapped about the goblin and Thane, but he didn't let go.

First Soul, I call to thee. Lend me your power to bind the night.

I was never one for spells, having learnt only a few necromantic chants at Nanny's knee, but I understood how they worked. The words focused your desires and instructed the magic to obey your will. As I grew more lightheaded, I needed that focus, so I made up something stupid. Another reason spells had never been my thing.

It worked though. The First Soul's own miasma encircled Harbinger's fog and ripped its coils from around us before forcing the vampire back into solid form. Yeah, that's what I'd been going for. I think.

I gasped for air, but not before giving Conrad a silent nudge. The guardsman pinned Harbinger's arms once more. The burnt brides cried piteously and tried to pull Conrad back as he dragged the vampire away, but they were too weak. The First Soul had ripped

Harbinger's power away, including that which sustained his fledglings.

I looked at Ilsa, asleep through everything. I hoped she might be released from Harbinger's curse, but she was dead. Vampires had a half-life, which meant they ruled the night but died when the sun rose. None but the most powerful could resist, and not even the brides qualified anymore. They collapsed. Only Harbinger still held to consciousness. I couldn't leave Ilsa in that crypt, one more person dead because of me. I heaved her over one shoulder. Thane helped me get her up the spiral stairs.

When we emerged in the great hall, I saw Conrad had dragged Harbinger to the main doors. They were barricaded with iron. The goblin unbarred them and threw them wide open. A rectangle of sunlight entered the room. It was dim from cloud cover but still sunlight.

Thane and I placed Ilsa in a shadowed corner, before swinging the throne back into place. I wedged a metal candelabra in the cracks to block the mechanism and seal the brides in.

"Shevic! Drasben!" Harbinger called for his Unmentionable cronies. When there was no answer, he cursed in a foreign language too ancient for me to recognize, but I gathered he wasn't happy.

"No one will help you," I told him. It's the same message he'd tried to give me, but I don't think it registered in his ancient brain. He continued to glare and snarl, more like a feral vamp now than the 'Lord of Night' or whatever he considered himself.

"How dare you cross us," Harbinger growled. "None have disobeyed the Unmentionables and lived. None have survived me!"

I stepped close to Harbinger and smiled, showing him the First Soul still clenched in my fist. "You made the mistake of over-reaching, vampire. When I told you to stay out of my way, you should have listened."

Kill him, the First Soul told me. It was so tired of others touching and longing for it. It wanted only me.

"Kill him," I echoed. Conrad obeyed like a good corpse. He dragged Harbinger into the sunlight, and I went outside to watch the vampire burn.

He screamed like his brides had. Weak. Pathetic.

Conrad let go, for although his flesh was already hardening like marble, it was vulnerable to fire. He took a step back, and I suddenly thought it a pity the Dead God would claim his soul soon. He was mine.

Ours, the First Soul told me. *The whole world can be ours. You can raise more like Conrad, and I can destroy all those like Harbinger who stand against you.*

"Yes," I whispered.

"Eva?" Thane said my name in that way he had, and a shiver went down my spine.

I looked about me, dazed. It felt like I'd been dreaming, but I was still in the dream. Only, it was a nightmare.

The vampire's screams stabbed my ears, the acrid smoke of his burning flesh made me gag. Even the goblin hid his normally detached and analytical gaze from the scene.

Why had I been smiling about it all only a moment ago?

Thane's full attention was on me, and his expression was as horrified as my own. "Say something."

"Hold this for me." I gave him the First Soul.

When his hand touched it, he hissed with pain and quickly shoved it into his belt pouch with a look of distaste.

"How can you bear it?" he asked. "The bleak and utter ... the oily ... it feels like disappointment and regret and like no soul I have ever seen. It is...."

"An abomination. I know." I shut the doors behind us so no light would creep across the floor of the great hall and reach Ilsa where she slept.

I forced myself to watch as Harbinger turned to ash. The first predator. But not the last.

"It's not the only abomination," I whispered. I was the one who wielded it.

Thane wrapped his arms around me, and I turned in his embrace to hide my face against his chest. I breathed in the cinnamon scent of him, and for a moment I could forget the black tendrils of the First Soul reaching for me. The thin barrier of leather separating the relic and I was as nothing. It was the symbolism of that separation that mattered.

I loved the First Soul unconditionally. I had to. Part of me knew it would destroy me if I didn't.

But I feared it too.

It would be jealous, because I had discovered the same thing the Soul craved. I knew how it felt to be accepted completely. I now understood how important that was. Being loved like that can change you. Can make you want to be better. Can let you forget what you truly are, for a little while. Maybe I could change the First Soul, maybe not. But I knew Thane had changed me.

21 EPILOGUE

Two days later, we were past the aqueduct and picking our way down the steep trail to the river plain. The silver light of predawn made the landscape black and white, like one of Sandy's daguerreotypes or a portrait from a Highcrowne photography parlor. The fires of Lili's army crept over the hills like an early sunrise.

"She's coming," I said. "She senses it." I was referring to the First Soul hidden in Thane's pack. It drew all evil to it. It was hard for him to bear its taint, but he rode with it for my sake. Seemed I was another one of the evil things drawn by it.

"Lili wants you more," he said.

"Then let's keep going before her forces cut us off. It may already be too late to make the river and find a ship."

I wished we'd built a coffin for Ilsa and brought a wagon to carry her. It felt wrong leaving my sister behind on the cold stones of that castle. But what was I to do? We were running out of time, and she had become something even more monstrous than before. Murder was her only means of survival now. She had no choice, and she was pushing me into not having one either.

I didn't want to kill Ilsa. I was more afraid of that more than anything. I was frightened of what it would do to me. Of how much worse I could become. Despite the lines I had already crossed and said I never would, I knew I could go farther. The First Soul whispered to me how of how sweet it would be.

"I'm not going with you," the goblin said. He hadn't tried to explain away what happened in Count Bram's castle. There was a passing reference to previous cases of spontaneous combustion when it came to Harbinger, but his theories were half-hearted. He kept looking at Conrad who marched beside us.

The guardsman did not speak unless I commanded it, did not walk or halt unless directed to, and he did not sleep. What he did do is stare in the direction of Solheim, unblinking.

Now, as the sun rose, he took his first step independent of me. I felt it, the loss of control. The presence of the Dead God.

Thane felt it too. He said, "You must send him away. Now."

"Goodbye," I told the small remnant of Conrad that remained in his flesh. My last command was as powerful as I could make it, and I sent him running headlong down the hill and east toward the rising sun. He would be the Dead God's servant soon. "I'm so sorry. For everything," I whispered after him. He couldn't hear me anymore.

Tears should have poured down my cheeks, but they wouldn't come. The last time I'd felt like this was after Viktor died. Feeling like this made me do crazy things. I became obsessed, and I felt my new obsession starting.

The First Soul was mine.... But what was it for? I had left slaves un-freed, Fharen's plant abominations running wild, had bound Conrad's soul and ruthlessly used a man who loved me—all to claim the relic. Yet I had no idea how to use it to defeat the Dead God. And even then, would I ever be free of it?

I wished I had my father, the keeper, to talk to. My uncle would have to do.

"Where will you go?" I asked the doctor.

The goblin shrugged. "My emperor would want me to do all I can to keep the Elf Lands and their army between Lili of Solheim and our swamps. I will rejoin

Princess Hilja and see if she needs my help stirring up trouble.”

“If Illul Faellion isn’t overrun yet, it soon will be,” Thane said.

“Never fear. I have many ways and resources.”

“Not Gas,” I said. He had coldly turned Conrad over to Harbinger. I thought he would bargain, but he’d sent me a message that he was not playing games. I didn’t know what he was playing at, but it could not be good. “Tell me you’ll stay away from Gas and his Upside Down Party?”

“I’ll tell you that.” The goblin smiled, finally, but I didn’t know if it was genuine or merely something to reassure me that he was alright. The doctor always landed on his feet, even if they were mechanical. I didn’t need to worry about him.

“Lili is certain to have left at least one Asheen necromancer behind to take the elf capital,” Thane warned. “Be careful, Doctor, for their power is unmatched. Tell the princess they can raise your own dead against you a heartbeat after they fall in battle. Their numbers ever increase while yours dwindle.”

I expected the goblin to argue the implausibility of magic or cite the ‘plague’ as the cause of the madness consuming such soldiers, but he merely nodded. Maybe not even the goblin had landed on his mental feet this time.

"And you?" the doctor asked me. "I do so hope we meet again, Miss Thorne. Where can I find you when my duties here are done?"

I tried not to feel the black tendrils of the First Soul reaching for me and took Thane's hand instead. I saw only warmth and light in his eyes, and the darkness ebbed.

Only then could I look to the east, to where Conrad's form had grown small with distance, to where the call of Solheim still reverberated through me. I would never stop hearing it, never be free of its pull, not until this was all over. One way or another.

My memory suddenly resurrected the feel of frozen cobblestones beneath my boots, the stink of crowded streets, and the clang of metal and hiss of steam from the machines built by the humans who had intruded on the ancient stillness of stone and snow. I could hear the laughter of my friends, see Morgan's raised eyebrows and feel uncle's shadow. I hoped Ulric had the answers I needed.

"Home," I said. "I'm going home. To Highcrowne.

Until Next Time...

Find out what happens next in the series finale,
Eva Thorne Book 4, War of Thornes,
available now.

Did you enjoy this book? Please leave a review!

Join our mailing list at **www.lorelclayton.com** for
updates on forthcoming novels by Lorel Clayton.

ABOUT THE AUTHORS

Lorel and Clayton were teen sweethearts, brought together by a fierce love of books (and hormones). Despite being married for 30 years, they are still madly in love and still writing. As writing partners, they meld logic, creativity, and genres. Fantasy, science-fiction, mystery, horror, steampunk, thrillers, the classics ...

they read them all, and if they can mix them, they
will!

Still reading? Want to know more?

Lorel has a PhD in molecular biology and Once Upon
a Time did cancer research before turning to the dark
side (aka marketing), but she uses her powers for good,
helping to raise funds for charity. She loves books,
movies and animals, and would gladly spend all day
with a cat on her lap and the wind in her hair (Conan
reference there), while tapping out a story on her key-
board. Or maybe a movie script. With coffee of course.
And lots of chocolate!

Clayton is an artist and has recently tackled digital
painting, mostly because there's a hyperactive eight-
year-old boy running around the house (their gorgeous
son, in case you were wondering if that's normal).
Clayton is severely dyslexic but loves books and story-
telling. He adds vast imagination and a discerning ear
for effective prose to their creative collaboration, not to
mention the book cover art.

Born and raised in the western United States, they
traveled to Sydney, Australia in 1997 and never left,

finding the sunshine and beaches of "Oz" too irresistible. Look them up if ever you're Down Under.

· *463* ·

Connect with Lorel Clayton

Website: http://www.lorelclayton.com/
Twitter: https://twitter.com/lorelclayton
Facebook: www.facebook.com/AuthorLorelClayton/